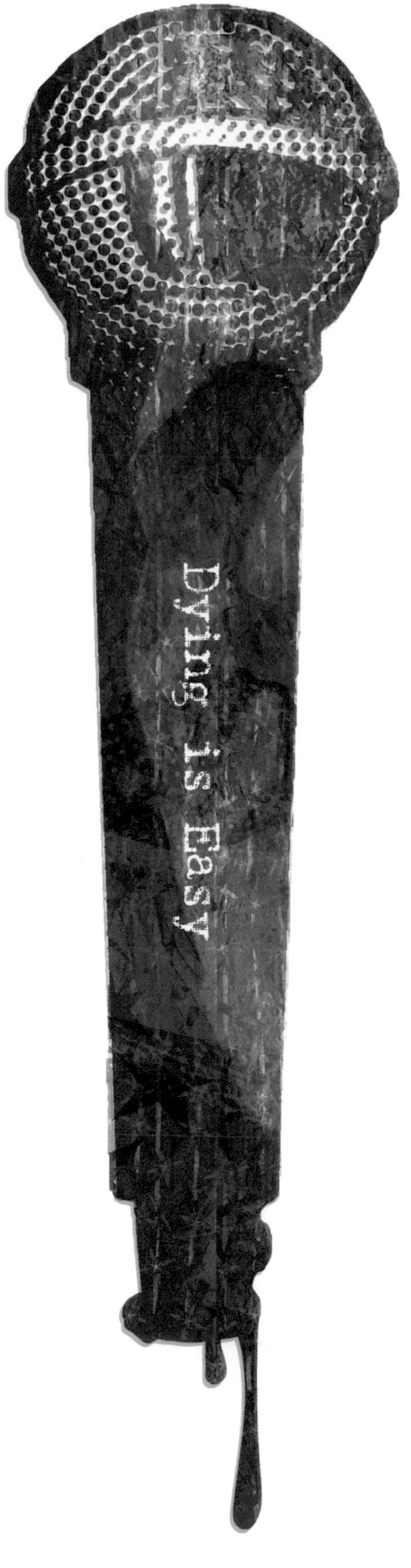
Dying is Easy

Dying is Easy created by **Joe Hill** and **Martin Simmonds**

Written by **Joe Hill**

Art by **Martin Simmonds**

Color Assists by **Dee Cunniffe**

Lettering/Design by **Shawn Lee**

Cover Artist
Martin Simmonds

Series Editors
Chris Ryall
Megan Brown

Collection Editors
Justin Eisinger
Alonzo Simon
Zac Boone

Chris Ryall, President & Publisher/CCO • Cara Morrison, Chief Financial Officer • Matthew Ruzicka, Chief Accounting Officer
John Barber, Editor-in-Chief • Justin Eisinger, Editorial Director, Graphic Novels and Collections • Scott Dunbier, Director, Special Projects
Jerry Bennington, VP of New Product Development • Lorelei Bunjes, VP of Technology & Information Services
Jud Meyers, Sales Director • Anna Morrow, Marketing Director • Tara McCrillis, Director of Design & Production
Mike Ford, Director of Operations • Shauna Monteforte, Manufacturing Operations Director • Rebekah Cahalin, General Manager

Ted Adams and Robbie Robbins, IDW Founders

Originally published as DYING IS EASY issues #1–5.

ISBN: 978-1-68405-703-0   23 22 21 20   1 2 3 4

 Facebook: facebook.com/idwpublishing   Twitter: @idwpublishing   Tumblr: tumblr.idwpublishing.com

YouTube: youtube.com/idwpublishing   Instagram: instagram.com/idwpublishing
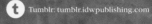

THIS **COP** IS A **STAND-UP** GUY

AN INTRODUCTION TO *DYING IS EASY*

"I always wondered what was the last thing to go through your sister's mind when she stepped in front of that truck. Probably the hood ornament, huh?"

Now that's cold. It's also a pretty good introduction to an ex-cop with a dark sense of humor, who does a truly fine job of acting out that eternal truth: While comedy is hard, dying is easy.

Syd Homes, as rendered by Joe Hill and Martin Simmonds, uses humor in a manner that won't be unfamiliar to readers of private eye fiction. Raymond Chandler gave Philip Marlowe the mouth of a wiseass, and no end of Marlowe's fictional descendants have littered the mean streets with their wisecracks.

That works pretty well in the books, but I have to wonder how often it happens outside of fiction. I've known a handful of private detectives over the years, and a diverse bunch they are, but I can't imagine a single one of them ever giving a lot of lip to a cop—or, truth to tell, even talking back to a toll-booth attendant.

But the notion of ex-cop as stand-up comic appealed to me, even though I knew right away you'd never encounter one in real life. Out of the question, right?

Wrong.

See for yourself. Google "ex-cop stand-up comedian" and look what pops up. And then be prepared to spend the next couple of hours on YouTube, watching Mike Armstrong and Alfie Moore and Michael Mancini do their stuff.

And it'll be a pleasant couple of hours, because they're pretty good. You'll get some laughs.

You'll get laughs from Syd Homes, too, even as he guides you through a dark and humorless world. And you'll also get a rattling good adventure in the form of a well-plotted detective story. The storyline's more intricate than I expected, with a couple of good twists at the end, and the resolution is solid. And, even as it leaves the reader wanting more, it hints that there may be more coming.

Let's hope so.

Lawrence Block
Lawrence Block's latest novel, Dead Girl Blues, *was released on June 24, 2020, Block's 82nd birthday*

1 • art by Martin Simmonds • 1

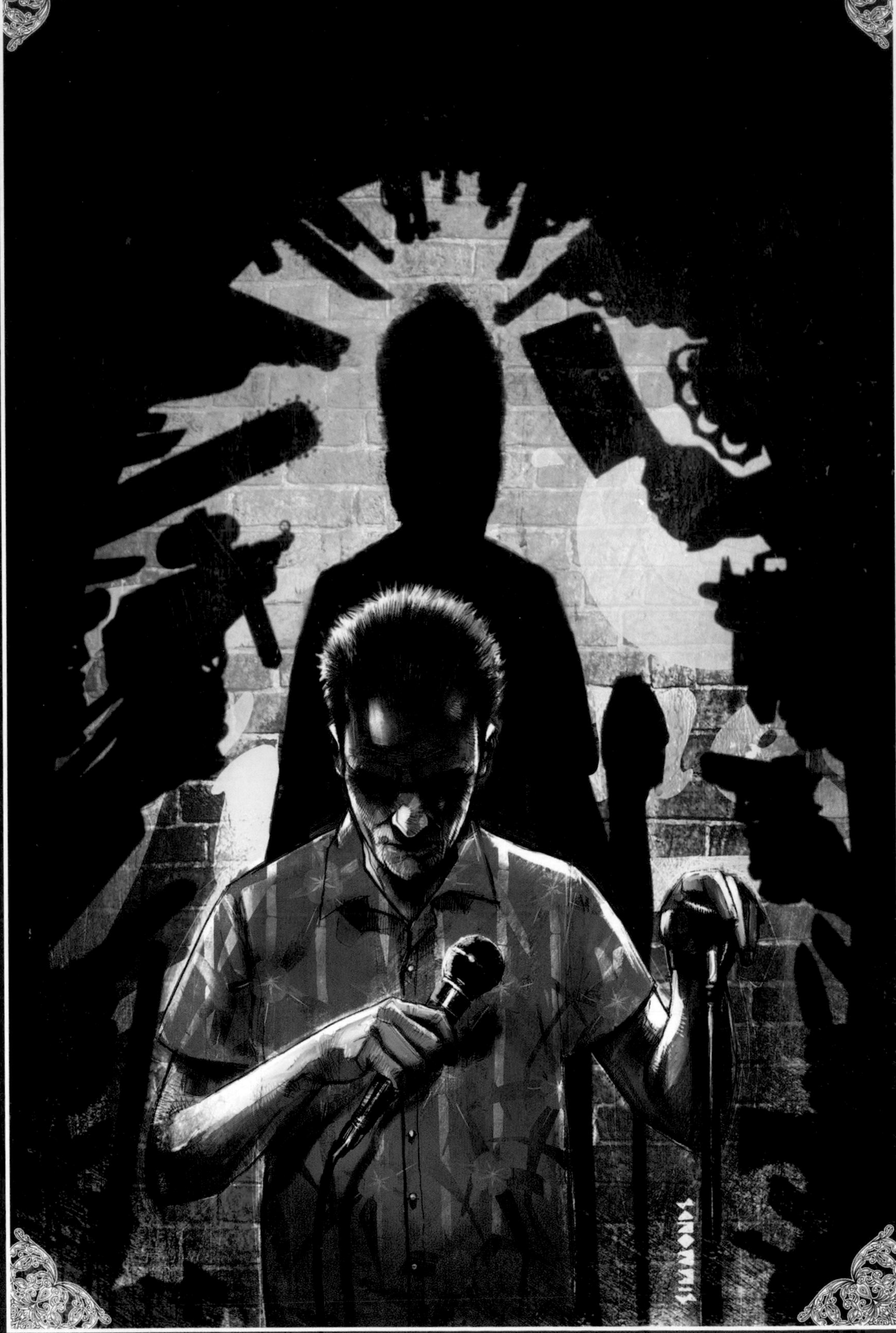
SIMMONDS

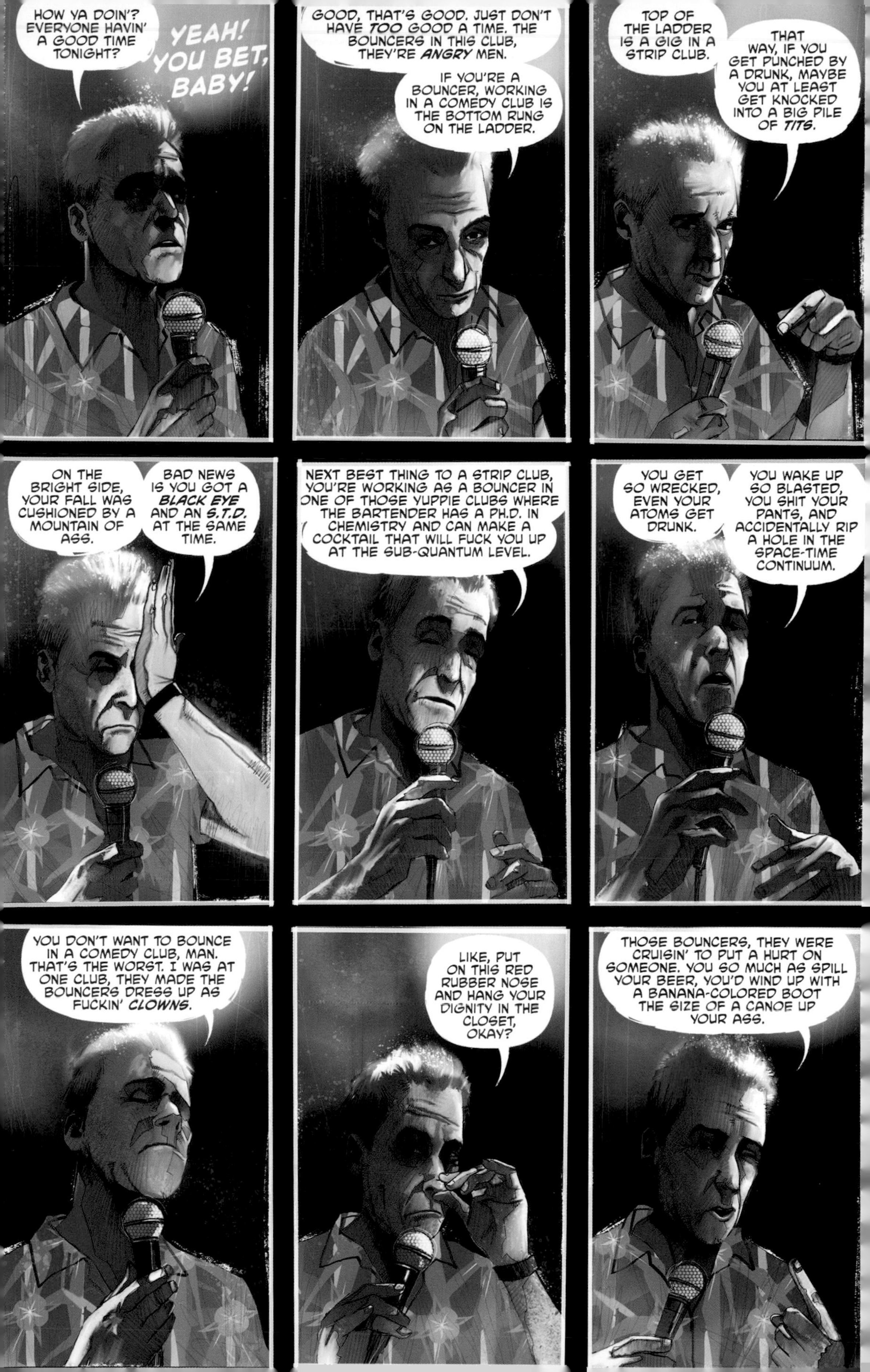
HOW YA DOIN'? EVERYONE HAVIN' A GOOD TIME TONIGHT?
YEAH! YOU BET, BABY!
GOOD, THAT'S GOOD. JUST DON'T HAVE TOO GOOD A TIME. THE BOUNCERS IN THIS CLUB, THEY'RE ANGRY MEN.
IF YOU'RE A BOUNCER, WORKING IN A COMEDY CLUB IS THE BOTTOM RUNG ON THE LADDER.
TOP OF THE LADDER IS A GIG IN A STRIP CLUB.
THAT WAY, IF YOU GET PUNCHED BY A DRUNK, MAYBE YOU AT LEAST GET KNOCKED INTO A BIG PILE OF TITS.
ON THE BRIGHT SIDE, YOUR FALL WAS CUSHIONED BY A MOUNTAIN OF ASS.
BAD NEWS IS YOU GOT A BLACK EYE AND AN S.T.D. AT THE SAME TIME.
NEXT BEST THING TO A STRIP CLUB, YOU'RE WORKING AS A BOUNCER IN ONE OF THOSE YUPPIE CLUBS WHERE THE BARTENDER HAS A PH.D. IN CHEMISTRY AND CAN MAKE A COCKTAIL THAT WILL FUCK YOU UP AT THE SUB-QUANTUM LEVEL.
YOU GET SO WRECKED, EVEN YOUR ATOMS GET DRUNK.
YOU WAKE UP SO BLASTED, YOU SHIT YOUR PANTS, AND ACCIDENTALLY RIP A HOLE IN THE SPACE-TIME CONTINUUM.
YOU DON'T WANT TO BOUNCE IN A COMEDY CLUB, MAN. THAT'S THE WORST. I WAS AT ONE CLUB, THEY MADE THE BOUNCERS DRESS UP AS FUCKIN' CLOWNS.
LIKE, PUT ON THIS RED RUBBER NOSE AND HANG YOUR DIGNITY IN THE CLOSET, OKAY?
THOSE BOUNCERS, THEY WERE CRUISIN' TO PUT A HURT ON SOMEONE. YOU SO MUCH AS SPILL YOUR BEER, YOU'D WIND UP WITH A BANANA-COLORED BOOT THE SIZE OF A CANOE UP YOUR ASS.

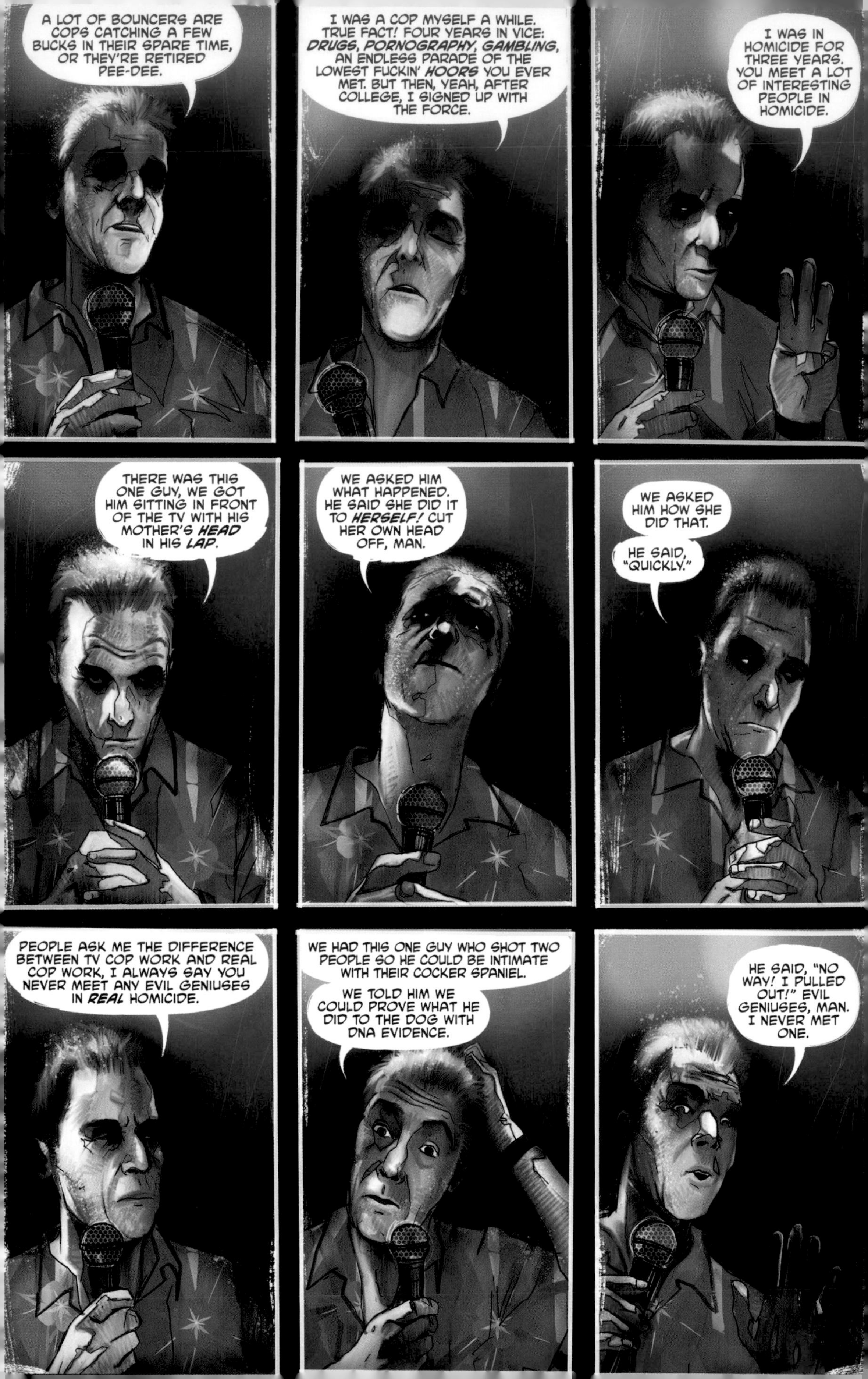
A LOT OF BOUNCERS ARE COPS CATCHING A FEW BUCKS IN THEIR SPARE TIME, OR THEY'RE RETIRED PEE-DEE.
I WAS A COP MYSELF A WHILE. TRUE FACT! FOUR YEARS IN VICE: DRUGS, PORNOGRAPHY, GAMBLING, AN ENDLESS PARADE OF THE LOWEST FUCKIN' HOORS YOU EVER MET. BUT THEN, YEAH, AFTER COLLEGE, I SIGNED UP WITH THE FORCE.
I WAS IN HOMICIDE FOR THREE YEARS. YOU MEET A LOT OF INTERESTING PEOPLE IN HOMICIDE.
THERE WAS THIS ONE GUY, WE GOT HIM SITTING IN FRONT OF THE TV WITH HIS MOTHER'S HEAD IN HIS LAP.
WE ASKED HIM WHAT HAPPENED. HE SAID SHE DID IT TO HERSELF! CUT HER OWN HEAD OFF, MAN.
WE ASKED HIM HOW SHE DID THAT.
HE SAID, "QUICKLY."
PEOPLE ASK ME THE DIFFERENCE BETWEEN TV COP WORK AND REAL COP WORK, I ALWAYS SAY YOU NEVER MEET ANY EVIL GENIUSES IN REAL HOMICIDE.
WE HAD THIS ONE GUY WHO SHOT TWO PEOPLE SO HE COULD BE INTIMATE WITH THEIR COCKER SPANIEL.
WE TOLD HIM WE COULD PROVE WHAT HE DID TO THE DOG WITH DNA EVIDENCE.
HE SAID, "NO WAY! I PULLED OUT!" EVIL GENIUSES, MAN. I NEVER MET ONE.

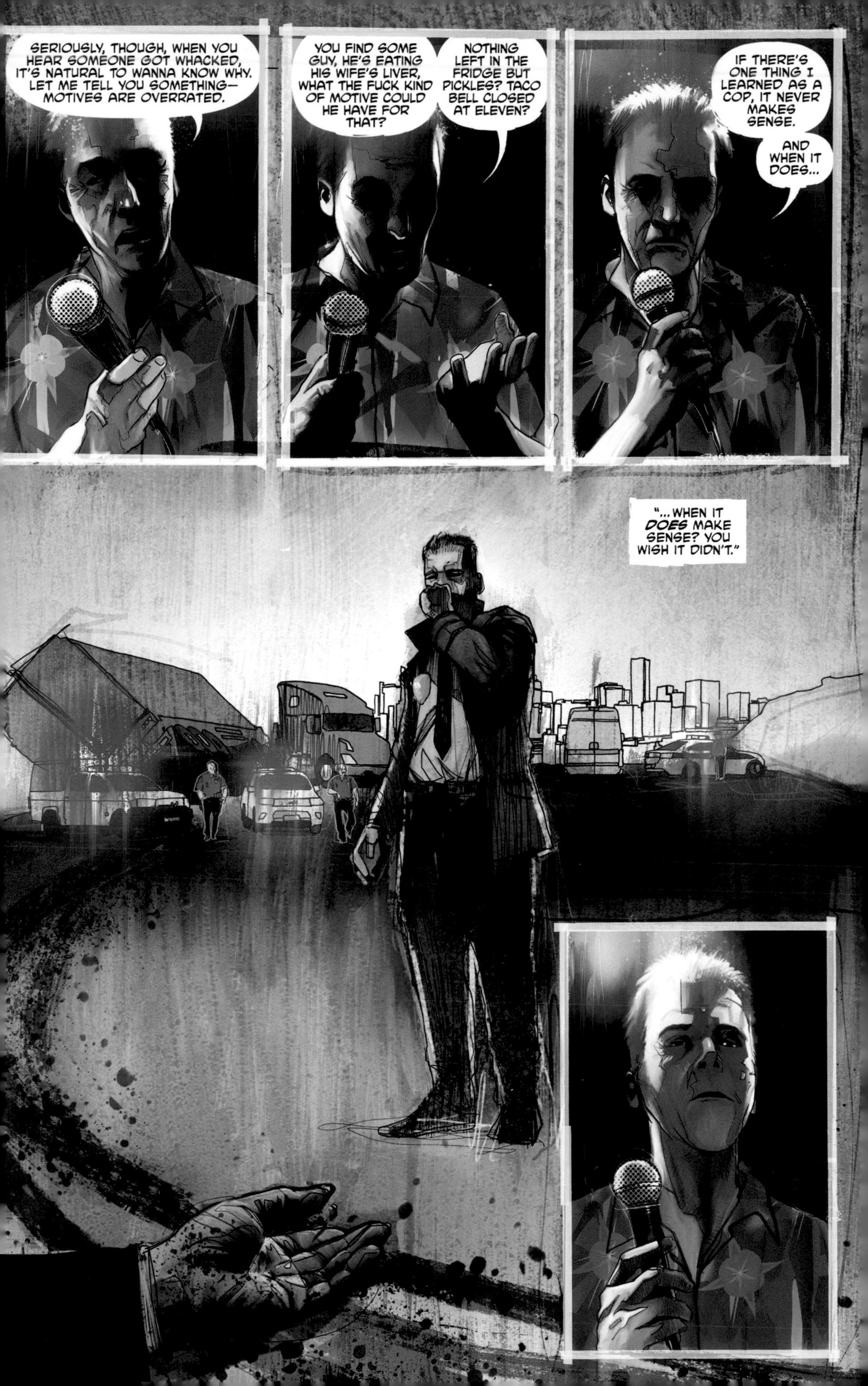
SERIOUSLY, THOUGH, WHEN YOU HEAR SOMEONE GOT WHACKED, IT'S NATURAL TO WANNA KNOW WHY. LET ME TELL YOU SOMETHING—MOTIVES ARE OVERRATED.
YOU FIND SOME GUY, HE'S EATING HIS WIFE'S LIVER, WHAT THE FUCK KIND OF MOTIVE COULD HE HAVE FOR THAT?
NOTHING LEFT IN THE FRIDGE BUT PICKLES? TACO BELL CLOSED AT ELEVEN?
IF THERE'S ONE THING I LEARNED AS A COP, IT NEVER MAKES SENSE.
AND WHEN IT DOES...
"...WHEN IT *DOES* MAKE SENSE? YOU WISH IT DIDN'T."

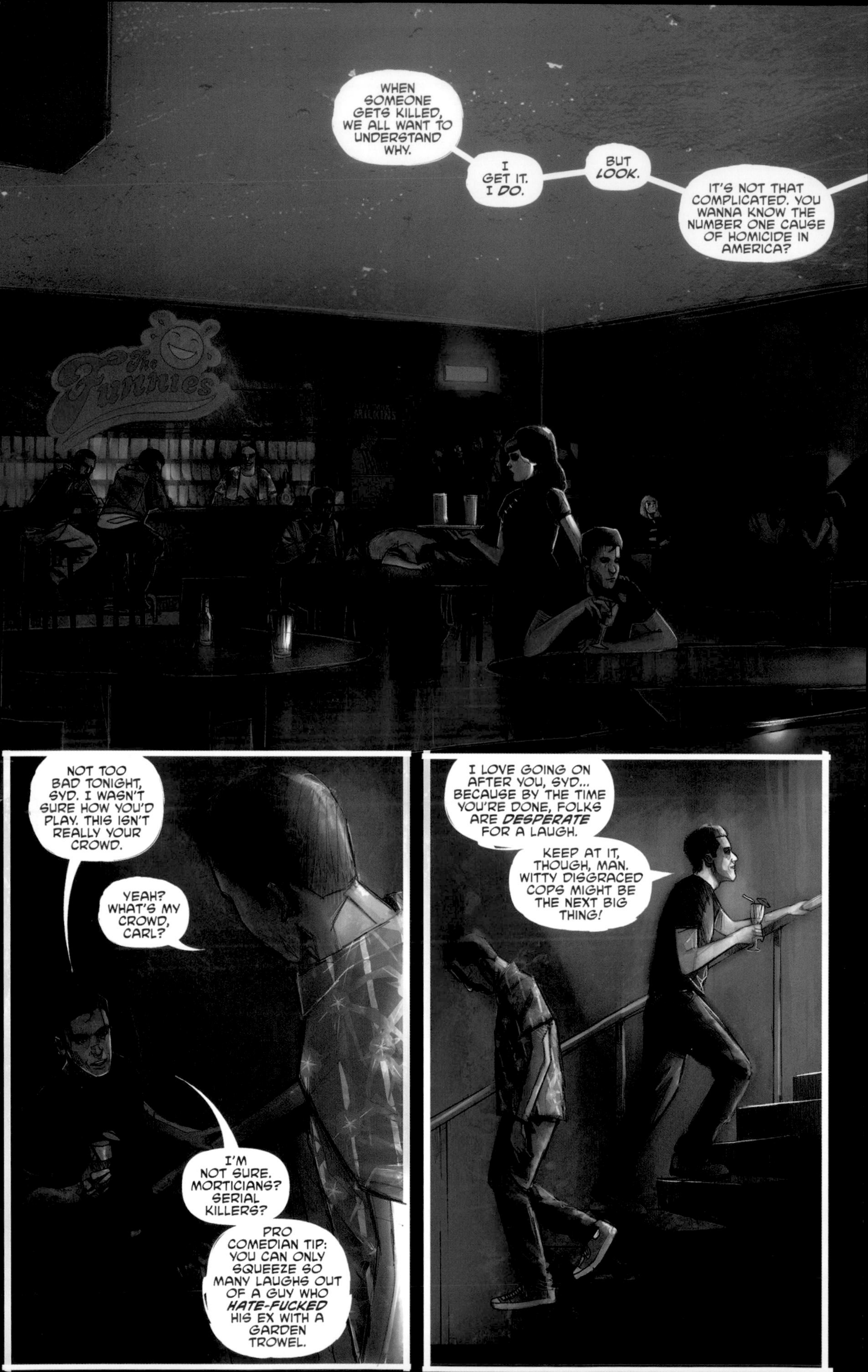
WHEN SOMEONE GETS KILLED, WE ALL WANT TO UNDERSTAND WHY.
I GET IT. I *DO*.
BUT *LOOK*.
IT'S NOT THAT COMPLICATED. YOU WANNA KNOW THE NUMBER ONE CAUSE OF HOMICIDE IN AMERICA?
The Funnies
NOT TOO BAD TONIGHT, SYD. I WASN'T SURE HOW YOU'D PLAY. THIS ISN'T REALLY YOUR CROWD.
YEAH? WHAT'S MY CROWD, CARL?
I'M NOT SURE. MORTICIANS? SERIAL KILLERS?
PRO COMEDIAN TIP: YOU CAN ONLY SQUEEZE SO MANY LAUGHS OUT OF A GUY WHO ***HATE-FUCKED*** HIS EX WITH A GARDEN TROWEL.
I LOVE GOING ON AFTER YOU, SYD... BECAUSE BY THE TIME YOU'RE DONE, FOLKS ARE ***DESPERATE*** FOR A LAUGH.
KEEP AT IT, THOUGH, MAN. WITTY DISGRACED COPS MIGHT BE THE NEXT BIG THING!

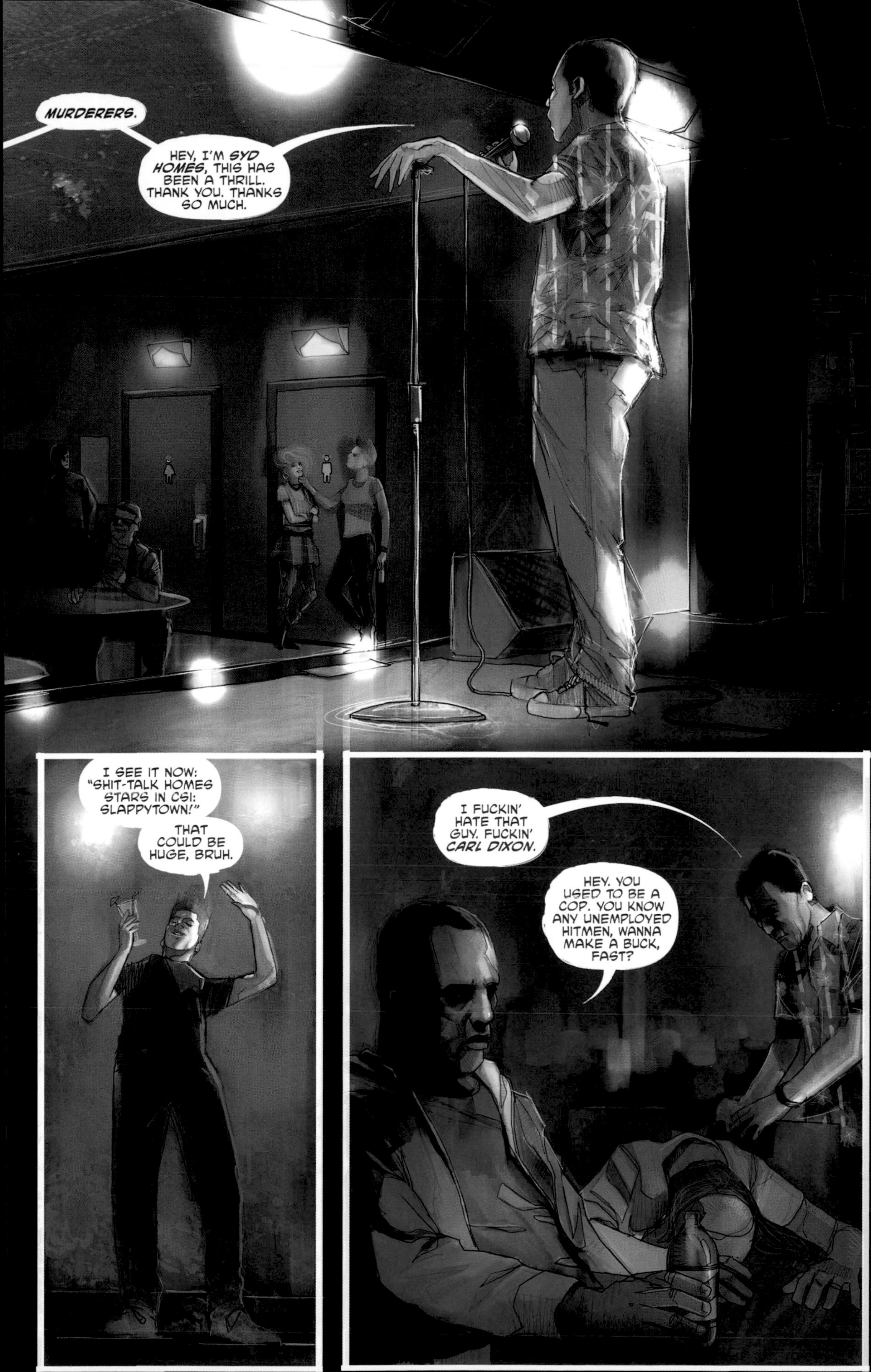
MURDERERS.
HEY, I'M SYD HOMES, THIS HAS BEEN A THRILL. THANK YOU. THANKS SO MUCH.
I SEE IT NOW: "SHIT-TALK HOMES STARS IN CSI: SLAPPYTOWN!"
THAT COULD BE HUGE, BRUH.
I FUCKIN' HATE THAT GUY. FUCKIN' CARL DIXON.
HEY. YOU USED TO BE A COP. YOU KNOW ANY UNEMPLOYED HITMEN, WANNA MAKE A BUCK, FAST?

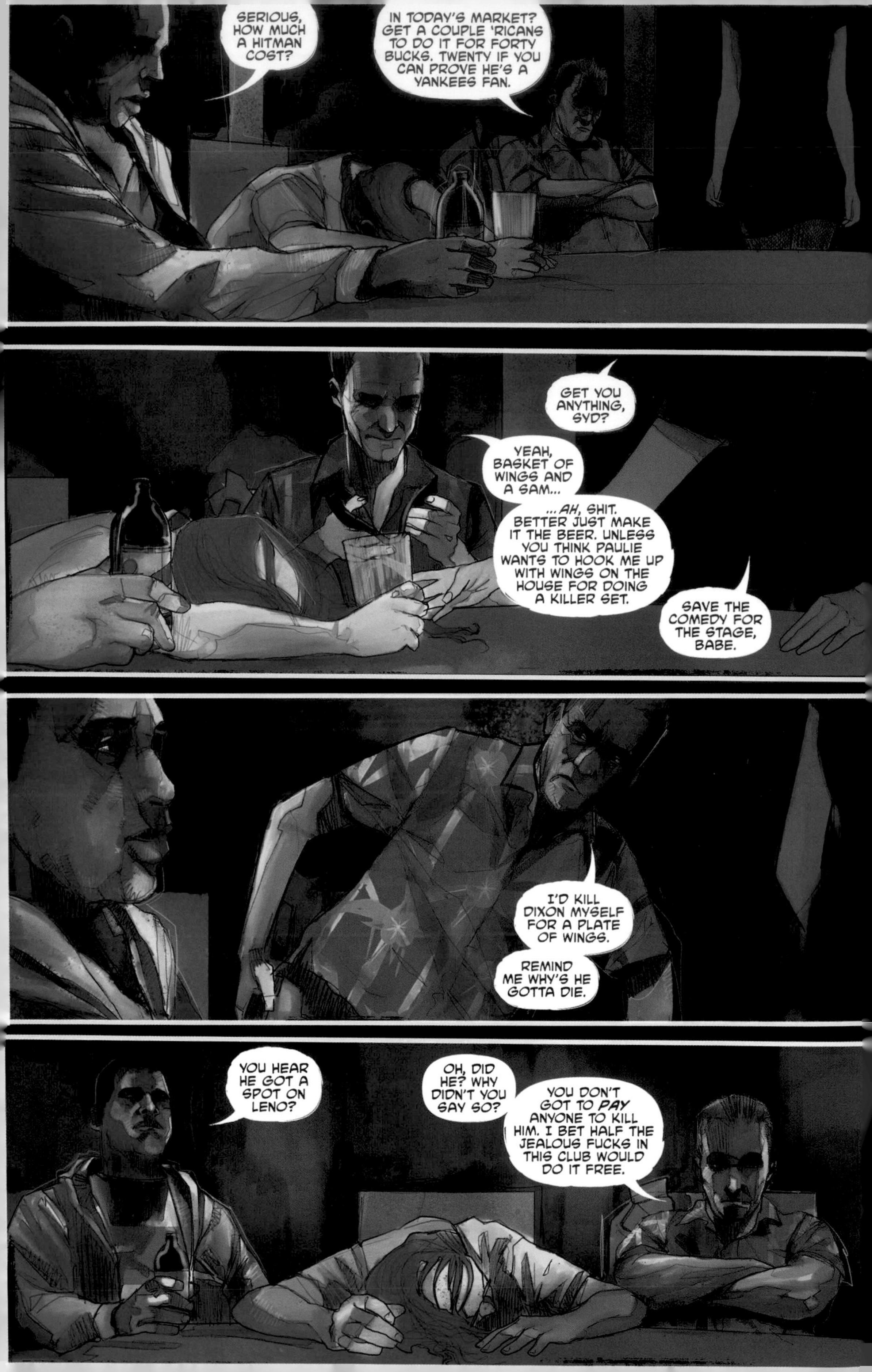
SERIOUS, HOW MUCH A HITMAN COST?
IN TODAY'S MARKET? GET A COUPLE 'RICANS TO DO IT FOR FORTY BUCKS. TWENTY IF YOU CAN PROVE HE'S A YANKEES FAN.
GET YOU ANYTHING, SYD?
YEAH, BASKET OF WINGS AND A SAM...
...AH, SHIT. BETTER JUST MAKE IT THE BEER. UNLESS YOU THINK PAULIE WANTS TO HOOK ME UP WITH WINGS ON THE HOUSE FOR DOING A KILLER SET.
SAVE THE COMEDY FOR THE STAGE, BABE.
I'D KILL DIXON MYSELF FOR A PLATE OF WINGS.
REMIND ME WHY'S HE GOTTA DIE.
YOU HEAR HE GOT A SPOT ON LENO?
OH, DID HE? WHY DIDN'T YOU SAY SO?
YOU DON'T GOT TO PAY ANYONE TO KILL HIM. I BET HALF THE JEALOUS FUCKS IN THIS CLUB WOULD DO IT FREE.

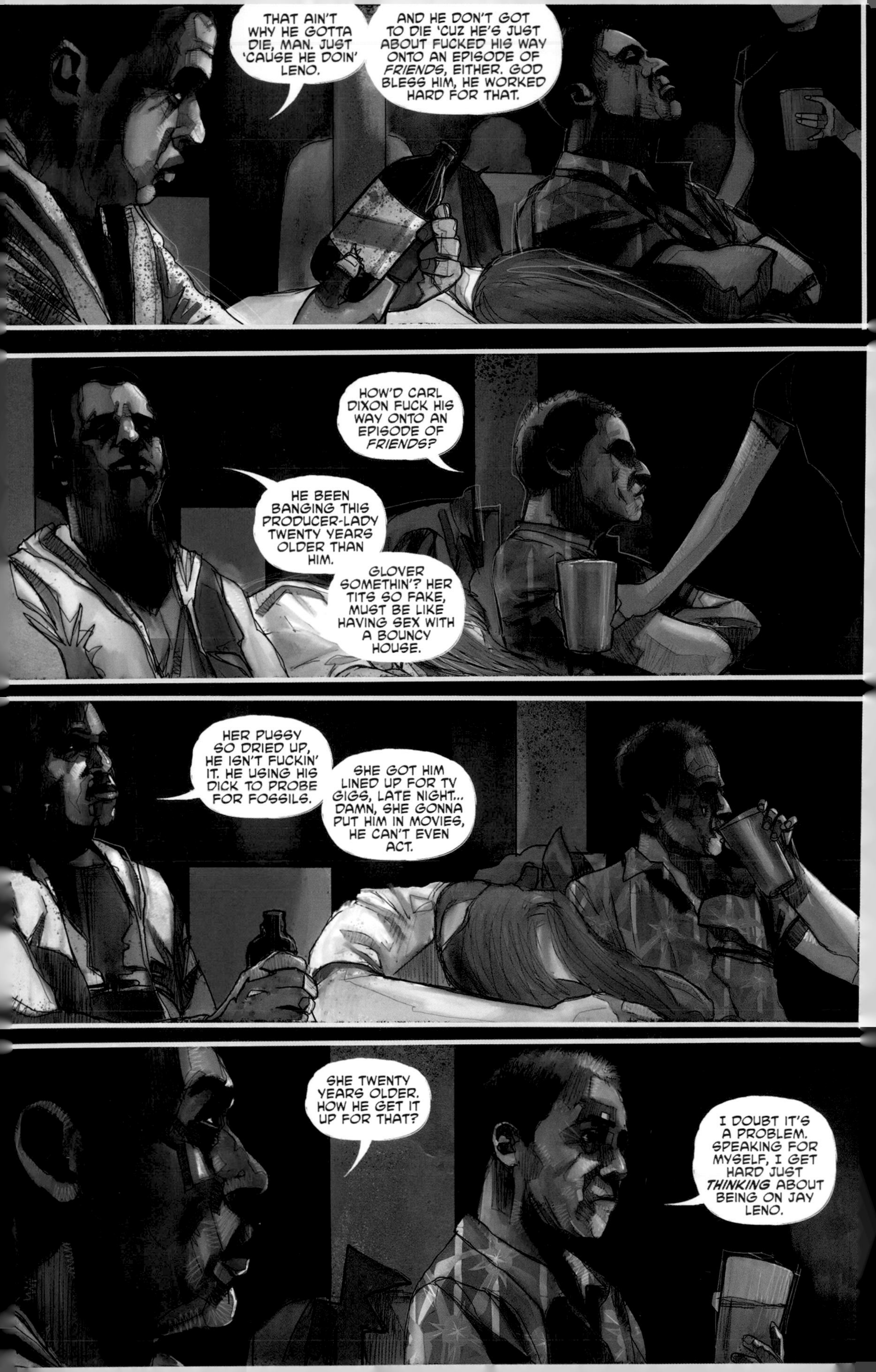
THAT AIN'T WHY HE GOTTA DIE, MAN. JUST 'CAUSE HE DOIN' LENO.
AND HE DON'T GOT TO DIE 'CUZ HE'S JUST ABOUT FUCKED HIS WAY ONTO AN EPISODE OF *FRIENDS*, EITHER. GOD BLESS HIM, HE WORKED HARD FOR THAT.
HOW'D CARL DIXON FUCK HIS WAY ONTO AN EPISODE OF *FRIENDS*?
HE BEEN BANGING THIS PRODUCER-LADY TWENTY YEARS OLDER THAN HIM.
GLOVER SOMETHIN'? HER TITS SO FAKE, MUST BE LIKE HAVING SEX WITH A BOUNCY HOUSE.
HER PUSSY SO DRIED UP, HE ISN'T FUCKIN' IT. HE USING HIS DICK TO PROBE FOR FOSSILS.
SHE GOT HIM LINED UP FOR TV GIGS, LATE NIGHT... DAMN, SHE GONNA PUT HIM IN MOVIES, HE CAN'T EVEN ACT.
SHE TWENTY YEARS OLDER. HOW HE GET IT UP FOR THAT?
I DOUBT IT'S A PROBLEM. SPEAKING FOR MYSELF, I GET HARD JUST *THINKING* ABOUT BEING ON JAY LENO.

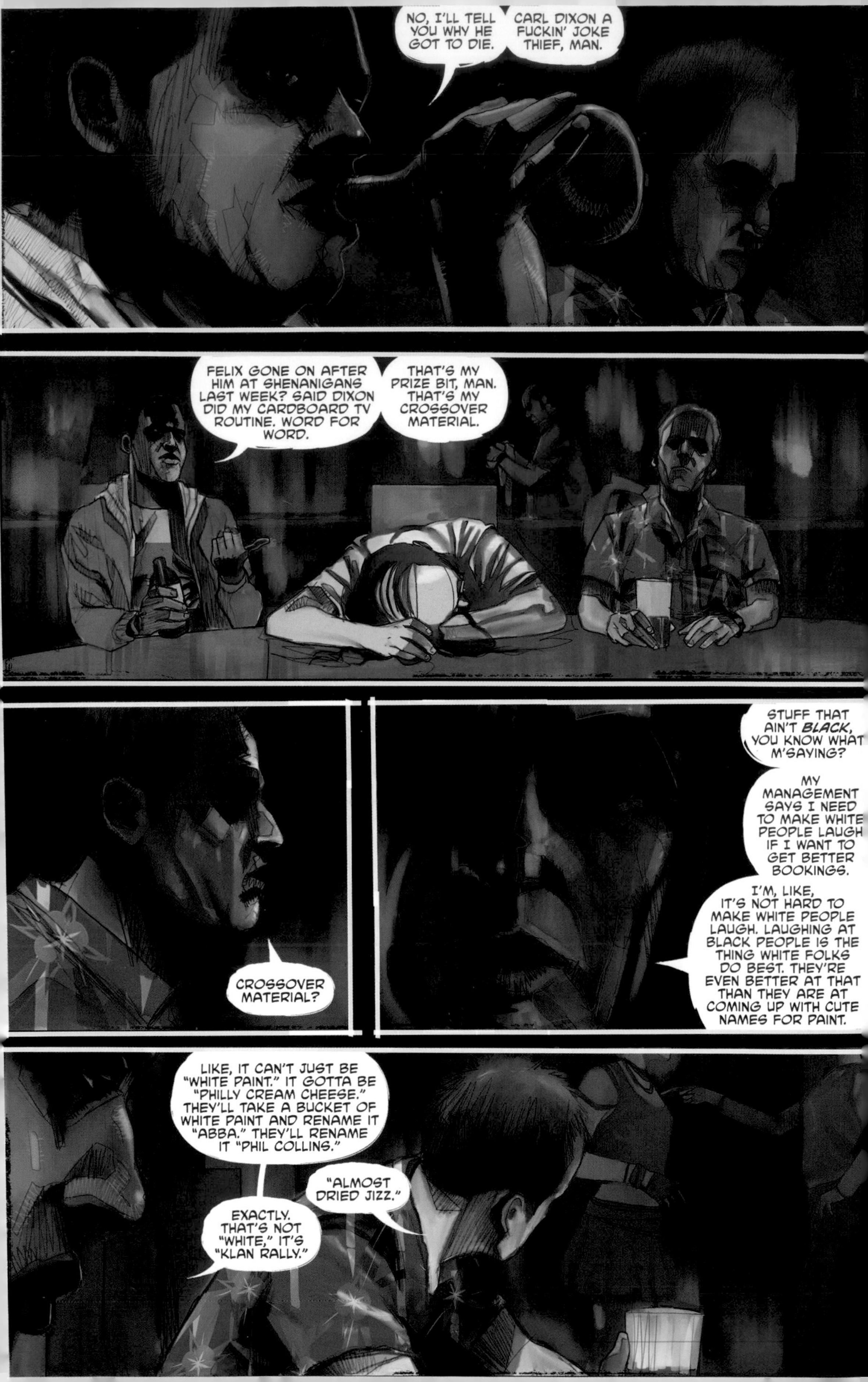
NO, I'LL TELL YOU WHY HE GOT TO DIE.
CARL DIXON A FUCKIN' JOKE THIEF, MAN.
FELIX GONE ON AFTER HIM AT SHENANIGANS LAST WEEK? SAID DIXON DID MY CARDBOARD TV ROUTINE. WORD FOR WORD.
THAT'S MY PRIZE BIT, MAN. THAT'S MY CROSSOVER MATERIAL.
CROSSOVER MATERIAL?
STUFF THAT AIN'T *BLACK*, YOU KNOW WHAT M'SAYING?
MY MANAGEMENT SAYS I NEED TO MAKE WHITE PEOPLE LAUGH IF I WANT TO GET BETTER BOOKINGS.
I'M, LIKE, IT'S NOT HARD TO MAKE WHITE PEOPLE LAUGH. LAUGHING AT BLACK PEOPLE IS THE THING WHITE FOLKS DO BEST. THEY'RE EVEN BETTER AT THAT THAN THEY ARE AT COMING UP WITH CUTE NAMES FOR PAINT.
LIKE, IT CAN'T JUST BE "WHITE PAINT." IT GOTTA BE "PHILLY CREAM CHEESE." THEY'LL TAKE A BUCKET OF WHITE PAINT AND RENAME IT "ABBA." THEY'LL RENAME IT "PHIL COLLINS."
"ALMOST DRIED JIZZ."
EXACTLY. THAT'S NOT "WHITE," IT'S "KLAN RALLY."

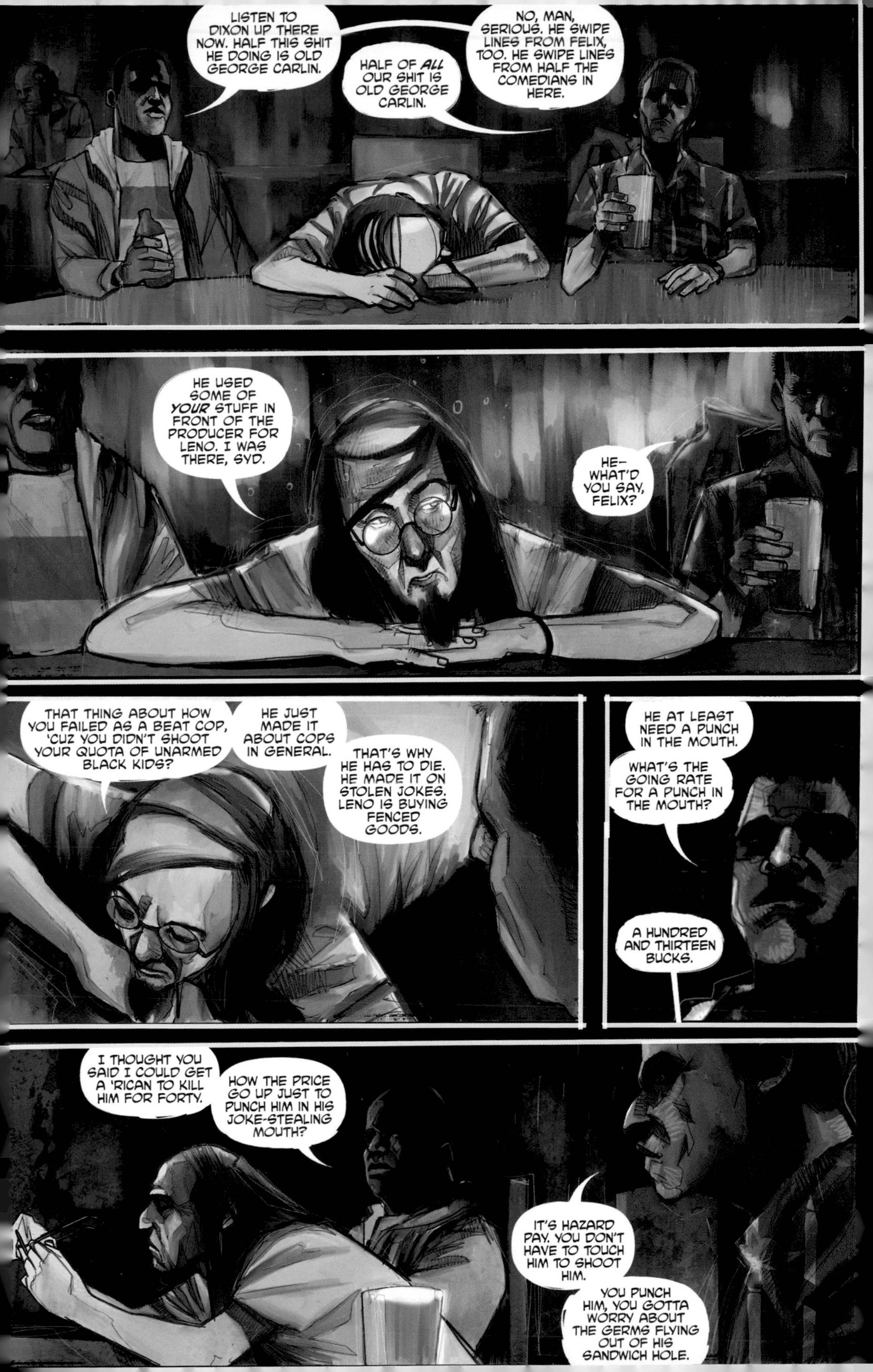
LISTEN TO DIXON UP THERE NOW. HALF THIS SHIT HE DOING IS OLD GEORGE CARLIN.
HALF OF *ALL* OUR SHIT IS OLD GEORGE CARLIN.
NO, MAN, SERIOUS. HE SWIPE LINES FROM FELIX, TOO. HE SWIPE LINES FROM HALF THE COMEDIANS IN HERE.
HE USED SOME OF ***YOUR*** STUFF IN FRONT OF THE PRODUCER FOR LENO. I WAS THERE, SYD.
HE— WHAT'D YOU SAY, FELIX?
THAT THING ABOUT HOW YOU FAILED AS A BEAT COP, 'CUZ YOU DIDN'T SHOOT YOUR QUOTA OF UNARMED BLACK KIDS?
HE JUST MADE IT ABOUT COPS IN GENERAL.
THAT'S WHY HE HAS TO DIE. HE MADE IT ON STOLEN JOKES. LENO IS BUYING FENCED GOODS.
HE AT LEAST NEED A PUNCH IN THE MOUTH.
WHAT'S THE GOING RATE FOR A PUNCH IN THE MOUTH?
A HUNDRED AND THIRTEEN BUCKS.
I THOUGHT YOU SAID I COULD GET A 'RICAN TO KILL HIM FOR FORTY.
HOW THE PRICE GO UP JUST TO PUNCH HIM IN HIS JOKE-STEALING MOUTH?
IT'S HAZARD PAY. YOU DON'T HAVE TO TOUCH HIM TO SHOOT HIM.
YOU PUNCH HIM, YOU GOTTA WORRY ABOUT THE GERMS FLYING OUT OF HIS SANDWICH HOLE.

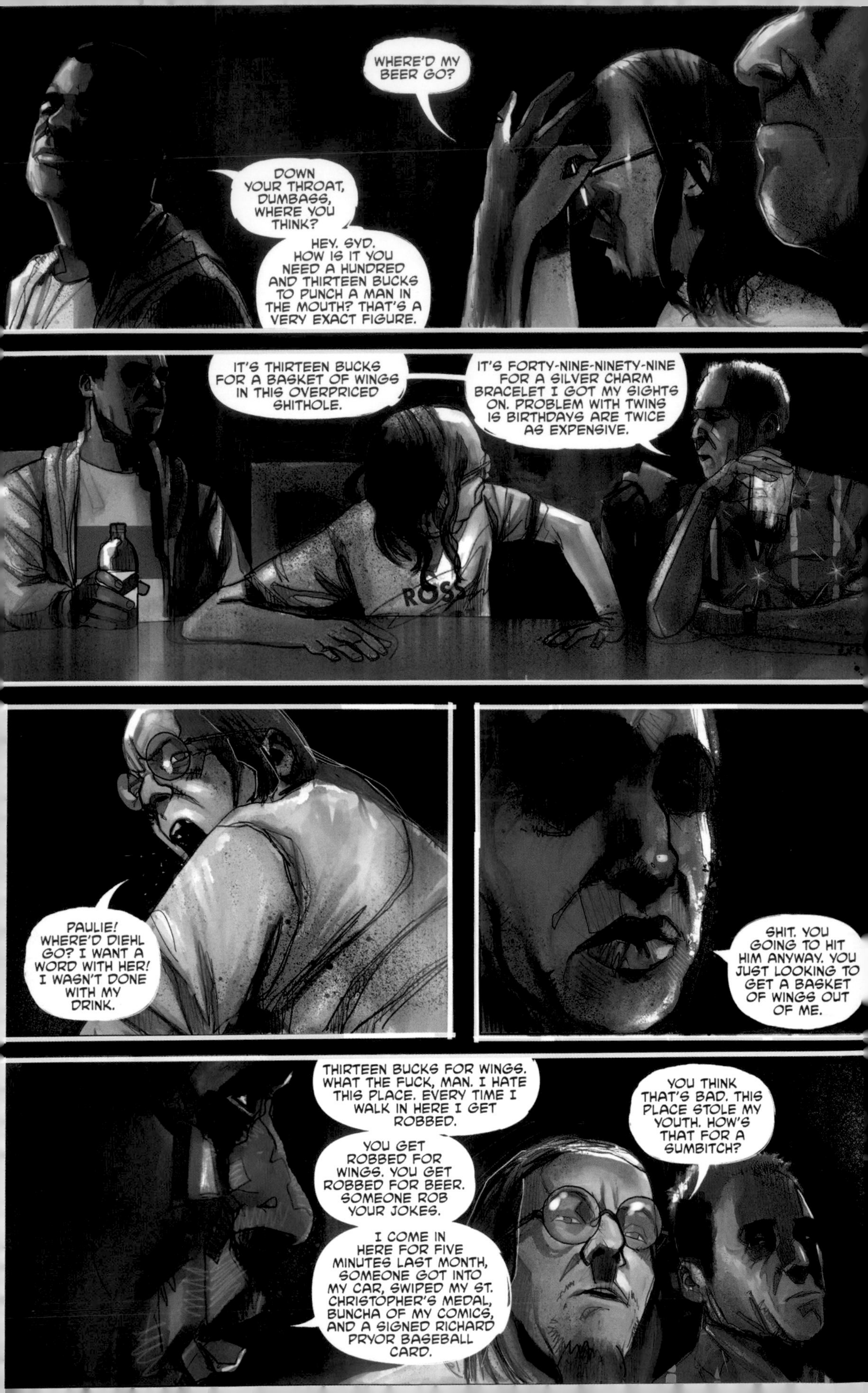
WHERE'D MY BEER GO?
DOWN YOUR THROAT, DUMBASS, WHERE YOU THINK?
HEY. SYD. HOW IS IT YOU NEED A HUNDRED AND THIRTEEN BUCKS TO PUNCH A MAN IN THE MOUTH? THAT'S A VERY EXACT FIGURE.
IT'S THIRTEEN BUCKS FOR A BASKET OF WINGS IN THIS OVERPRICED SHITHOLE.
IT'S FORTY-NINE-NINETY-NINE FOR A SILVER CHARM BRACELET I GOT MY SIGHTS ON. PROBLEM WITH TWINS IS BIRTHDAYS ARE TWICE AS EXPENSIVE.
ROSS
PAULIE! WHERE'D DIEHL GO? I WANT A WORD WITH HER! I WASN'T DONE WITH MY DRINK.
SHIT. YOU GOING TO HIT HIM ANYWAY. YOU JUST LOOKING TO GET A BASKET OF WINGS OUT OF ME.
THIRTEEN BUCKS FOR WINGS. WHAT THE FUCK, MAN. I HATE THIS PLACE. EVERY TIME I WALK IN HERE I GET ROBBED.
YOU GET ROBBED FOR WINGS. YOU GET ROBBED FOR BEER. SOMEONE ROB YOUR JOKES.
I COME IN HERE FOR FIVE MINUTES LAST MONTH, SOMEONE GOT INTO MY CAR, SWIPED MY ST. CHRISTOPHER'S MEDAL, BUNCHA OF MY COMICS, AND A SIGNED RICHARD PRYOR BASEBALL CARD.
YOU THINK THAT'S BAD. THIS PLACE STOLE MY YOUTH. HOW'S THAT FOR A SUMBITCH?

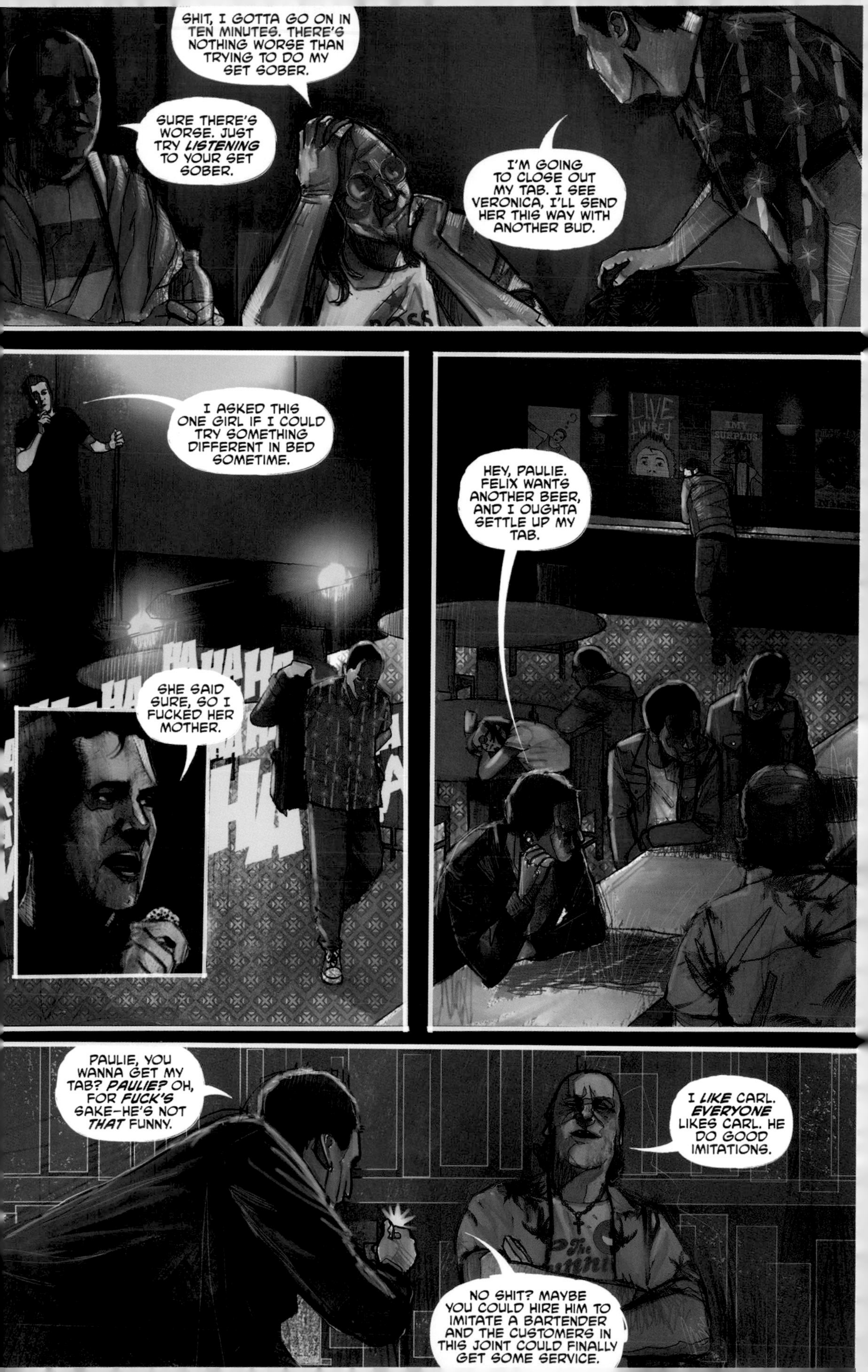
SHIT, I GOTTA GO ON IN TEN MINUTES. THERE'S NOTHING WORSE THAN TRYING TO DO MY SET SOBER.
SURE THERE'S WORSE. JUST TRY *LISTENING* TO YOUR SET SOBER.
I'M GOING TO CLOSE OUT MY TAB. I SEE VERONICA, I'LL SEND HER THIS WAY WITH ANOTHER BUD.
I ASKED THIS ONE GIRL IF I COULD TRY SOMETHING DIFFERENT IN BED SOMETIME.
HAHAHA
SHE SAID SURE, SO I FUCKED HER MOTHER.
HEY, PAULIE. FELIX WANTS ANOTHER BEER, AND I OUGHTA SETTLE UP MY TAB.
PAULIE, YOU WANNA GET MY TAB? *PAULIE?* OH, FOR *FUCK'S* SAKE–HE'S NOT *THAT* FUNNY.
I *LIKE* CARL. *EVERYONE* LIKES CARL. HE DO GOOD IMITATIONS.
NO SHIT? MAYBE YOU COULD HIRE HIM TO IMITATE A BARTENDER AND THE CUSTOMERS IN THIS JOINT COULD FINALLY GET SOME SERVICE.

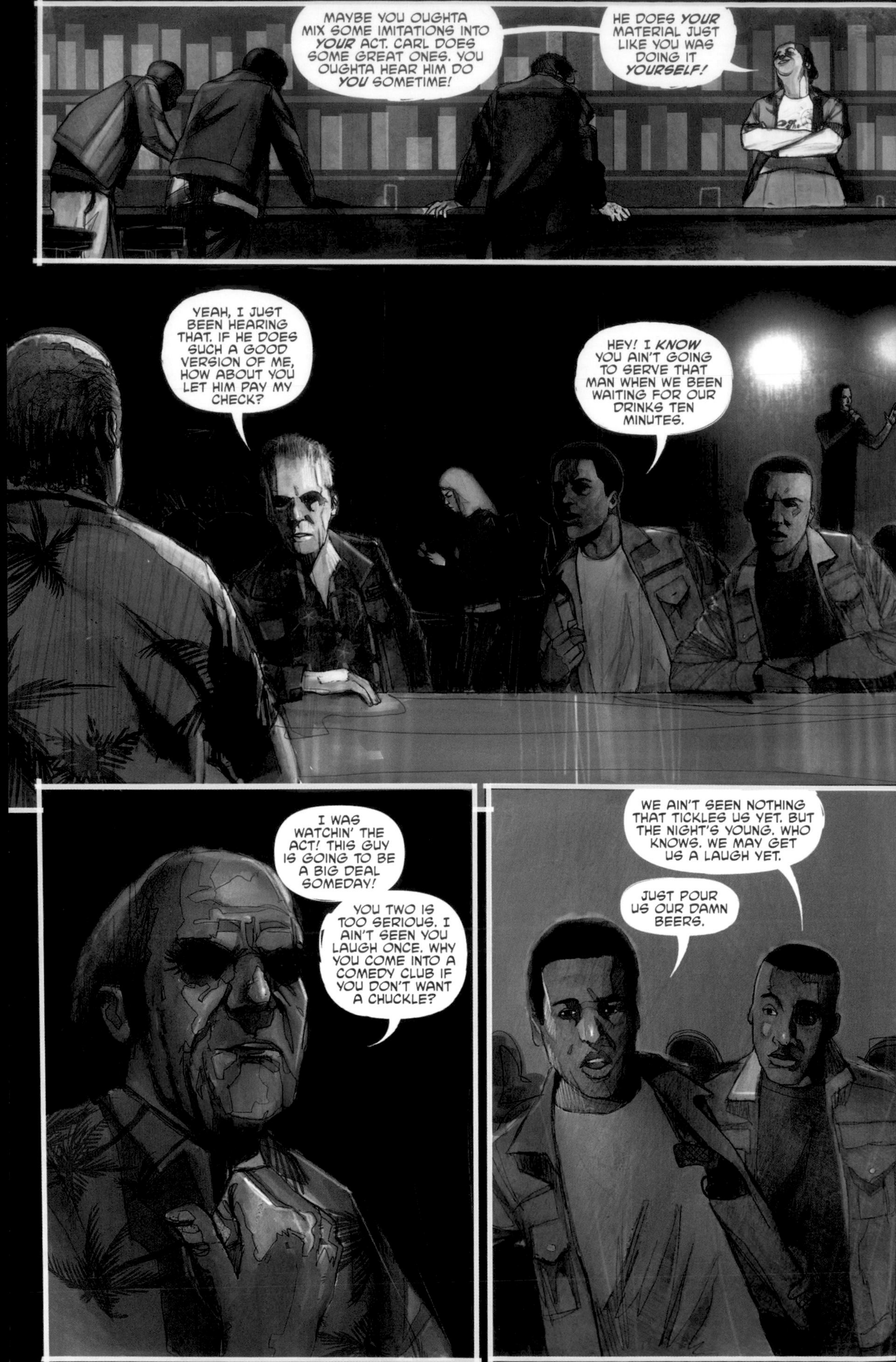
MAYBE YOU OUGHTA MIX SOME IMITATIONS INTO YOUR ACT. CARL DOES SOME GREAT ONES. YOU OUGHTA HEAR HIM DO YOU SOMETIME!
HE DOES YOUR MATERIAL JUST LIKE YOU WAS DOING IT YOURSELF!
YEAH, I JUST BEEN HEARING THAT. IF HE DOES SUCH A GOOD VERSION OF ME, HOW ABOUT YOU LET HIM PAY MY CHECK?
HEY! I KNOW YOU AIN'T GOING TO SERVE THAT MAN WHEN WE BEEN WAITING FOR OUR DRINKS TEN MINUTES.
I WAS WATCHIN' THE ACT! THIS GUY IS GOING TO BE A BIG DEAL SOMEDAY!
YOU TWO IS TOO SERIOUS. I AIN'T SEEN YOU LAUGH ONCE. WHY YOU COME INTO A COMEDY CLUB IF YOU DON'T WANT A CHUCKLE?
WE AIN'T SEEN NOTHING THAT TICKLES US YET. BUT THE NIGHT'S YOUNG. WHO KNOWS. WE MAY GET US A LAUGH YET.
JUST POUR US OUR DAMN BEERS.

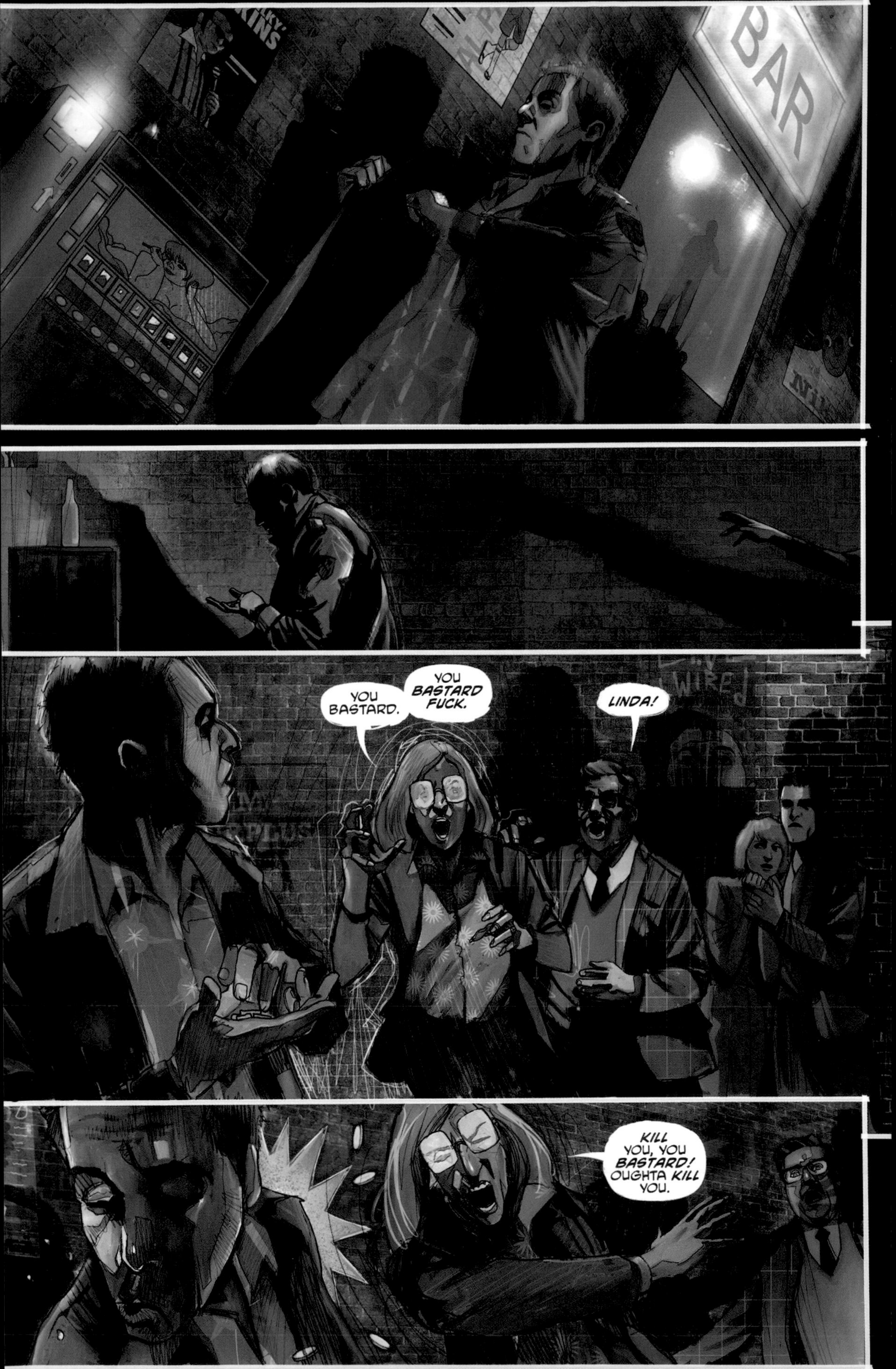
BAR
YOU BASTARD.
YOU BASTARD FUCK.
LINDA!
KILL YOU, YOU BASTARD! OUGHTA KILL YOU.

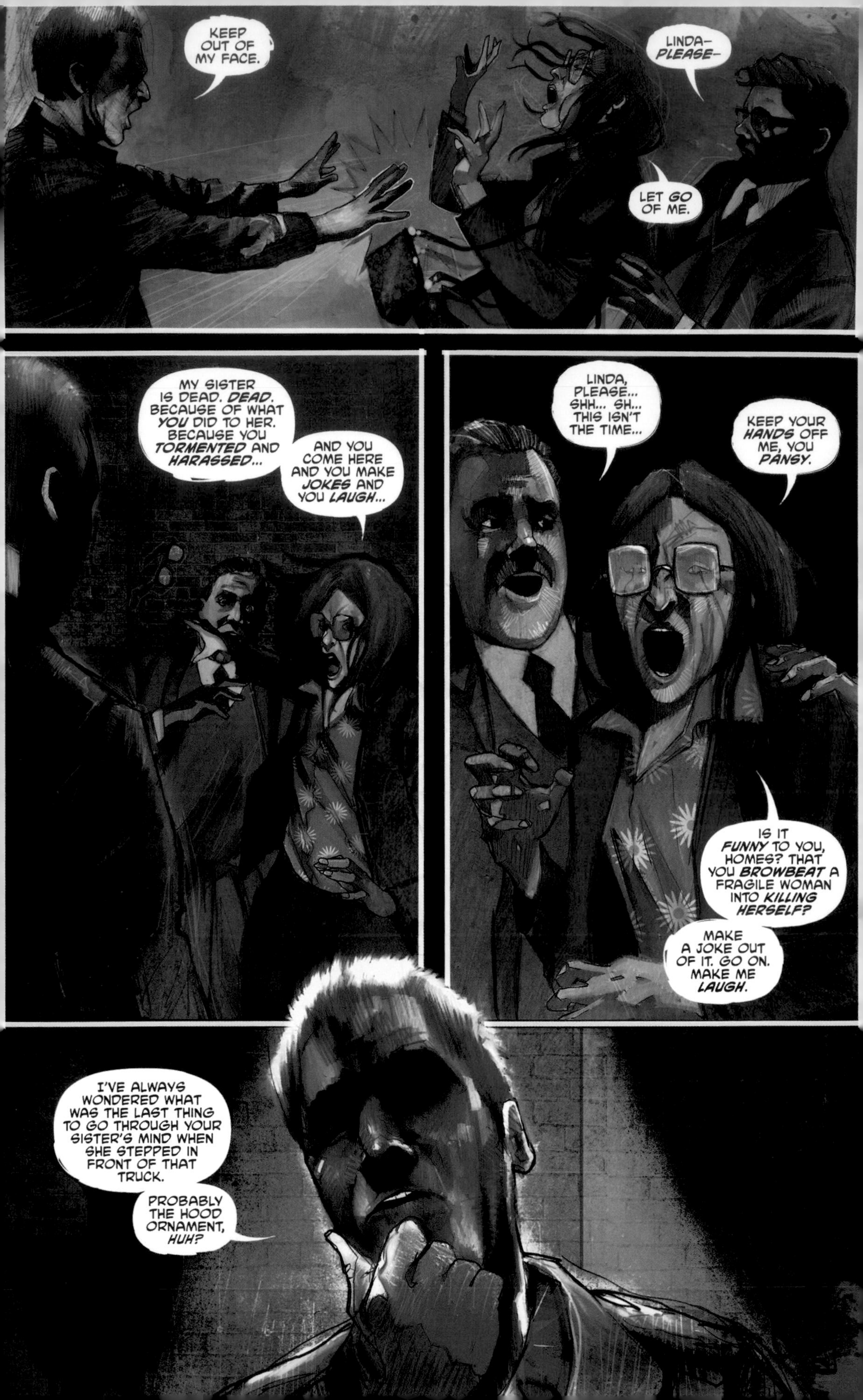

KEEP OUT OF MY FACE.
LINDA—PLEASE—
LET GO OF ME.
MY SISTER IS DEAD. DEAD. BECAUSE OF WHAT YOU DID TO HER. BECAUSE YOU TORMENTED AND HARASSED...
AND YOU COME HERE AND YOU MAKE JOKES AND YOU LAUGH...
LINDA, PLEASE... SHH... SH... THIS ISN'T THE TIME...
KEEP YOUR HANDS OFF ME, YOU PANSY.
IS IT FUNNY TO YOU, HOMES? THAT YOU BROWBEAT A FRAGILE WOMAN INTO KILLING HERSELF?
MAKE A JOKE OUT OF IT. GO ON. MAKE ME LAUGH.
I'VE ALWAYS WONDERED WHAT WAS THE LAST THING TO GO THROUGH YOUR SISTER'S MIND WHEN SHE STEPPED IN FRONT OF THAT TRUCK.
PROBABLY THE HOOD ORNAMENT, HUH?

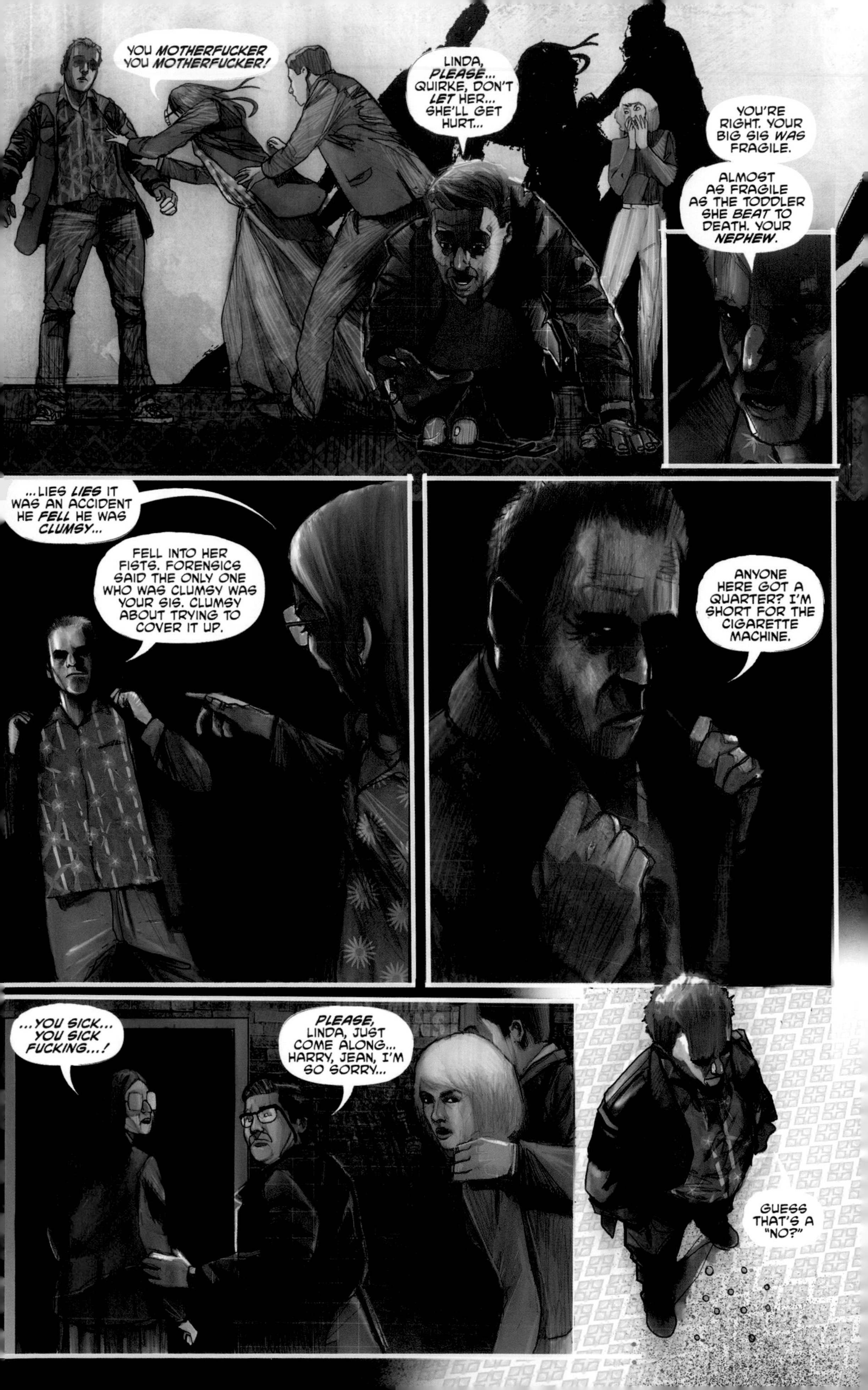
YOU MOTHERFUCKER YOU MOTHERFUCKER!
LINDA, PLEASE... QUIRKE, DON'T LET HER... SHE'LL GET HURT...
YOU'RE RIGHT. YOUR BIG SIS WAS FRAGILE.
ALMOST AS FRAGILE AS THE TODDLER SHE BEAT TO DEATH. YOUR NEPHEW.
...LIES LIES IT WAS AN ACCIDENT HE FELL HE WAS CLUMSY...
FELL INTO HER FISTS. FORENSICS SAID THE ONLY ONE WHO WAS CLUMSY WAS YOUR SIS. CLUMSY ABOUT TRYING TO COVER IT UP.
ANYONE HERE GOT A QUARTER? I'M SHORT FOR THE CIGARETTE MACHINE.
...YOU SICK... YOU SICK FUCKING...!
PLEASE, LINDA, JUST COME ALONG... HARRY, JEAN, I'M SO SORRY...
GUESS THAT'S A "NO?"

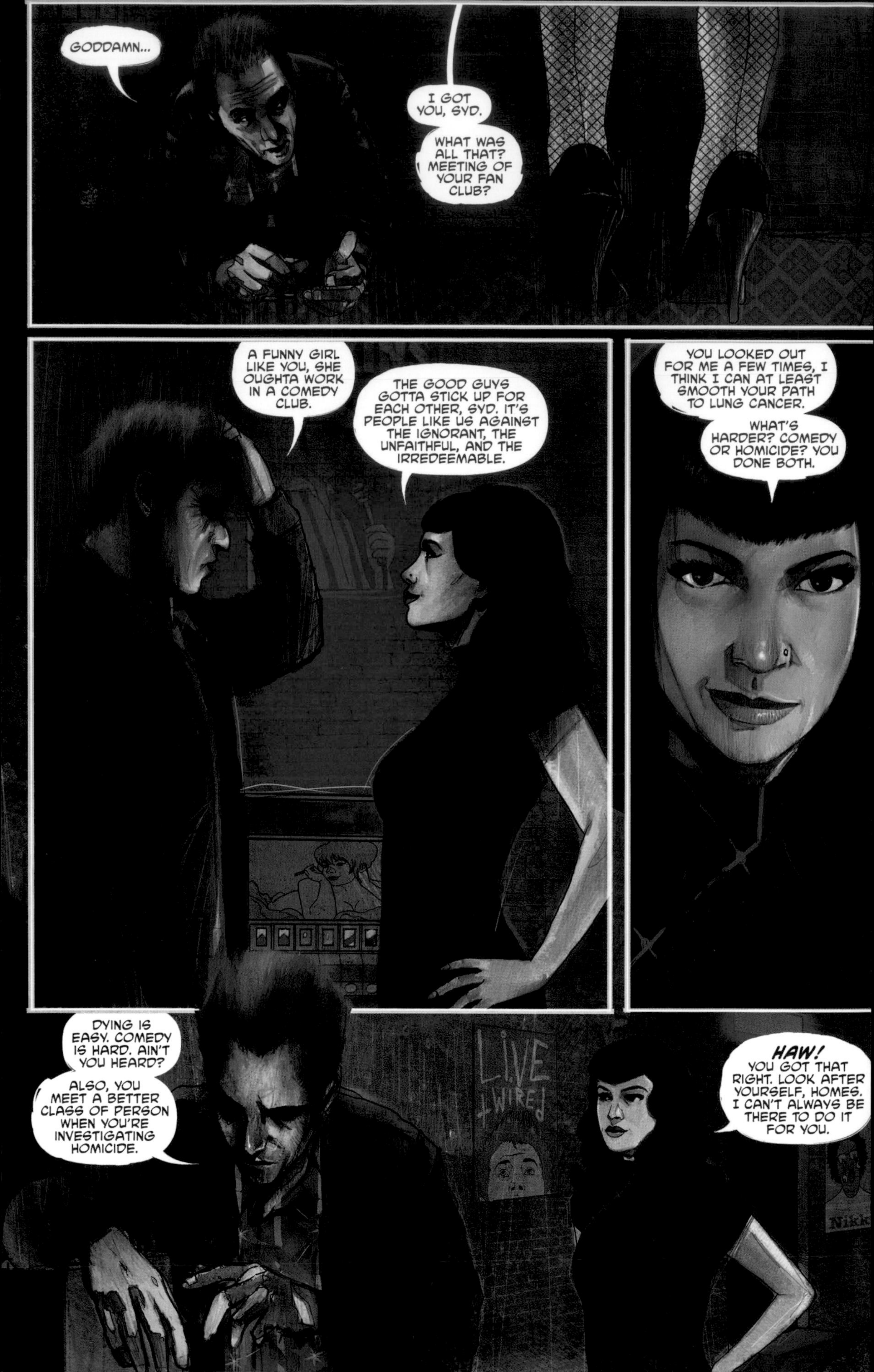
GODDAMN...
I GOT YOU, SYD.
WHAT WAS ALL THAT? MEETING OF YOUR FAN CLUB?
A FUNNY GIRL LIKE YOU, SHE OUGHTA WORK IN A COMEDY CLUB.
THE GOOD GUYS GOTTA STICK UP FOR EACH OTHER, SYD. IT'S PEOPLE LIKE US AGAINST THE IGNORANT, THE UNFAITHFUL, AND THE IRREDEEMABLE.
YOU LOOKED OUT FOR ME A FEW TIMES, I THINK I CAN AT LEAST SMOOTH YOUR PATH TO LUNG CANCER.
WHAT'S HARDER? COMEDY OR HOMICIDE? YOU DONE BOTH.
DYING IS EASY. COMEDY IS HARD. AIN'T YOU HEARD?
ALSO, YOU MEET A BETTER CLASS OF PERSON WHEN YOU'RE INVESTIGATING HOMICIDE.
LIVE WIRED
HAW! YOU GOT THAT RIGHT. LOOK AFTER YOURSELF, HOMES. I CAN'T ALWAYS BE THERE TO DO IT FOR YOU.

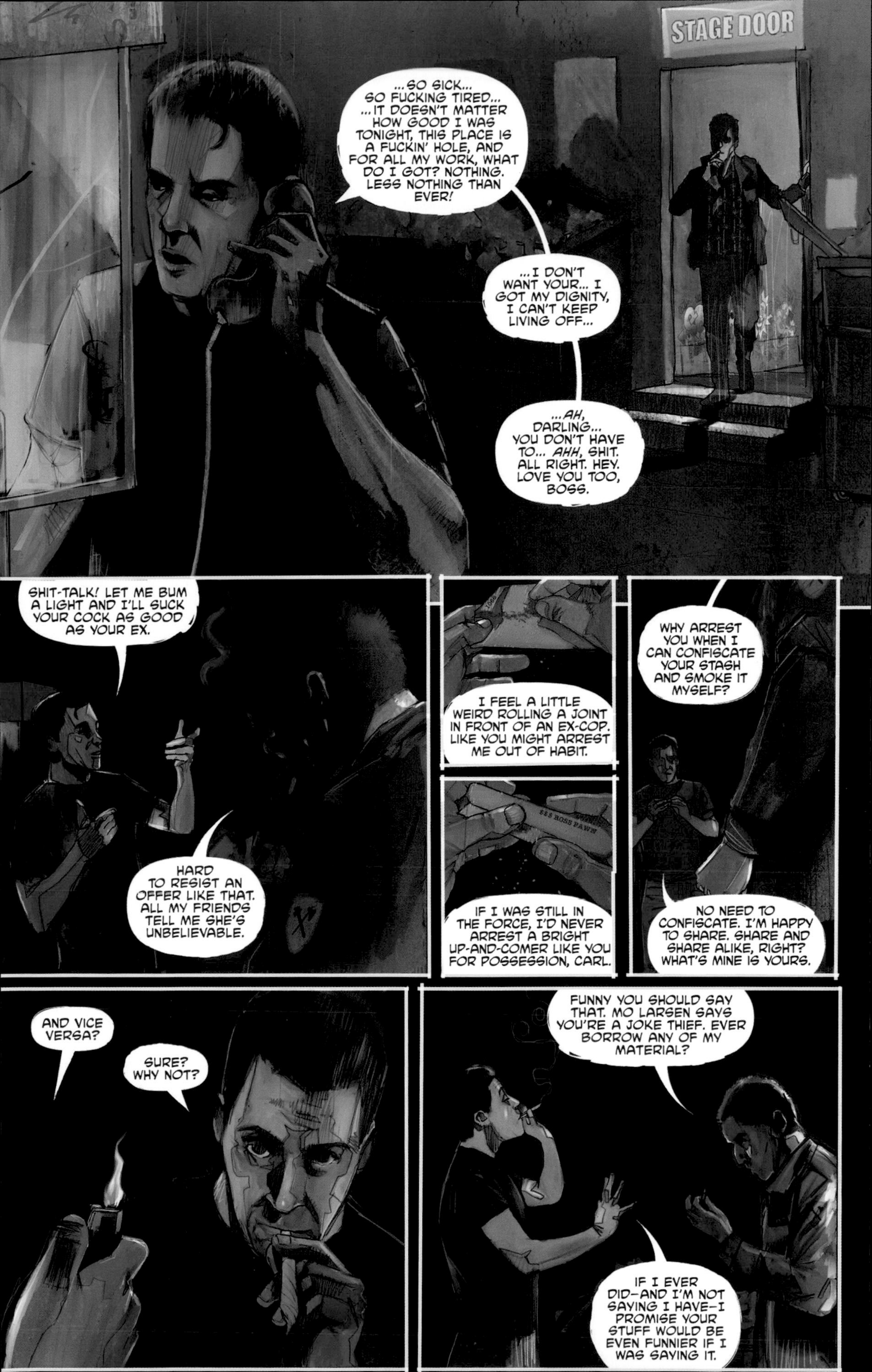
STAGE DOOR
...SO SICK... SO FUCKING TIRED... ...IT DOESN'T MATTER HOW GOOD I WAS TONIGHT, THIS PLACE IS A FUCKIN' HOLE, AND FOR ALL MY WORK, WHAT DO I GOT? NOTHING. LESS NOTHING THAN EVER!
...I DON'T WANT YOUR... I GOT MY DIGNITY, I CAN'T KEEP LIVING OFF...
...AH, DARLING... YOU DON'T HAVE TO... AHH, SHIT. ALL RIGHT. HEY. LOVE YOU TOO, BOSS.
SHIT-TALK! LET ME BUM A LIGHT AND I'LL SUCK YOUR COCK AS GOOD AS YOUR EX.
HARD TO RESIST AN OFFER LIKE THAT. ALL MY FRIENDS TELL ME SHE'S UNBELIEVABLE.
I FEEL A LITTLE WEIRD ROLLING A JOINT IN FRONT OF AN EX-COP. LIKE YOU MIGHT ARREST ME OUT OF HABIT.
IF I WAS STILL IN THE FORCE, I'D NEVER ARREST A BRIGHT UP-AND-COMER LIKE YOU FOR POSSESSION, CARL.
WHY ARREST YOU WHEN I CAN CONFISCATE YOUR STASH AND SMOKE IT MYSELF?
NO NEED TO CONFISCATE. I'M HAPPY TO SHARE. SHARE AND SHARE ALIKE, RIGHT? WHAT'S MINE IS YOURS.
AND VICE VERSA?
SURE? WHY NOT?
FUNNY YOU SHOULD SAY THAT. MO LARSEN SAYS YOU'RE A JOKE THIEF. EVER BORROW ANY OF MY MATERIAL?
IF I EVER DID—AND I'M NOT SAYING I HAVE—I PROMISE YOUR STUFF WOULD BE EVEN FUNNIER IF I WAS SAYING IT.

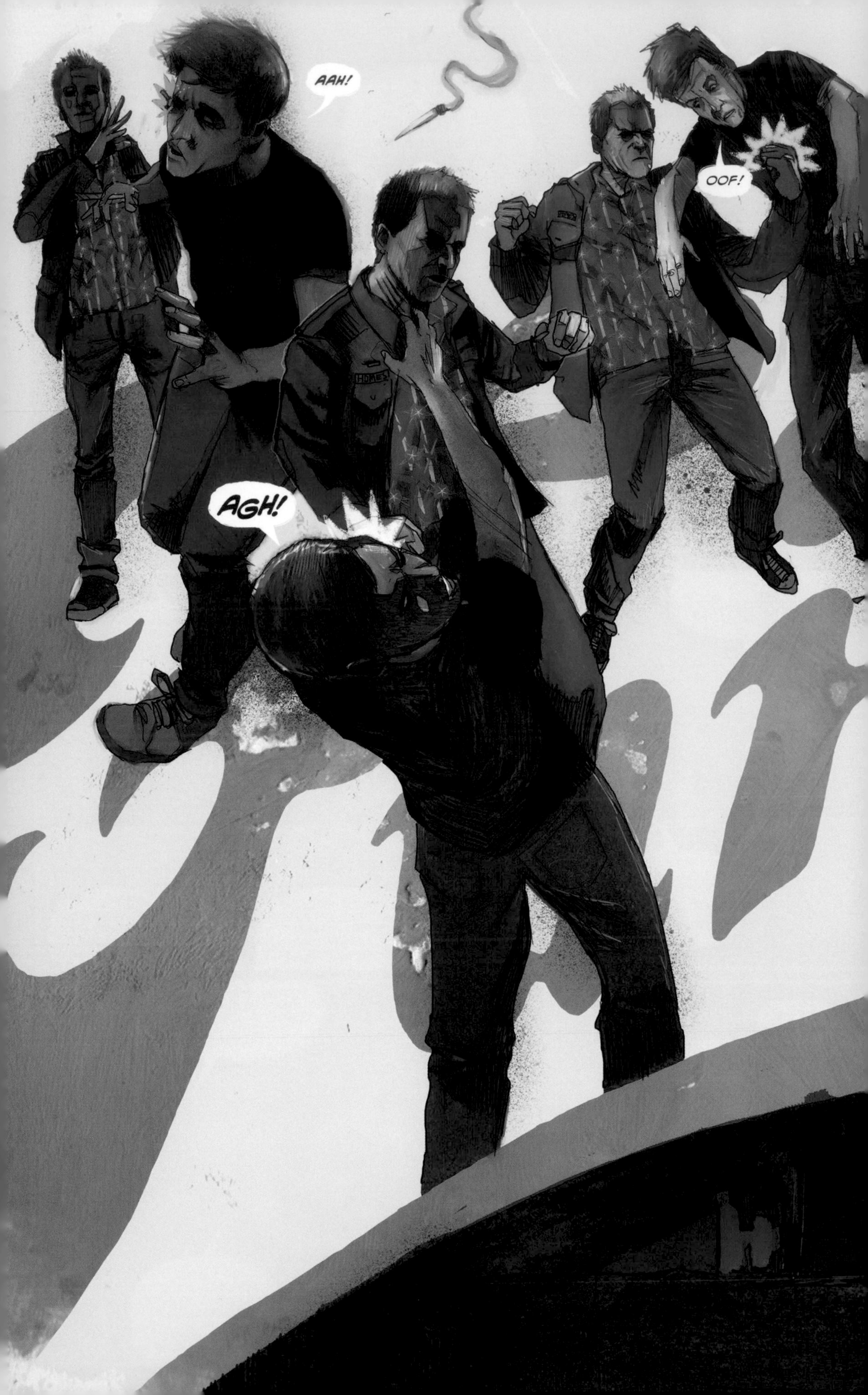
AAH!
OOF!
AGH!

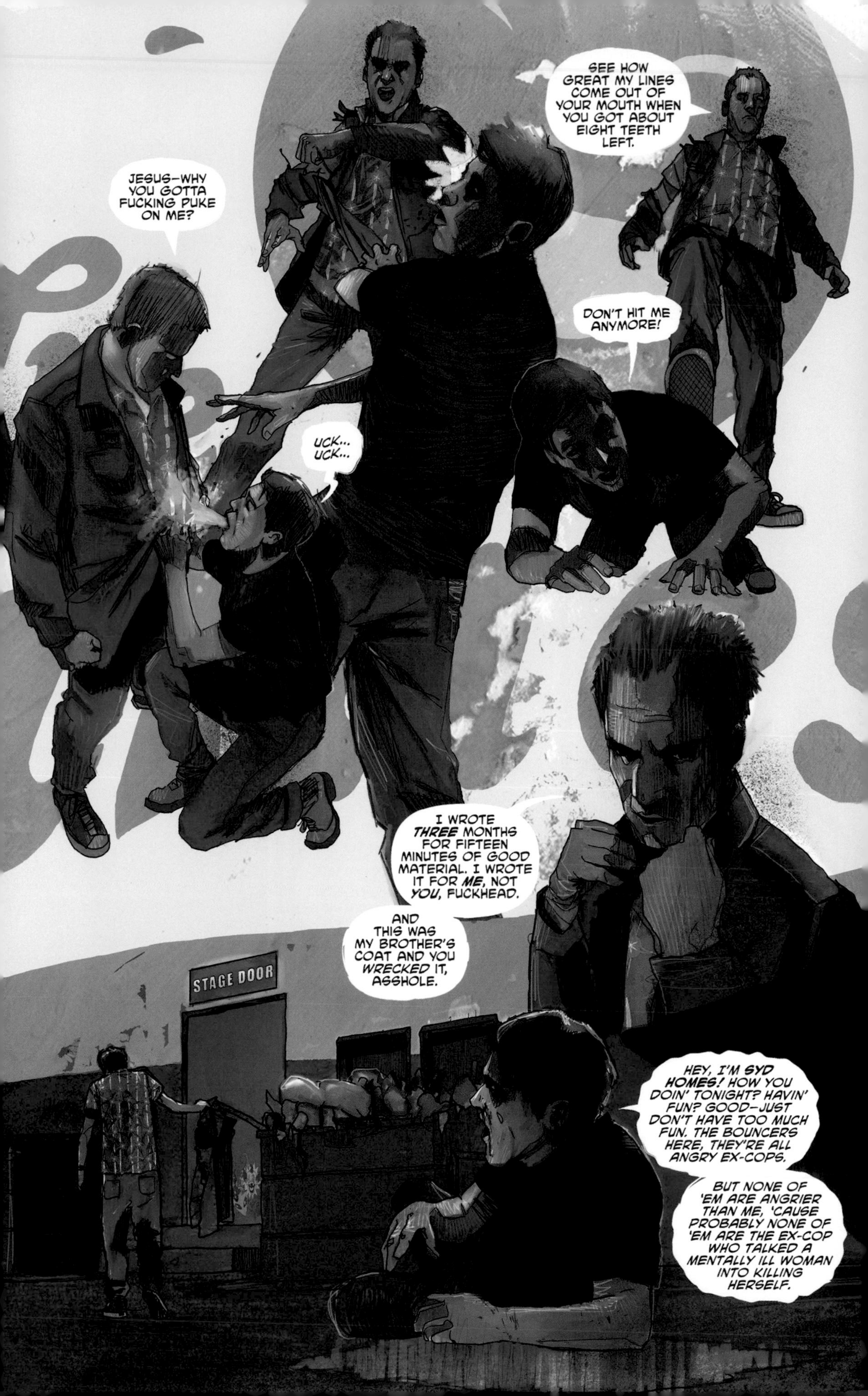
JESUS—WHY YOU GOTTA FUCKING PUKE ON ME?
SEE HOW GREAT MY LINES COME OUT OF YOUR MOUTH WHEN YOU GOT ABOUT EIGHT TEETH LEFT.
DON'T HIT ME ANYMORE!
UCK... UCK...
I WROTE *THREE* MONTHS FOR FIFTEEN MINUTES OF GOOD MATERIAL. I WROTE IT FOR *ME*, NOT *YOU*, FUCKHEAD.
AND THIS WAS MY BROTHER'S COAT AND YOU *WRECKED* IT, ASSHOLE.
STAGE DOOR
*HEY, I'M **SYD HOMES!** HOW YOU DOIN' TONIGHT? HAVIN' FUN? GOOD—JUST DON'T HAVE TOO MUCH FUN. THE BOUNCERS HERE, THEY'RE ALL ANGRY EX-COPS.*
BUT NONE OF 'EM ARE ANGRIER THAN ME, 'CAUSE PROBABLY NONE OF 'EM ARE THE EX-COP WHO TALKED A MENTALLY ILL WOMAN INTO KILLING HERSELF.

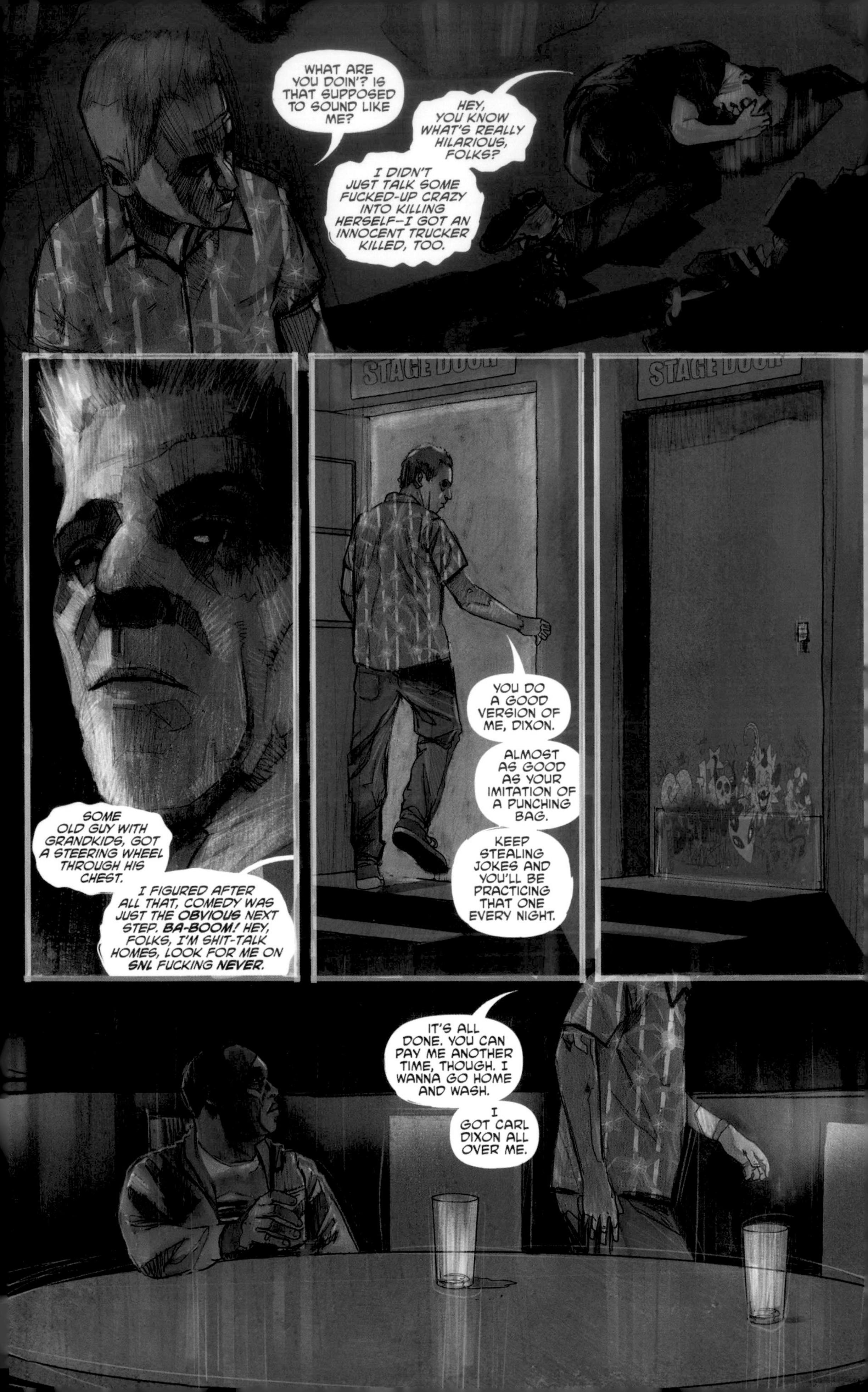
WHAT ARE YOU DOIN'? IS THAT SUPPOSED TO SOUND LIKE ME?
HEY, YOU KNOW WHAT'S REALLY HILARIOUS, FOLKS?
I DIDN'T JUST TALK SOME FUCKED-UP CRAZY INTO KILLING HERSELF—I GOT AN INNOCENT TRUCKER KILLED, TOO.
SOME OLD GUY WITH GRANDKIDS, GOT A STEERING WHEEL THROUGH HIS CHEST.
I FIGURED AFTER ALL THAT, COMEDY WAS JUST THE **OBVIOUS** NEXT STEP. **BA-BOOM!** HEY, FOLKS, I'M SHIT-TALK HOMES, LOOK FOR ME ON **SNL** FUCKING **NEVER**.
STAGE DOOR
YOU DO A GOOD VERSION OF ME, DIXON.
ALMOST AS GOOD AS YOUR IMITATION OF A PUNCHING BAG.
KEEP STEALING JOKES AND YOU'LL BE PRACTICING THAT ONE EVERY NIGHT.
STAGE DOOR
IT'S ALL DONE. YOU CAN PAY ME ANOTHER TIME, THOUGH. I WANNA GO HOME AND WASH.
I GOT CARL DIXON ALL OVER ME.

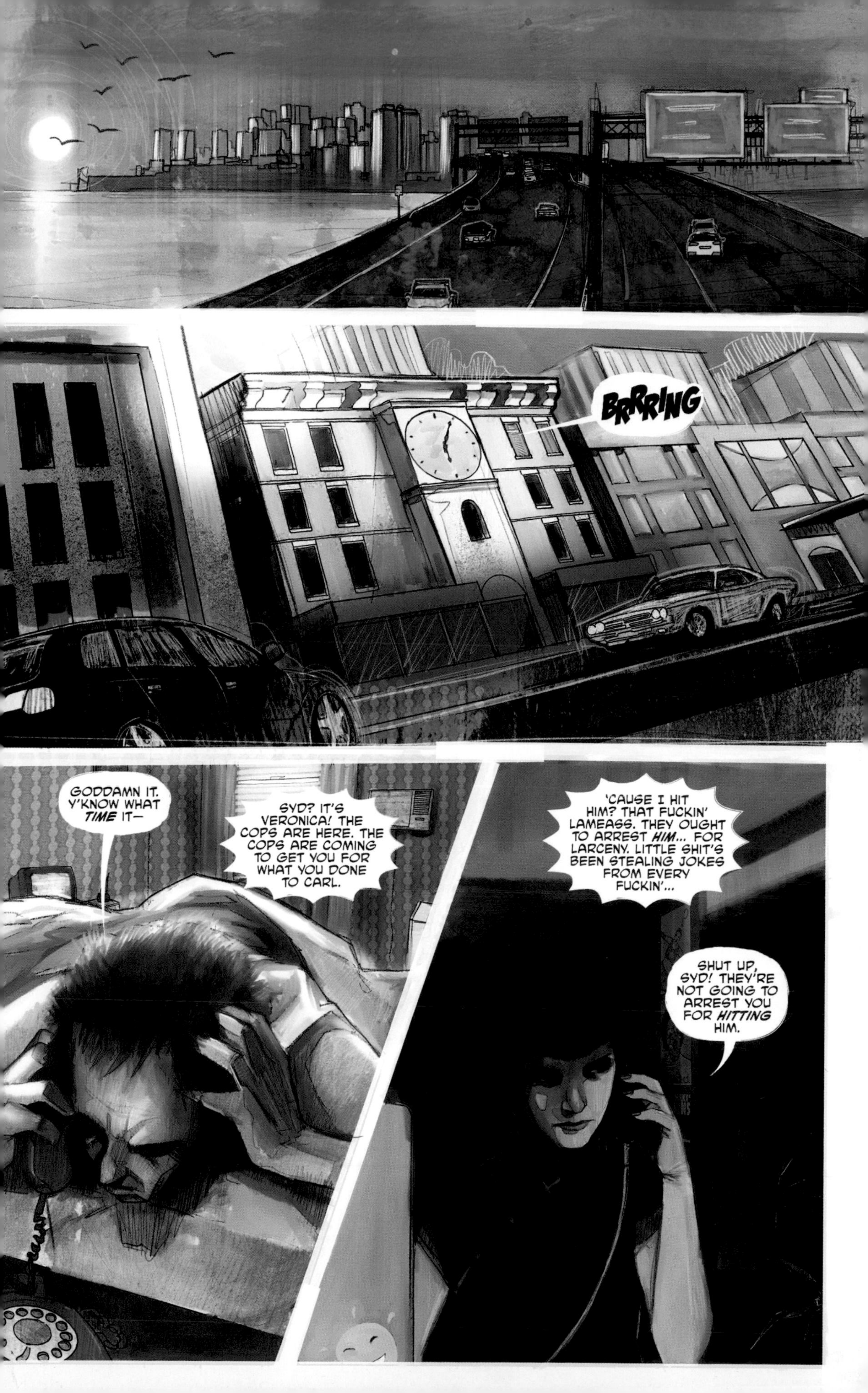
BRRRING
GODDAMN IT. Y'KNOW WHAT *TIME* IT—
SYD? IT'S VERONICA! THE COPS ARE HERE. THE COPS ARE COMING TO GET YOU FOR WHAT YOU DONE TO CARL.
'CAUSE I HIT HIM? THAT FUCKIN' LAMEASS. THEY OUGHT TO ARREST *HIM*... FOR LARCENY. LITTLE SHIT'S BEEN STEALING JOKES FROM EVERY FUCKIN'...
SHUT UP, SYD! THEY'RE NOT GOING TO ARREST YOU FOR *HITTING* HIM.

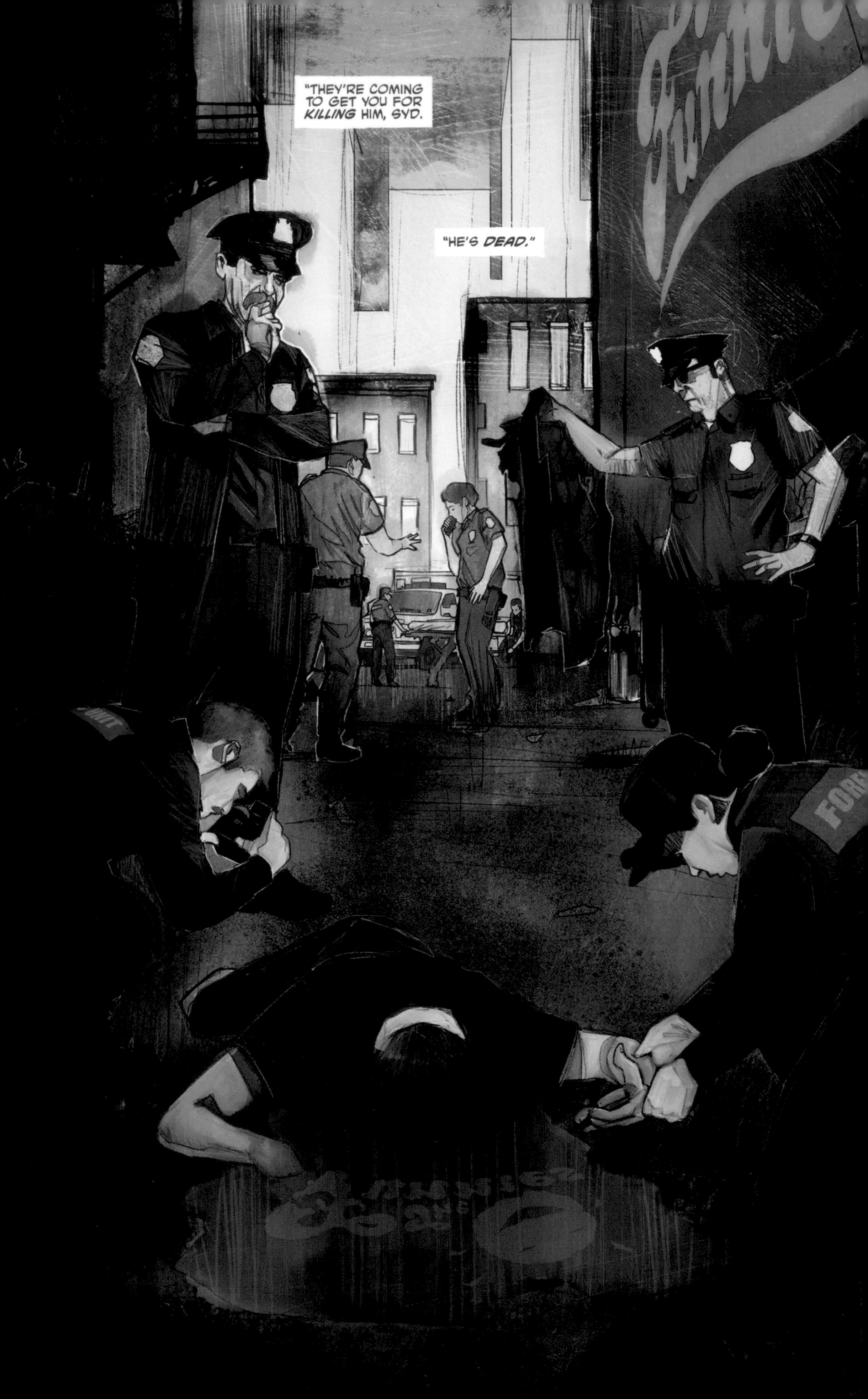
"THEY'RE COMING TO GET YOU FOR *KILLING* HIM, SYD.
"HE'S *DEAD.*"

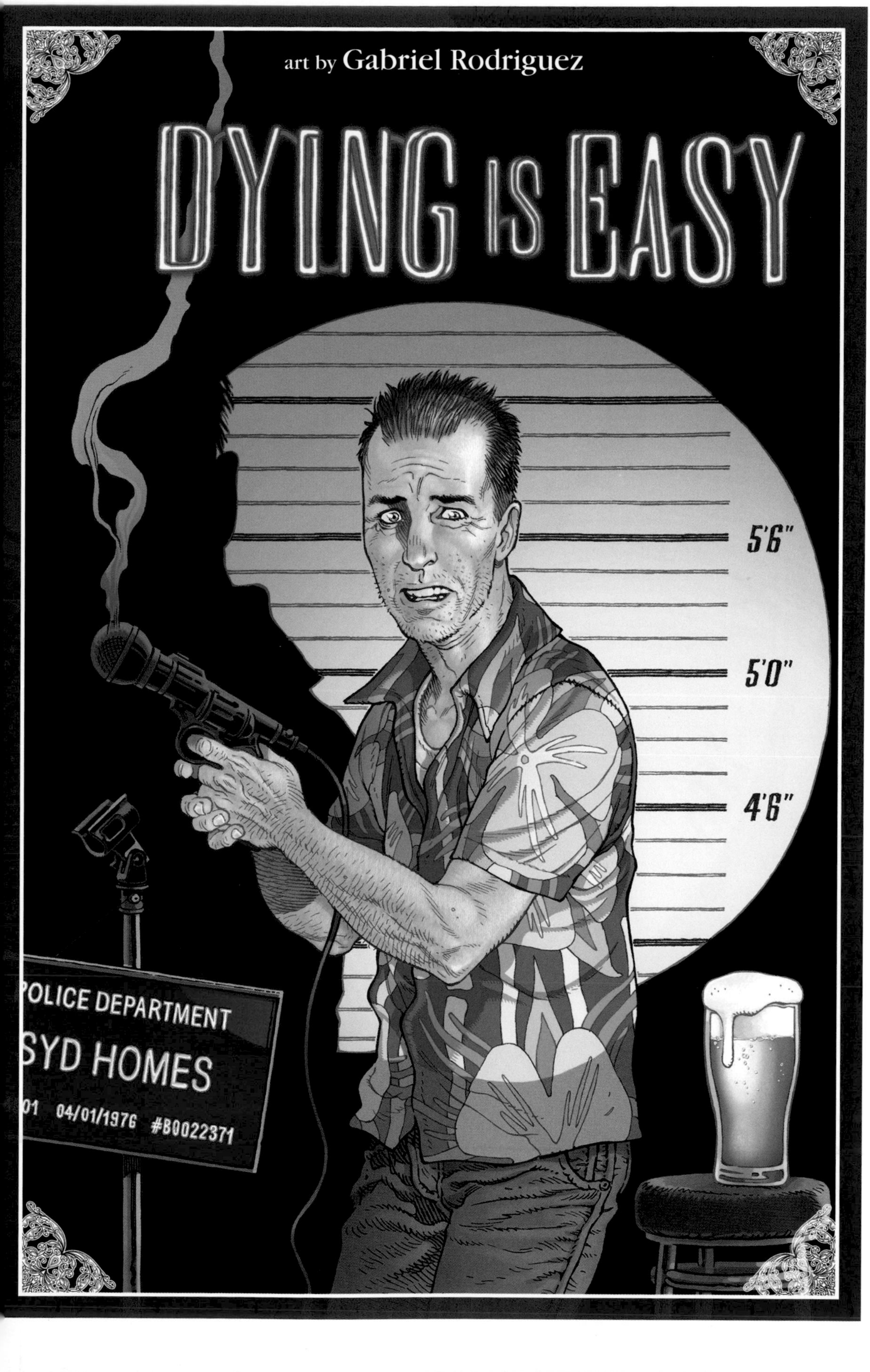
art by Gabriel Rodriguez
DYING IS EASY
5'6"
5'0"
4'6"
POLICE DEPARTMENT
SYD HOMES
01 04/01/1976 #B0022371

2 • art by Martin Simmonds • 2

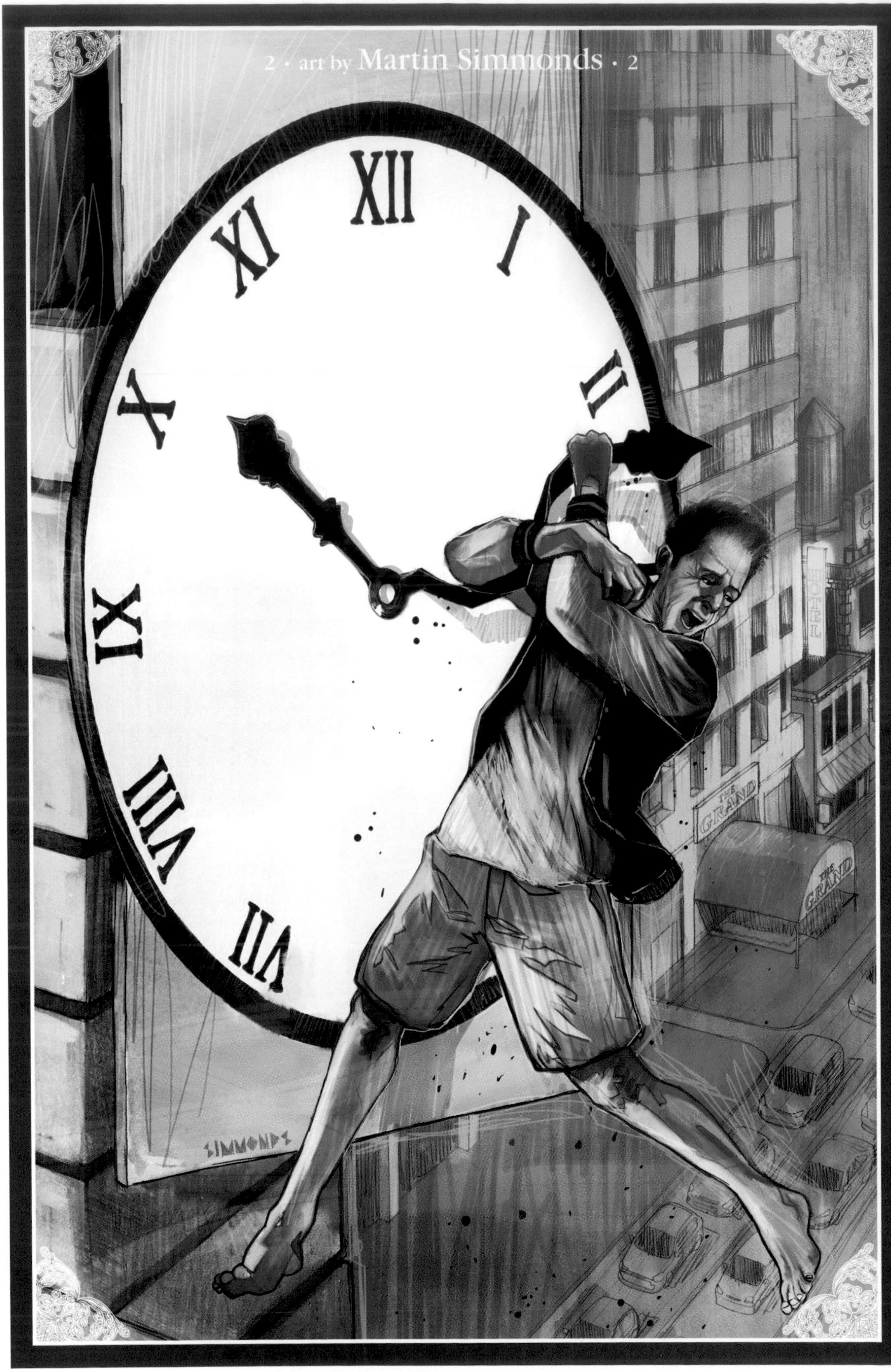

SIMMONDS
HOTEL
THE GRAND
THE GRAND

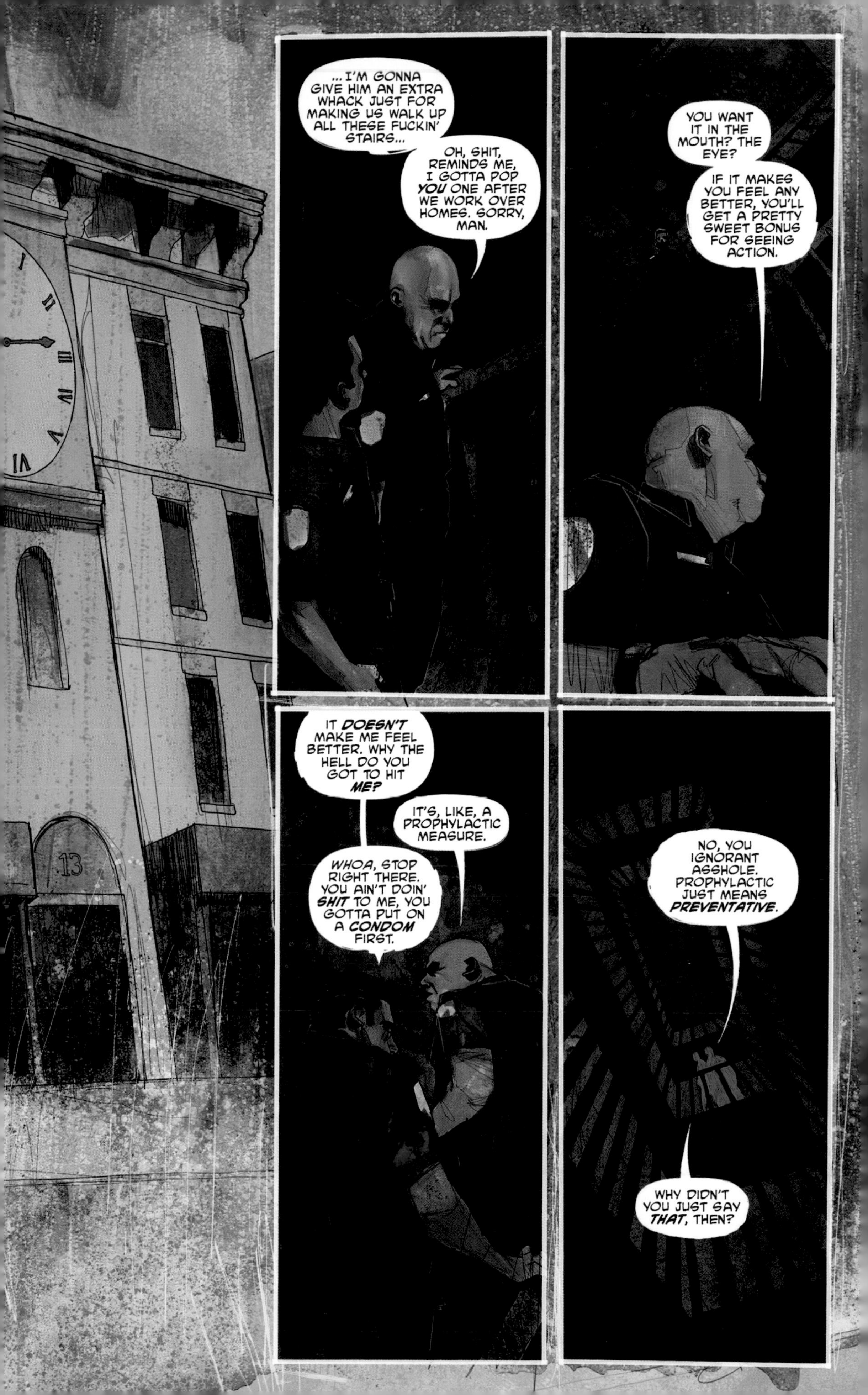

... I'M GONNA GIVE HIM AN EXTRA WHACK JUST FOR MAKING US WALK UP ALL THESE FUCKIN' STAIRS...
OH, SHIT, REMINDS ME, I GOTTA POP *YOU* ONE AFTER WE WORK OVER HOMES. SORRY, MAN.
YOU WANT IT IN THE MOUTH? THE EYE?
IF IT MAKES YOU FEEL ANY BETTER, YOU'LL GET A PRETTY SWEET BONUS FOR SEEING ACTION.
IT *DOESN'T* MAKE ME FEEL BETTER. WHY THE HELL DO YOU GOT TO HIT *ME?*
IT'S, LIKE, A PROPHYLACTIC MEASURE.
WHOA, STOP RIGHT THERE. YOU AIN'T DOIN' *SHIT* TO ME, YOU GOTTA PUT ON A *CONDOM* FIRST.
NO, YOU IGNORANT ASSHOLE. PROPHYLACTIC JUST MEANS *PREVENTATIVE*.
WHY DIDN'T YOU JUST SAY *THAT*, THEN?

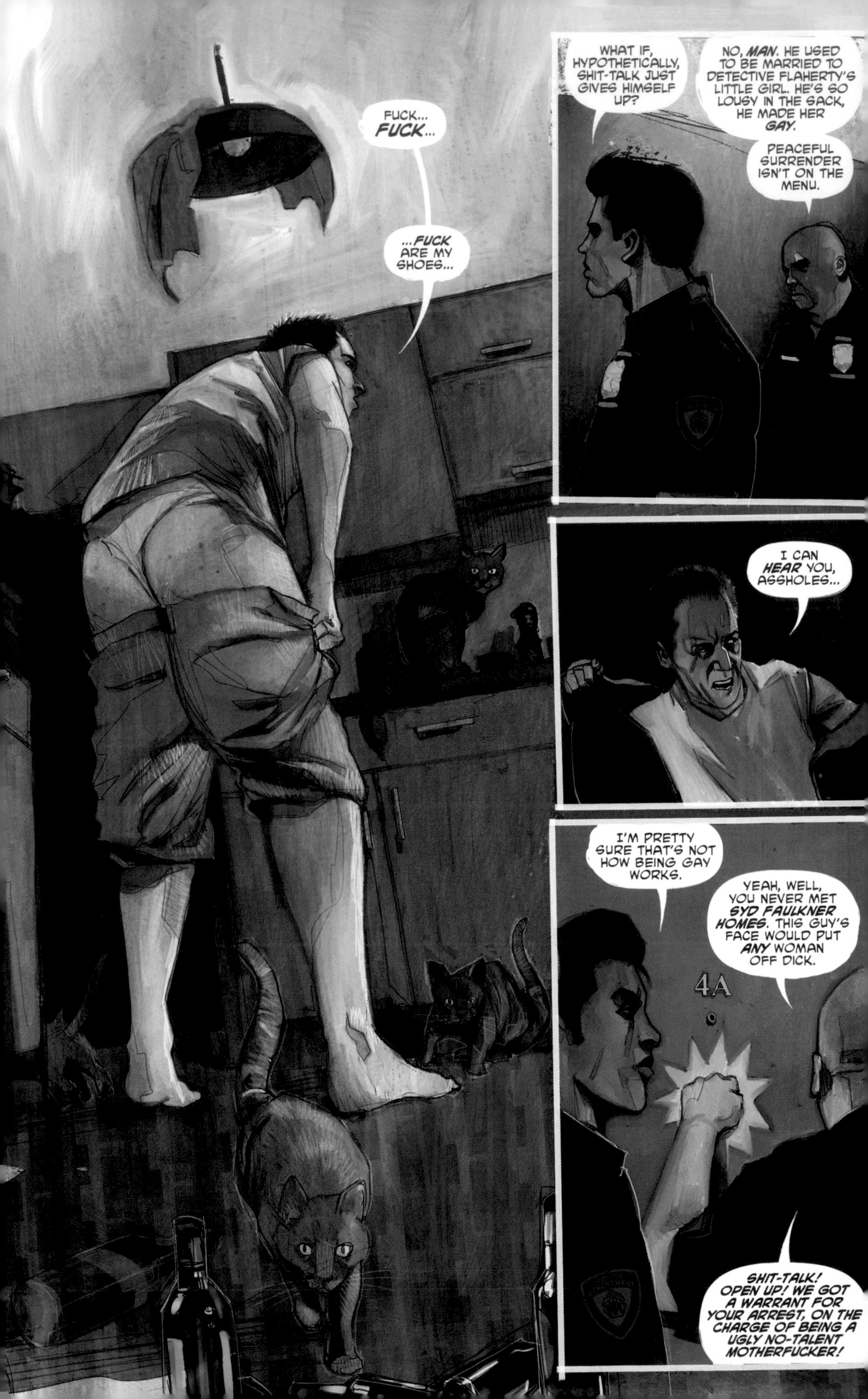
FUCK... FUCK...
...FUCK ARE MY SHOES...
WHAT IF, HYPOTHETICALLY, SHIT-TALK JUST GIVES HIMSELF UP?
NO, MAN. HE USED TO BE MARRIED TO DETECTIVE FLAHERTY'S LITTLE GIRL. HE'S SO LOUSY IN THE SACK, HE MADE HER GAY.
PEACEFUL SURRENDER ISN'T ON THE MENU.
I CAN HEAR YOU, ASSHOLES...
I'M PRETTY SURE THAT'S NOT HOW BEING GAY WORKS.
YEAH, WELL, YOU NEVER MET SYD FAULKNER HOMES. THIS GUY'S FACE WOULD PUT ANY WOMAN OFF DICK.
4A
SHIT-TALK! OPEN UP! WE GOT A WARRANT FOR YOUR ARREST, ON THE CHARGE OF BEING A UGLY NO-TALENT MOTHERFUCKER!

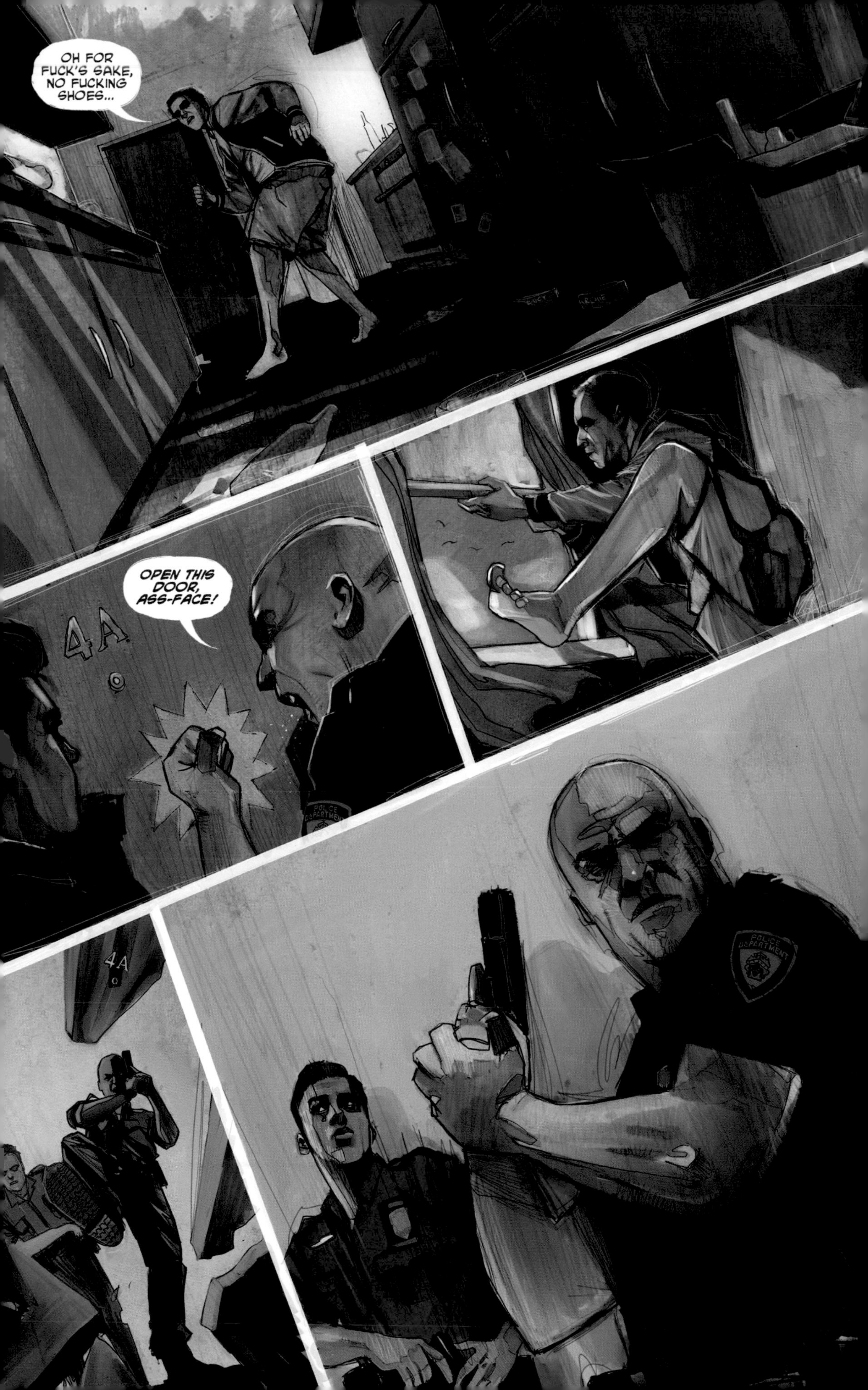
OH FOR FUCK'S SAKE, NO FUCKING SHOES...
OPEN THIS DOOR, ASS-FACE!
4A
POLICE DEPARTMENT

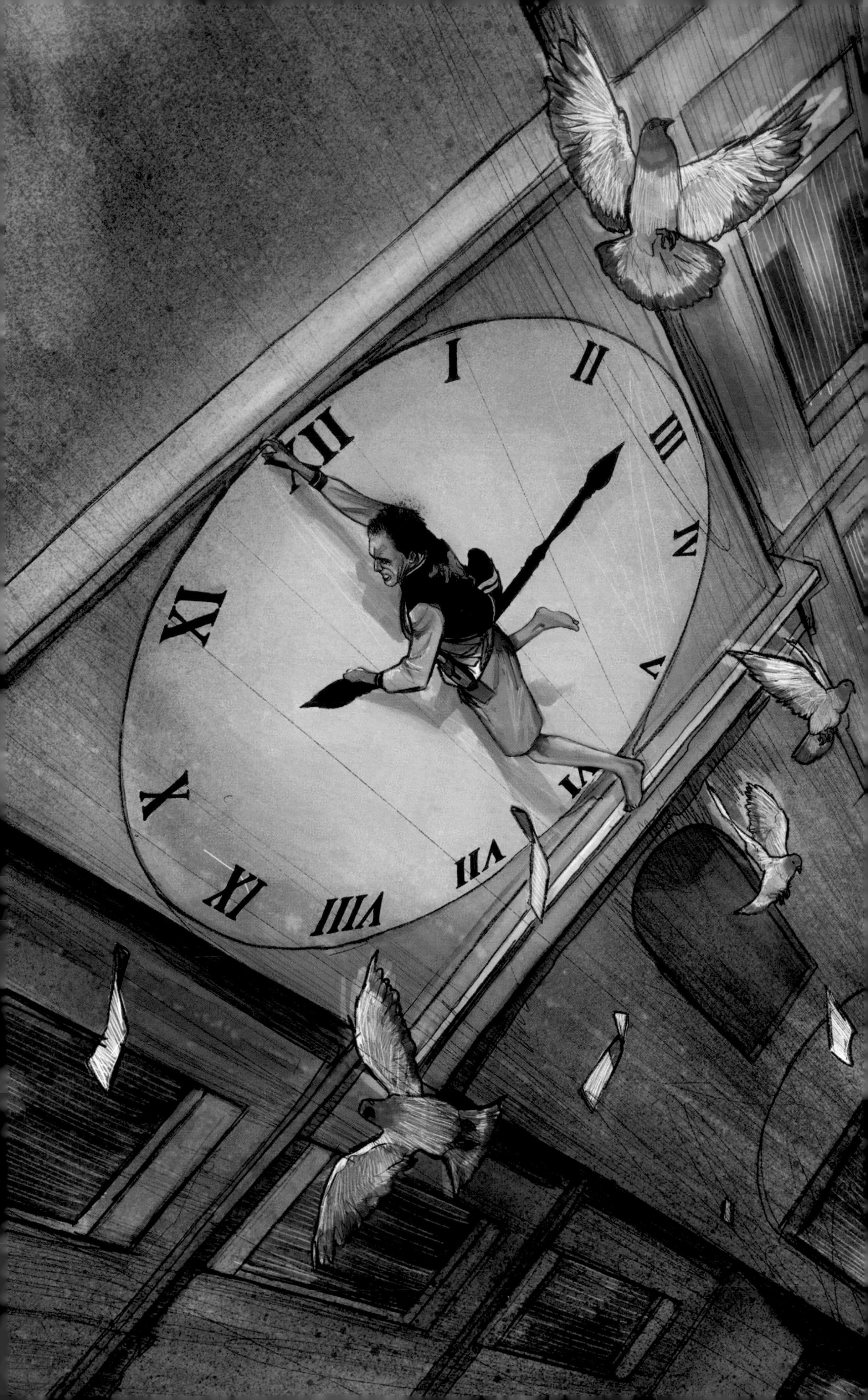

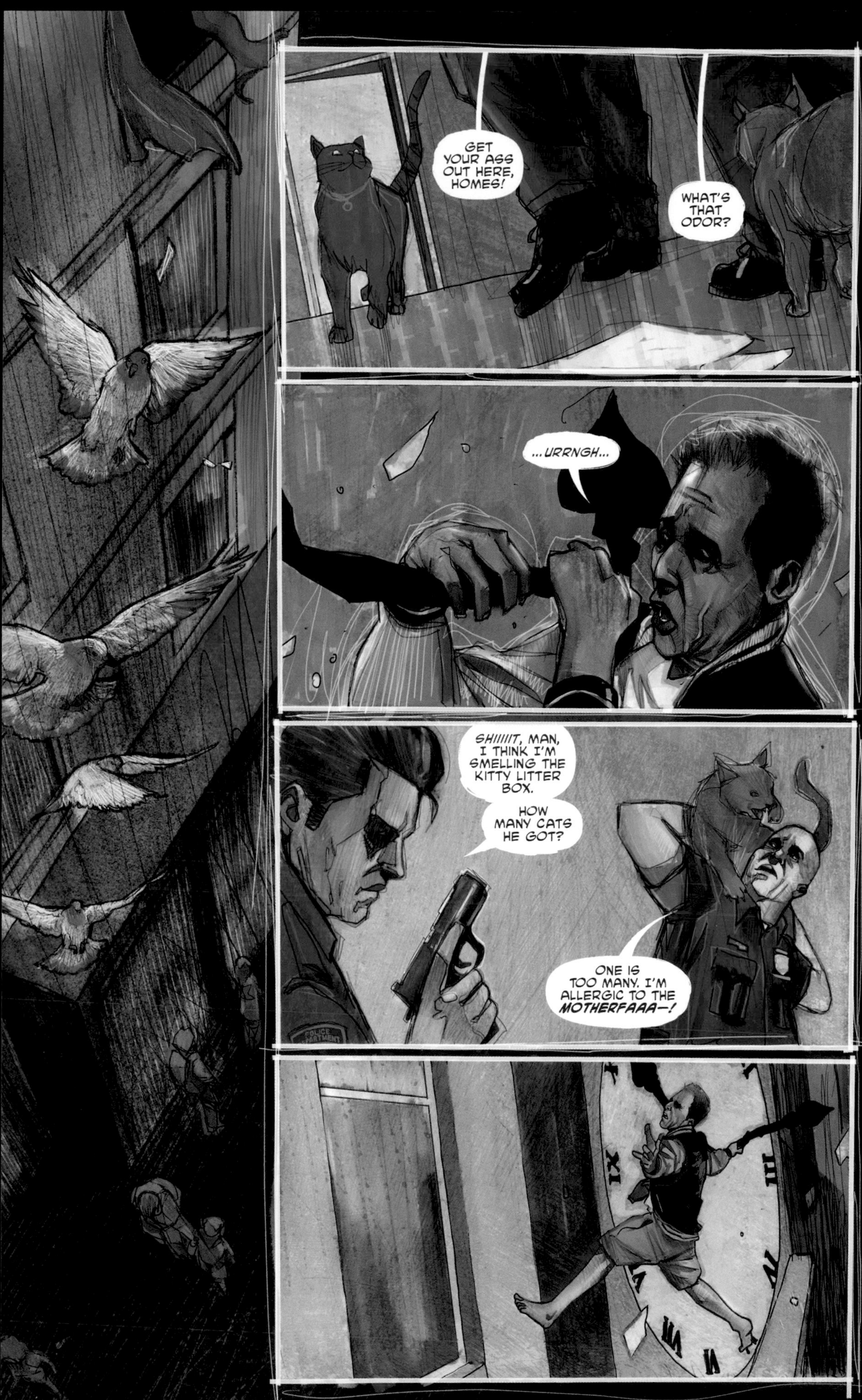
GET YOUR ASS OUT HERE, HOMES!
WHAT'S THAT ODOR?
...URRNGH...
SHIIIIIT, MAN, I THINK I'M SMELLING THE KITTY LITTER BOX.
HOW MANY CATS HE GOT?
ONE IS TOO MANY. I'M ALLERGIC TO THE MOTHERFAAA—!
POLICE DEPARTMENT

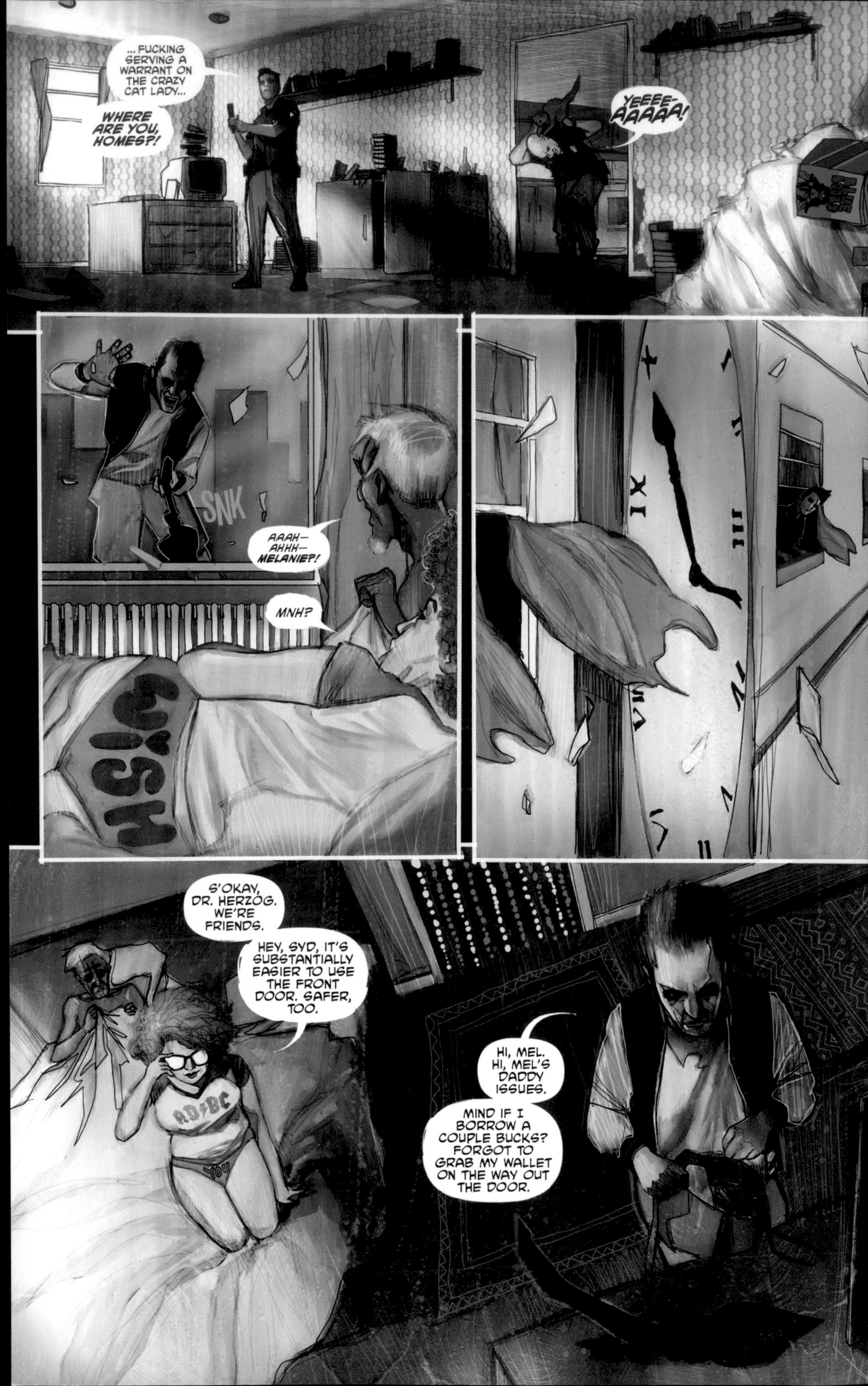

...FUCKING SERVING A WARRANT ON THE CRAZY CAT LADY...
WHERE ARE YOU, HOMES?!
YEEEE-AAAAA!
SNK
AAAH— AHHH— MELANIE?!
MNH?
S'OKAY, DR. HERZOG. WE'RE FRIENDS.
HEY, SYD, IT'S SUBSTANTIALLY EASIER TO USE THE FRONT DOOR. SAFER, TOO.
HI, MEL. HI, MEL'S DADDY ISSUES.
MIND IF I BORROW A COUPLE BUCKS? FORGOT TO GRAB MY WALLET ON THE WAY OUT THE DOOR.

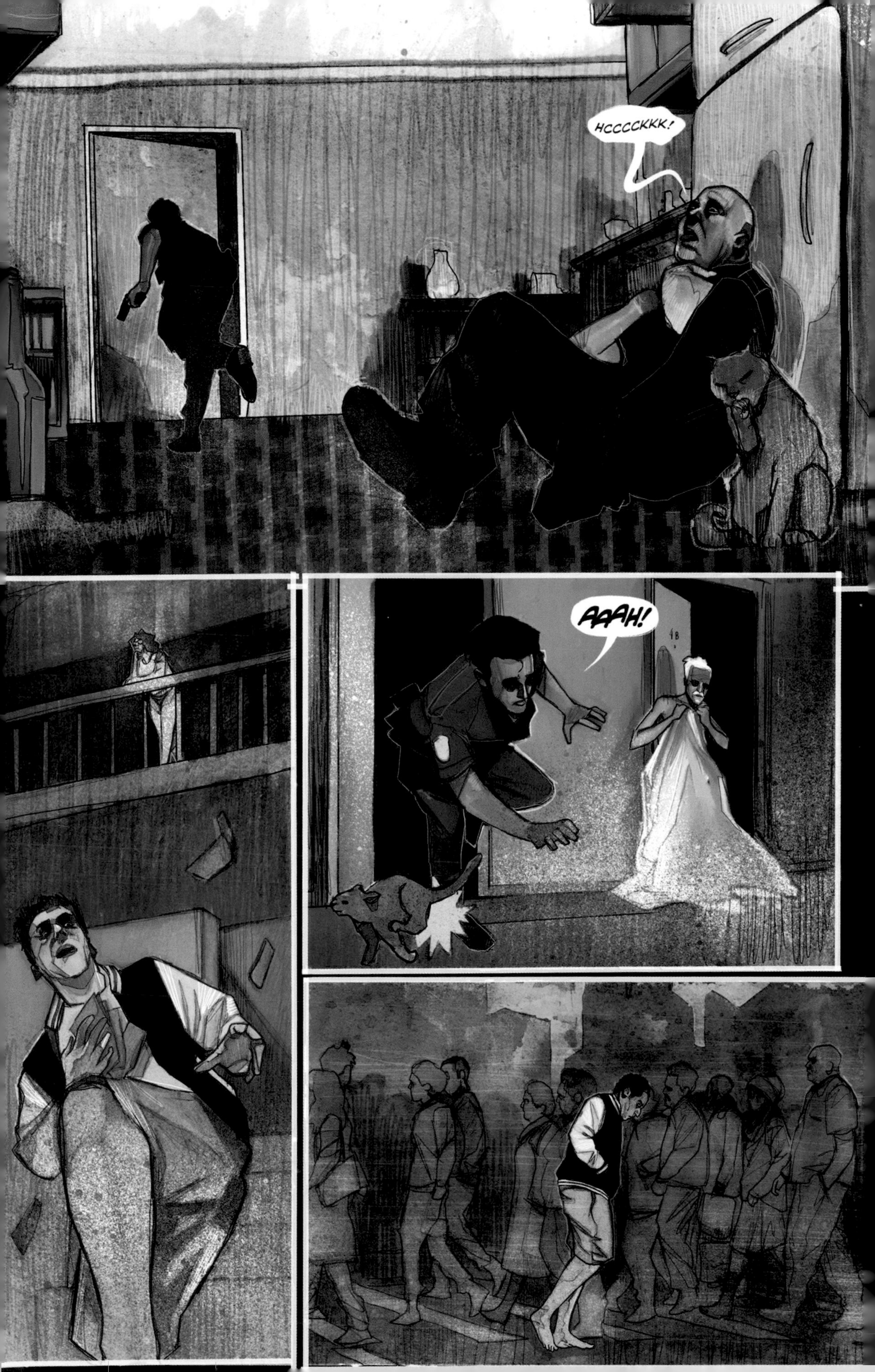
HCCCCKKK!
AAAH!

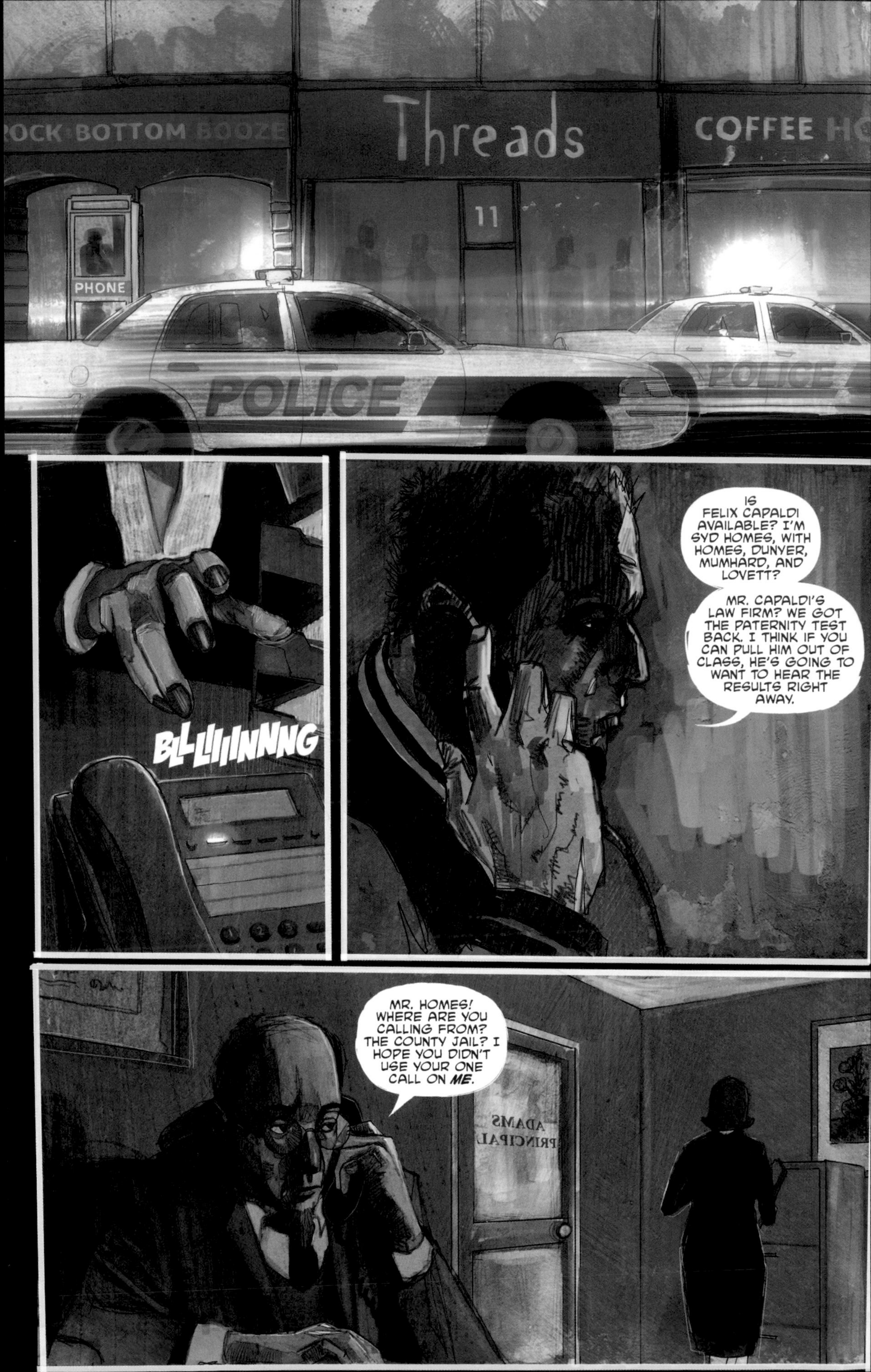

ROCK BOTTOM BOOZE
Threads
COFFEE HO
11
PHONE
POLICE
POLICE
BLLLIIIINNNG
IS FELIX CAPALDI AVAILABLE? I'M SYD HOMES, WITH HOMES, DUNYER, MUMHARD, AND LOVETT?
MR. CAPALDI'S LAW FIRM? WE GOT THE PATERNITY TEST BACK. I THINK IF YOU CAN PULL HIM OUT OF CLASS, HE'S GOING TO WANT TO HEAR THE RESULTS RIGHT AWAY.
MR. HOMES! WHERE ARE YOU CALLING FROM? THE COUNTY JAIL? I HOPE YOU DIDN'T USE YOUR ONE CALL ON *ME*.

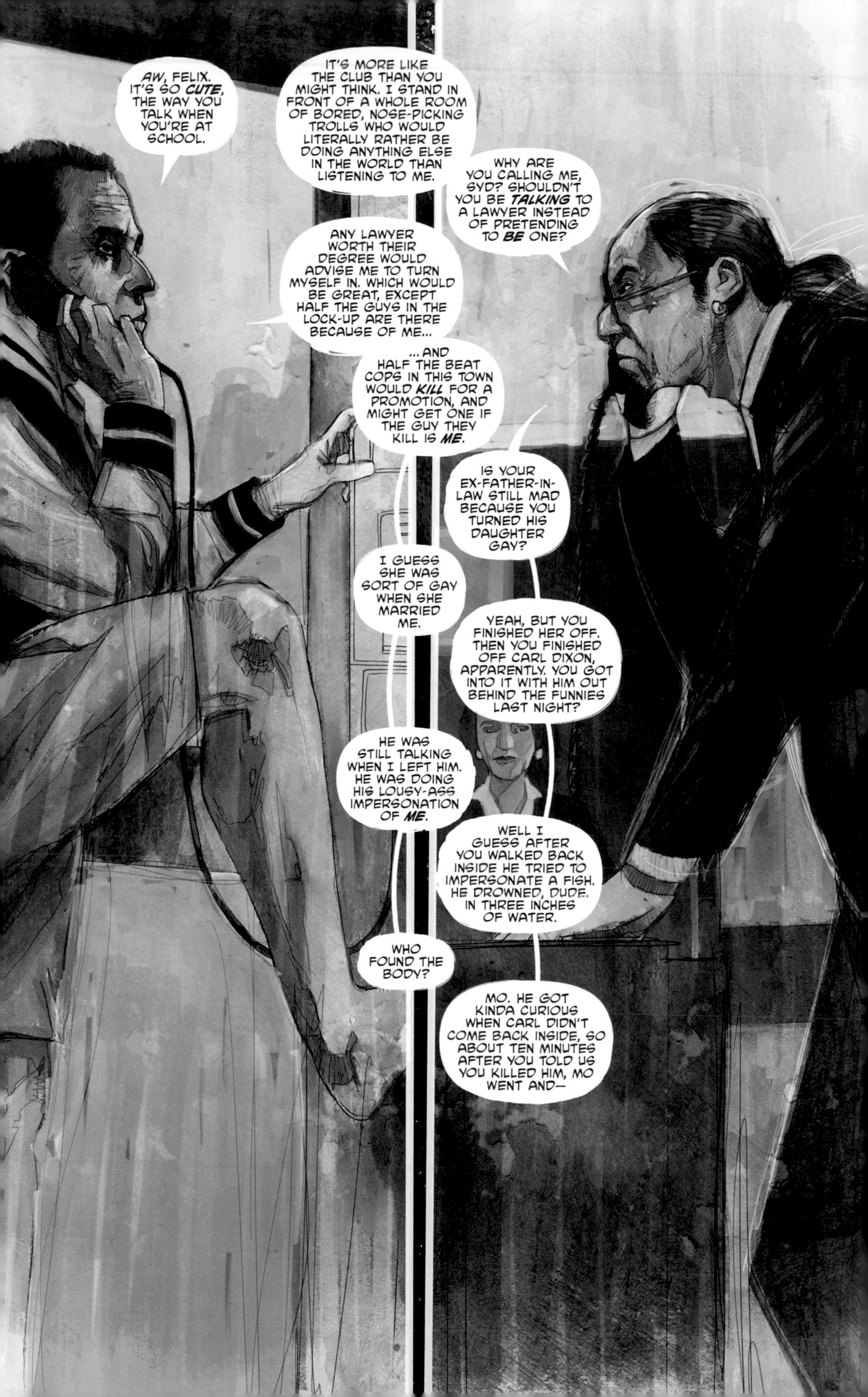
AW, FELIX. IT'S SO CUTE, THE WAY YOU TALK WHEN YOU'RE AT SCHOOL.
IT'S MORE LIKE THE CLUB THAN YOU MIGHT THINK. I STAND IN FRONT OF A WHOLE ROOM OF BORED, NOSE-PICKING TROLLS WHO WOULD LITERALLY RATHER BE DOING ANYTHING ELSE IN THE WORLD THAN LISTENING TO ME.
WHY ARE YOU CALLING ME, SYD? SHOULDN'T YOU BE TALKING TO A LAWYER INSTEAD OF PRETENDING TO BE ONE?
ANY LAWYER WORTH THEIR DEGREE WOULD ADVISE ME TO TURN MYSELF IN. WHICH WOULD BE GREAT, EXCEPT HALF THE GUYS IN THE LOCK-UP ARE THERE BECAUSE OF ME...
...AND HALF THE BEAT COPS IN THIS TOWN WOULD KILL FOR A PROMOTION, AND MIGHT GET ONE IF THE GUY THEY KILL IS ME.
IS YOUR EX-FATHER-IN-LAW STILL MAD BECAUSE YOU TURNED HIS DAUGHTER GAY?
I GUESS SHE WAS SORT OF GAY WHEN SHE MARRIED ME.
YEAH, BUT YOU FINISHED HER OFF. THEN YOU FINISHED OFF CARL DIXON, APPARENTLY. YOU GOT INTO IT WITH HIM OUT BEHIND THE FUNNIES LAST NIGHT?
HE WAS STILL TALKING WHEN I LEFT HIM. HE WAS DOING HIS LOUSY-ASS IMPERSONATION OF ME.
WELL I GUESS AFTER YOU WALKED BACK INSIDE HE TRIED TO IMPERSONATE A FISH. HE DROWNED, DUDE. IN THREE INCHES OF WATER.
WHO FOUND THE BODY?
MO. HE GOT KINDA CURIOUS WHEN CARL DIDN'T COME BACK INSIDE, SO ABOUT TEN MINUTES AFTER YOU TOLD US YOU KILLED HIM, MO WENT AND—

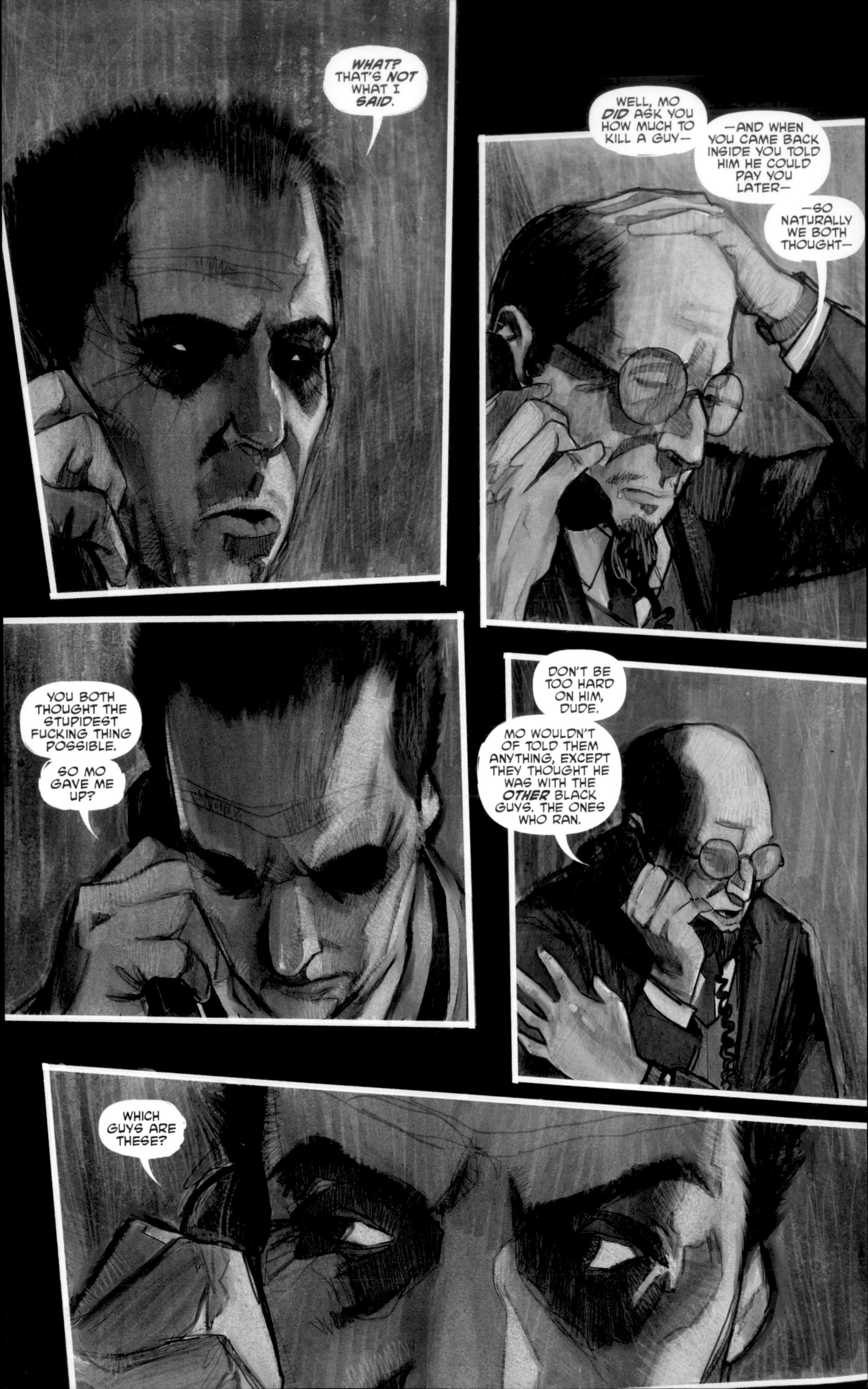
WHAT? THAT'S NOT WHAT I SAID.
WELL, MO DID ASK YOU HOW MUCH TO KILL A GUY—
—AND WHEN YOU CAME BACK INSIDE YOU TOLD HIM HE COULD PAY YOU LATER—
—SO NATURALLY WE BOTH THOUGHT—
YOU BOTH THOUGHT THE STUPIDEST FUCKING THING POSSIBLE.
SO MO GAVE ME UP?
DON'T BE TOO HARD ON HIM, DUDE.
MO WOULDN'T OF TOLD THEM ANYTHING, EXCEPT THEY THOUGHT HE WAS WITH THE OTHER BLACK GUYS. THE ONES WHO RAN.
WHICH GUYS ARE THESE?

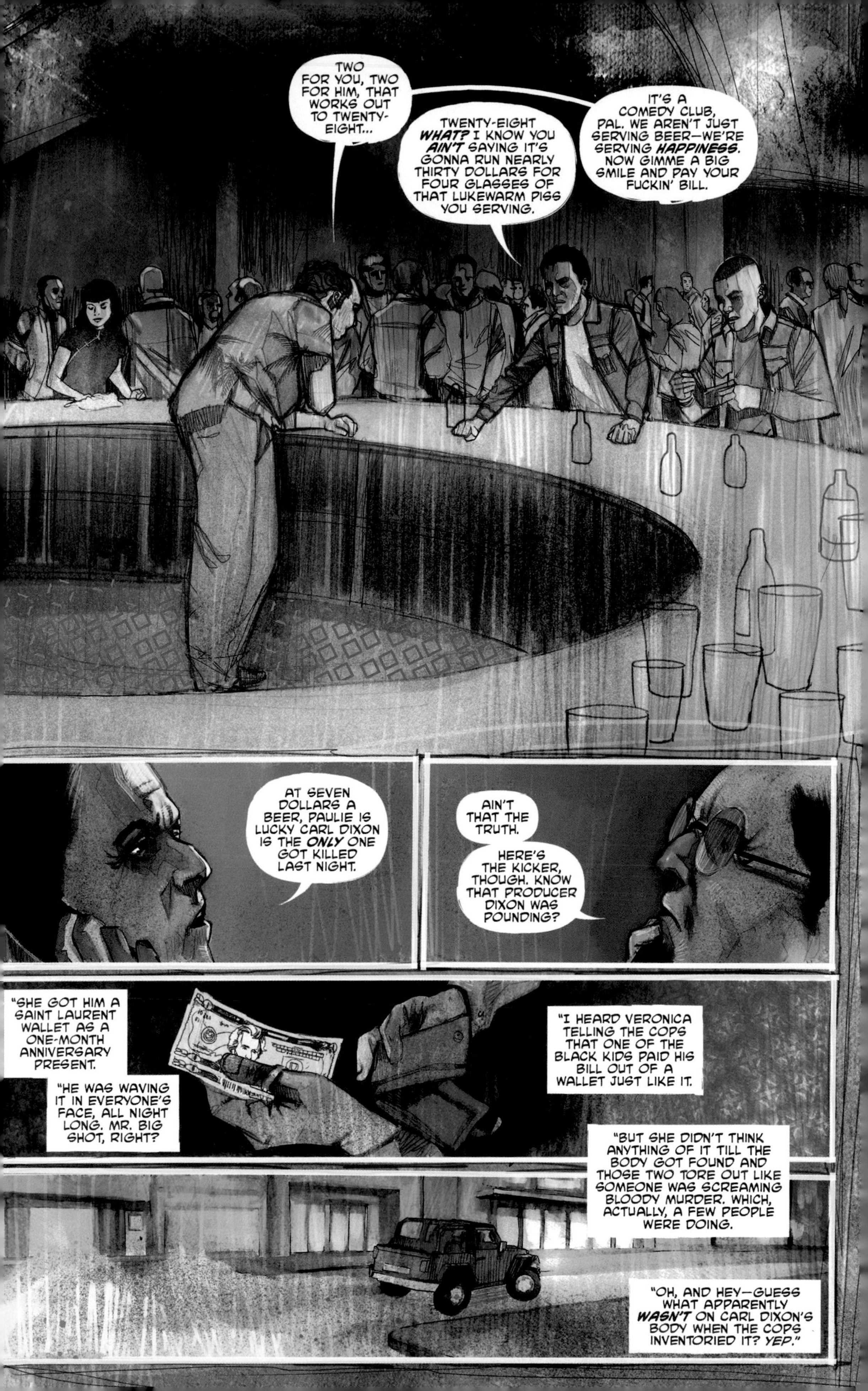

TWO FOR YOU, TWO FOR HIM, THAT WORKS OUT TO TWENTY-EIGHT...
TWENTY-EIGHT *WHAT?* I KNOW YOU *AIN'T* SAYING IT'S GONNA RUN NEARLY THIRTY DOLLARS FOR FOUR GLASSES OF THAT LUKEWARM PISS YOU SERVING.
IT'S A COMEDY CLUB, PAL. WE AREN'T JUST SERVING BEER—WE'RE SERVING *HAPPINESS*. NOW GIMME A BIG SMILE AND PAY YOUR FUCKIN' BILL.
AT SEVEN DOLLARS A BEER, PAULIE IS LUCKY CARL DIXON IS THE *ONLY* ONE GOT KILLED LAST NIGHT.
AIN'T THAT THE TRUTH.
HERE'S THE KICKER, THOUGH. KNOW THAT PRODUCER DIXON WAS POUNDING?
"SHE GOT HIM A SAINT LAURENT WALLET AS A ONE-MONTH ANNIVERSARY PRESENT.
"HE WAS WAVING IT IN EVERYONE'S FACE, ALL NIGHT LONG. MR. BIG SHOT, RIGHT?
"I HEARD VERONICA TELLING THE COPS THAT ONE OF THE BLACK KIDS PAID HIS BILL OUT OF A WALLET JUST LIKE IT.
"BUT SHE DIDN'T THINK ANYTHING OF IT TILL THE BODY GOT FOUND AND THOSE TWO TORE OUT LIKE SOMEONE WAS SCREAMING BLOODY MURDER. WHICH, ACTUALLY, A FEW PEOPLE WERE DOING.
"OH, AND HEY—GUESS WHAT APPARENTLY *WASN'T* ON CARL DIXON'S BODY WHEN THE COPS INVENTORIED IT? *YEP*."

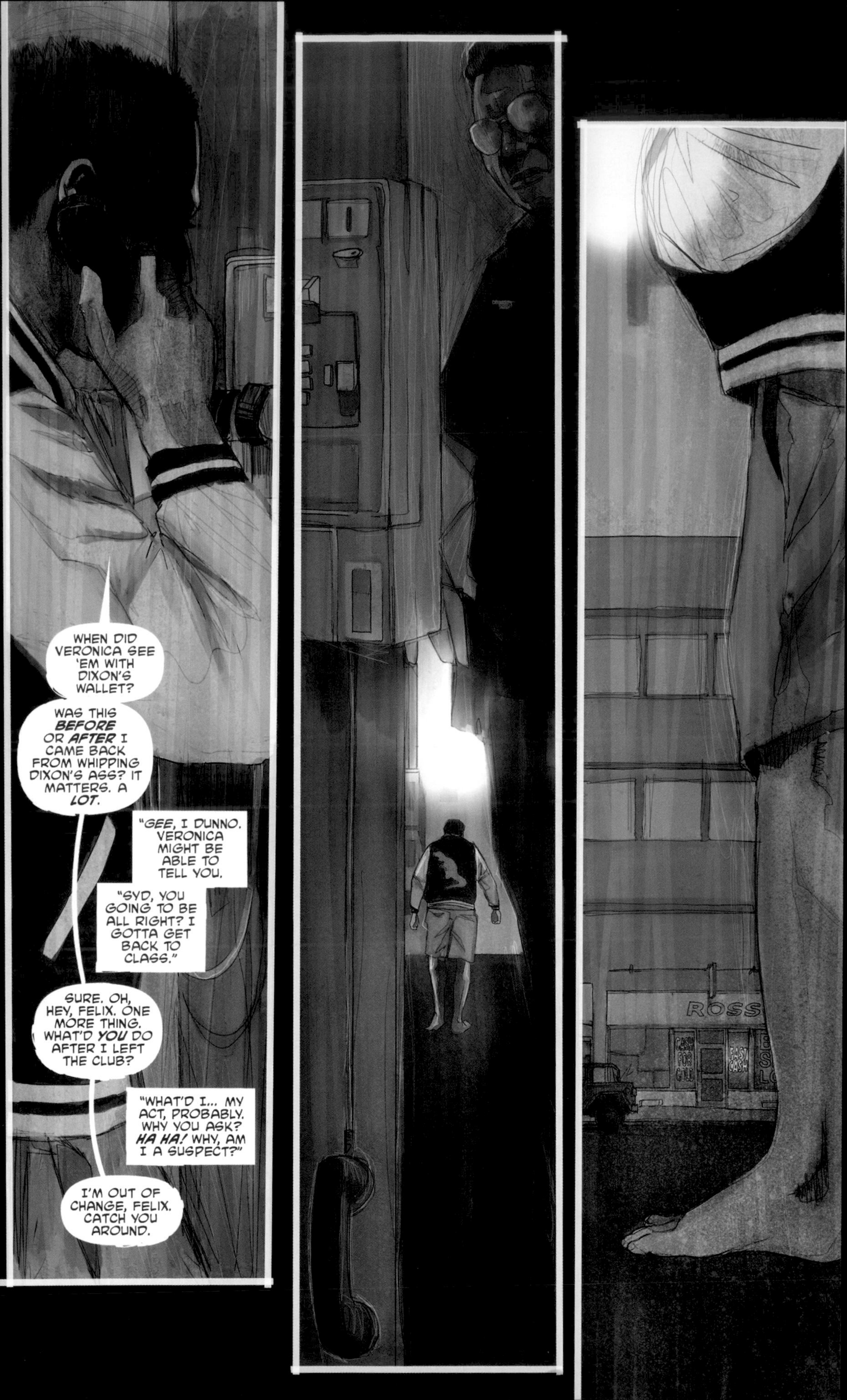
WHEN DID VERONICA SEE 'EM WITH DIXON'S WALLET?
WAS THIS BEFORE OR AFTER I CAME BACK FROM WHIPPING DIXON'S ASS? IT MATTERS. A LOT.
"GEE, I DUNNO. VERONICA MIGHT BE ABLE TO TELL YOU.
"SYD, YOU GOING TO BE ALL RIGHT? I GOTTA GET BACK TO CLASS."
SURE. OH, HEY, FELIX. ONE MORE THING. WHAT'D YOU DO AFTER I LEFT THE CLUB?
"WHAT'D I... MY ACT, PROBABLY. WHY YOU ASK? HA HA! WHY, AM I A SUSPECT?"
I'M OUT OF CHANGE, FELIX. CATCH YOU AROUND.
ROSS
CASH FOR GOLD
FAST CASH

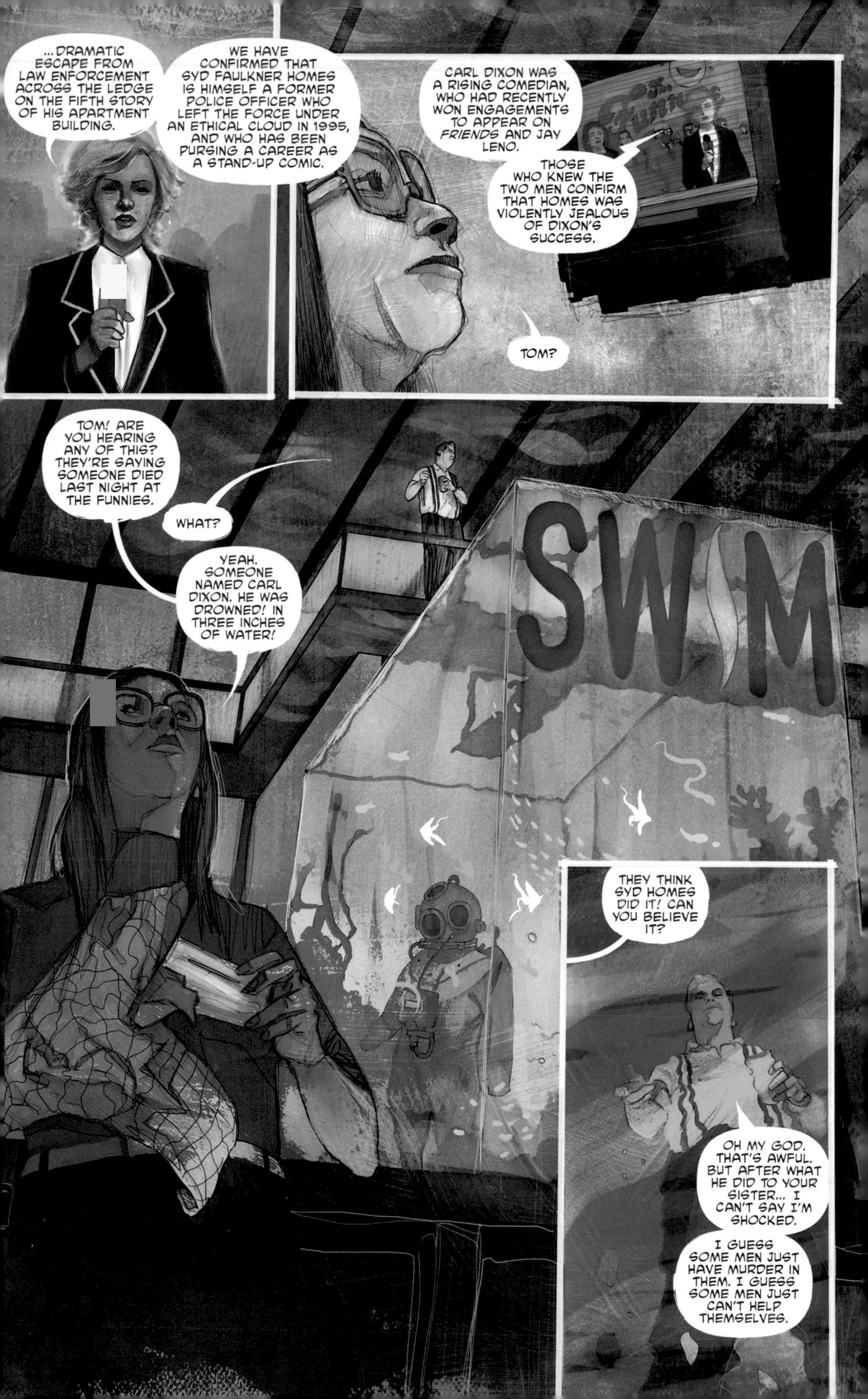
...DRAMATIC ESCAPE FROM LAW ENFORCEMENT ACROSS THE LEDGE ON THE FIFTH STORY OF HIS APARTMENT BUILDING.
WE HAVE CONFIRMED THAT SYD FAULKNER HOMES IS HIMSELF A FORMER POLICE OFFICER WHO LEFT THE FORCE UNDER AN ETHICAL CLOUD IN 1995, AND WHO HAS BEEN PURSING A CAREER AS A STAND-UP COMIC.
CARL DIXON WAS A RISING COMEDIAN, WHO HAD RECENTLY WON ENGAGEMENTS TO APPEAR ON *FRIENDS* AND JAY LENO.
THOSE WHO KNEW THE TWO MEN CONFIRM THAT HOMES WAS VIOLENTLY JEALOUS OF DIXON'S SUCCESS.
TOM?
TOM! ARE YOU HEARING ANY OF THIS? THEY'RE SAYING SOMEONE DIED LAST NIGHT AT THE FUNNIES.
WHAT?
YEAH. SOMEONE NAMED CARL DIXON. HE WAS DROWNED! IN THREE INCHES OF WATER!
SWIM
THEY THINK SYD HOMES DID IT! CAN YOU BELIEVE IT?
OH MY GOD. THAT'S AWFUL. BUT AFTER WHAT HE DID TO YOUR SISTER... I CAN'T SAY I'M SHOCKED.
I GUESS SOME MEN JUST HAVE MURDER IN THEM. I GUESS SOME MEN JUST CAN'T HELP THEMSELVES.

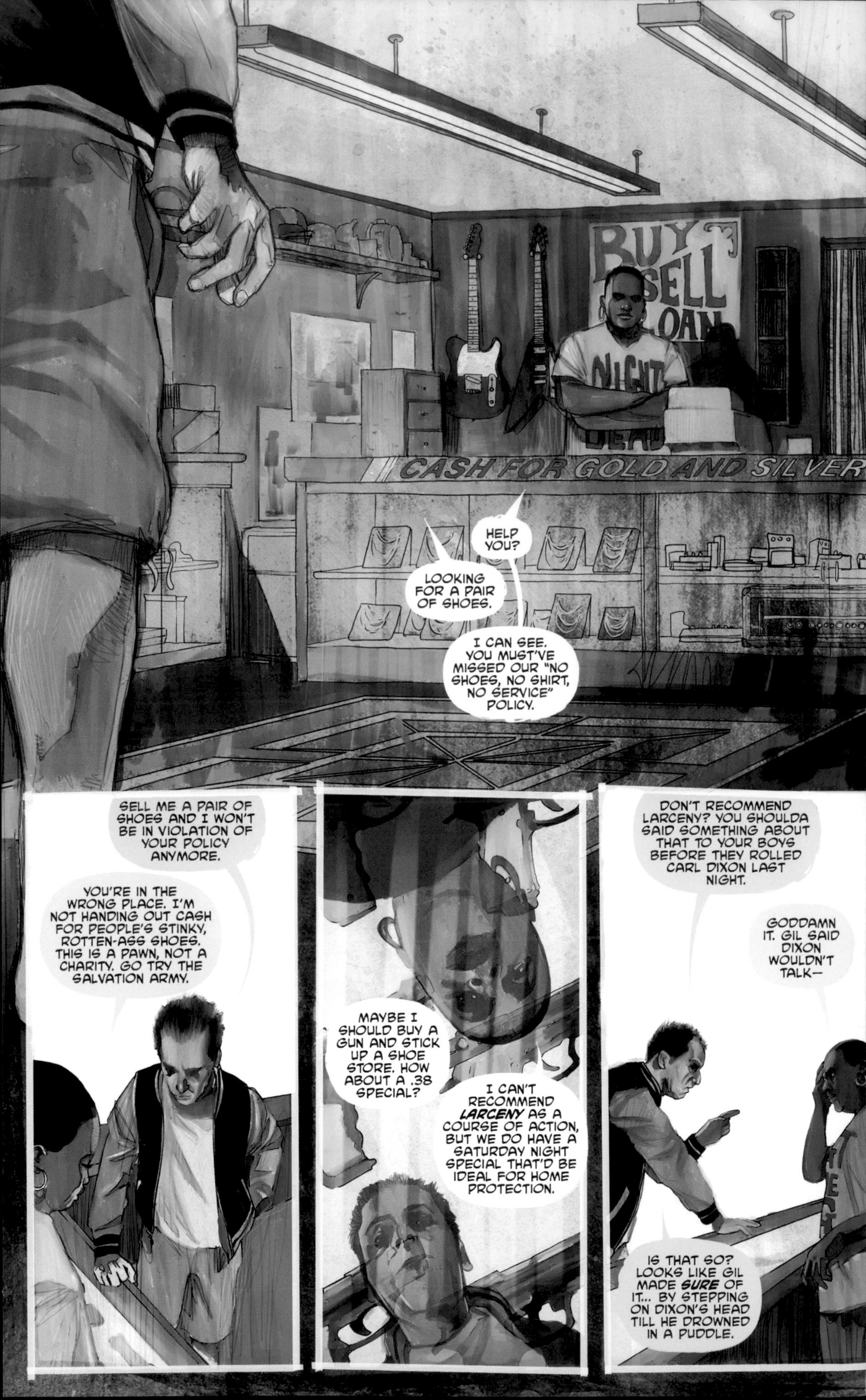
BUY
SELL
LOAN
CASH FOR GOLD AND SILVER
HELP YOU?
LOOKING FOR A PAIR OF SHOES.
I CAN SEE. YOU MUST'VE MISSED OUR "NO SHOES, NO SHIRT, NO SERVICE" POLICY.
SELL ME A PAIR OF SHOES AND I WON'T BE IN VIOLATION OF YOUR POLICY ANYMORE.
YOU'RE IN THE WRONG PLACE. I'M NOT HANDING OUT CASH FOR PEOPLE'S STINKY, ROTTEN-ASS SHOES. THIS IS A PAWN, NOT A CHARITY. GO TRY THE SALVATION ARMY.
MAYBE I SHOULD BUY A GUN AND STICK UP A SHOE STORE. HOW ABOUT A .38 SPECIAL?
I CAN'T RECOMMEND *LARCENY* AS A COURSE OF ACTION, BUT WE DO HAVE A SATURDAY NIGHT SPECIAL THAT'D BE IDEAL FOR HOME PROTECTION.
DON'T RECOMMEND LARCENY? YOU SHOULDA SAID SOMETHING ABOUT THAT TO YOUR BOYS BEFORE THEY ROLLED CARL DIXON LAST NIGHT.
GODDAMN IT. GIL SAID DIXON WOULDN'T TALK—
IS THAT SO? LOOKS LIKE GIL MADE *SURE* OF IT... BY STEPPING ON DIXON'S HEAD TILL HE DROWNED IN A PUDDLE.

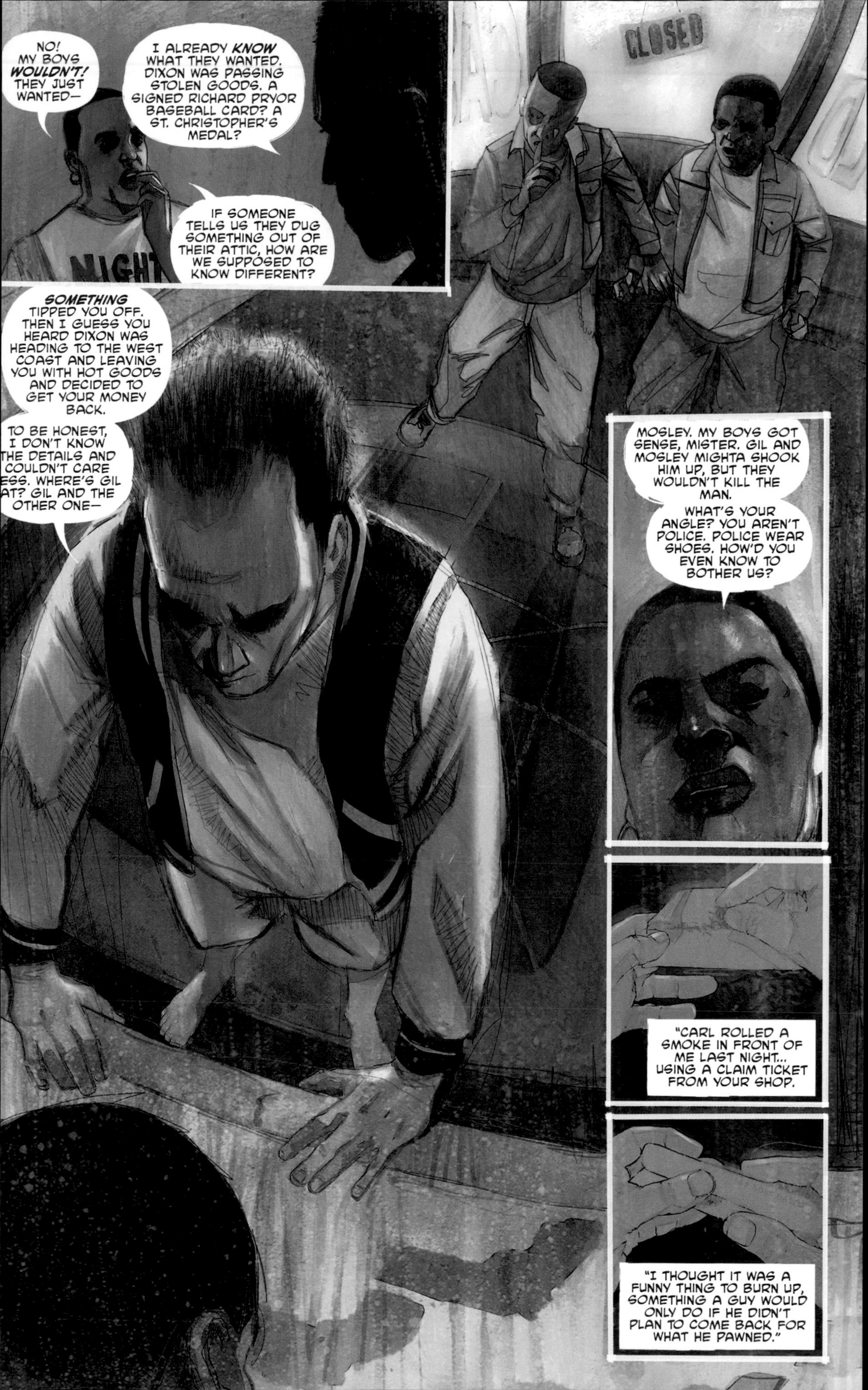
NO! MY BOYS WOULDN'T! THEY JUST WANTED—
I ALREADY KNOW WHAT THEY WANTED. DIXON WAS PASSING STOLEN GOODS. A SIGNED RICHARD PRYOR BASEBALL CARD? A ST. CHRISTOPHER'S MEDAL?
IF SOMEONE TELLS US THEY DUG SOMETHING OUT OF THEIR ATTIC, HOW ARE WE SUPPOSED TO KNOW DIFFERENT?
CLOSED
SOMETHING TIPPED YOU OFF. THEN I GUESS YOU HEARD DIXON WAS HEADING TO THE WEST COAST AND LEAVING YOU WITH HOT GOODS AND DECIDED TO GET YOUR MONEY BACK.
TO BE HONEST, I DON'T KNOW THE DETAILS AND COULDN'T CARE LESS. WHERE'S GIL AT? GIL AND THE OTHER ONE—
MOSLEY. MY BOYS GOT SENSE, MISTER. GIL AND MOSLEY MIGHTA SHOOK HIM UP, BUT THEY WOULDN'T KILL THE MAN.
WHAT'S YOUR ANGLE? YOU AREN'T POLICE. POLICE WEAR SHOES. HOW'D YOU EVEN KNOW TO BOTHER US?
"CARL ROLLED A SMOKE IN FRONT OF ME LAST NIGHT... USING A CLAIM TICKET FROM YOUR SHOP.
"I THOUGHT IT WAS A FUNNY THING TO BURN UP, SOMETHING A GUY WOULD ONLY DO IF HE DIDN'T PLAN TO COME BACK FOR WHAT HE PAWNED."

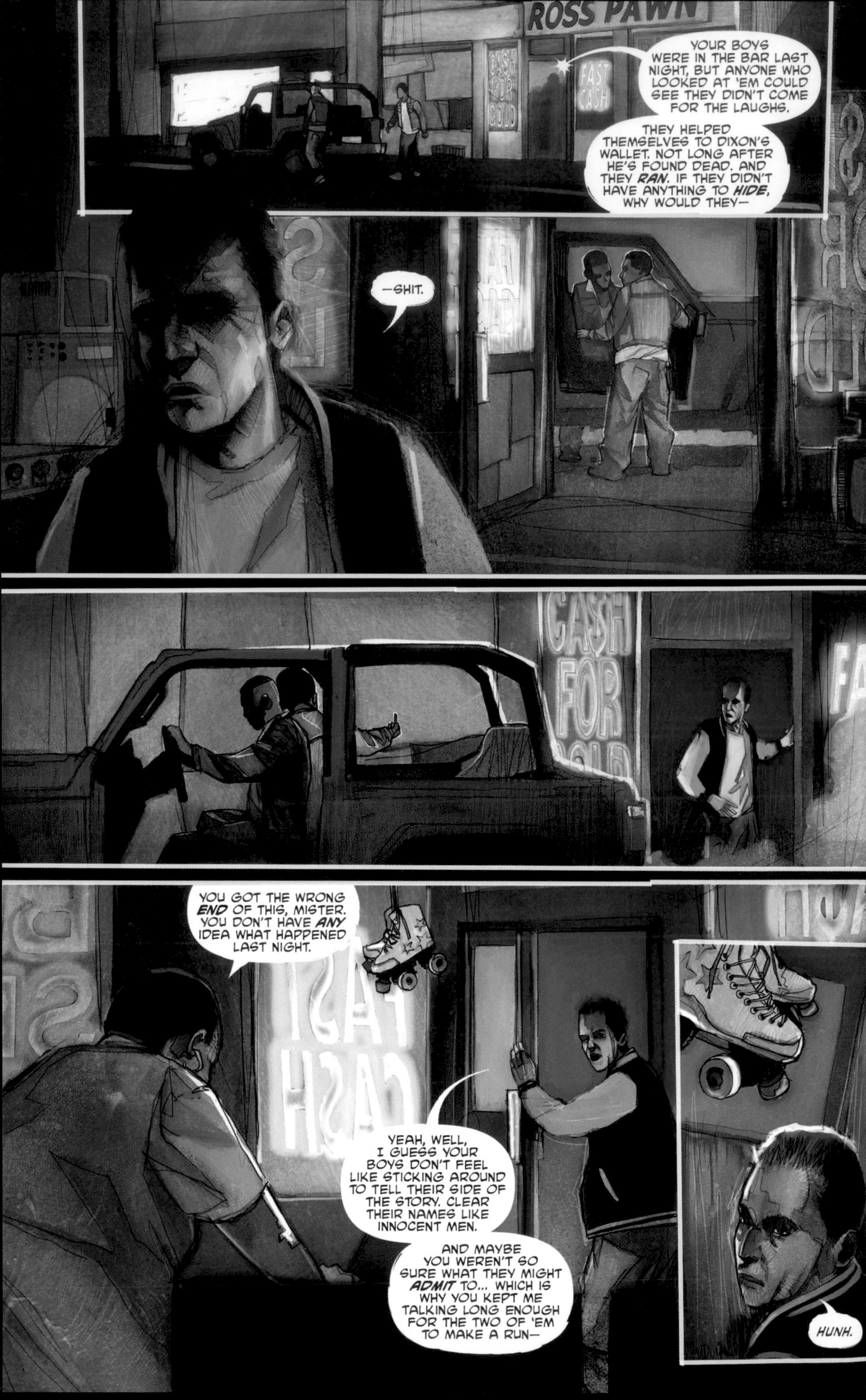
ROSS PAWN
YOUR BOYS WERE IN THE BAR LAST NIGHT, BUT ANYONE WHO LOOKED AT 'EM COULD SEE THEY DIDN'T COME FOR THE LAUGHS.
THEY HELPED THEMSELVES TO DIXON'S WALLET. NOT LONG AFTER HE'S FOUND DEAD. AND THEY *RAN*. IF THEY DIDN'T HAVE ANYTHING TO *HIDE*, WHY WOULD THEY—
—SHIT.
CASH FOR GOLD
YOU GOT THE WRONG *END* OF THIS, MISTER. YOU DON'T HAVE *ANY* IDEA WHAT HAPPENED LAST NIGHT.
YEAH, WELL, I GUESS YOUR BOYS DON'T FEEL LIKE STICKING AROUND TO TELL THEIR SIDE OF THE STORY. CLEAR THEIR NAMES LIKE INNOCENT MEN.
AND MAYBE YOU WEREN'T SO SURE WHAT THEY MIGHT *ADMIT* TO... WHICH IS WHY YOU KEPT ME TALKING LONG ENOUGH FOR THE TWO OF 'EM TO MAKE A RUN—
HUNH.

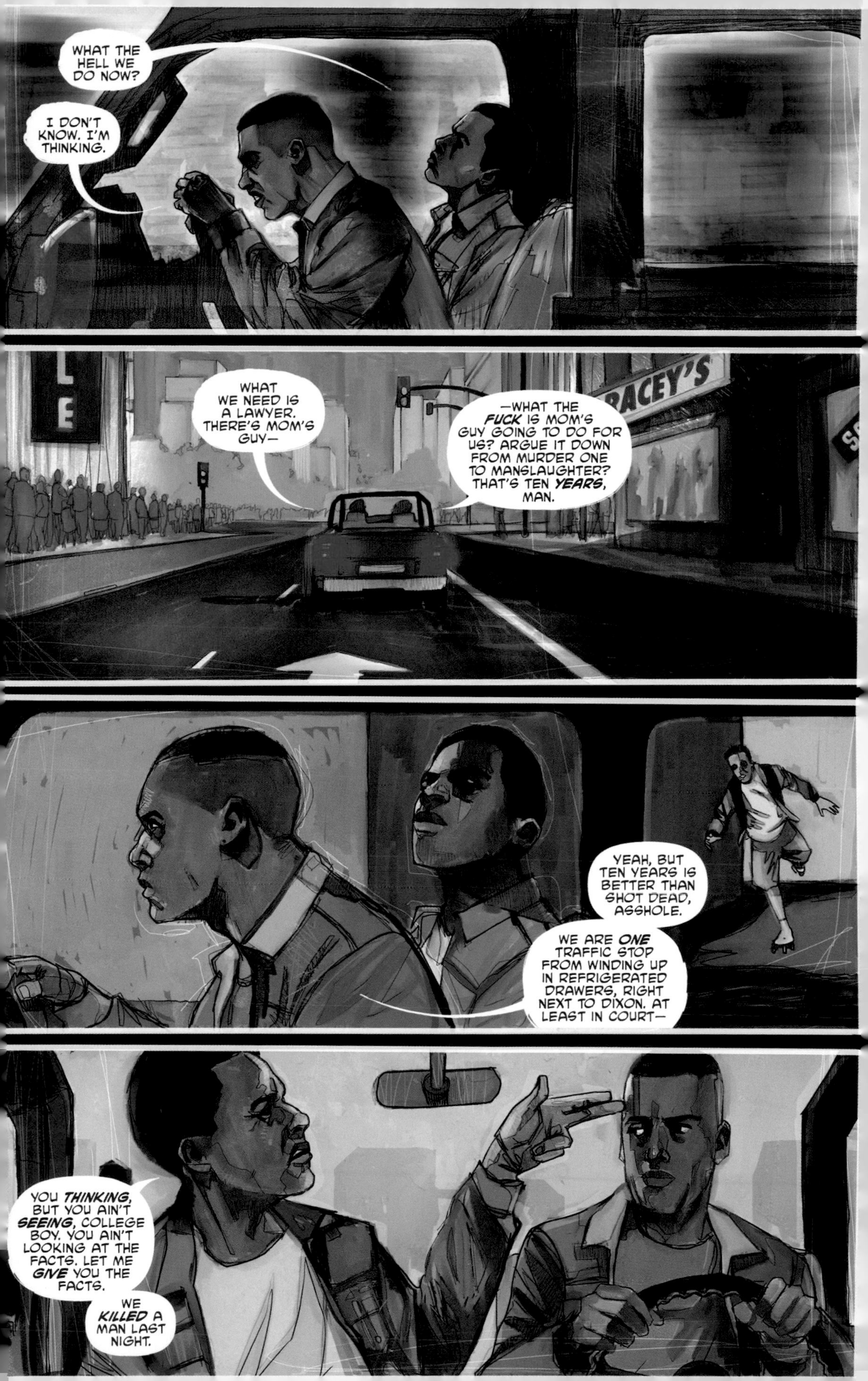
WHAT THE HELL WE DO NOW?
I DON'T KNOW. I'M THINKING.
WHAT WE NEED IS A LAWYER. THERE'S MOM'S GUY—
—WHAT THE FUCK IS MOM'S GUY GOING TO DO FOR US? ARGUE IT DOWN FROM MURDER ONE TO MANSLAUGHTER? THAT'S TEN YEARS, MAN.
YEAH, BUT TEN YEARS IS BETTER THAN SHOT DEAD, ASSHOLE.
WE ARE ONE TRAFFIC STOP FROM WINDING UP IN REFRIGERATED DRAWERS, RIGHT NEXT TO DIXON. AT LEAST IN COURT—
YOU THINKING, BUT YOU AIN'T SEEING, COLLEGE BOY. YOU AIN'T LOOKING AT THE FACTS. LET ME GIVE YOU THE FACTS.
WE KILLED A MAN LAST NIGHT.

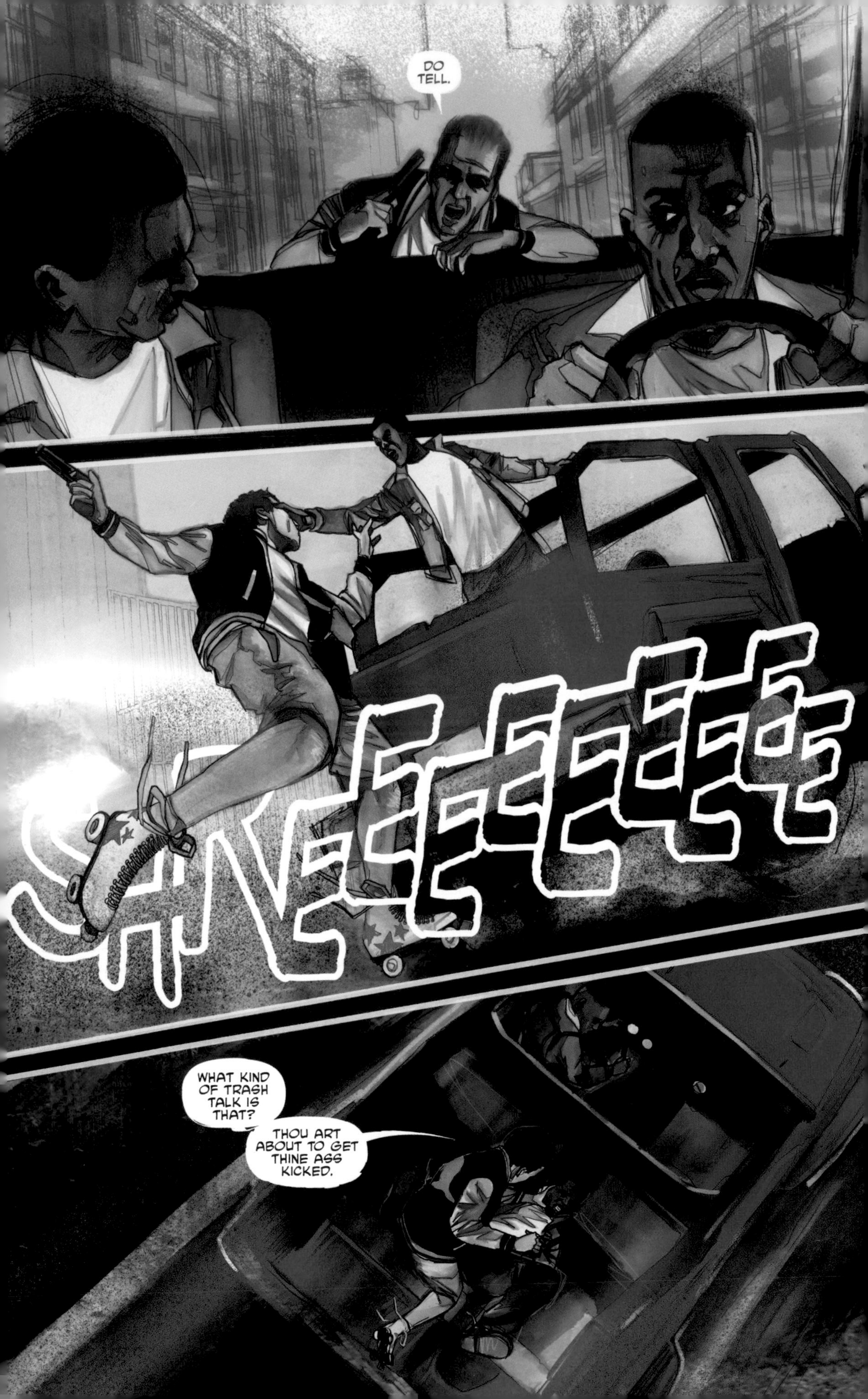
DO TELL.
SHREEEEEEEE
WHAT KIND OF TRASH TALK IS THAT?
THOU ART ABOUT TO GET THINE ASS KICKED.

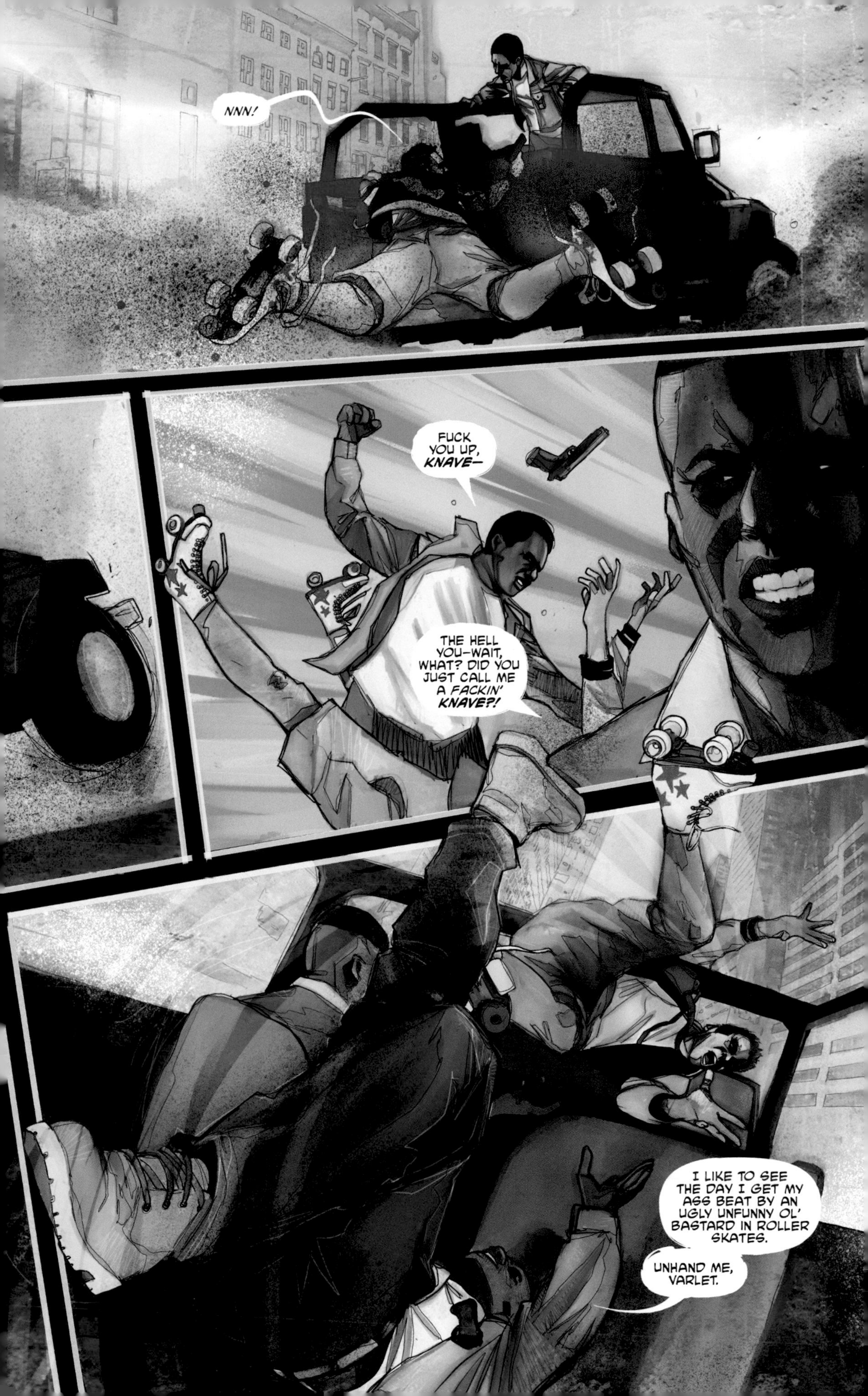
NNN!
FUCK YOU UP, KNAVE—
THE HELL YOU—WAIT, WHAT? DID YOU JUST CALL ME A FACKIN' KNAVE?!
I LIKE TO SEE THE DAY I GET MY ASS BEAT BY AN UGLY UNFUNNY OL' BASTARD IN ROLLER SKATES.
UNHAND ME, VARLET.

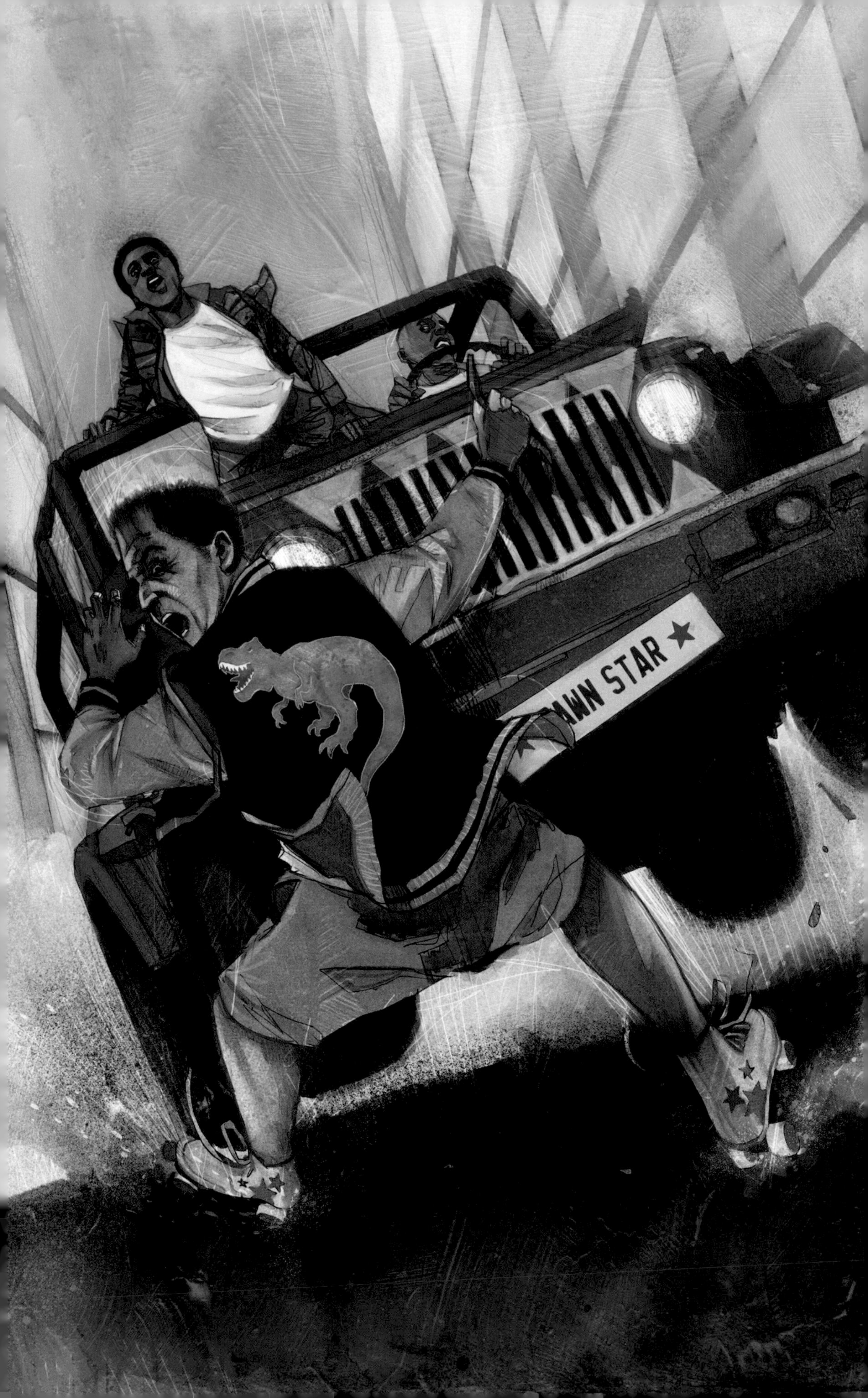
AWN STAR

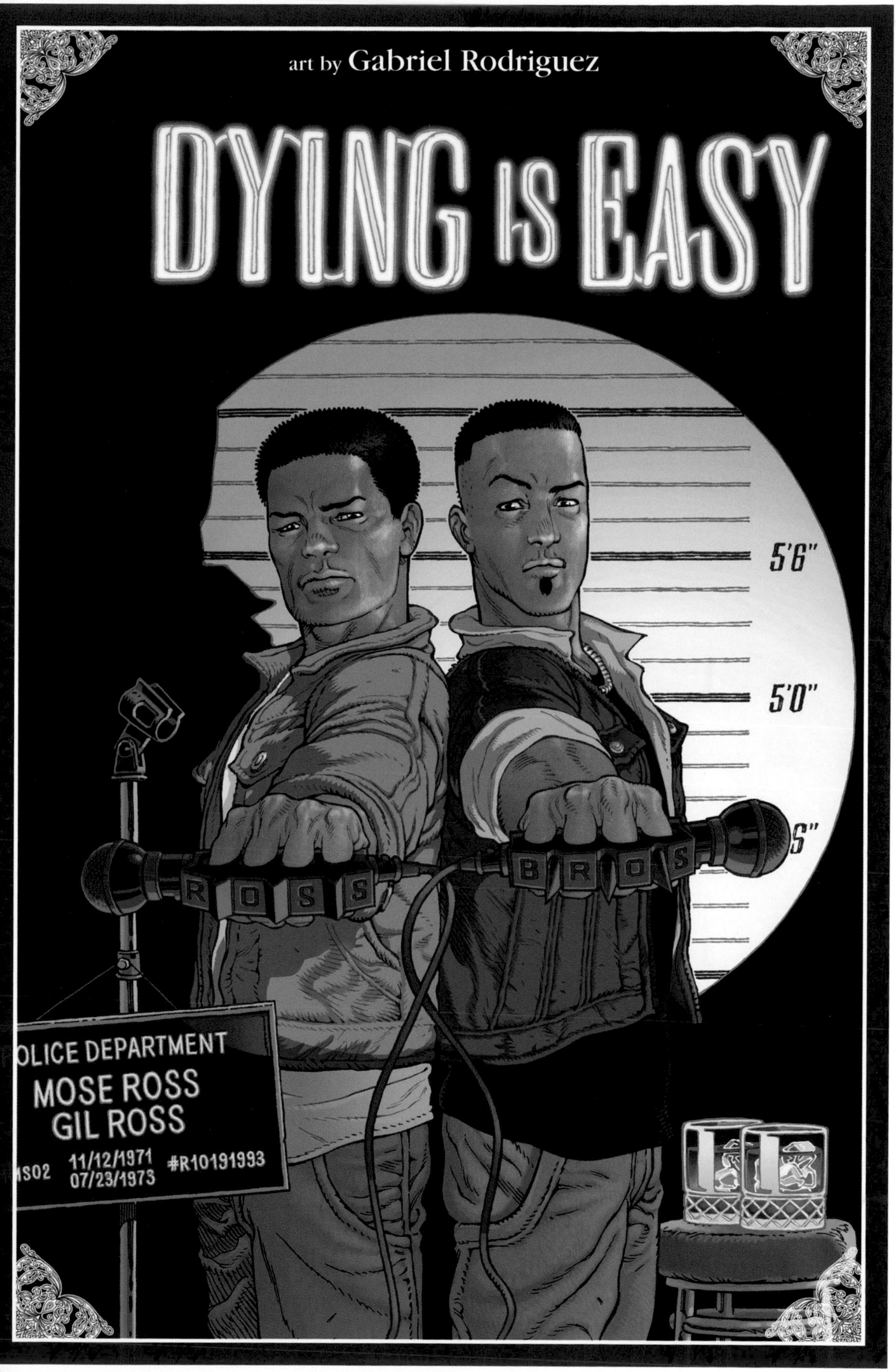
art by Gabriel Rodriguez
DYING IS EASY
5'6"
5'0"
ROSS
BROS
OLICE DEPARTMENT
MOSE ROSS
GIL ROSS
1S02
11/12/1971
07/23/1973
#R10191993

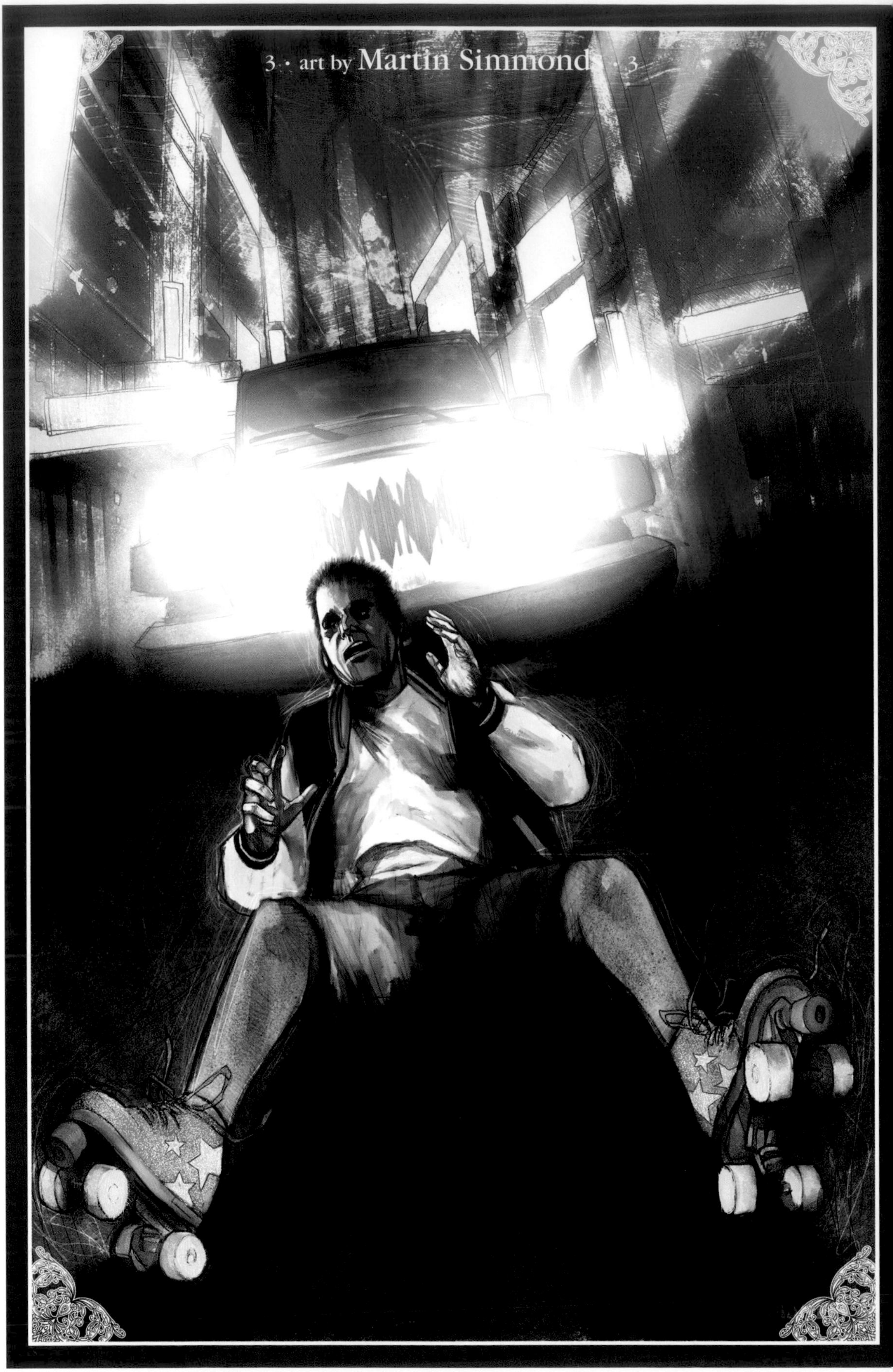
3 • art by Martin Simmonds • 3

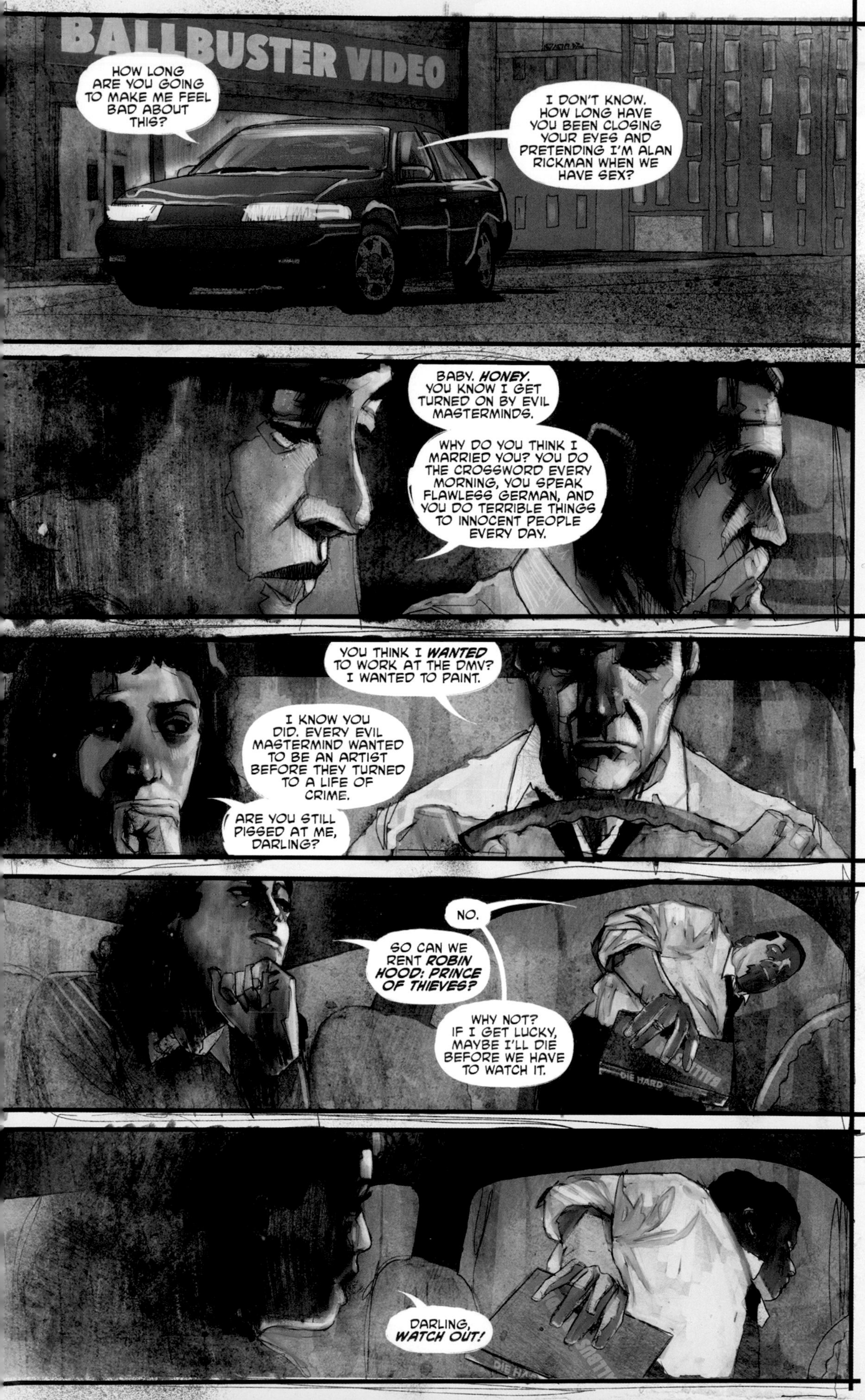
BALLBUSTER VIDEO
HOW LONG ARE YOU GOING TO MAKE ME FEEL BAD ABOUT THIS?
I DON'T KNOW. HOW LONG HAVE YOU BEEN CLOSING YOUR EYES AND PRETENDING I'M ALAN RICKMAN WHEN WE HAVE SEX?
BABY. *HONEY.* YOU KNOW I GET TURNED ON BY EVIL MASTERMINDS.
WHY DO YOU THINK I MARRIED YOU? YOU DO THE CROSSWORD EVERY MORNING, YOU SPEAK FLAWLESS GERMAN, AND YOU DO TERRIBLE THINGS TO INNOCENT PEOPLE EVERY DAY.
YOU THINK I *WANTED* TO WORK AT THE DMV? I WANTED TO PAINT.
I KNOW YOU DID. EVERY EVIL MASTERMIND WANTED TO BE AN ARTIST BEFORE THEY TURNED TO A LIFE OF CRIME.
ARE YOU STILL PISSED AT ME, DARLING?
NO.
SO CAN WE RENT *ROBIN HOOD: PRINCE OF THIEVES?*
WHY NOT? IF I GET LUCKY, MAYBE I'LL DIE BEFORE WE HAVE TO WATCH IT.
DIE HARD
DARLING, *WATCH OUT!*
DIE HARD

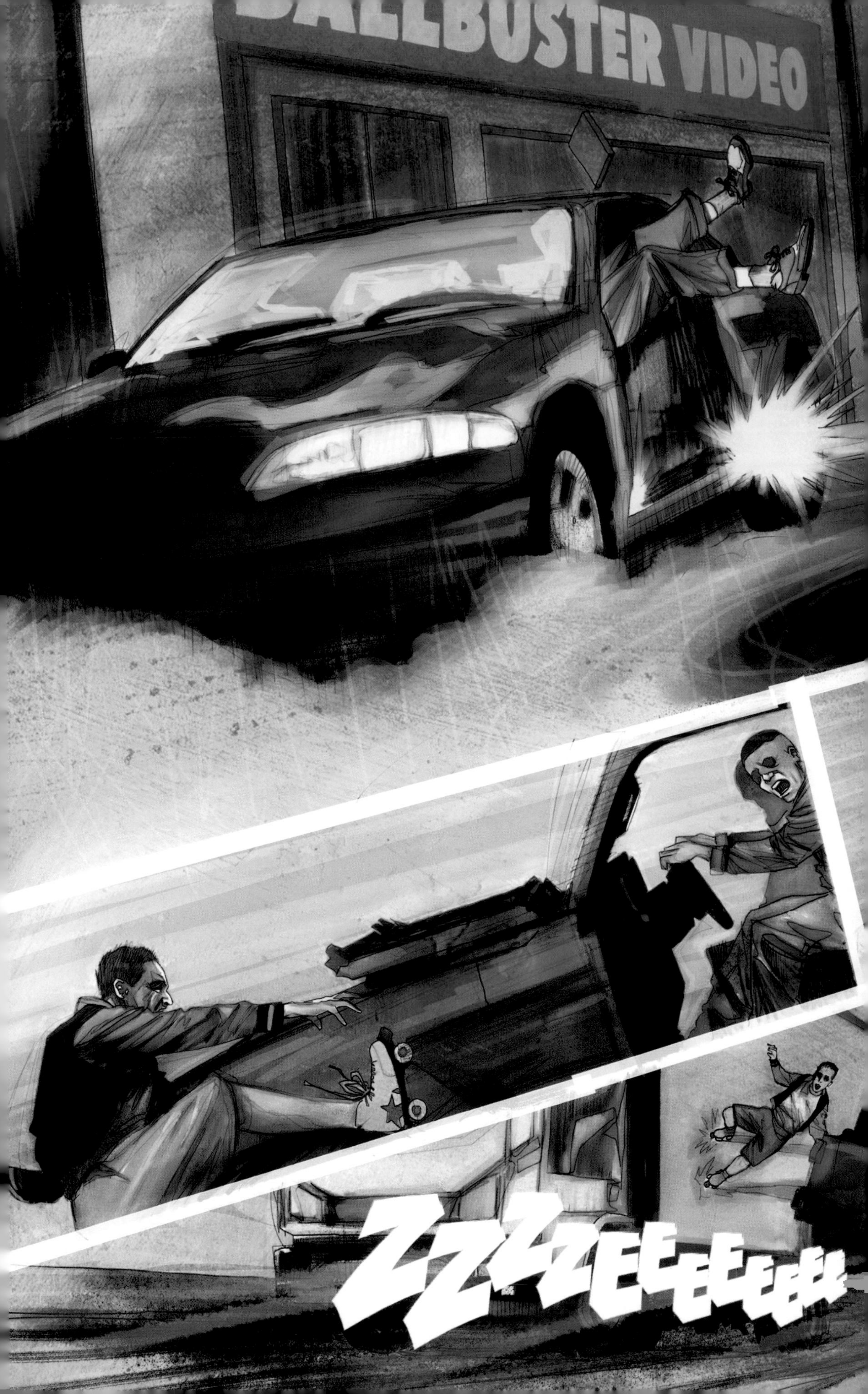
BALLBUSTER VIDEO
ZZZZEEEEEEEEL

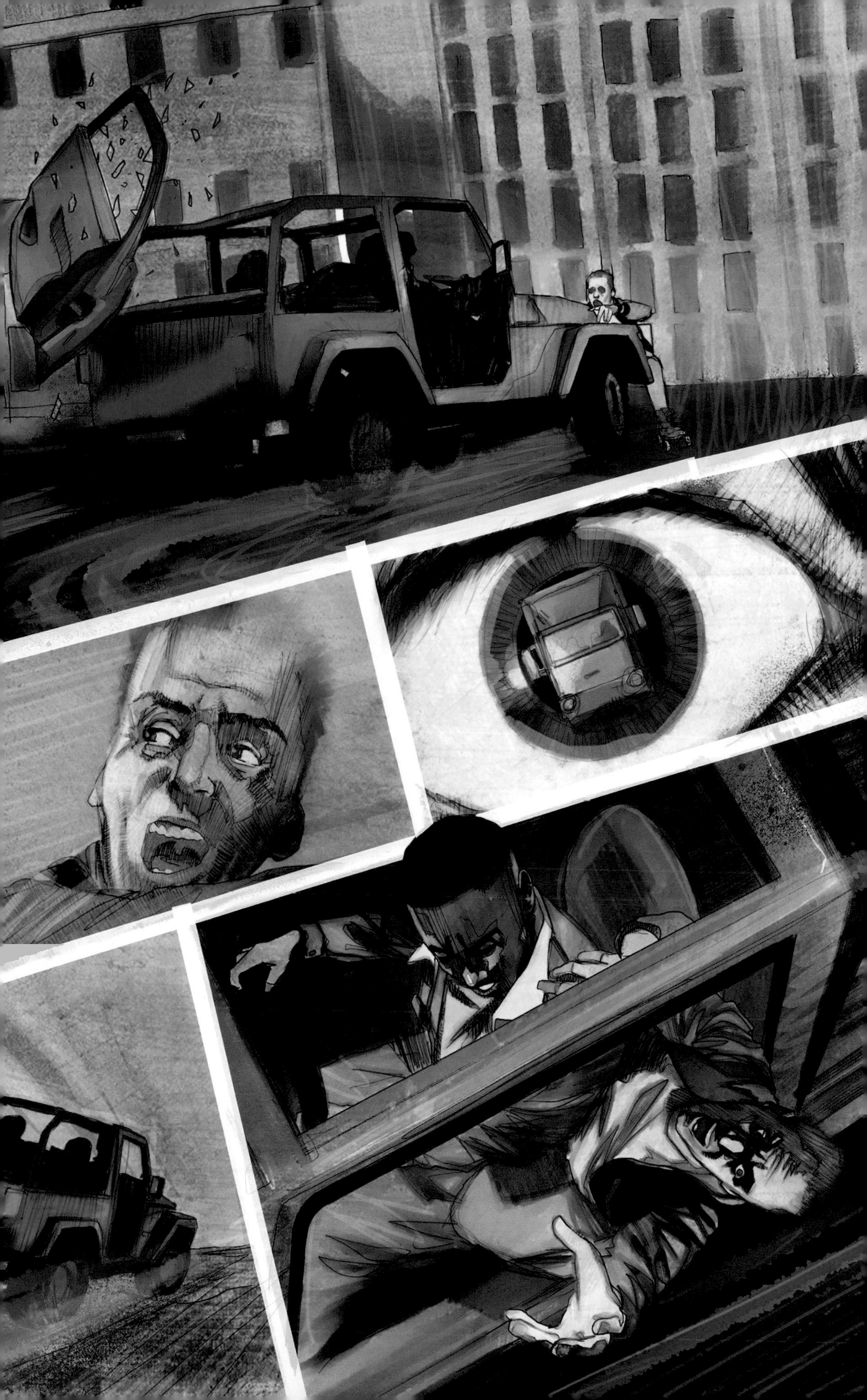

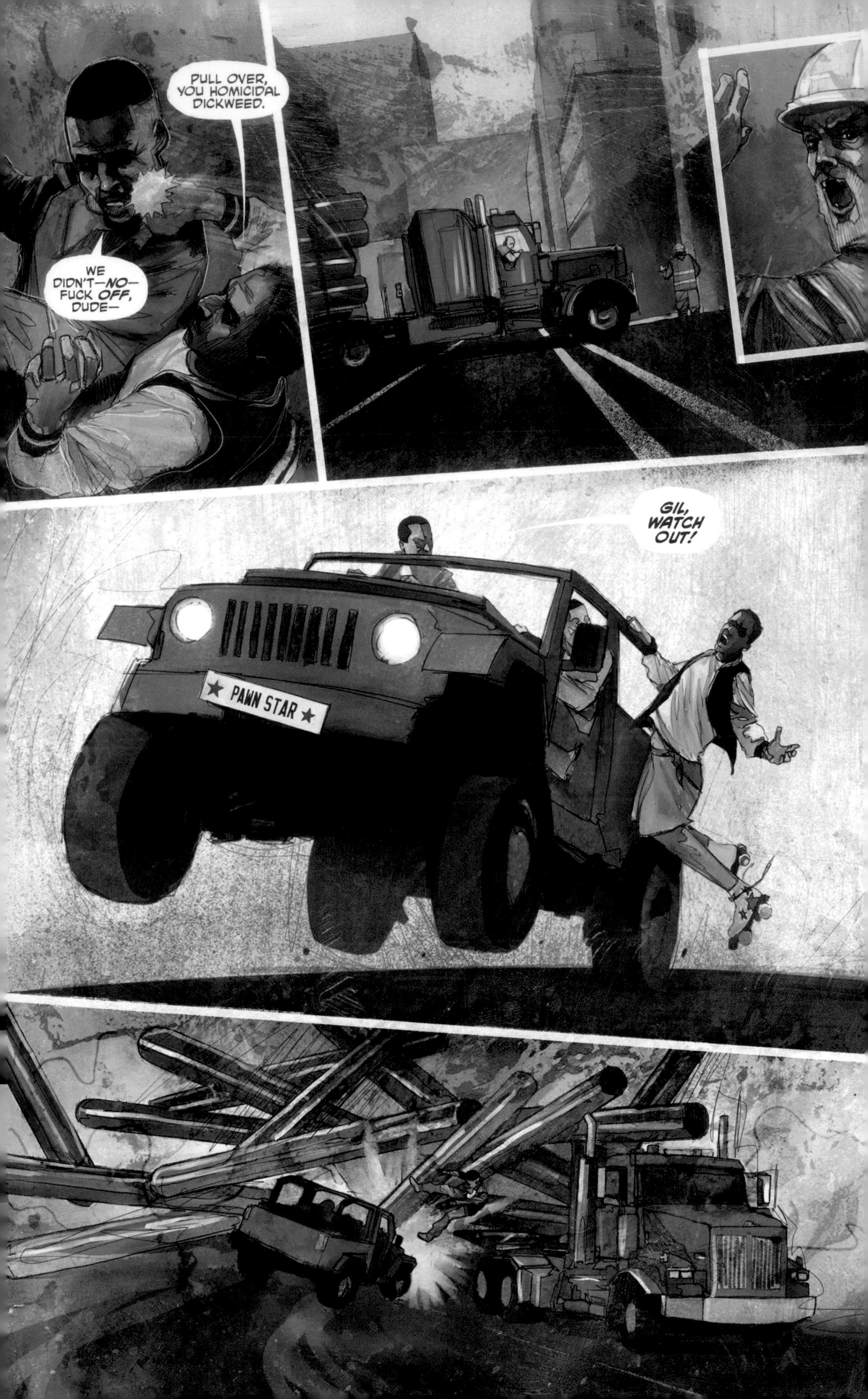
PULL OVER, YOU HOMICIDAL DICKWEED.
WE DIDN'T—NO—FUCK OFF, DUDE—
GIL, WATCH OUT!
PAWN STAR

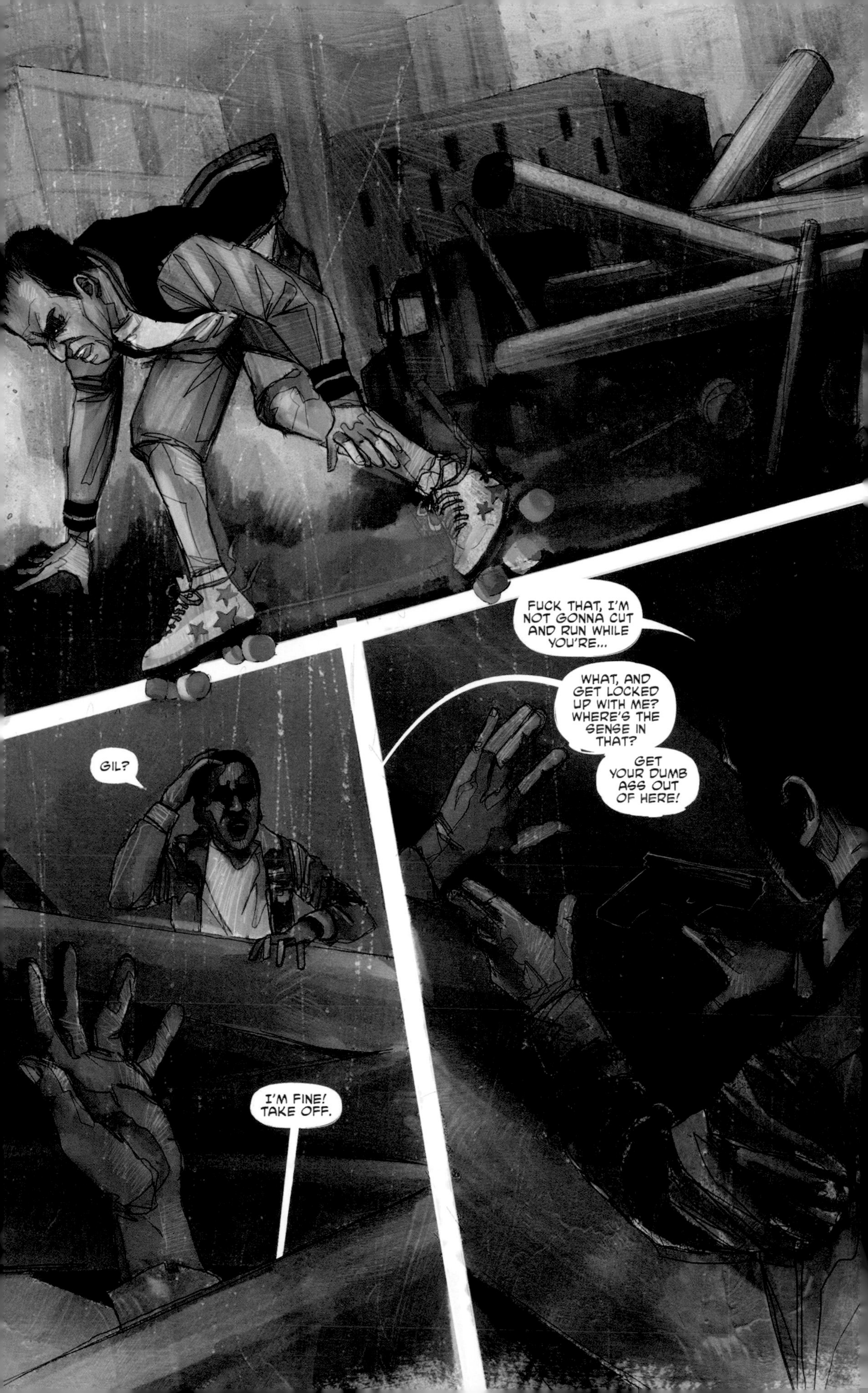
GIL?
I'M FINE! TAKE OFF.
FUCK THAT, I'M NOT GONNA CUT AND RUN WHILE YOU'RE...
WHAT, AND GET LOCKED UP WITH ME? WHERE'S THE SENSE IN THAT?
GET YOUR DUMB ASS OUT OF HERE!

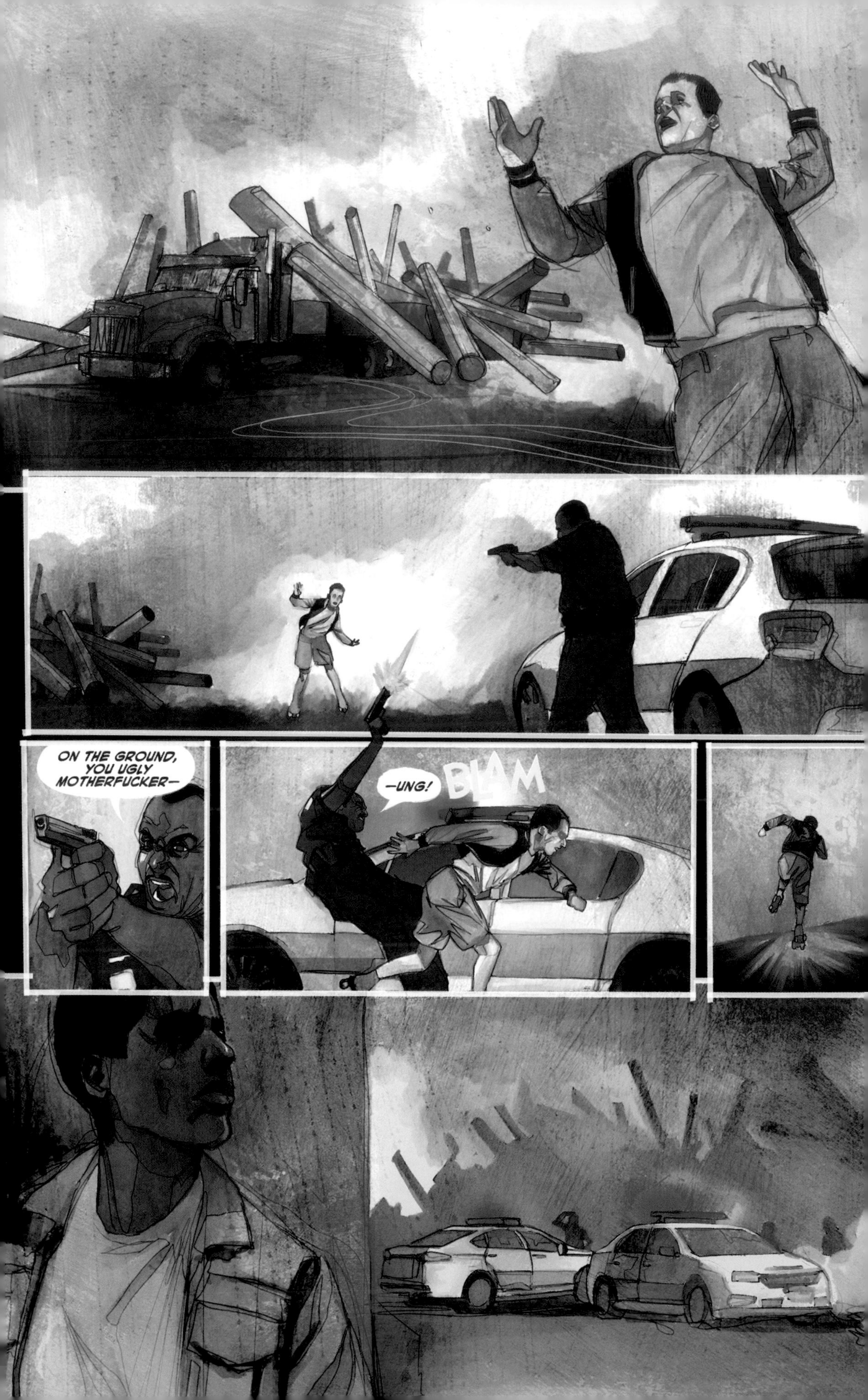
ON THE GROUND, YOU UGLY MOTHERFUCKER—
—UNG!
BLAM

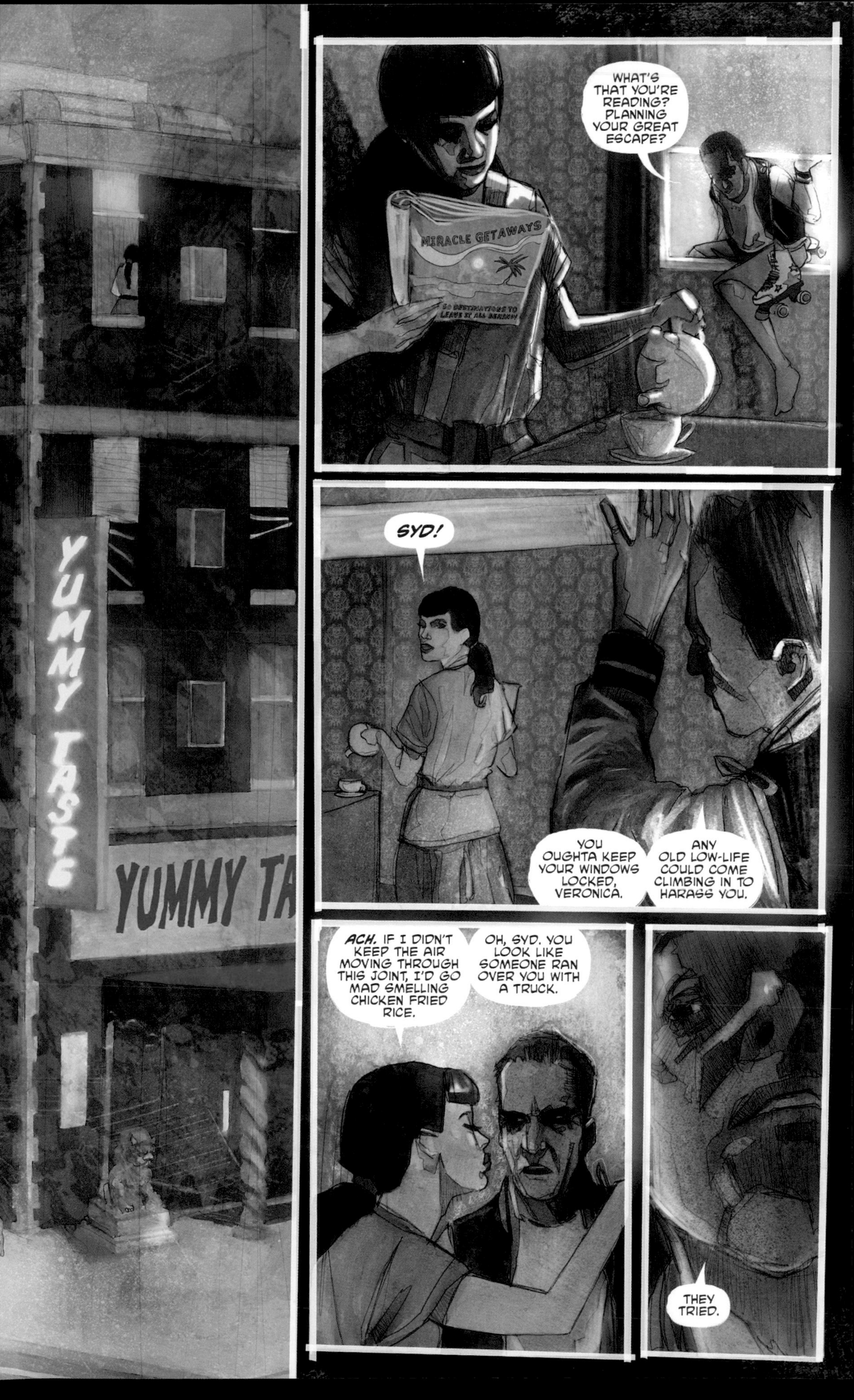
YUMMY TASTE
YUMMY TA
MIRACLE GETAWAYS
WHAT'S THAT YOU'RE READING? PLANNING YOUR GREAT ESCAPE?
SYD!
YOU OUGHTA KEEP YOUR WINDOWS LOCKED, VERONICA.
ANY OLD LOW-LIFE COULD COME CLIMBING IN TO HARASS YOU.
ACH. IF I DIDN'T KEEP THE AIR MOVING THROUGH THIS JOINT, I'D GO MAD SMELLING CHICKEN FRIED RICE.
OH, SYD. YOU LOOK LIKE SOMEONE RAN OVER YOU WITH A TRUCK.
THEY TRIED.

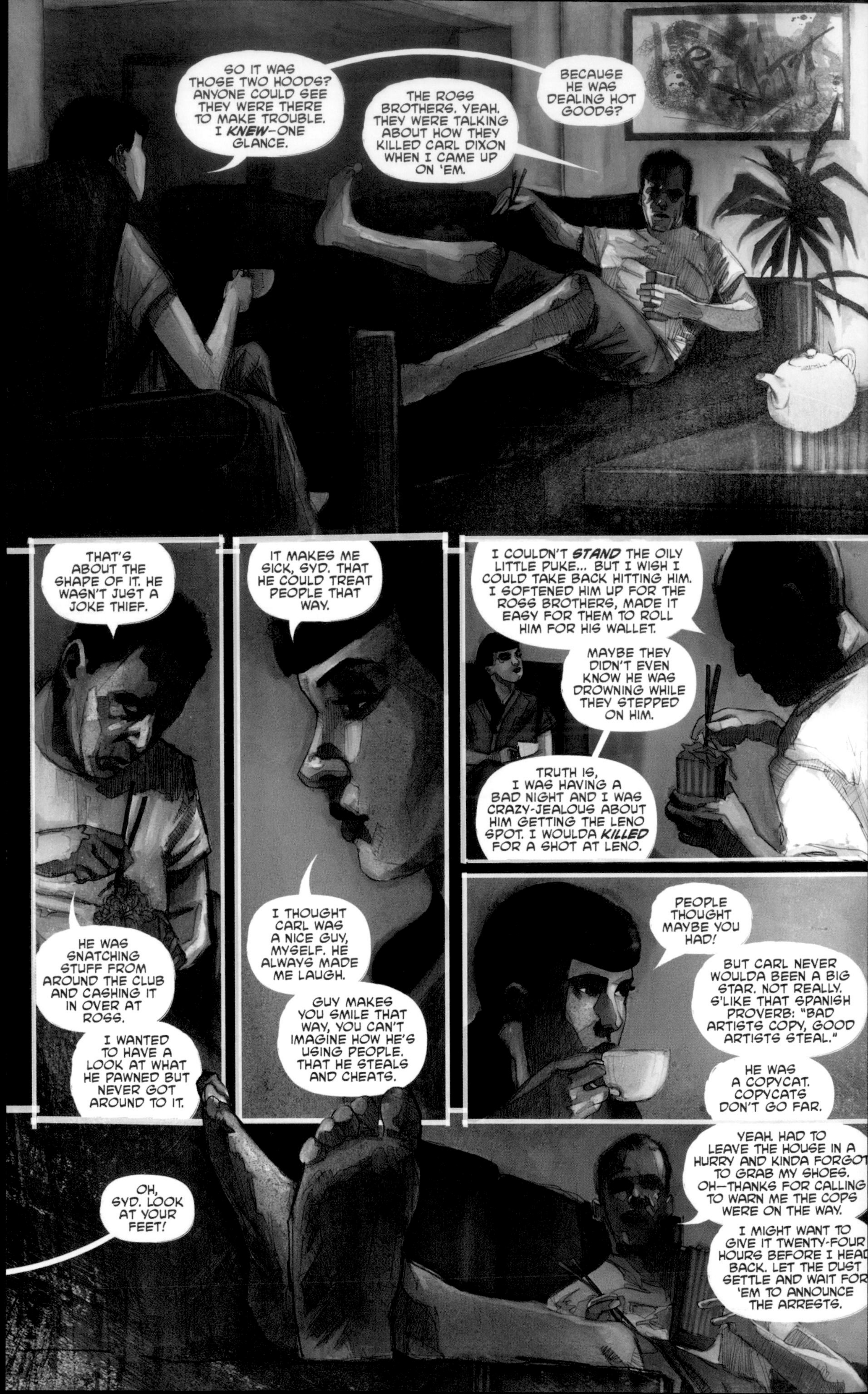
SO IT WAS THOSE TWO HOODS? ANYONE COULD SEE THEY WERE THERE TO MAKE TROUBLE. I *KNEW*—ONE GLANCE.
THE ROSS BROTHERS. YEAH. THEY WERE TALKING ABOUT HOW THEY KILLED CARL DIXON WHEN I CAME UP ON 'EM.
BECAUSE HE WAS DEALING HOT GOODS?
THAT'S ABOUT THE SHAPE OF IT. HE WASN'T JUST A JOKE THIEF.
HE WAS SNATCHING STUFF FROM AROUND THE CLUB AND CASHING IT IN OVER AT ROSS.
I WANTED TO HAVE A LOOK AT WHAT HE PAWNED BUT NEVER GOT AROUND TO IT.
IT MAKES ME SICK, SYD. THAT HE COULD TREAT PEOPLE THAT WAY.
I THOUGHT CARL WAS A NICE GUY, MYSELF. HE ALWAYS MADE ME LAUGH.
GUY MAKES YOU SMILE THAT WAY, YOU CAN'T IMAGINE HOW HE'S USING PEOPLE. THAT HE STEALS AND CHEATS.
I COULDN'T *STAND* THE OILY LITTLE PUKE... BUT I WISH I COULD TAKE BACK HITTING HIM. I SOFTENED HIM UP FOR THE ROSS BROTHERS, MADE IT EASY FOR THEM TO ROLL HIM FOR HIS WALLET.
MAYBE THEY DIDN'T EVEN KNOW HE WAS DROWNING WHILE THEY STEPPED ON HIM.
TRUTH IS, I WAS HAVING A BAD NIGHT AND I WAS CRAZY-JEALOUS ABOUT HIM GETTING THE LENO SPOT. I WOULDA *KILLED* FOR A SHOT AT LENO.
PEOPLE THOUGHT MAYBE YOU HAD!
BUT CARL NEVER WOULDA BEEN A BIG STAR. NOT REALLY. S'LIKE THAT SPANISH PROVERB: "BAD ARTISTS COPY, GOOD ARTISTS STEAL."
HE WAS A COPYCAT. COPYCATS DON'T GO FAR.
OH, SYD. LOOK AT YOUR FEET!
YEAH. HAD TO LEAVE THE HOUSE IN A HURRY AND KINDA FORGOT TO GRAB MY SHOES. OH—THANKS FOR CALLING TO WARN ME THE COPS WERE ON THE WAY.
I MIGHT WANT TO GIVE IT TWENTY-FOUR HOURS BEFORE I HEAD BACK. LET THE DUST SETTLE AND WAIT FOR 'EM TO ANNOUNCE THE ARRESTS.

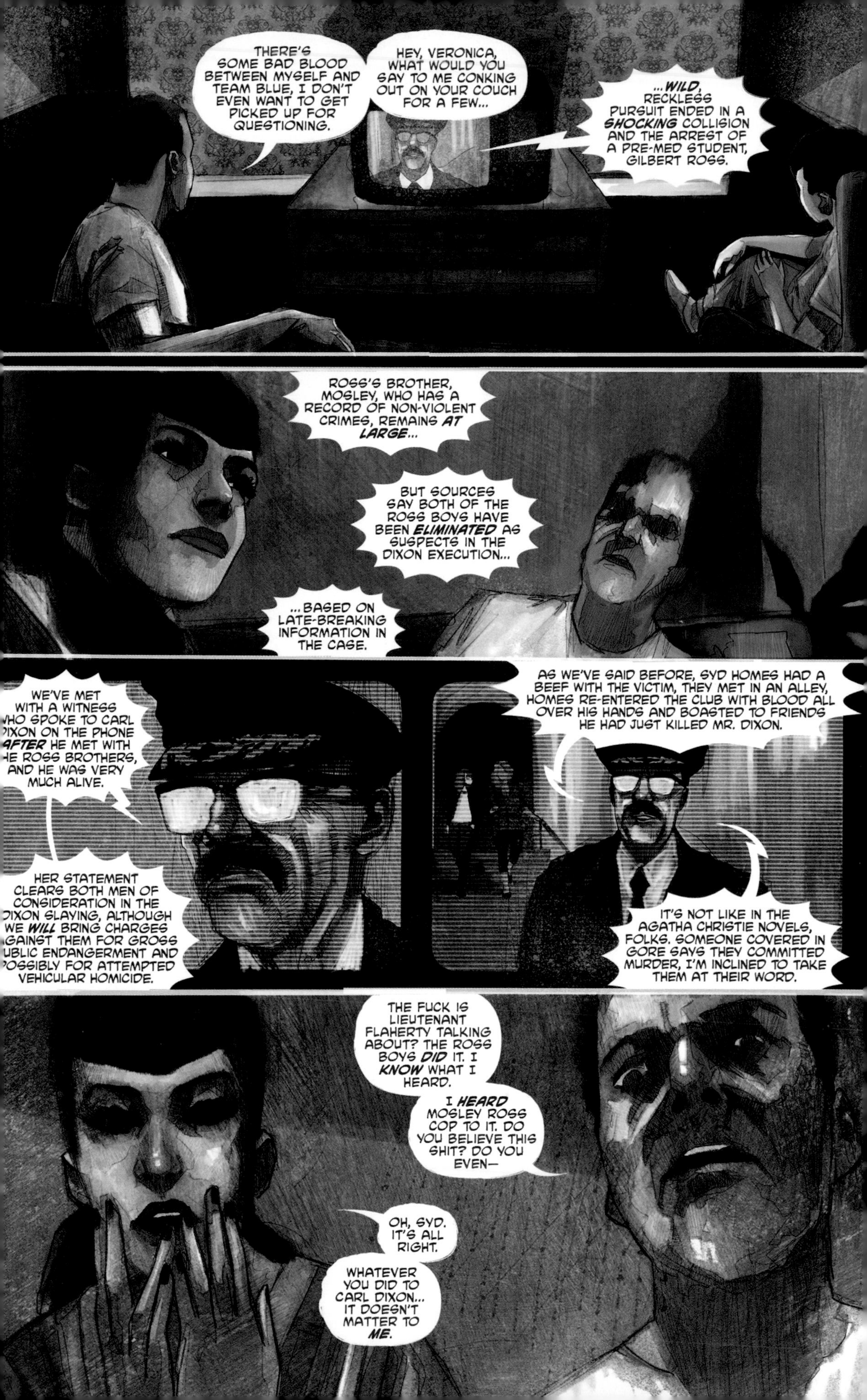
THERE'S SOME BAD BLOOD BETWEEN MYSELF AND TEAM BLUE, I DON'T EVEN WANT TO GET PICKED UP FOR QUESTIONING.
HEY, VERONICA, WHAT WOULD YOU SAY TO ME CONKING OUT ON YOUR COUCH FOR A FEW...
...WILD, RECKLESS PURSUIT ENDED IN A SHOCKING COLLISION AND THE ARREST OF A PRE-MED STUDENT, GILBERT ROSS.
ROSS'S BROTHER, MOSLEY, WHO HAS A RECORD OF NON-VIOLENT CRIMES, REMAINS AT LARGE...
BUT SOURCES SAY BOTH OF THE ROSS BOYS HAVE BEEN ELIMINATED AS SUSPECTS IN THE DIXON EXECUTION...
...BASED ON LATE-BREAKING INFORMATION IN THE CASE.
WE'VE MET WITH A WITNESS WHO SPOKE TO CARL DIXON ON THE PHONE AFTER HE MET WITH THE ROSS BROTHERS, AND HE WAS VERY MUCH ALIVE.
HER STATEMENT CLEARS BOTH MEN OF CONSIDERATION IN THE DIXON SLAYING, ALTHOUGH WE WILL BRING CHARGES AGAINST THEM FOR GROSS PUBLIC ENDANGERMENT AND POSSIBLY FOR ATTEMPTED VEHICULAR HOMICIDE.
AS WE'VE SAID BEFORE, SYD HOMES HAD A BEEF WITH THE VICTIM, THEY MET IN AN ALLEY, HOMES RE-ENTERED THE CLUB WITH BLOOD ALL OVER HIS HANDS AND BOASTED TO FRIENDS HE HAD JUST KILLED MR. DIXON.
IT'S NOT LIKE IN THE AGATHA CHRISTIE NOVELS, FOLKS. SOMEONE COVERED IN GORE SAYS THEY COMMITTED MURDER, I'M INCLINED TO TAKE THEM AT THEIR WORD.
THE FUCK IS LIEUTENANT FLAHERTY TALKING ABOUT? THE ROSS BOYS DID IT. I KNOW WHAT I HEARD.
I HEARD MOSLEY ROSS COP TO IT. DO YOU BELIEVE THIS SHIT? DO YOU EVEN—
OH, SYD. IT'S ALL RIGHT.
WHATEVER YOU DID TO CARL DIXON... IT DOESN'T MATTER TO ME.

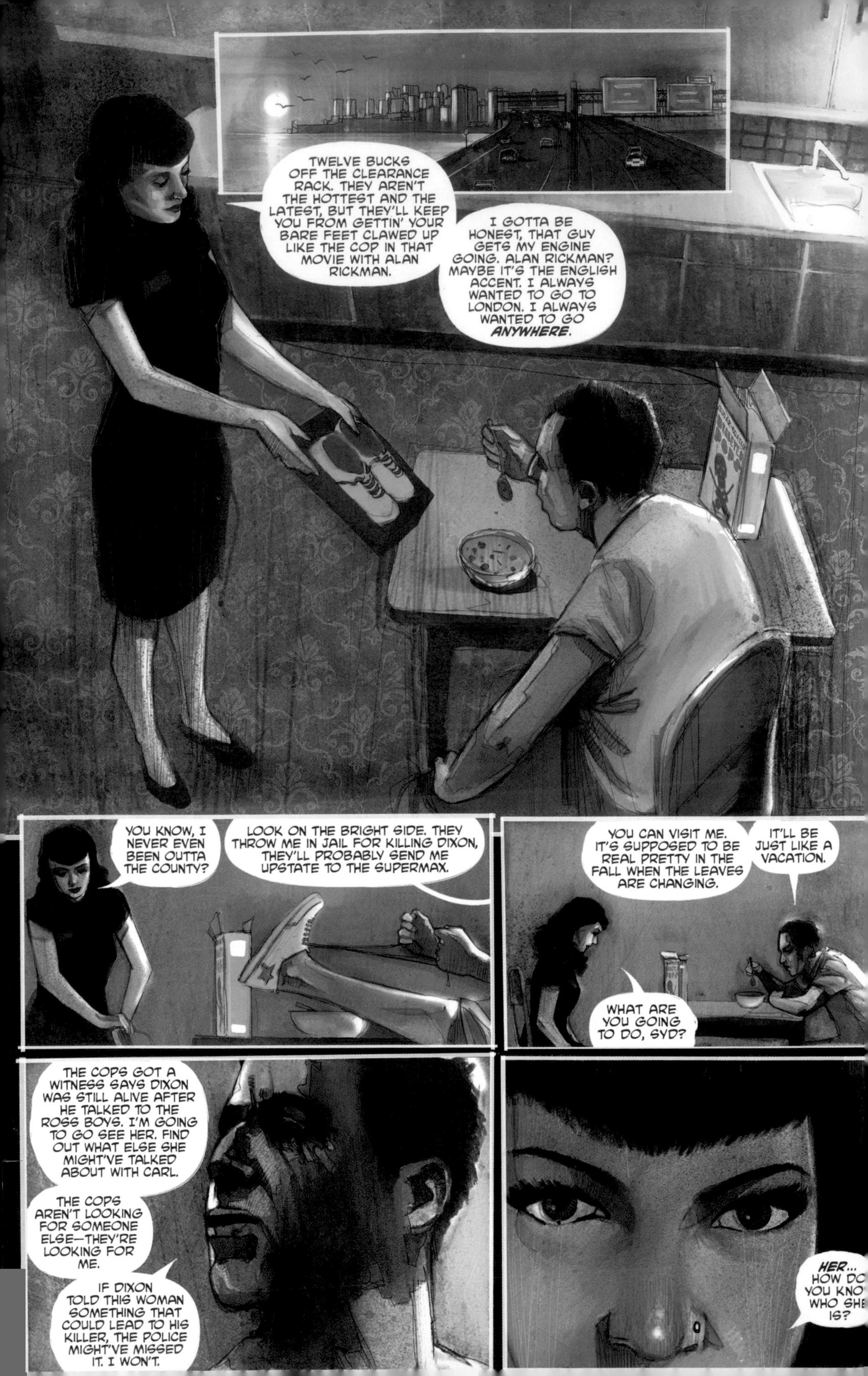
TWELVE BUCKS OFF THE CLEARANCE RACK. THEY AREN'T THE HOTTEST AND THE LATEST, BUT THEY'LL KEEP YOU FROM GETTIN' YOUR BARE FEET CLAWED UP LIKE THE COP IN THAT MOVIE WITH ALAN RICKMAN.
I GOTTA BE HONEST, THAT GUY GETS MY ENGINE GOING. ALAN RICKMAN? MAYBE IT'S THE ENGLISH ACCENT. I ALWAYS WANTED TO GO TO LONDON. I ALWAYS WANTED TO GO ***ANYWHERE***.
YOU KNOW, I NEVER EVEN BEEN OUTTA THE COUNTY?
LOOK ON THE BRIGHT SIDE. THEY THROW ME IN JAIL FOR KILLING DIXON, THEY'LL PROBABLY SEND ME UPSTATE TO THE SUPERMAX.
YOU CAN VISIT ME. IT'S SUPPOSED TO BE REAL PRETTY IN THE FALL WHEN THE LEAVES ARE CHANGING.
IT'LL BE JUST LIKE A VACATION.
WHAT ARE YOU GOING TO DO, SYD?
THE COPS GOT A WITNESS SAYS DIXON WAS STILL ALIVE AFTER HE TALKED TO THE ROSS BOYS. I'M GOING TO GO SEE HER. FIND OUT WHAT ELSE SHE MIGHT'VE TALKED ABOUT WITH CARL.
THE COPS AREN'T LOOKING FOR SOMEONE ELSE—THEY'RE LOOKING FOR ME.
IF DIXON TOLD THIS WOMAN SOMETHING THAT COULD LEAD TO HIS KILLER, THE POLICE MIGHT'VE MISSED IT. I WON'T.
HER... HOW DO YOU KNOW WHO SHE IS?

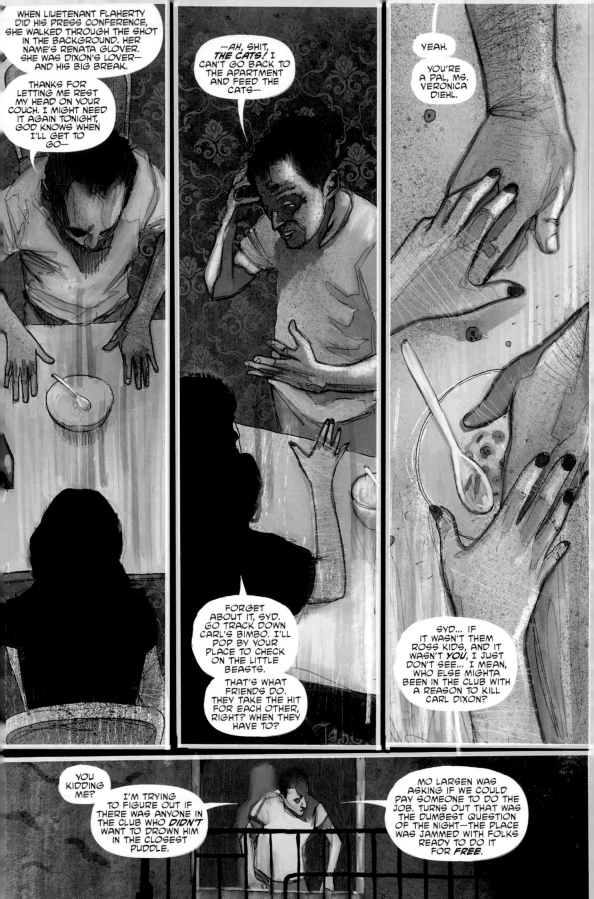

WHEN LIEUTENANT FLAHERTY DID HIS PRESS CONFERENCE, SHE WALKED THROUGH THE SHOT IN THE BACKGROUND. HER NAME'S RENATA GLOVER. SHE WAS DIXON'S LOVER— AND HIS BIG BREAK.

THANKS FOR LETTING ME REST MY HEAD ON YOUR COUCH. I MIGHT NEED IT AGAIN TONIGHT, GOD KNOWS WHEN I'LL GET TO GO—

—AH, SHIT, *THE CATS!* I CAN'T GO BACK TO THE APARTMENT AND FEED THE CATS—

YEAH.

YOU'RE A PAL, MS. VERONICA DIEHL.

FORGET ABOUT IT, SYD. GO TRACK DOWN CARL'S BIMBO. I'LL POP BY YOUR PLACE TO CHECK ON THE LITTLE BEASTS.

THAT'S WHAT FRIENDS DO. THEY TAKE THE HIT FOR EACH OTHER, RIGHT? WHEN THEY HAVE TO?

SYD... IF IT WASN'T THEM ROSS KIDS, AND IT WASN'T *YOU*, I JUST DON'T SEE... I MEAN, WHO ELSE MIGHTA BEEN IN THE CLUB WITH A REASON TO KILL CARL DIXON?

YOU KIDDING ME?

I'M TRYING TO FIGURE OUT IF THERE WAS ANYONE IN THE CLUB WHO *DIDN'T* WANT TO DROWN HIM IN THE CLOSEST PUDDLE.

MO LARSEN WAS ASKING IF WE COULD PAY SOMEONE TO DO THE JOB. TURNS OUT THAT WAS THE DUMBEST QUESTION OF THE NIGHT—THE PLACE WAS JAMMED WITH FOLKS READY TO DO IT FOR *FREE*.

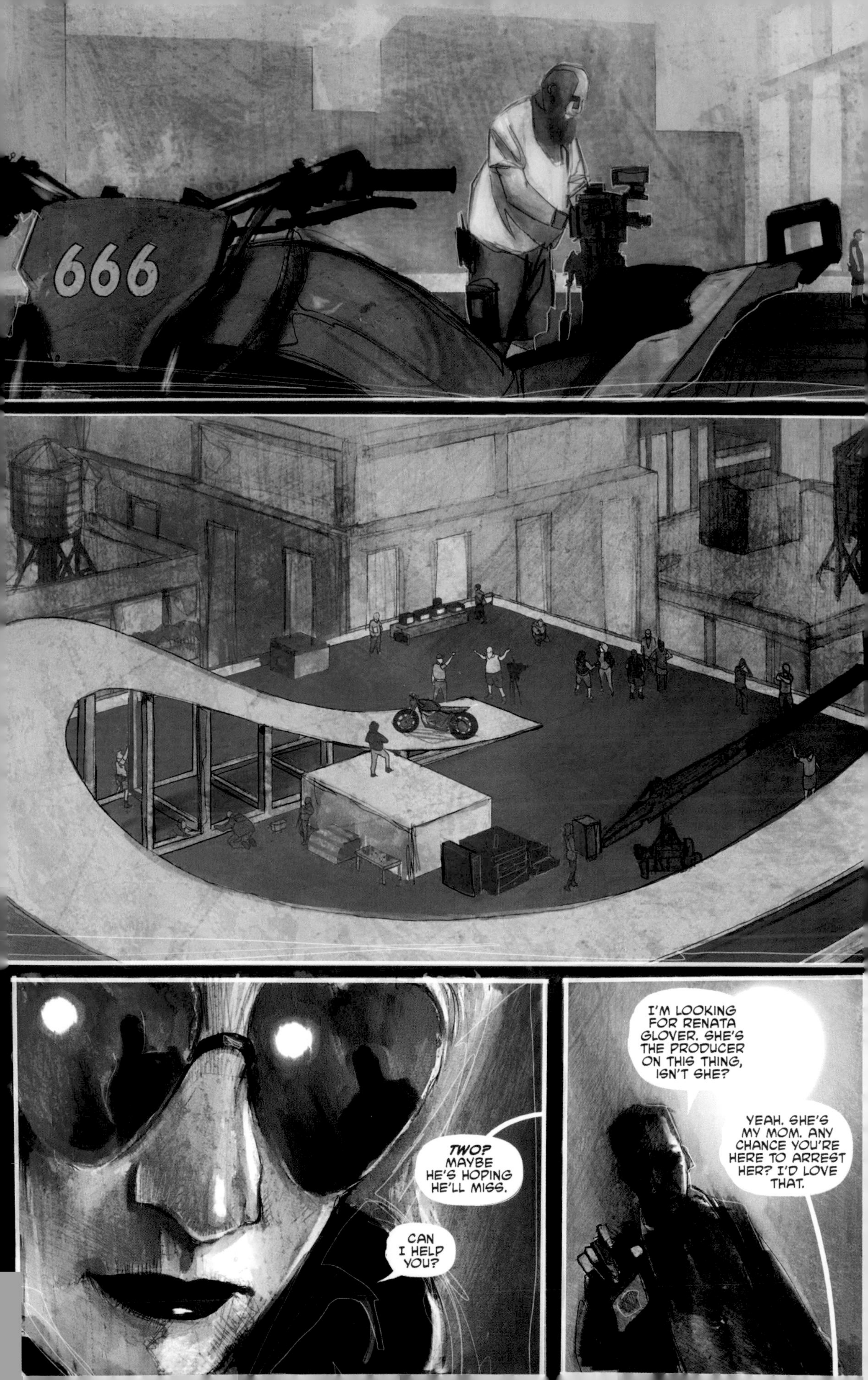

666
TWO? MAYBE HE'S HOPING HE'LL MISS.
CAN I HELP YOU?
I'M LOOKING FOR RENATA GLOVER. SHE'S THE PRODUCER ON THIS THING, ISN'T SHE?
YEAH. SHE'S MY MOM. ANY CHANCE YOU'RE HERE TO ARREST HER? I'D LOVE THAT.

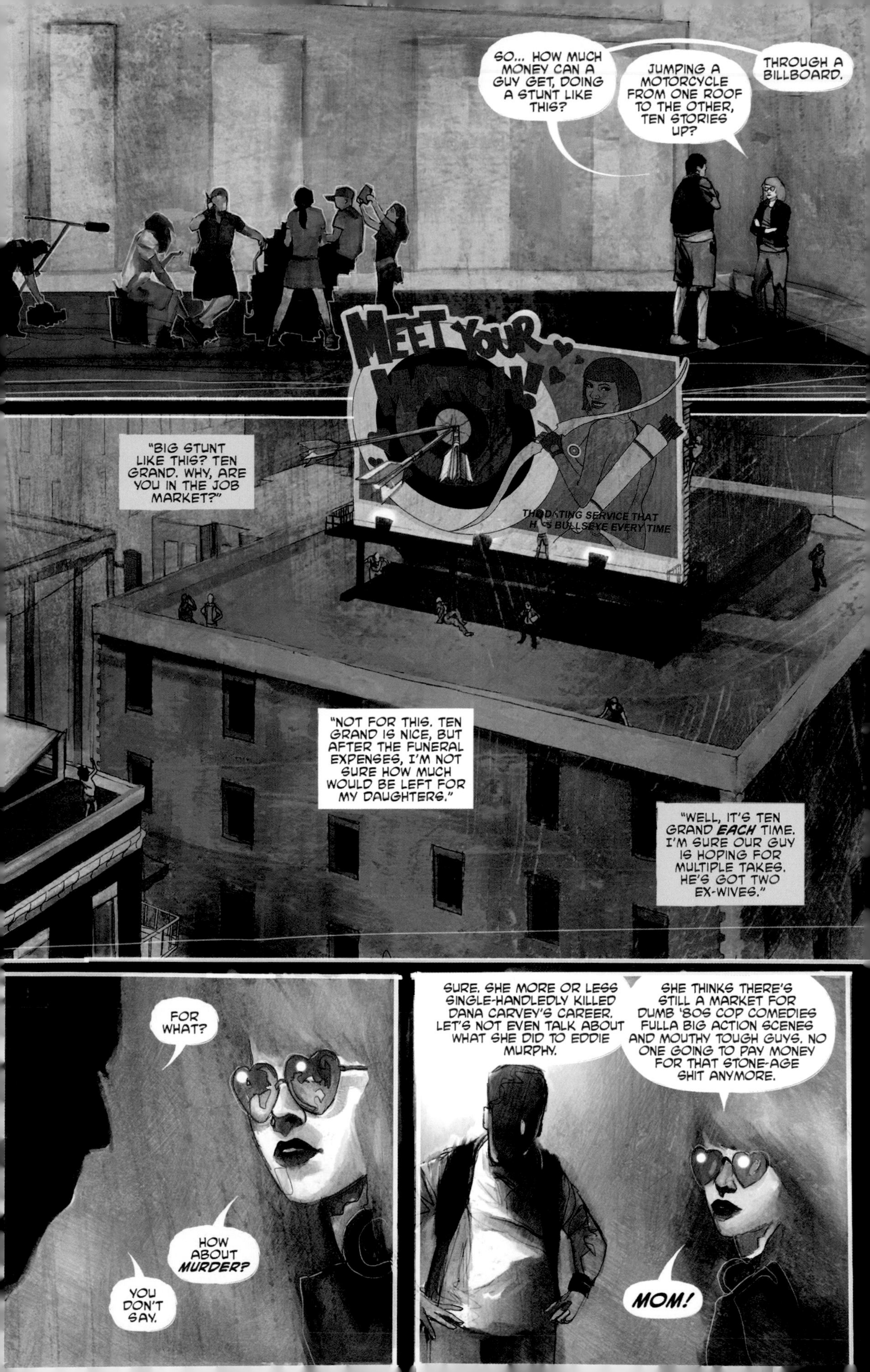
SO... HOW MUCH MONEY CAN A GUY GET, DOING A STUNT LIKE THIS?
JUMPING A MOTORCYCLE FROM ONE ROOF TO THE OTHER, TEN STORIES UP?
THROUGH A BILLBOARD.
MEET YOUR MATCH!
THE DATING SERVICE THAT HITS BULLSEYE EVERY TIME
"BIG STUNT LIKE THIS? TEN GRAND. WHY, ARE YOU IN THE JOB MARKET?"
"NOT FOR THIS. TEN GRAND IS NICE, BUT AFTER THE FUNERAL EXPENSES, I'M NOT SURE HOW MUCH WOULD BE LEFT FOR MY DAUGHTERS."
"WELL, IT'S TEN GRAND EACH TIME. I'M SURE OUR GUY IS HOPING FOR MULTIPLE TAKES. HE'S GOT TWO EX-WIVES."
FOR WHAT?
HOW ABOUT MURDER?
YOU DON'T SAY.
SURE. SHE MORE OR LESS SINGLE-HANDLEDLY KILLED DANA CARVEY'S CAREER. LET'S NOT EVEN TALK ABOUT WHAT SHE DID TO EDDIE MURPHY.
SHE THINKS THERE'S STILL A MARKET FOR DUMB '80S COP COMEDIES FULLA BIG ACTION SCENES AND MOUTHY TOUGH GUYS. NO ONE GOING TO PAY MONEY FOR THAT STONE-AGE SHIT ANYMORE.
MOM!

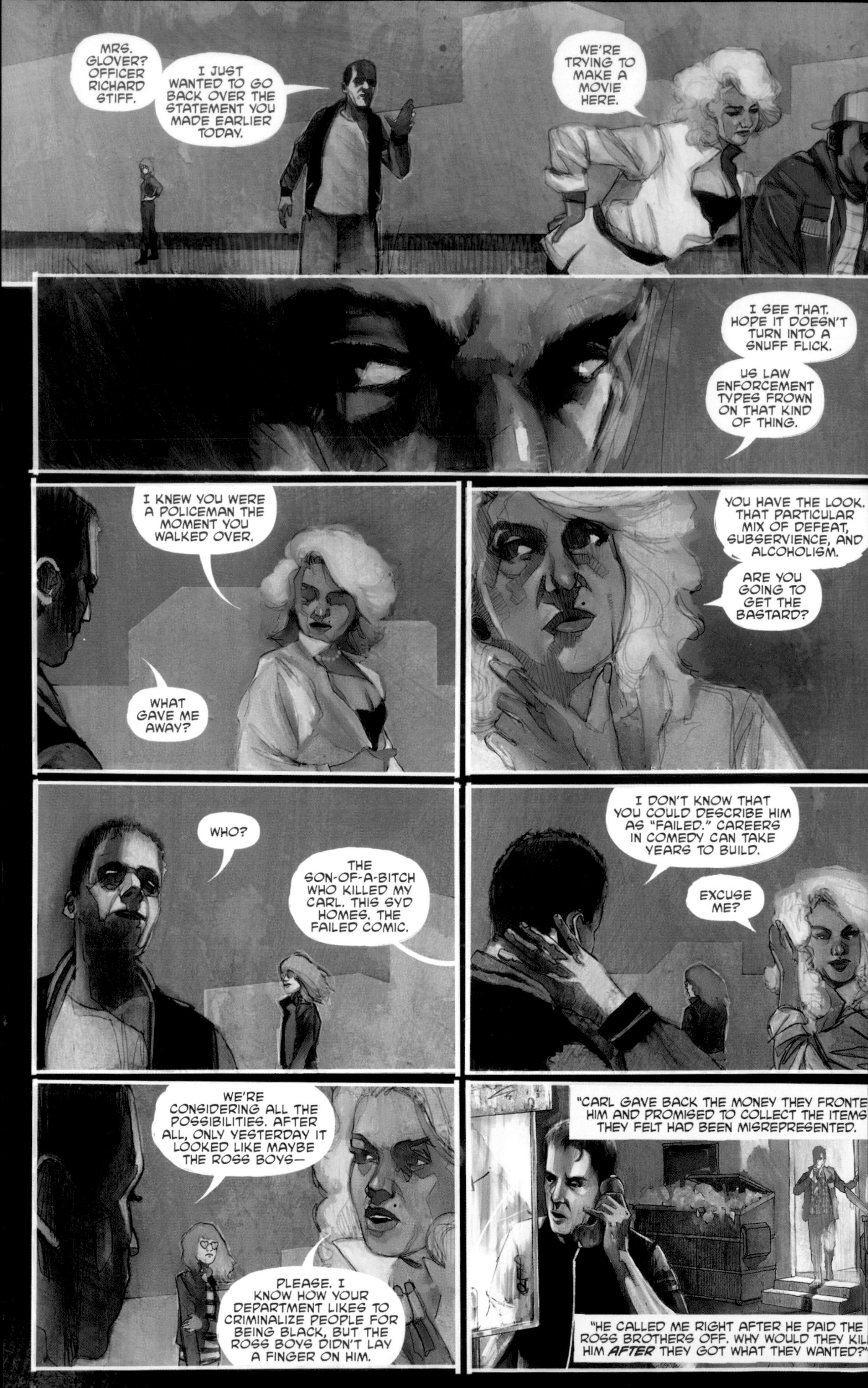
MRS. GLOVER? OFFICER RICHARD STIFF.
I JUST WANTED TO GO BACK OVER THE STATEMENT YOU MADE EARLIER TODAY.
WE'RE TRYING TO MAKE A MOVIE HERE.
I SEE THAT. HOPE IT DOESN'T TURN INTO A SNUFF FLICK.
US LAW ENFORCEMENT TYPES FROWN ON THAT KIND OF THING.
I KNEW YOU WERE A POLICEMAN THE MOMENT YOU WALKED OVER.
WHAT GAVE ME AWAY?
YOU HAVE THE LOOK. THAT PARTICULAR MIX OF DEFEAT, SUBSERVIENCE, AND ALCOHOLISM.
ARE YOU GOING TO GET THE BASTARD?
WHO?
THE SON-OF-A-BITCH WHO KILLED MY CARL. THIS SYD HOMES. THE FAILED COMIC.
I DON'T KNOW THAT YOU COULD DESCRIBE HIM AS "FAILED." CAREERS IN COMEDY CAN TAKE YEARS TO BUILD.
EXCUSE ME?
WE'RE CONSIDERING ALL THE POSSIBILITIES. AFTER ALL, ONLY YESTERDAY IT LOOKED LIKE MAYBE THE ROSS BOYS—
PLEASE. I KNOW HOW YOUR DEPARTMENT LIKES TO CRIMINALIZE PEOPLE FOR BEING BLACK, BUT THE ROSS BOYS DIDN'T LAY A FINGER ON HIM.
"CARL GAVE BACK THE MONEY THEY FRONTE HIM AND PROMISED TO COLLECT THE ITEMS THEY FELT HAD BEEN MISREPRESENTED.
"HE CALLED ME RIGHT AFTER HE PAID THE ROSS BROTHERS OFF. WHY WOULD THEY KIL HIM AFTER THEY GOT WHAT THEY WANTED?"

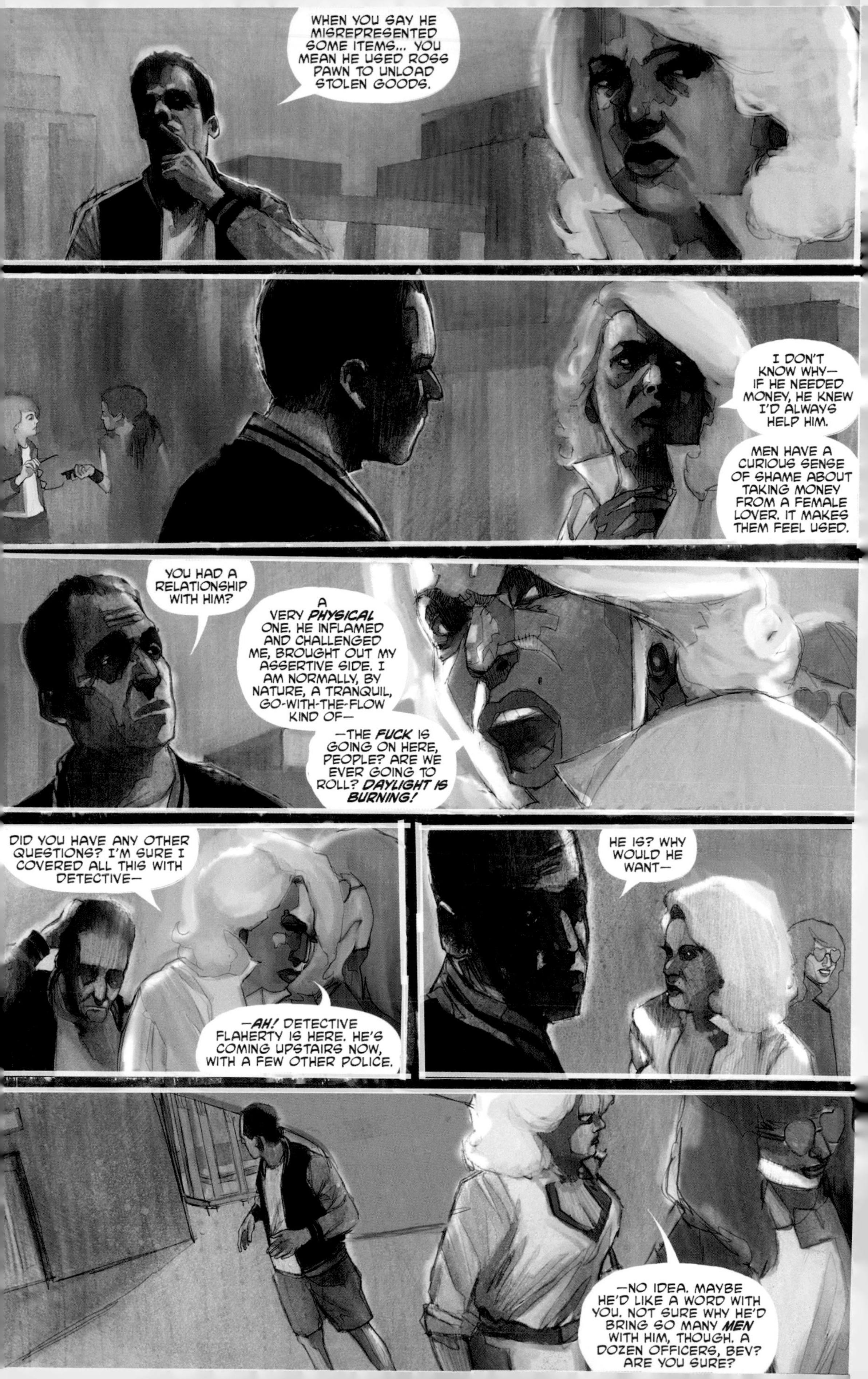
WHEN YOU SAY HE MISREPRESENTED SOME ITEMS... YOU MEAN HE USED ROSS PAWN TO UNLOAD STOLEN GOODS.
I DON'T KNOW WHY— IF HE NEEDED MONEY, HE KNEW I'D ALWAYS HELP HIM.
MEN HAVE A CURIOUS SENSE OF SHAME ABOUT TAKING MONEY FROM A FEMALE LOVER. IT MAKES THEM FEEL USED.
YOU HAD A RELATIONSHIP WITH HIM?
A VERY PHYSICAL ONE. HE INFLAMED AND CHALLENGED ME, BROUGHT OUT MY ASSERTIVE SIDE. I AM NORMALLY, BY NATURE, A TRANQUIL, GO-WITH-THE-FLOW KIND OF—
—THE FUCK IS GOING ON HERE, PEOPLE? ARE WE EVER GOING TO ROLL? DAYLIGHT IS BURNING!
DID YOU HAVE ANY OTHER QUESTIONS? I'M SURE I COVERED ALL THIS WITH DETECTIVE—
—AH! DETECTIVE FLAHERTY IS HERE. HE'S COMING UPSTAIRS NOW, WITH A FEW OTHER POLICE.
HE IS? WHY WOULD HE WANT—
—NO IDEA. MAYBE HE'D LIKE A WORD WITH YOU. NOT SURE WHY HE'D BRING SO MANY MEN WITH HIM, THOUGH. A DOZEN OFFICERS, BEV? ARE YOU SURE?

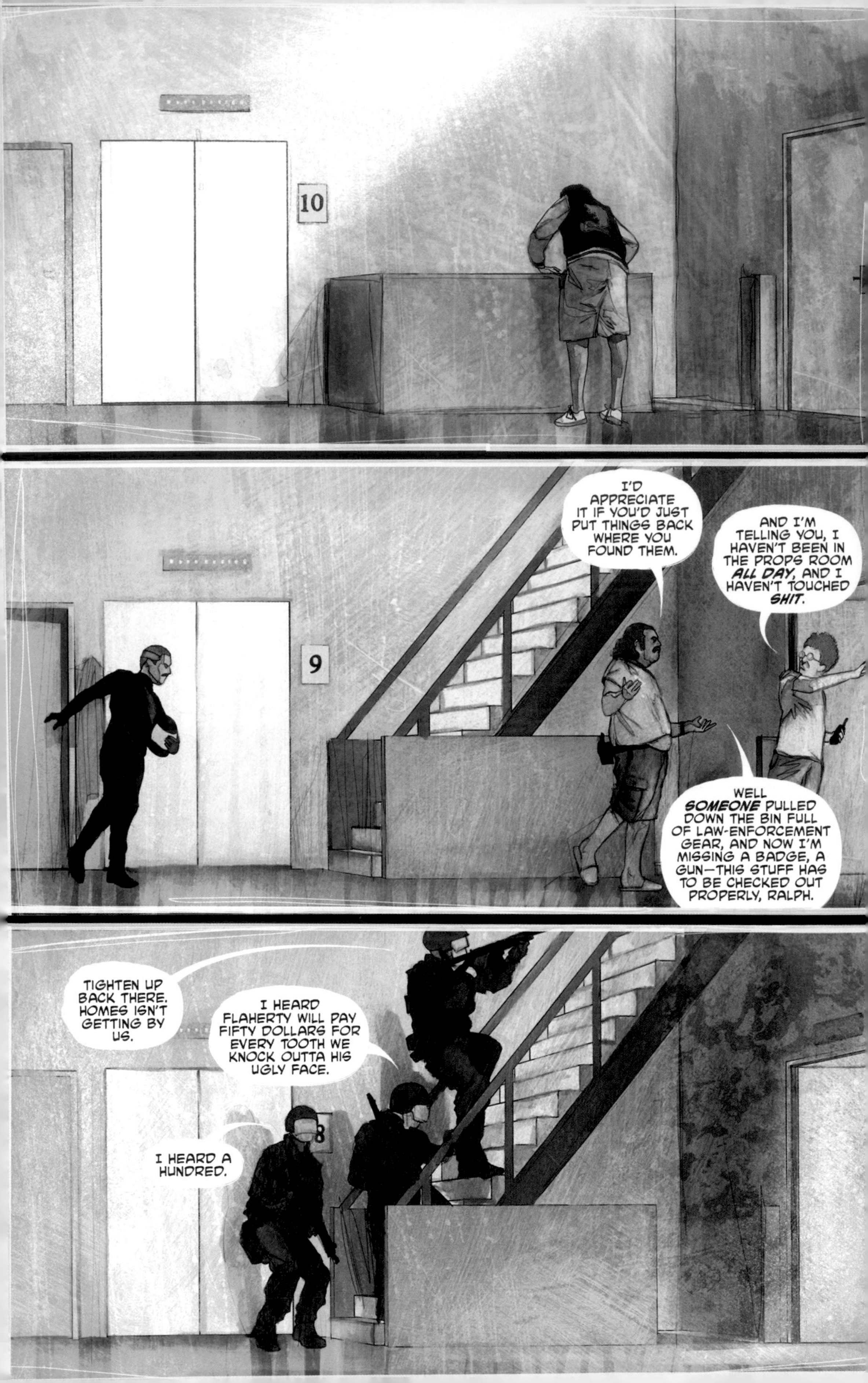
10
I'D APPRECIATE IT IF YOU'D JUST PUT THINGS BACK WHERE YOU FOUND THEM.
AND I'M TELLING YOU, I HAVEN'T BEEN IN THE PROPS ROOM ALL DAY, AND I HAVEN'T TOUCHED SHIT.
9
WELL SOMEONE PULLED DOWN THE BIN FULL OF LAW-ENFORCEMENT GEAR, AND NOW I'M MISSING A BADGE, A GUN—THIS STUFF HAS TO BE CHECKED OUT PROPERLY, RALPH.
TIGHTEN UP BACK THERE. HOMES ISN'T GETTING BY US.
I HEARD FLAHERTY WILL PAY FIFTY DOLLARS FOR EVERY TOOTH WE KNOCK OUTTA HIS UGLY FACE.
I HEARD A HUNDRED.

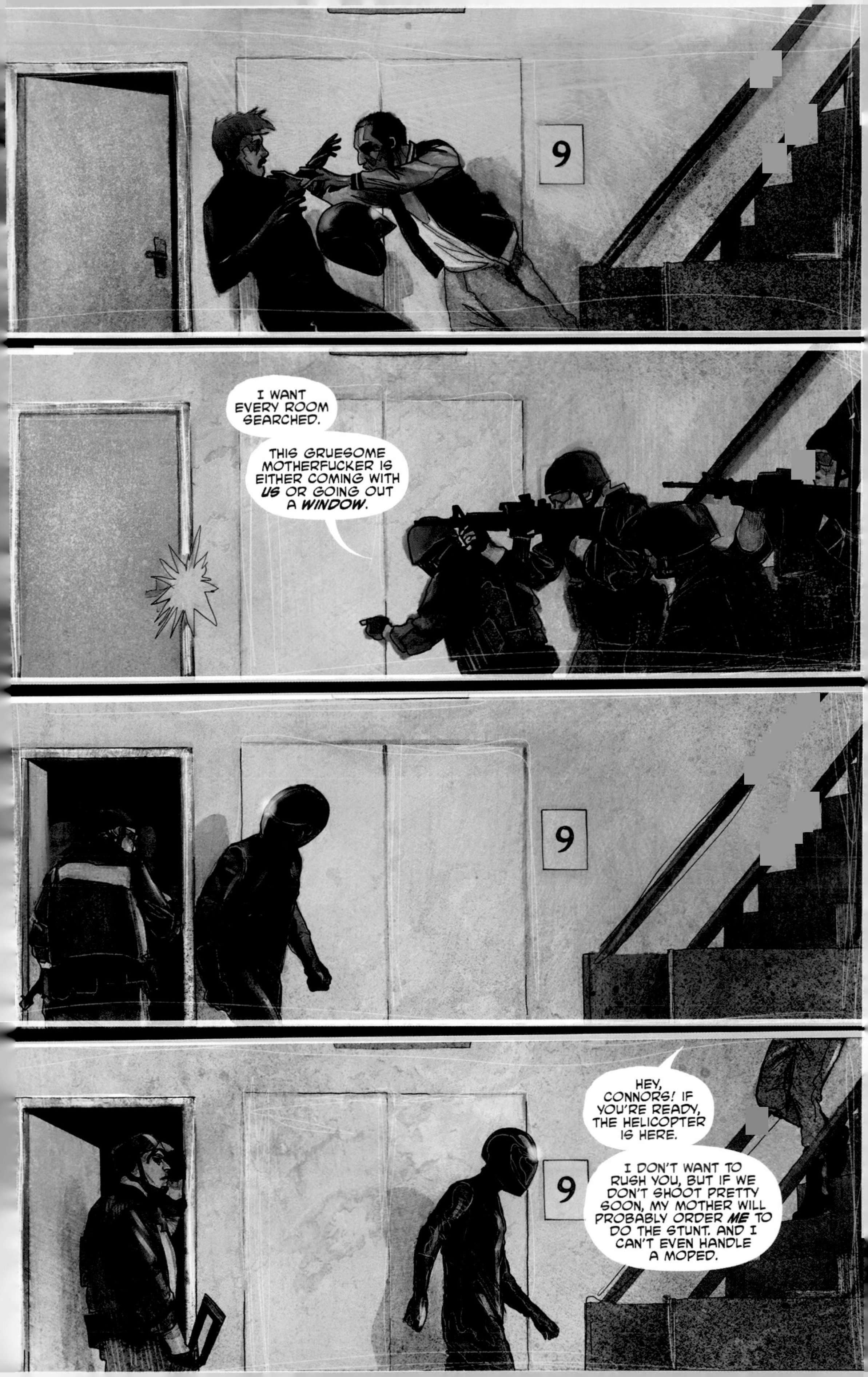
I WANT EVERY ROOM SEARCHED.
THIS GRUESOME MOTHERFUCKER IS EITHER COMING WITH *US* OR GOING OUT A *WINDOW*.
HEY, CONNORS! IF YOU'RE READY, THE HELICOPTER IS HERE.
I DON'T WANT TO RUSH YOU, BUT IF WE DON'T SHOOT PRETTY SOON, MY MOTHER WILL PROBABLY ORDER *ME* TO DO THE STUNT. AND I CAN'T EVEN HANDLE A MOPED.
9

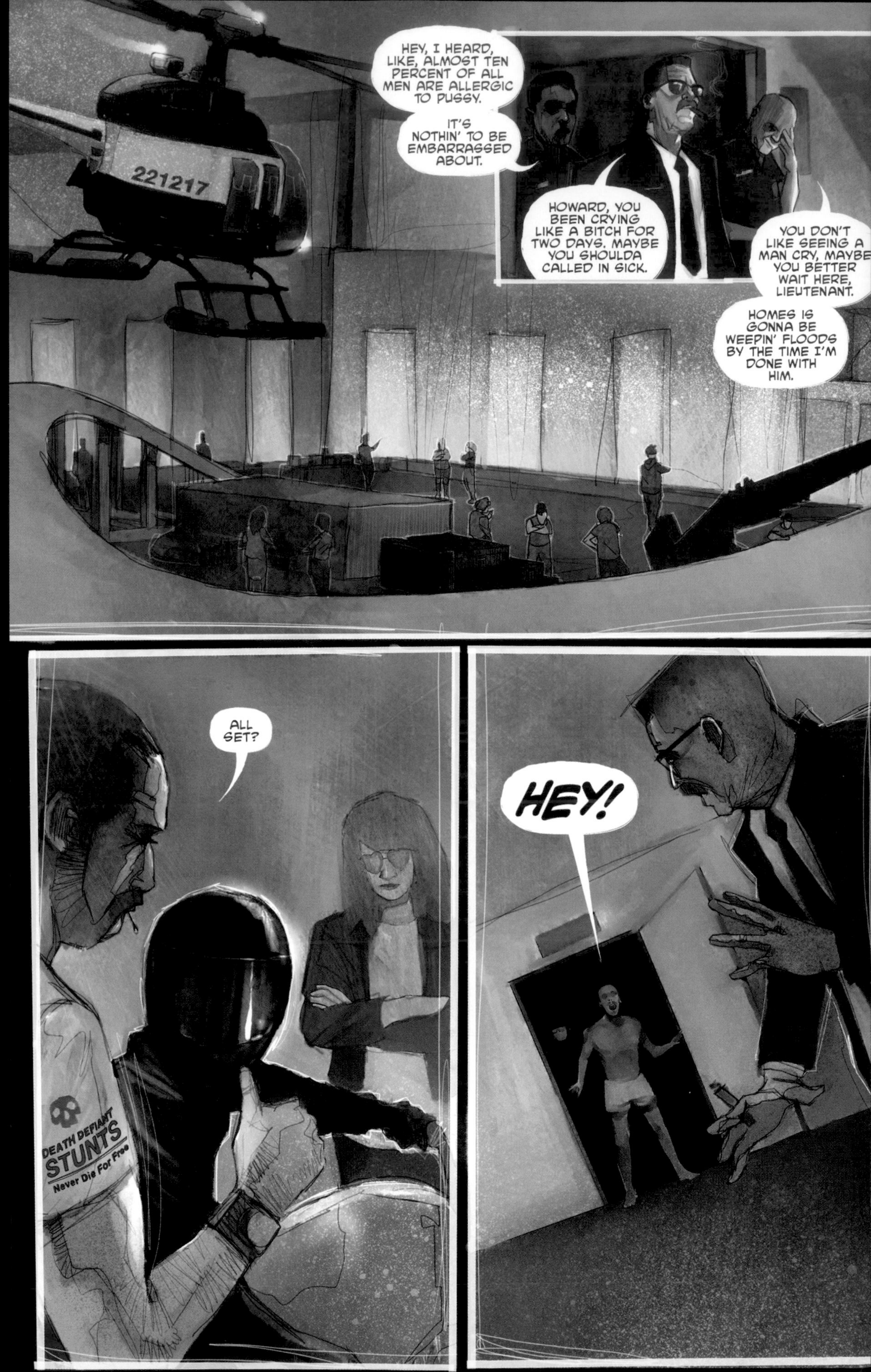
HEY, I HEARD, LIKE, ALMOST TEN PERCENT OF ALL MEN ARE ALLERGIC TO PUSSY.
IT'S NOTHIN' TO BE EMBARRASSED ABOUT.
221217
HOWARD, YOU BEEN CRYING LIKE A BITCH FOR TWO DAYS. MAYBE YOU SHOULDA CALLED IN SICK.
YOU DON'T LIKE SEEING A MAN CRY, MAYBE YOU BETTER WAIT HERE, LIEUTENANT.
HOMES IS GONNA BE WEEPIN' FLOODS BY THE TIME I'M DONE WITH HIM.
ALL SET?
DEATH DEFIANT STUNTS Never Die For Free
HEY!

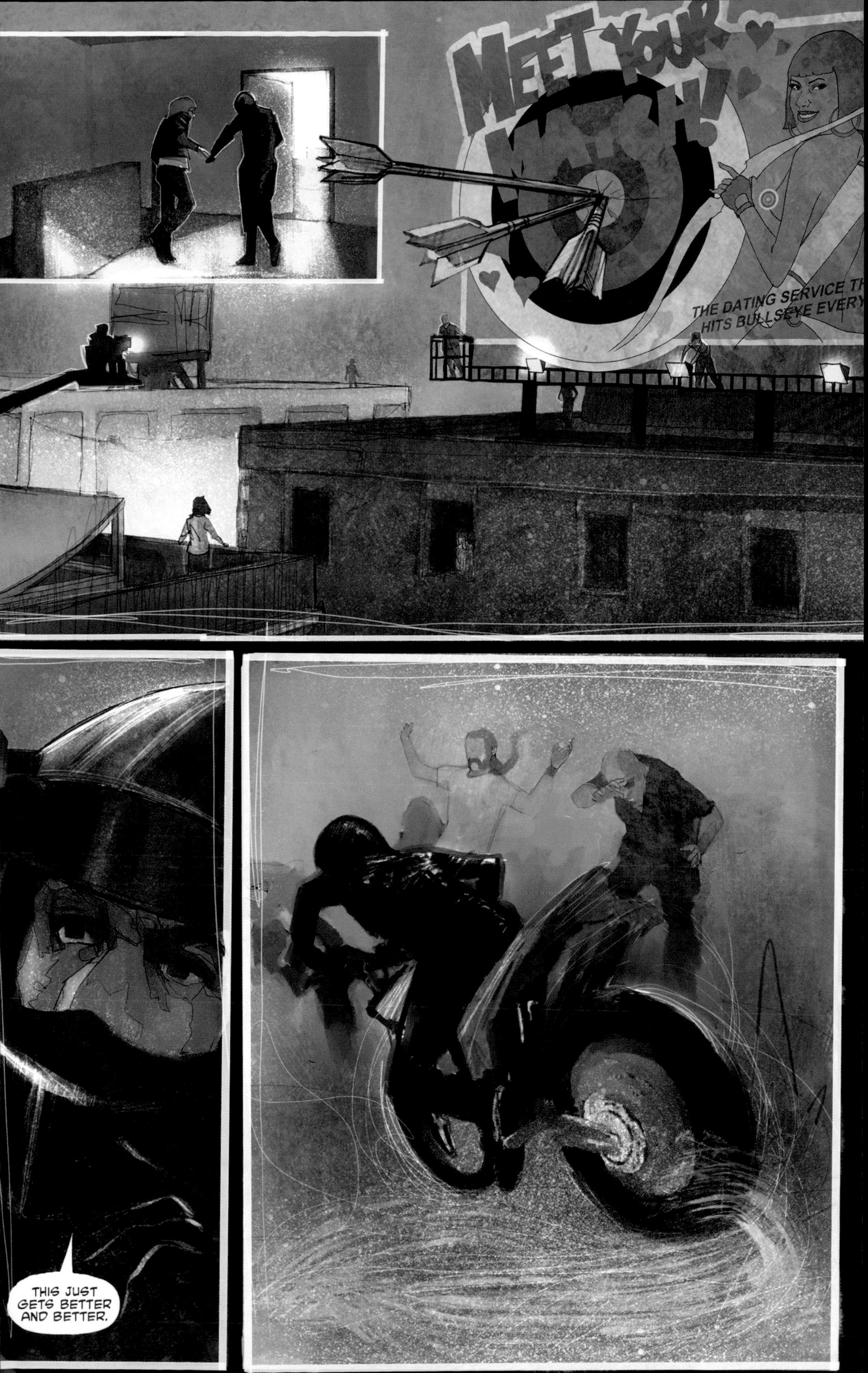
MEET YOUR MATCH!
THE DATING SERVICE TH
HITS BULLSEYE EVERY
THIS JUST GETS BETTER AND BETTER.

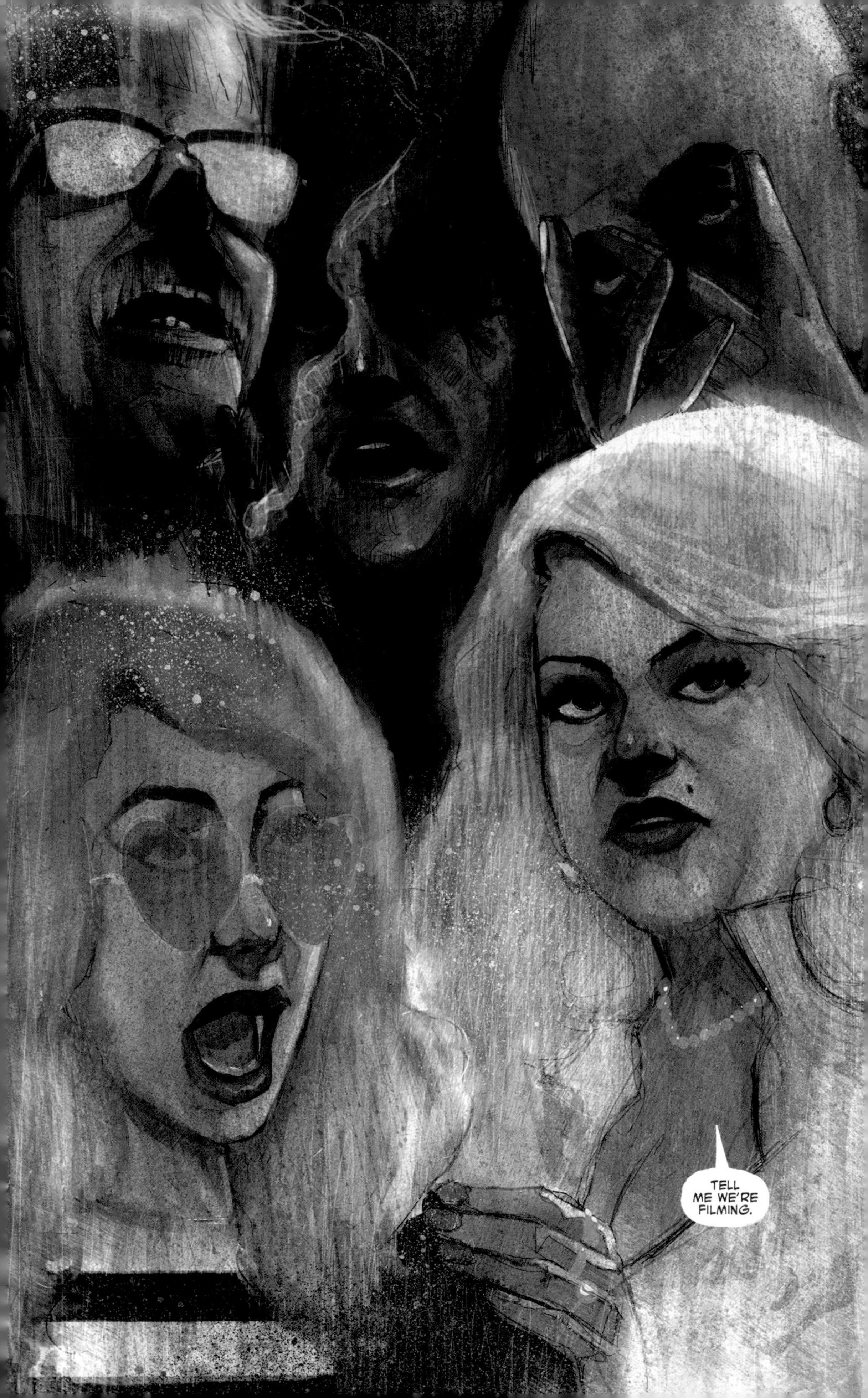
TELL ME WE'RE FILMING.

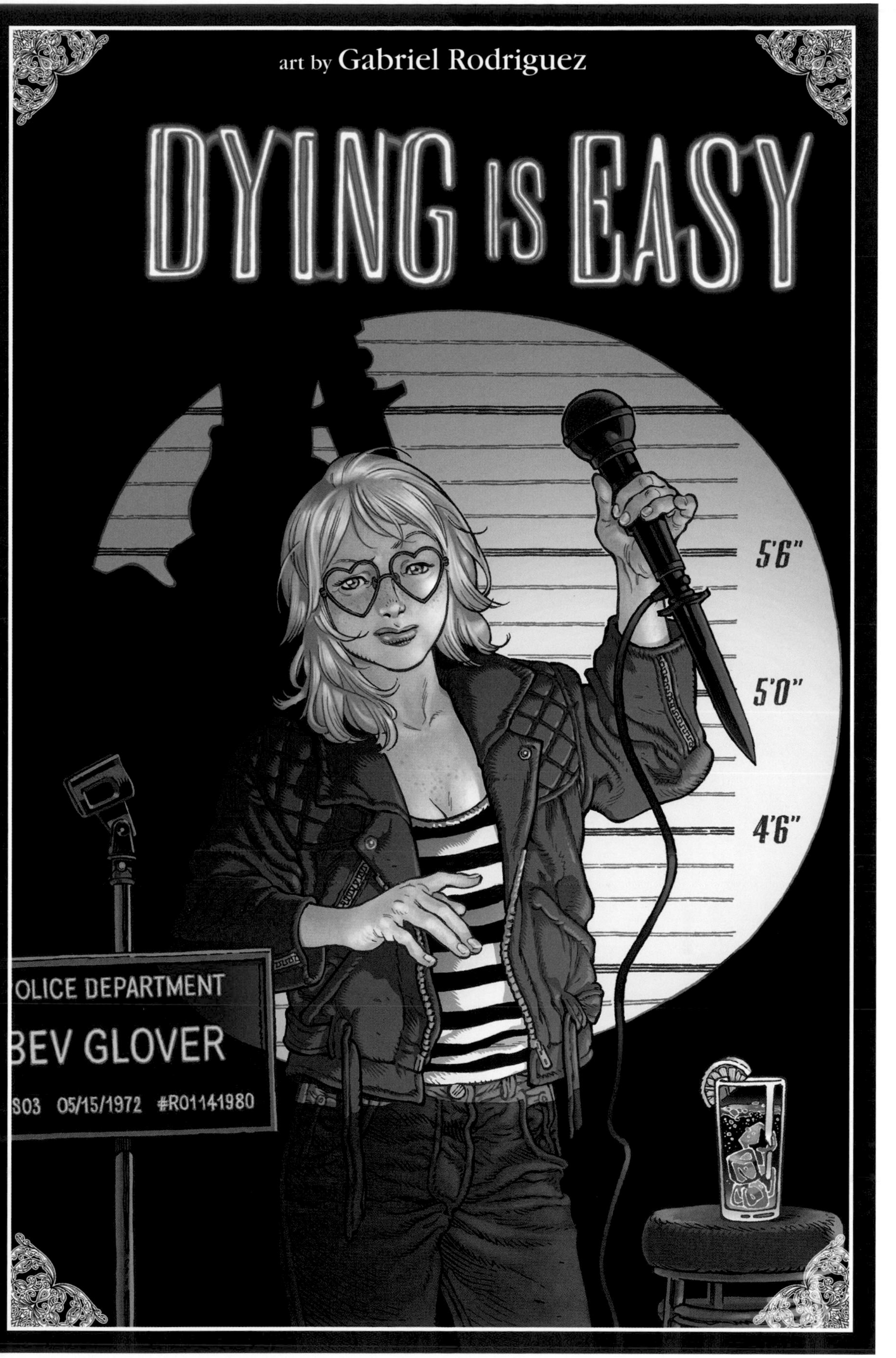
art by Gabriel Rodriguez
DYING IS EASY
5'6"
5'0"
4'6"
OLICE DEPARTMENT
BEV GLOVER
S03 05/15/1972 #R01141980

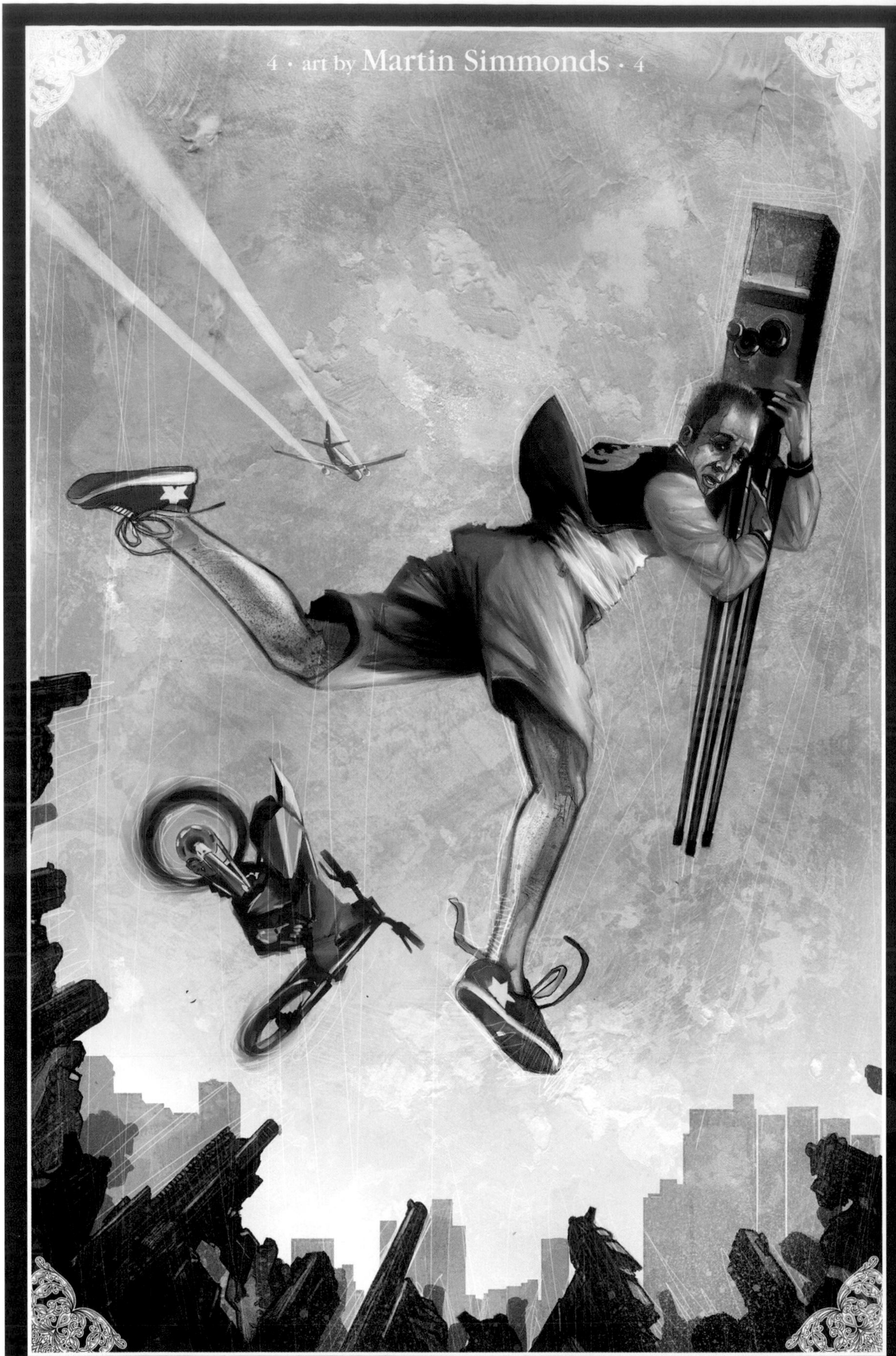
4 · art by Martin Simmonds · 4

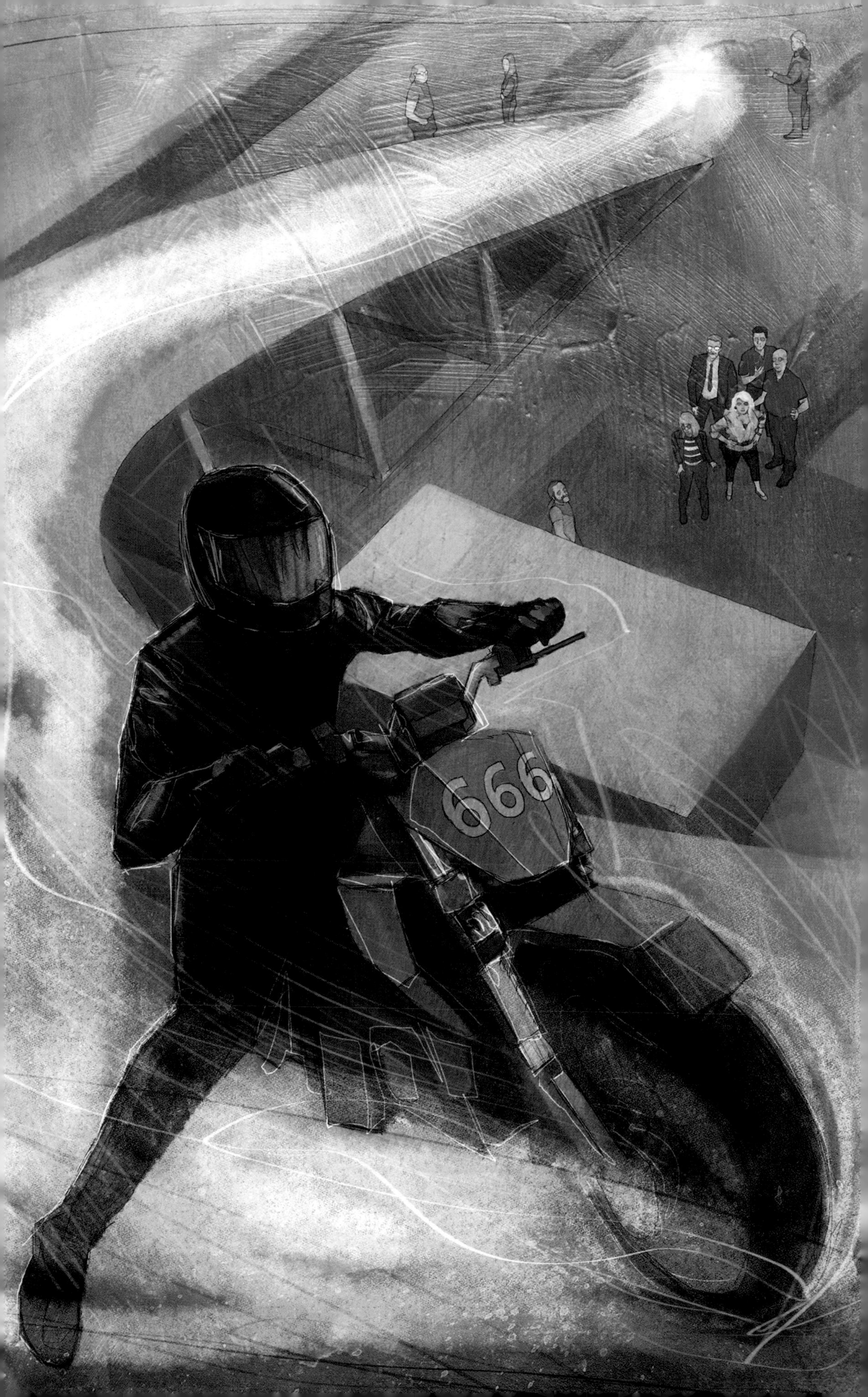
666

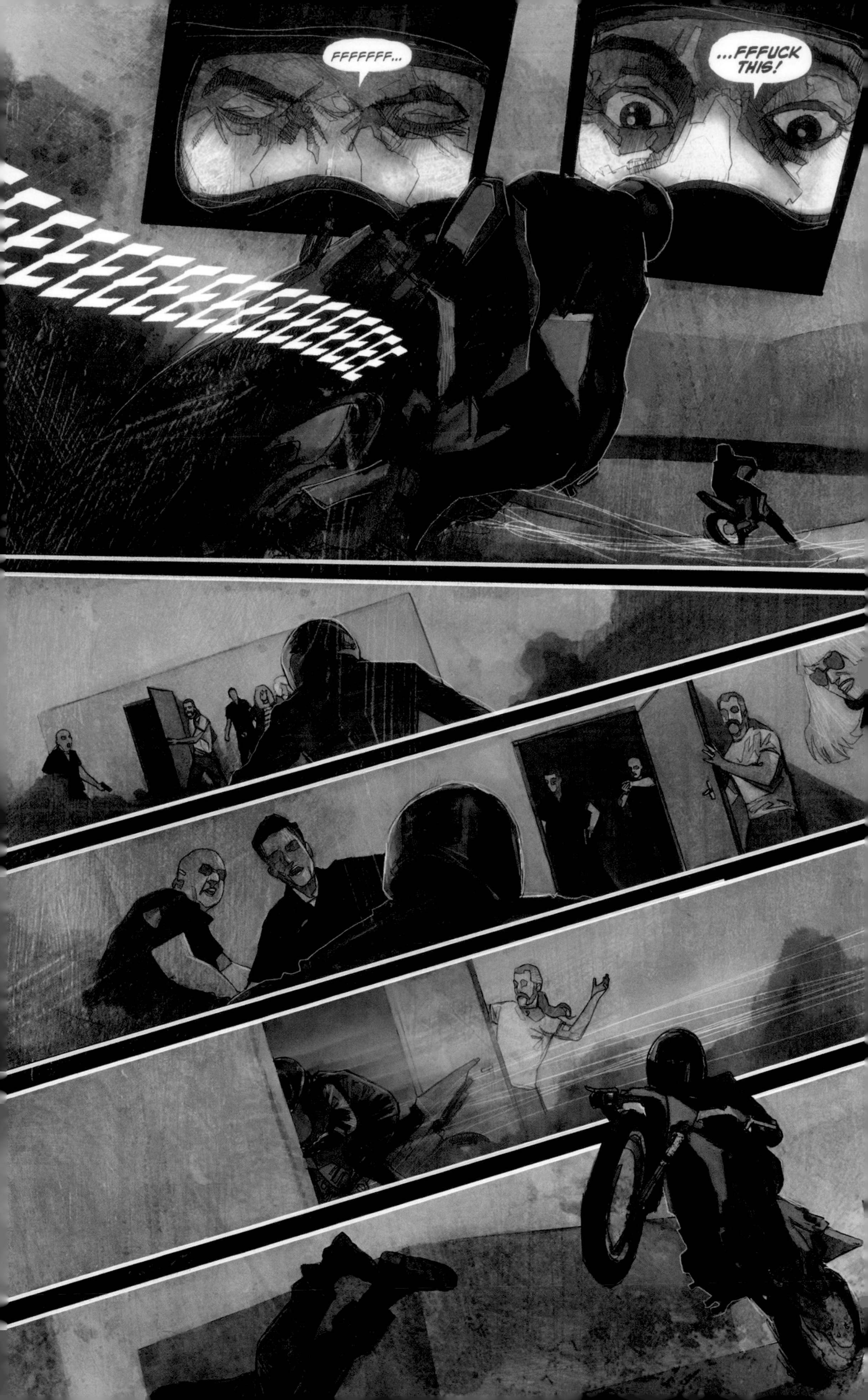
FFFFFFF...
...FFFUCK THIS!
EEEEEEEEEEEEEEEE

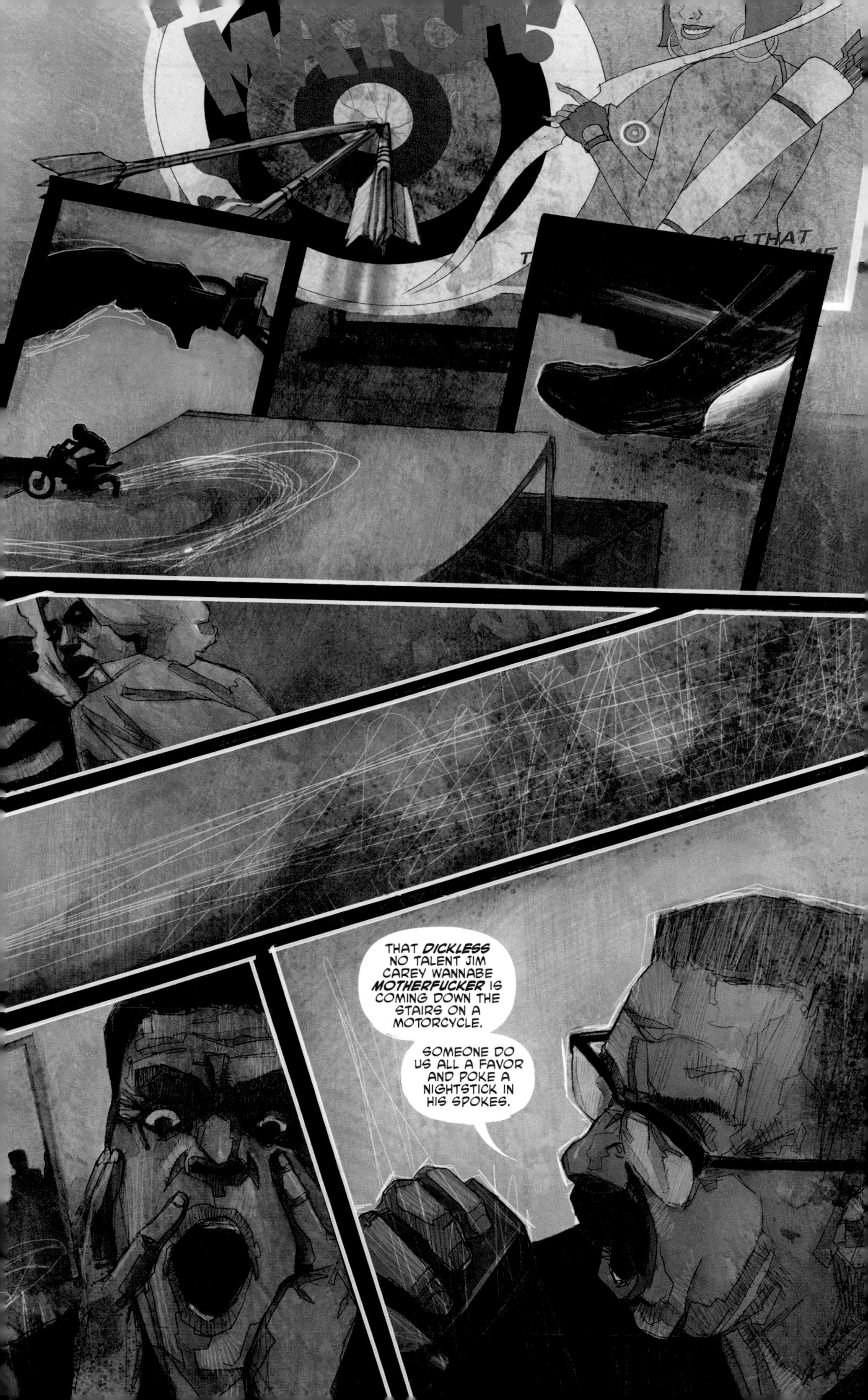
THAT DICKLESS NO TALENT JIM CAREY WANNABE MOTHERFUCKER IS COMING DOWN THE STAIRS ON A MOTORCYCLE.
SOMEONE DO US ALL A FAVOR AND POKE A NIGHTSTICK IN HIS SPOKES.

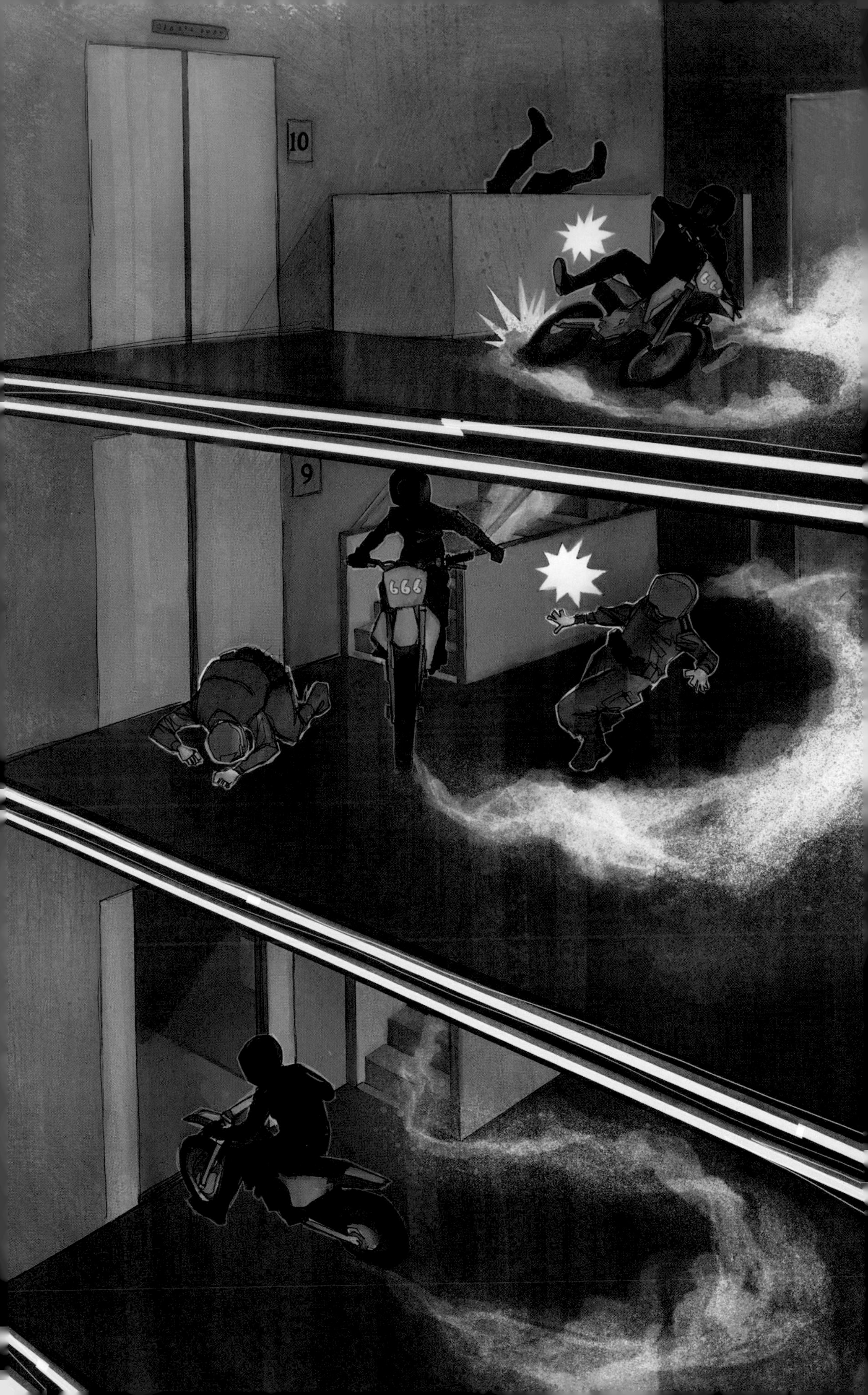
10
666
9
666

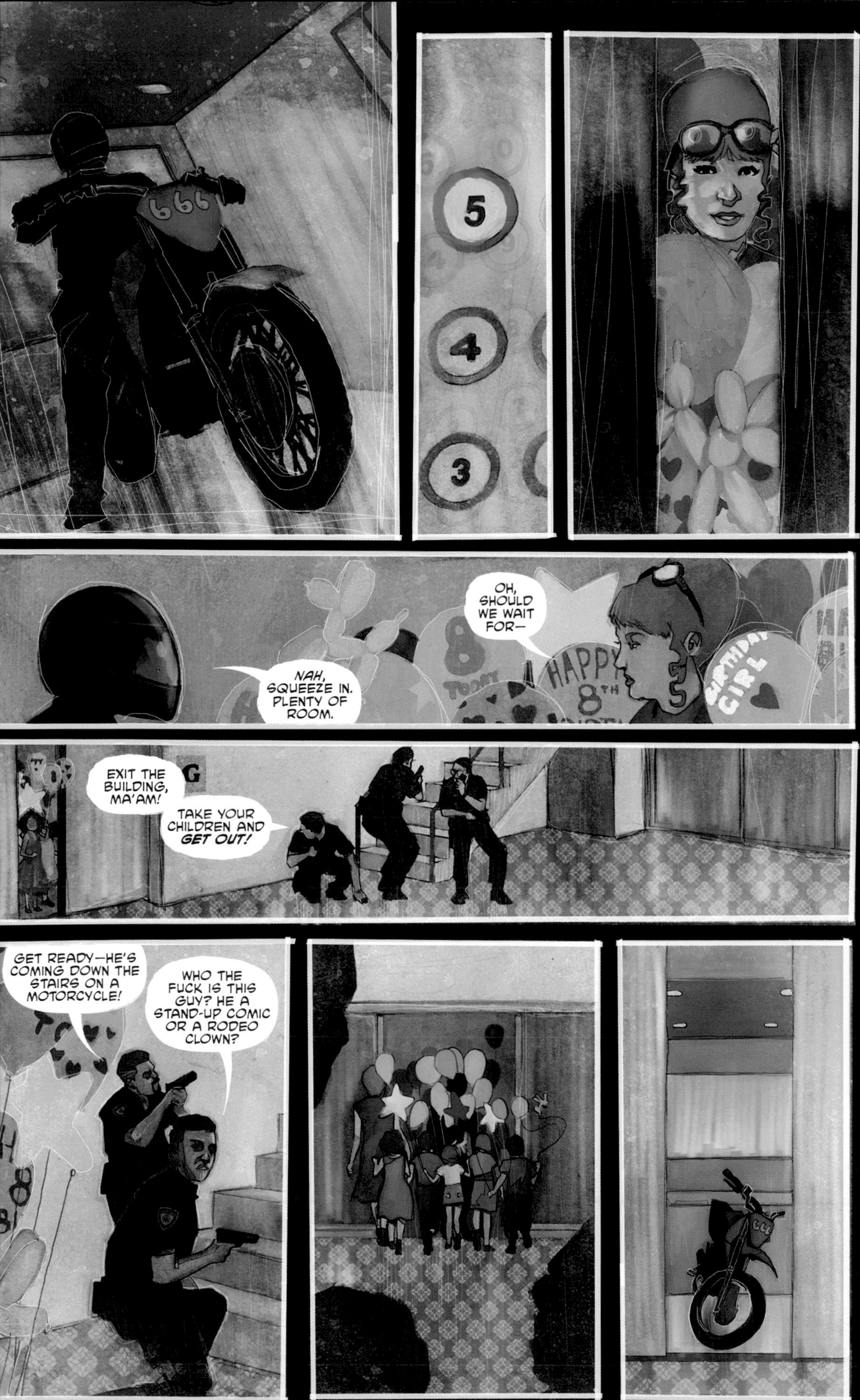
666
5
4
3
OH, SHOULD WE WAIT FOR—
NAH, SQUEEZE IN. PLENTY OF ROOM.
HAPPY 8TH
BIRTHDAY GIRL
G
EXIT THE BUILDING, MA'AM!
TAKE YOUR CHILDREN AND *GET OUT!*
GET READY—HE'S COMING DOWN THE STAIRS ON A MOTORCYCLE!
WHO THE FUCK IS THIS GUY? HE A STAND-UP COMIC OR A RODEO CLOWN?

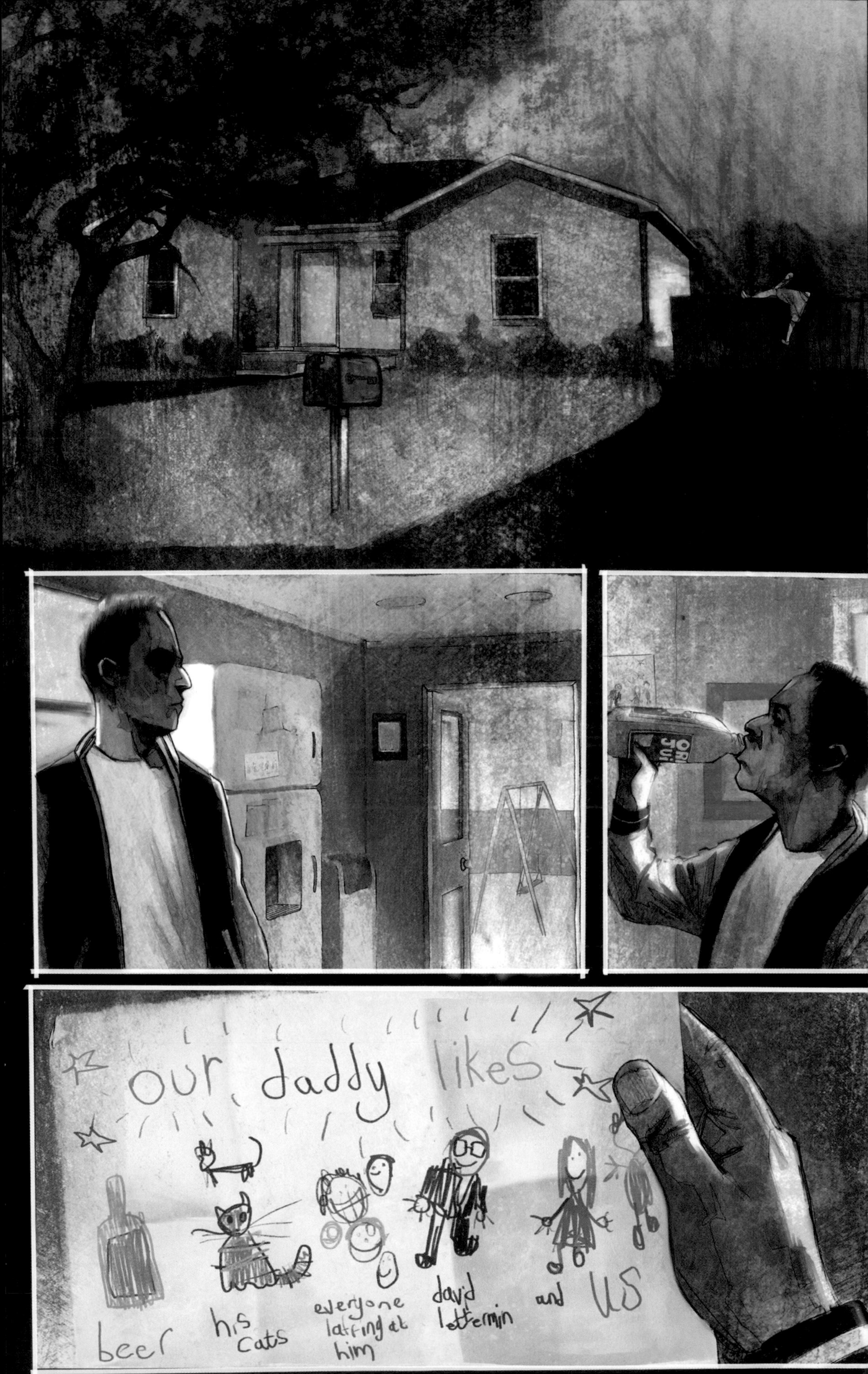
our daddy likes
beer
his cats
everyone laffing at him
david lettermin
and us

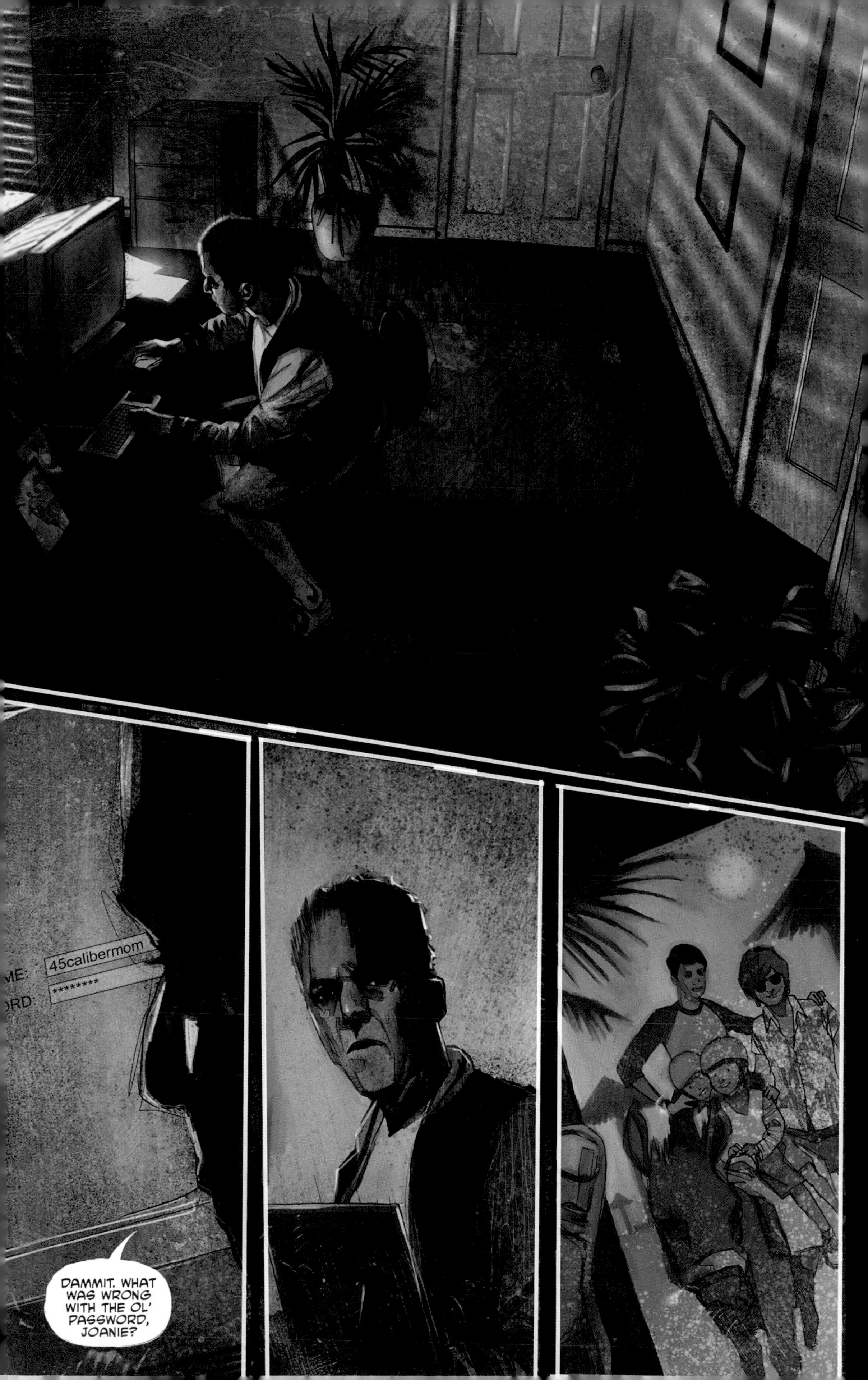

ME: 45calibermom
RD: ********
DAMMIT. WHAT WAS WRONG WITH THE OL' PASSWORD, JOANIE?

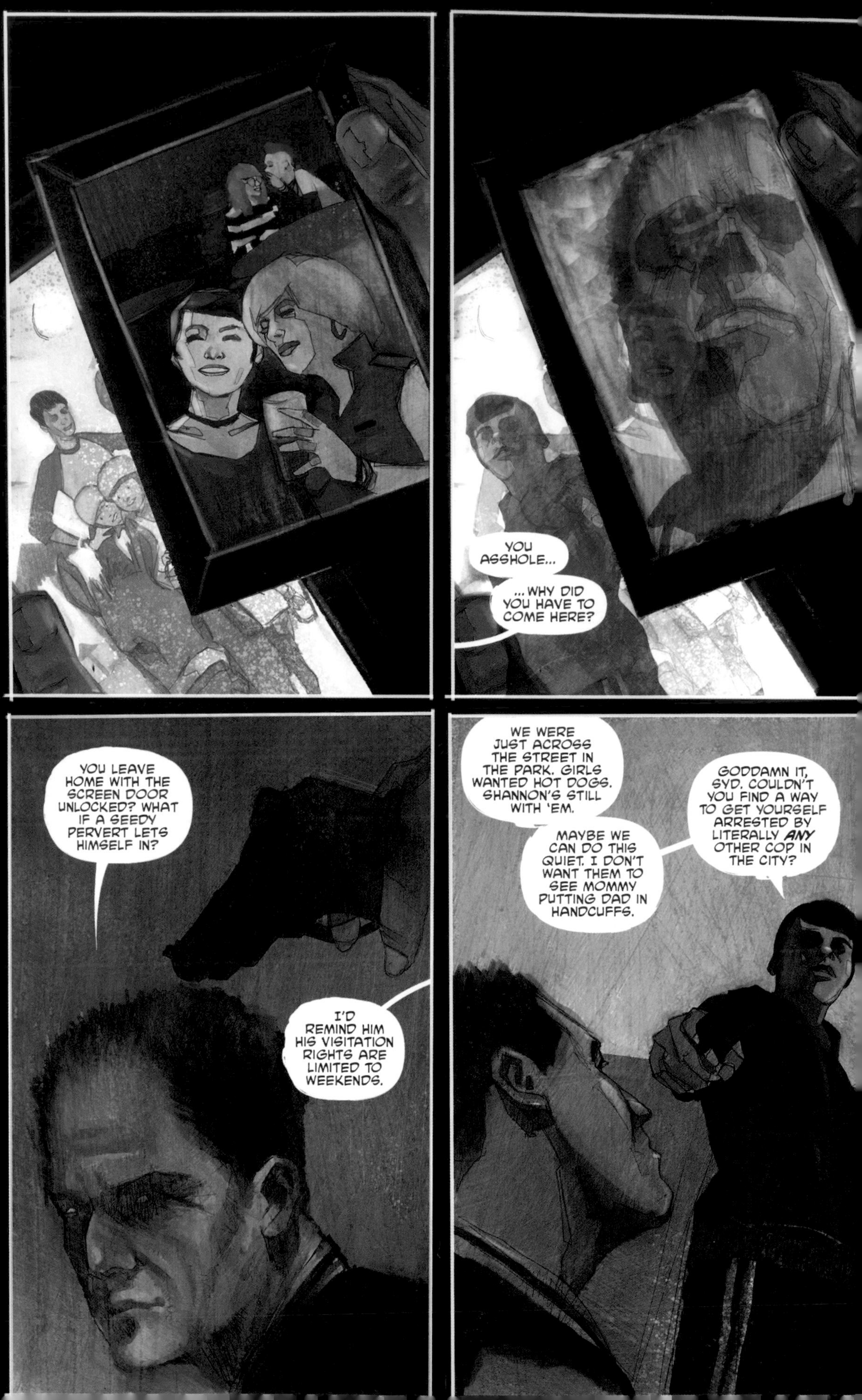
YOU ASSHOLE...
...WHY DID YOU HAVE TO COME HERE?
YOU LEAVE HOME WITH THE SCREEN DOOR UNLOCKED? WHAT IF A SEEDY PERVERT LETS HIMSELF IN?
I'D REMIND HIM HIS VISITATION RIGHTS ARE LIMITED TO WEEKENDS.
WE WERE JUST ACROSS THE STREET IN THE PARK. GIRLS WANTED HOT DOGS. SHANNON'S STILL WITH 'EM.
MAYBE WE CAN DO THIS QUIET. I DON'T WANT THEM TO SEE MOMMY PUTTING DAD IN HANDCUFFS.
GODDAMN IT, SYD. COULDN'T YOU FIND A WAY TO GET YOURSELF ARRESTED BY LITERALLY ANY OTHER COP IN THE CITY?

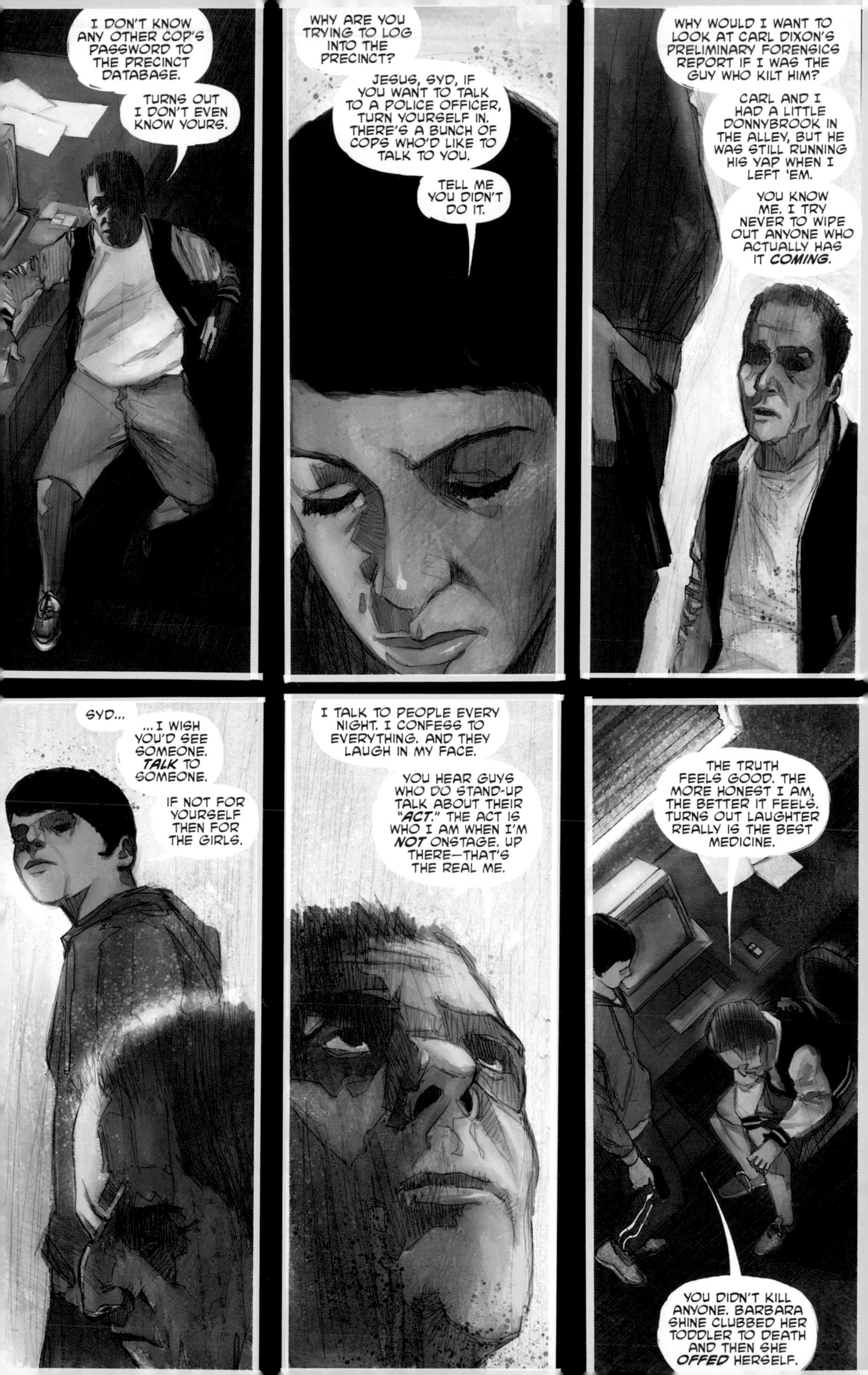
I DON'T KNOW ANY OTHER COP'S PASSWORD TO THE PRECINCT DATABASE.
TURNS OUT I DON'T EVEN KNOW YOURS.
WHY ARE YOU TRYING TO LOG INTO THE PRECINCT?
JESUS, SYD, IF YOU WANT TO TALK TO A POLICE OFFICER, TURN YOURSELF IN. THERE'S A BUNCH OF COPS WHO'D LIKE TO TALK TO YOU.
TELL ME YOU DIDN'T DO IT.
WHY WOULD I WANT TO LOOK AT CARL DIXON'S PRELIMINARY FORENSICS REPORT IF I WAS THE GUY WHO KILT HIM?
CARL AND I HAD A LITTLE DONNYBROOK IN THE ALLEY, BUT HE WAS STILL RUNNING HIS YAP WHEN I LEFT 'EM.
YOU KNOW ME. I TRY NEVER TO WIPE OUT ANYONE WHO ACTUALLY HAS IT *COMING*.
SYD...
...I WISH YOU'D SEE SOMEONE. ***TALK*** TO SOMEONE.
IF NOT FOR YOURSELF THEN FOR THE GIRLS.
I TALK TO PEOPLE EVERY NIGHT. I CONFESS TO EVERYTHING. AND THEY LAUGH IN MY FACE.
YOU HEAR GUYS WHO DO STAND-UP TALK ABOUT THEIR "*ACT*." THE ACT IS WHO I AM WHEN I'M ***NOT*** ONSTAGE. UP THERE—THAT'S THE REAL ME.
THE TRUTH FEELS GOOD. THE MORE HONEST I AM, THE BETTER IT FEELS. TURNS OUT LAUGHTER REALLY IS THE BEST MEDICINE.
YOU DIDN'T KILL ANYONE. BARBARA SHINE CLUBBED HER TODDLER TO DEATH AND THEN SHE ***OFFED*** HERSELF.

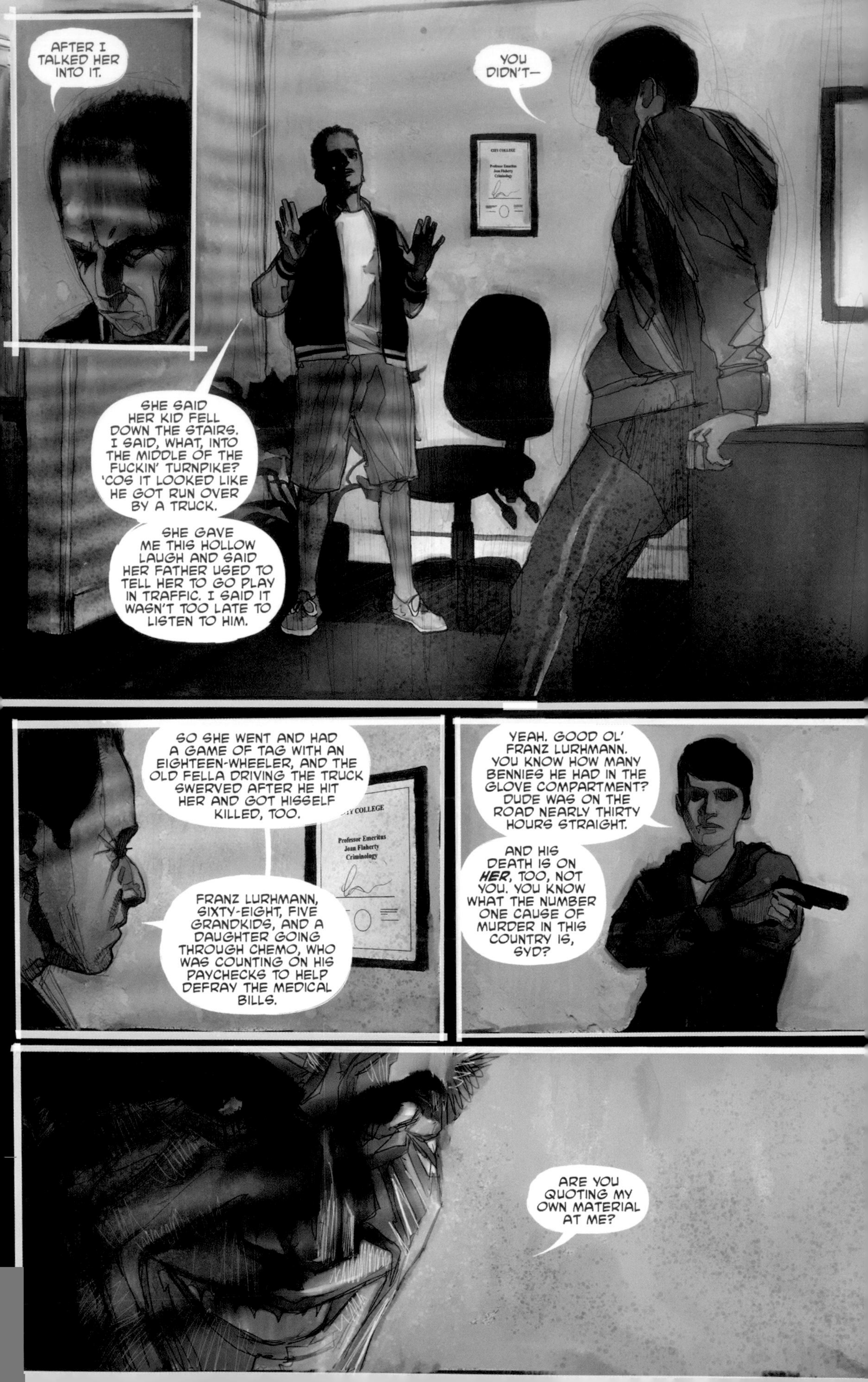

AFTER I TALKED HER INTO IT.
YOU DIDN'T—
SHE SAID HER KID FELL DOWN THE STAIRS. I SAID, WHAT, INTO THE MIDDLE OF THE FUCKIN' TURNPIKE? 'COS IT LOOKED LIKE HE GOT RUN OVER BY A TRUCK.
SHE GAVE ME THIS HOLLOW LAUGH AND SAID HER FATHER USED TO TELL HER TO GO PLAY IN TRAFFIC. I SAID IT WASN'T TOO LATE TO LISTEN TO HIM.
SO SHE WENT AND HAD A GAME OF TAG WITH AN EIGHTEEN-WHEELER, AND THE OLD FELLA DRIVING THE TRUCK SWERVED AFTER HE HIT HER AND GOT HISSELF KILLED, TOO.
Professor Emeritus
Jean Flaherty
Criminology
FRANZ LURHMANN, SIXTY-EIGHT, FIVE GRANDKIDS, AND A DAUGHTER GOING THROUGH CHEMO, WHO WAS COUNTING ON HIS PAYCHECKS TO HELP DEFRAY THE MEDICAL BILLS.
YEAH. GOOD OL' FRANZ LURHMANN. YOU KNOW HOW MANY BENNIES HE HAD IN THE GLOVE COMPARTMENT? DUDE WAS ON THE ROAD NEARLY THIRTY HOURS STRAIGHT.
AND HIS DEATH IS ON *HER*, TOO, NOT YOU. YOU KNOW WHAT THE NUMBER ONE CAUSE OF MURDER IN THIS COUNTRY IS, SYD?
ARE YOU QUOTING MY OWN MATERIAL AT ME?

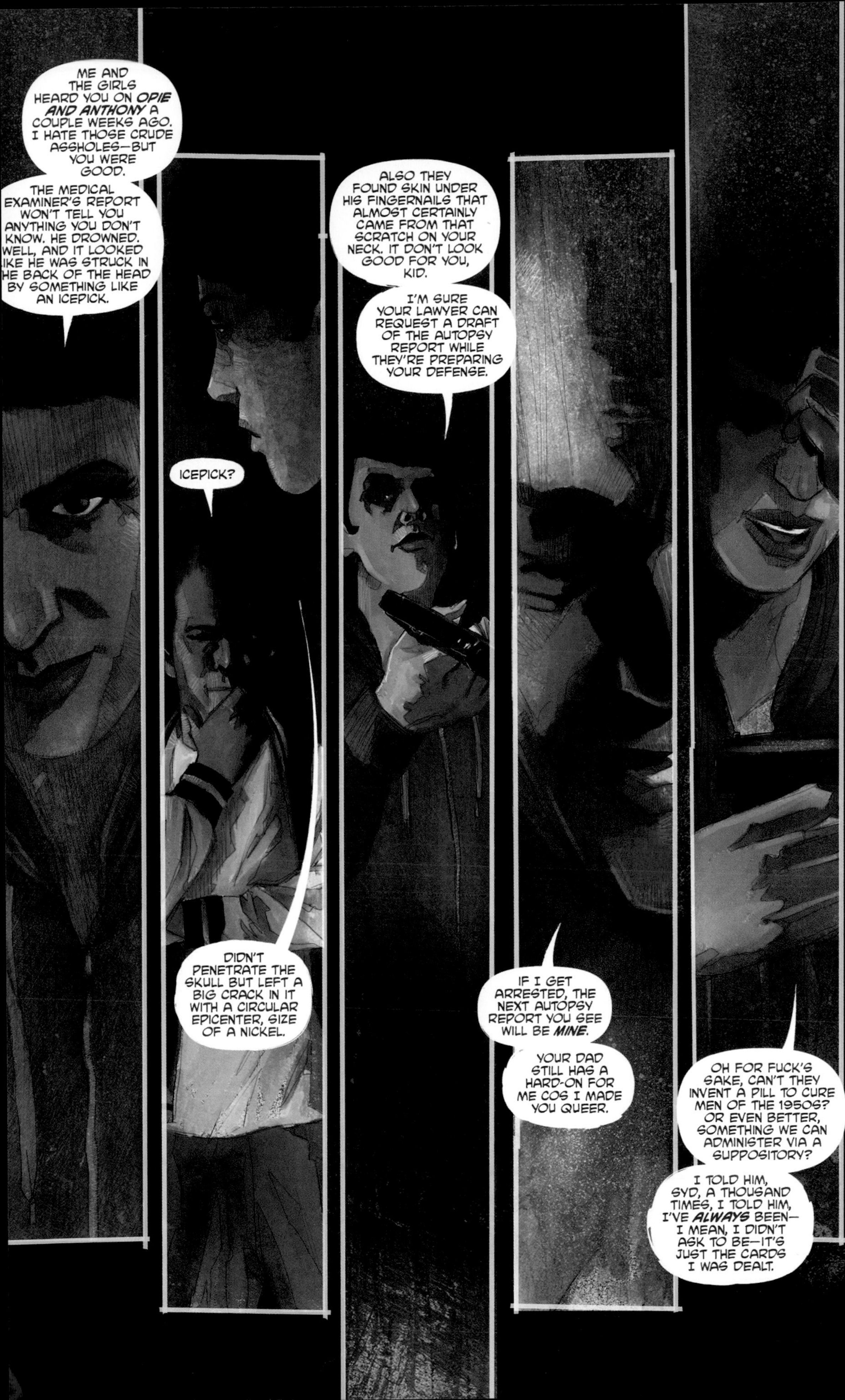
ME AND THE GIRLS HEARD YOU ON *OPIE AND ANTHONY* A COUPLE WEEKS AGO. I HATE THOSE CRUDE ASSHOLES—BUT YOU WERE GOOD.
THE MEDICAL EXAMINER'S REPORT WON'T TELL YOU ANYTHING YOU DON'T KNOW. HE DROWNED. WELL, AND IT LOOKED LIKE HE WAS STRUCK IN THE BACK OF THE HEAD BY SOMETHING LIKE AN ICEPICK.
ICEPICK?
DIDN'T PENETRATE THE SKULL BUT LEFT A BIG CRACK IN IT WITH A CIRCULAR EPICENTER, SIZE OF A NICKEL.
ALSO THEY FOUND SKIN UNDER HIS FINGERNAILS THAT ALMOST CERTAINLY CAME FROM THAT SCRATCH ON YOUR NECK. IT DON'T LOOK GOOD FOR YOU, KID.
I'M SURE YOUR LAWYER CAN REQUEST A DRAFT OF THE AUTOPSY REPORT WHILE THEY'RE PREPARING YOUR DEFENSE.
IF I GET ARRESTED, THE NEXT AUTOPSY REPORT YOU SEE WILL BE *MINE*.
YOUR DAD STILL HAS A HARD-ON FOR ME COS I MADE YOU QUEER.
OH FOR FUCK'S SAKE, CAN'T THEY INVENT A PILL TO CURE MEN OF THE 1950S? OR EVEN BETTER, SOMETHING WE CAN ADMINISTER VIA A SUPPOSITORY?
I TOLD HIM, SYD, A THOUSAND TIMES, I TOLD HIM, I'VE *ALWAYS* BEEN— I MEAN, I DIDN'T ASK TO BE—IT'S JUST THE CARDS I WAS DEALT.

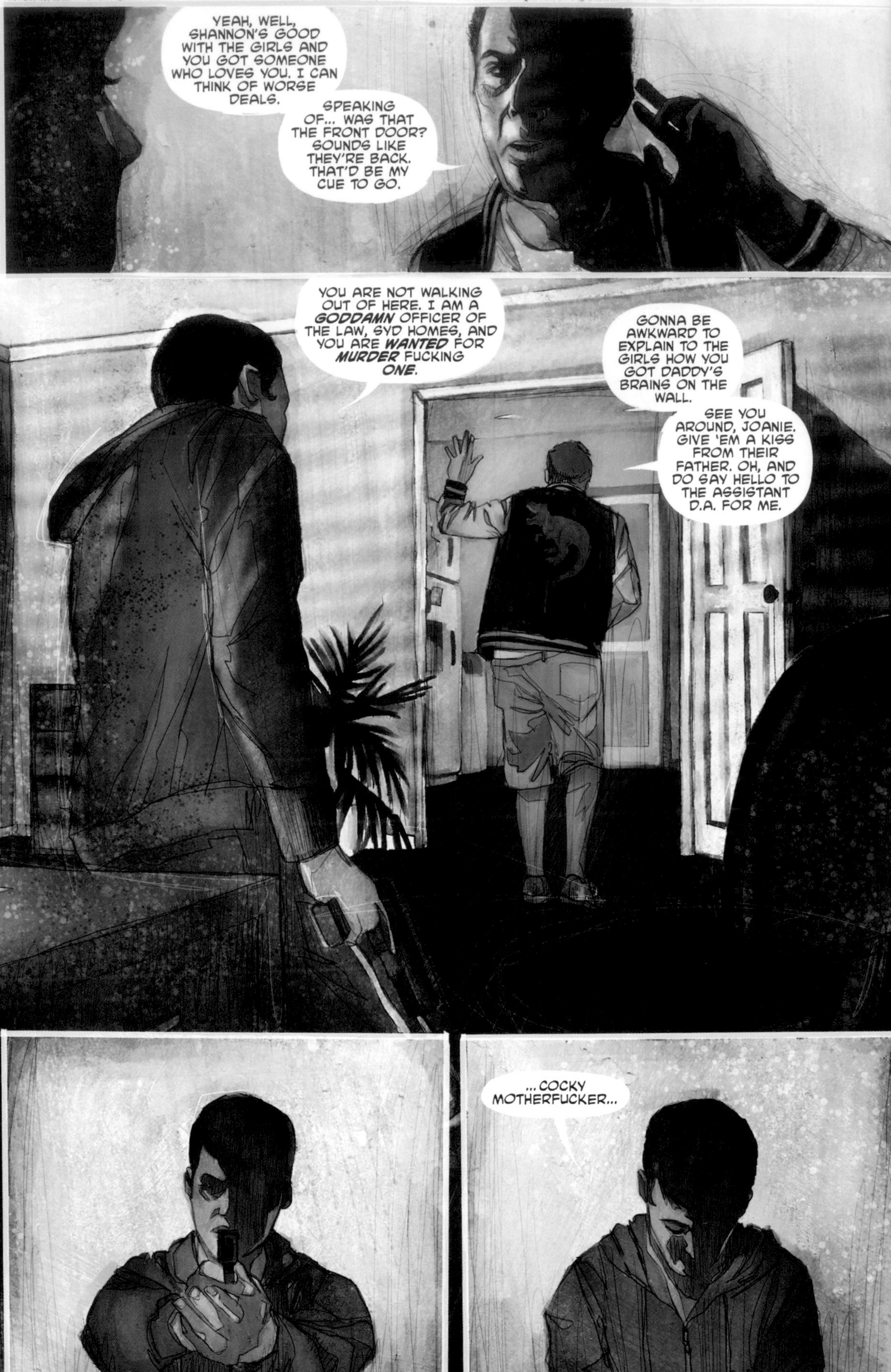
YEAH, WELL, SHANNON'S GOOD WITH THE GIRLS AND YOU GOT SOMEONE WHO LOVES YOU. I CAN THINK OF WORSE DEALS.
SPEAKING OF... WAS THAT THE FRONT DOOR? SOUNDS LIKE THEY'RE BACK. THAT'D BE MY CUE TO GO.
YOU ARE NOT WALKING OUT OF HERE. I AM A GODDAMN OFFICER OF THE LAW, SYD HOMES, AND YOU ARE WANTED FOR MURDER FUCKING ONE.
GONNA BE AWKWARD TO EXPLAIN TO THE GIRLS HOW YOU GOT DADDY'S BRAINS ON THE WALL.
SEE YOU AROUND, JOANIE. GIVE 'EM A KISS FROM THEIR FATHER. OH, AND DO SAY HELLO TO THE ASSISTANT D.A. FOR ME.
...COCKY MOTHERFUCKER...

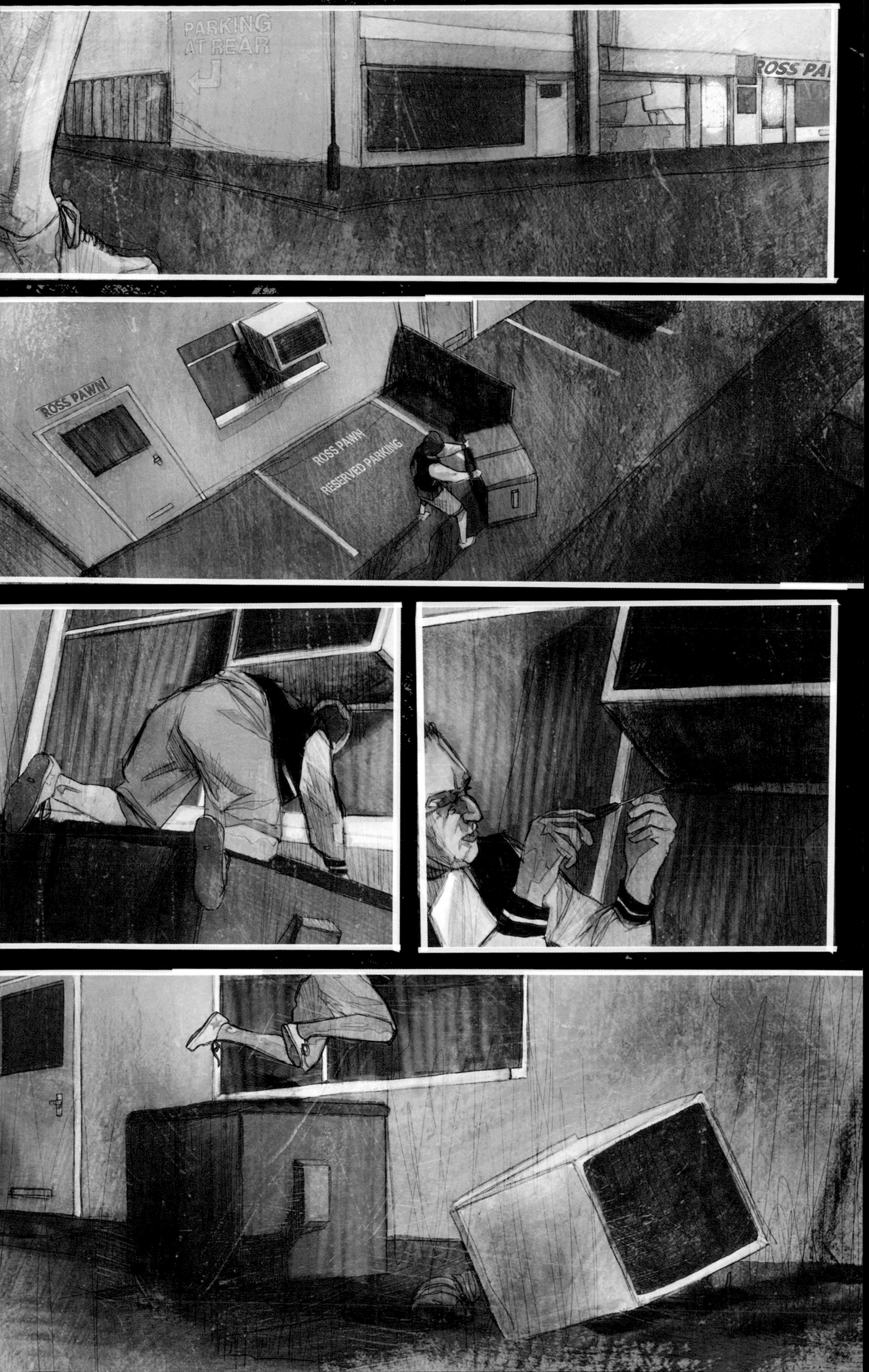

PARKING
AT REAR
ROSS PAWN
ROSS PAWN
RESERVED PARKING

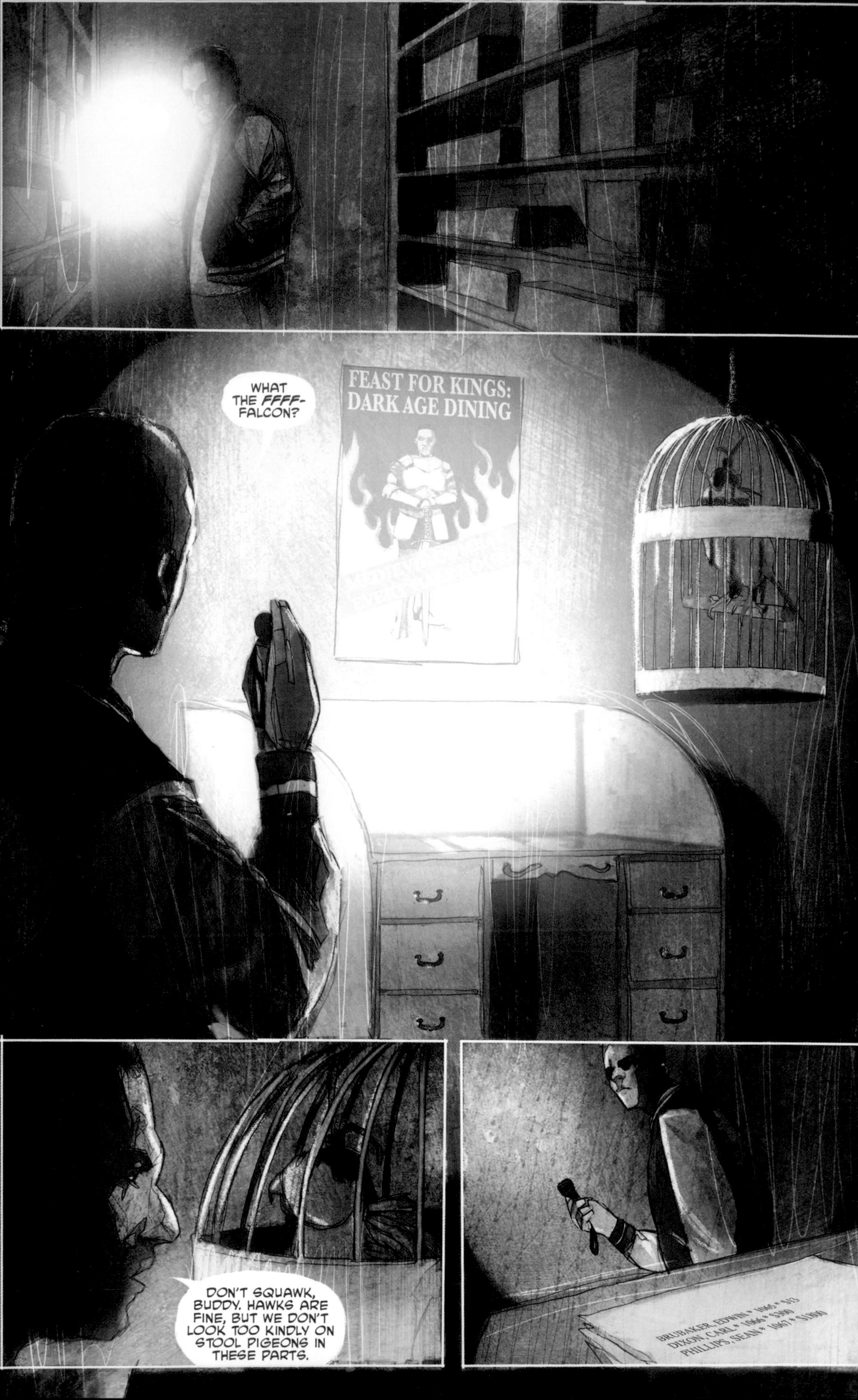
WHAT THE FFFF-FALCON?
FEAST FOR KINGS: DARK AGE DINING
DON'T SQUAWK, BUDDY. HAWKS ARE FINE, BUT WE DON'T LOOK TOO KINDLY ON STOOL PIGEONS IN THESE PARTS.
BRUBAKER, EDWIN * 1065 * $13
DIXON, CARL * 1066 * $300
PHILLIPS, SEAN * 1067 * $1800

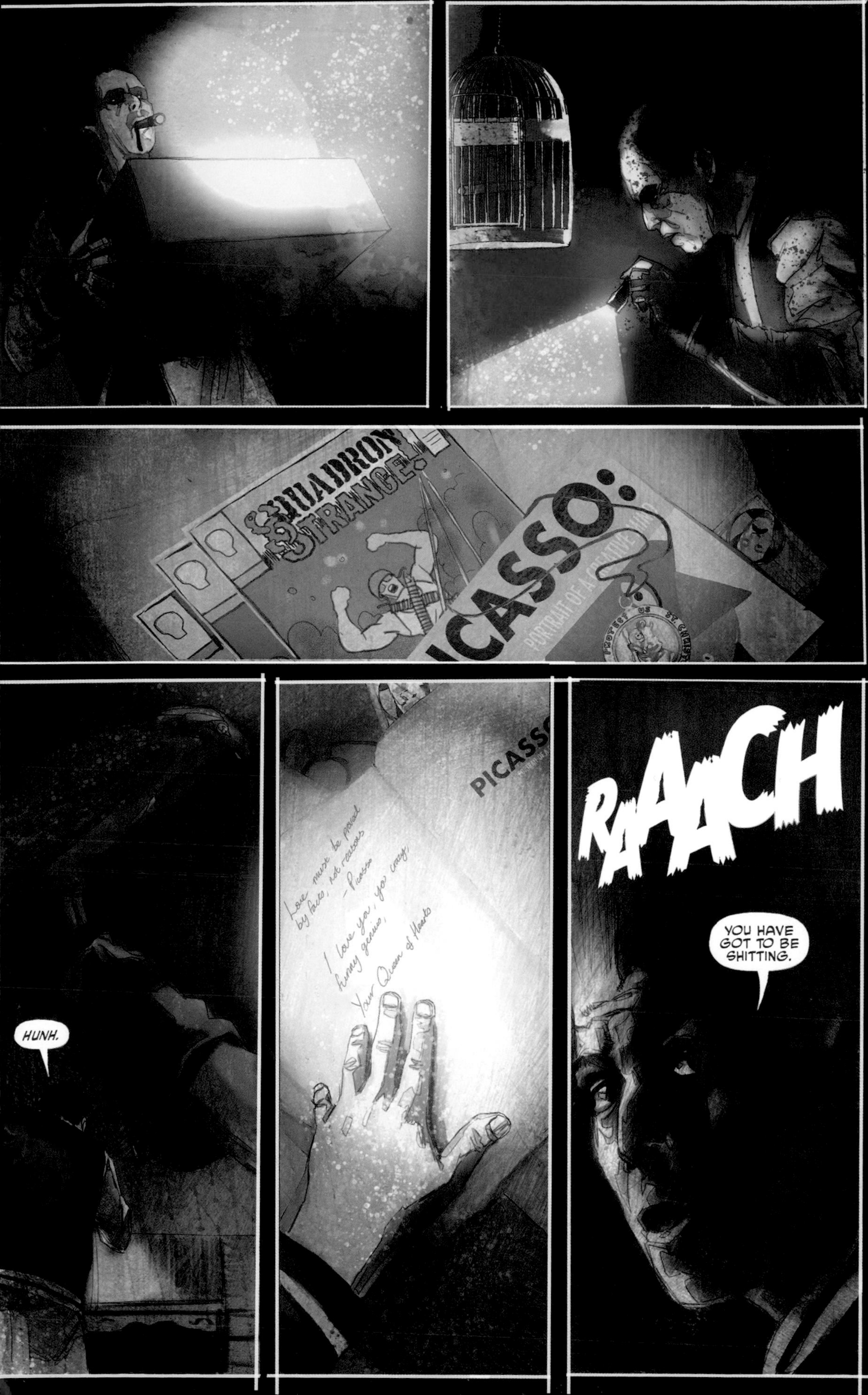
SQUADRON STRANGE!
PICASSO:
PORTRAIT OF A CREATIVE MIND
HUNH.
PICASSO
Love must be proved by facts, not reasons
-Picasso
I love you, you crazy, funny genius,
Your Queen of Hearts
RAAACH
YOU HAVE GOT TO BE SHITTING.

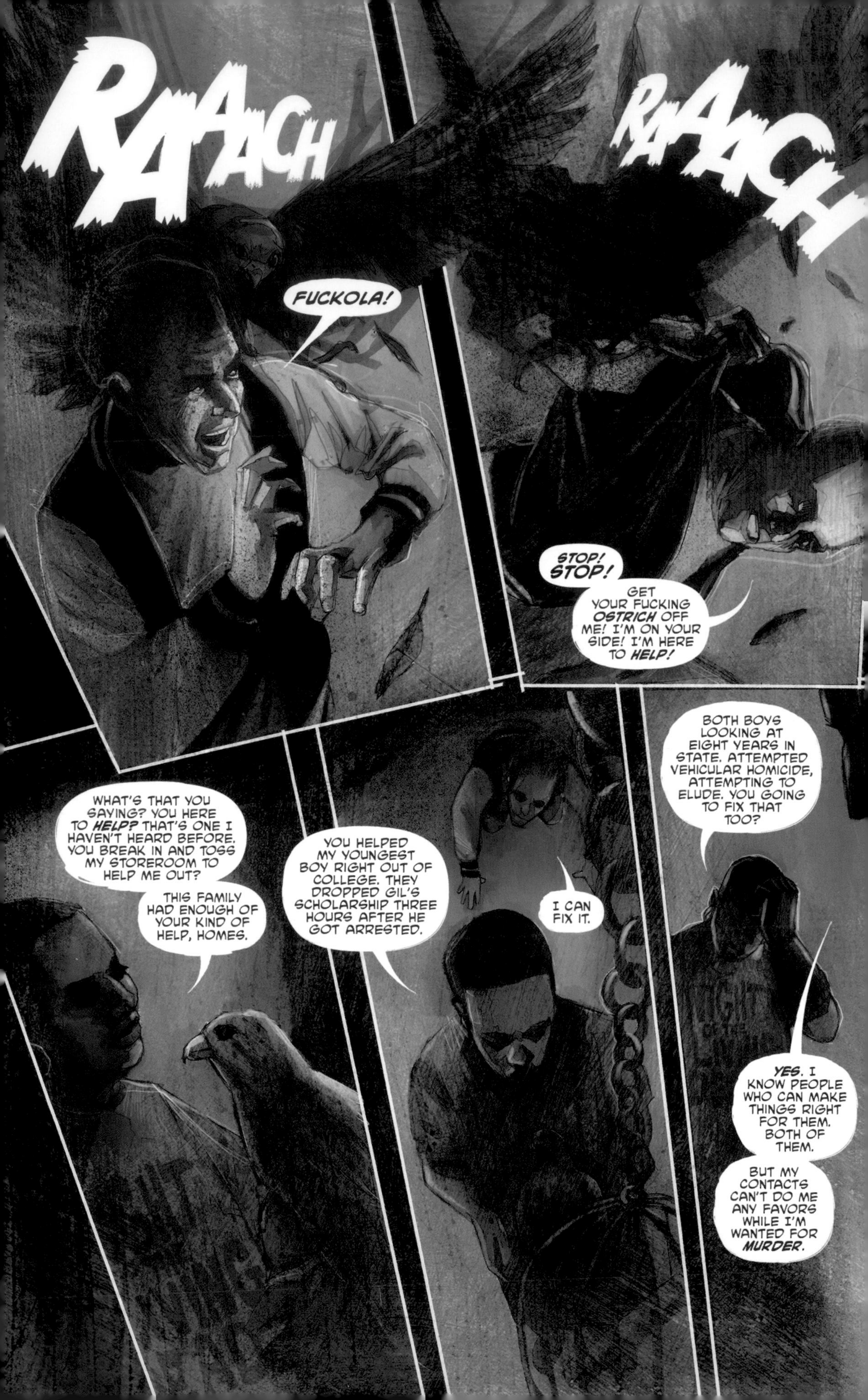
RAAACH
FUCKOLA!
RAAACH
STOP! STOP!
GET YOUR FUCKING OSTRICH OFF ME! I'M ON YOUR SIDE! I'M HERE TO HELP!
WHAT'S THAT YOU SAYING? YOU HERE TO HELP? THAT'S ONE I HAVEN'T HEARD BEFORE. YOU BREAK IN AND TOSS MY STOREROOM TO HELP ME OUT?
THIS FAMILY HAD ENOUGH OF YOUR KIND OF HELP, HOMES.
YOU HELPED MY YOUNGEST BOY RIGHT OUT OF COLLEGE. THEY DROPPED GIL'S SCHOLARSHIP THREE HOURS AFTER HE GOT ARRESTED.
I CAN FIX IT.
BOTH BOYS LOOKING AT EIGHT YEARS IN STATE. ATTEMPTED VEHICULAR HOMICIDE, ATTEMPTING TO ELUDE. YOU GOING TO FIX THAT TOO?
YES. I KNOW PEOPLE WHO CAN MAKE THINGS RIGHT FOR THEM. BOTH OF THEM.
BUT MY CONTACTS CAN'T DO ME ANY FAVORS WHILE I'M WANTED FOR MURDER.

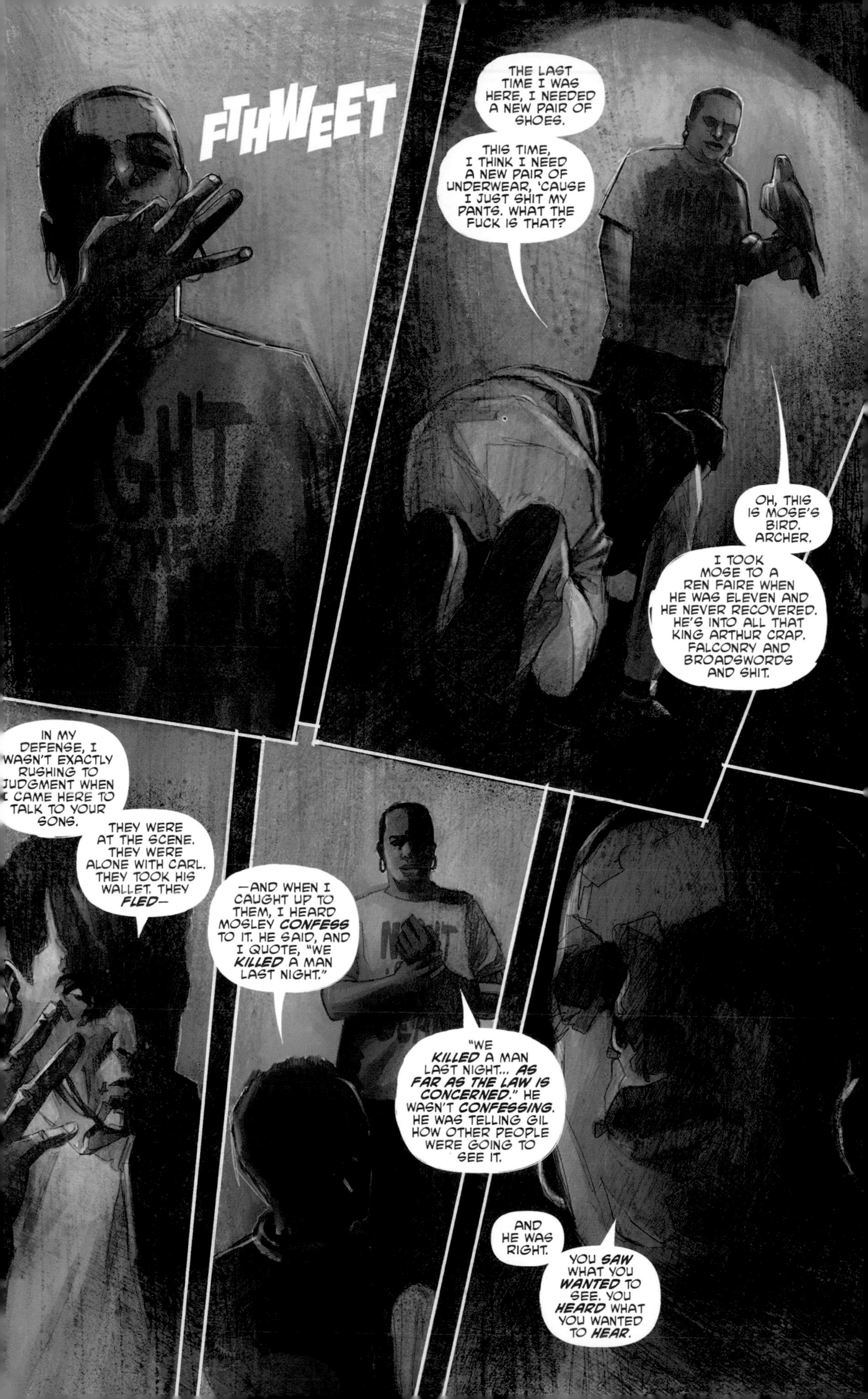
FTHWEET
THE LAST TIME I WAS HERE, I NEEDED A NEW PAIR OF SHOES.
THIS TIME, I THINK I NEED A NEW PAIR OF UNDERWEAR, 'CAUSE I JUST SHIT MY PANTS. WHAT THE FUCK IS THAT?
OH, THIS IS MOSE'S BIRD. ARCHER.
I TOOK MOSE TO A REN FAIRE WHEN HE WAS ELEVEN AND HE NEVER RECOVERED. HE'S INTO ALL THAT KING ARTHUR CRAP. FALCONRY AND BROADSWORDS AND SHIT.
IN MY DEFENSE, I WASN'T EXACTLY RUSHING TO JUDGMENT WHEN I CAME HERE TO TALK TO YOUR SONS.
THEY WERE AT THE SCENE. THEY WERE ALONE WITH CARL. THEY TOOK HIS WALLET. THEY FLED—
—AND WHEN I CAUGHT UP TO THEM, I HEARD MOSLEY CONFESS TO IT. HE SAID, AND I QUOTE, "WE KILLED A MAN LAST NIGHT."
"WE KILLED A MAN LAST NIGHT... AS FAR AS THE LAW IS CONCERNED." HE WASN'T CONFESSING. HE WAS TELLING GIL HOW OTHER PEOPLE WERE GOING TO SEE IT.
AND HE WAS RIGHT.
YOU SAW WHAT YOU WANTED TO SEE. YOU HEARD WHAT YOU WANTED TO HEAR.

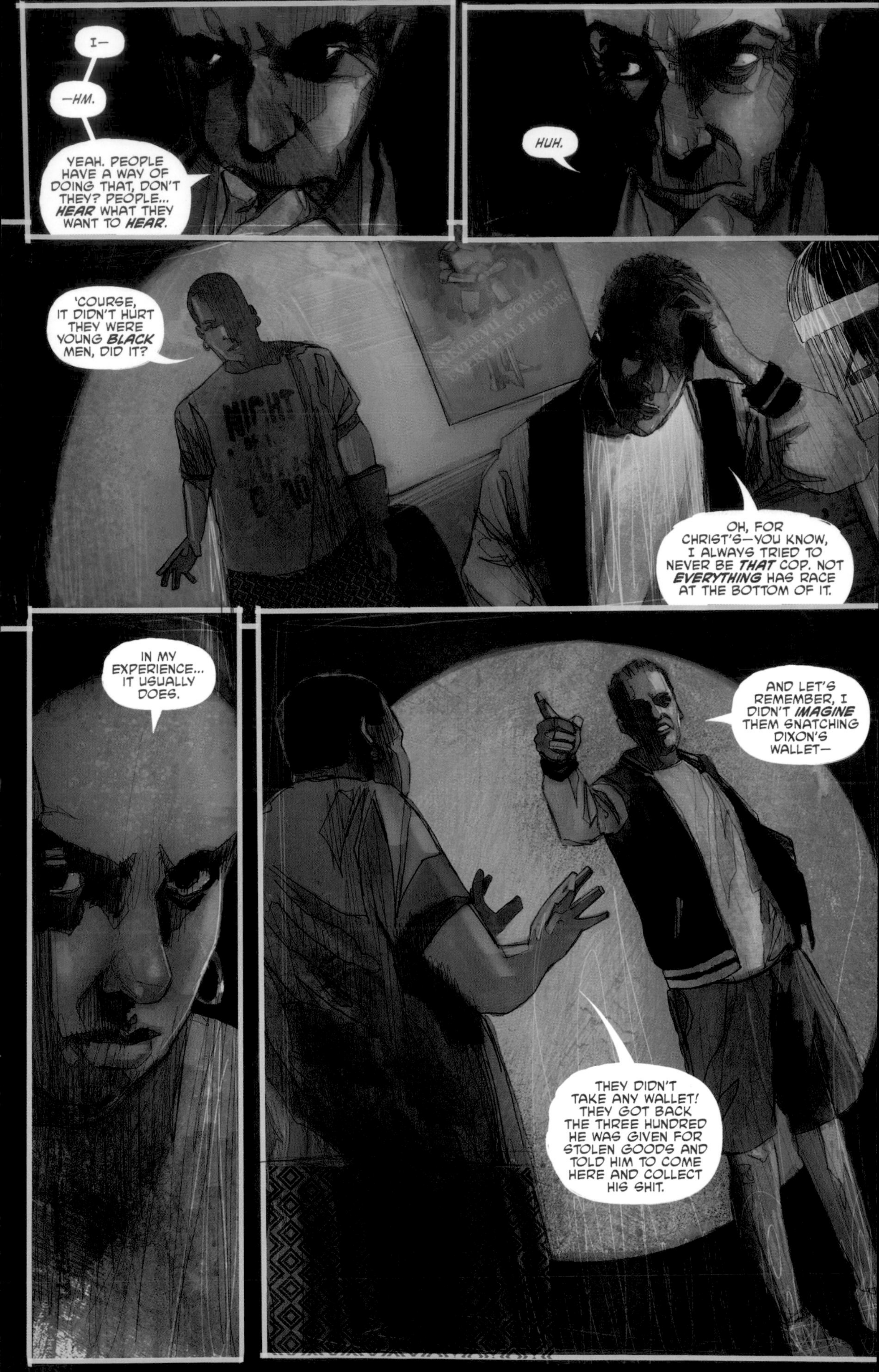
I—
—HM.
YEAH. PEOPLE HAVE A WAY OF DOING THAT, DON'T THEY? PEOPLE... HEAR WHAT THEY WANT TO HEAR.
HUH.
'COURSE, IT DIDN'T HURT THEY WERE YOUNG BLACK MEN, DID IT?
OH, FOR CHRIST'S—YOU KNOW, I ALWAYS TRIED TO NEVER BE THAT COP. NOT EVERYTHING HAS RACE AT THE BOTTOM OF IT.
IN MY EXPERIENCE... IT USUALLY DOES.
AND LET'S REMEMBER, I DIDN'T IMAGINE THEM SNATCHING DIXON'S WALLET—
THEY DIDN'T TAKE ANY WALLET! THEY GOT BACK THE THREE HUNDRED HE WAS GIVEN FOR STOLEN GOODS AND TOLD HIM TO COME HERE AND COLLECT HIS SHIT.

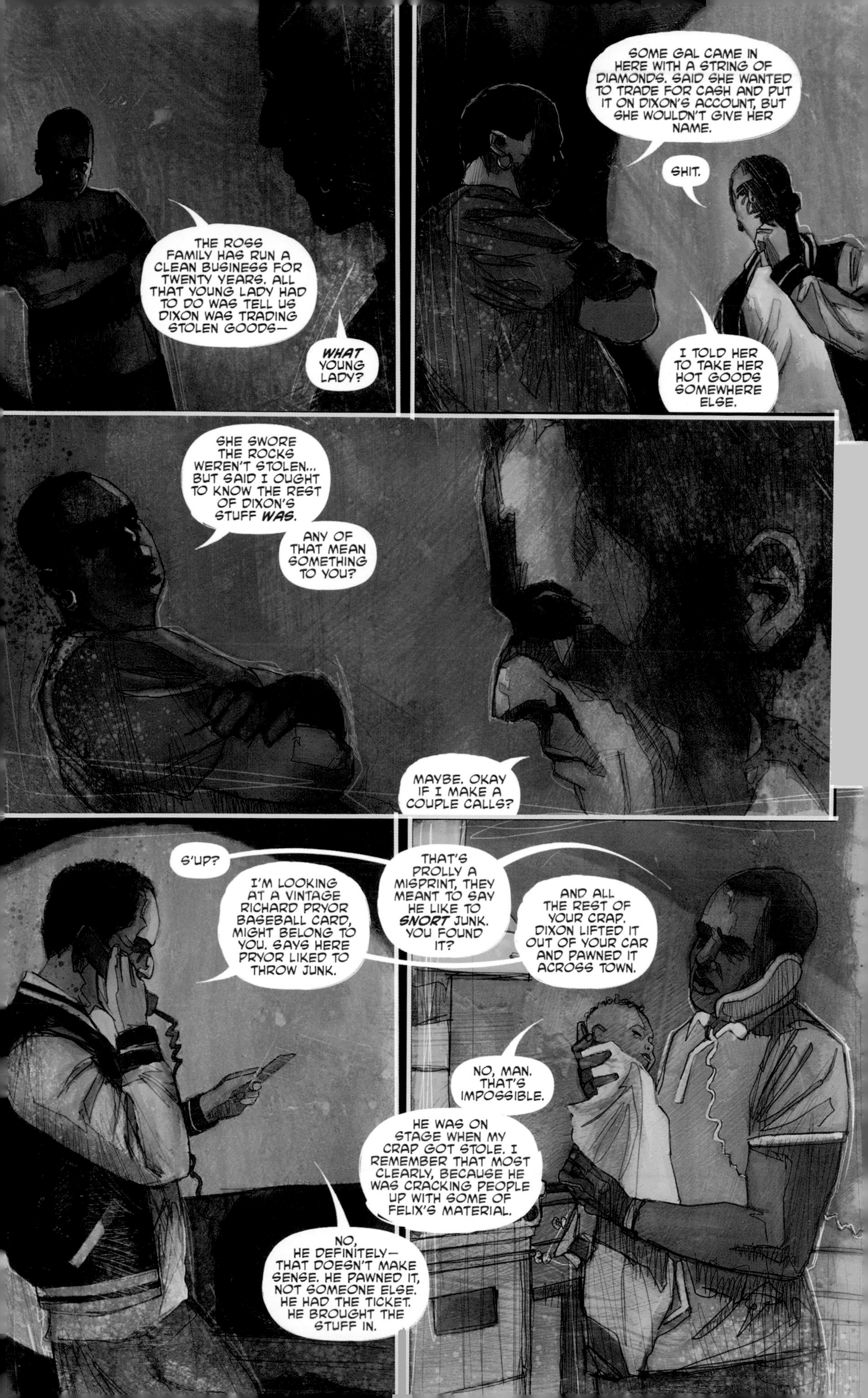
THE ROSS FAMILY HAS RUN A CLEAN BUSINESS FOR TWENTY YEARS. ALL THAT YOUNG LADY HAD TO DO WAS TELL US DIXON WAS TRADING STOLEN GOODS—
WHAT YOUNG LADY?
SOME GAL CAME IN HERE WITH A STRING OF DIAMONDS. SAID SHE WANTED TO TRADE FOR CASH AND PUT IT ON DIXON'S ACCOUNT, BUT SHE WOULDN'T GIVE HER NAME.
SHIT.
I TOLD HER TO TAKE HER HOT GOODS SOMEWHERE ELSE.
SHE SWORE THE ROCKS WEREN'T STOLEN... BUT SAID I OUGHT TO KNOW THE REST OF DIXON'S STUFF *WAS*.
ANY OF THAT MEAN SOMETHING TO YOU?
MAYBE. OKAY IF I MAKE A COUPLE CALLS?
S'UP?
I'M LOOKING AT A VINTAGE RICHARD PRYOR BASEBALL CARD, MIGHT BELONG TO YOU. SAYS HERE PRYOR LIKED TO THROW JUNK.
THAT'S PROLLY A MISPRINT, THEY MEANT TO SAY HE LIKE TO *SNORT* JUNK. YOU FOUND IT?
AND ALL THE REST OF YOUR CRAP. DIXON LIFTED IT OUT OF YOUR CAR AND PAWNED IT ACROSS TOWN.
NO, MAN. THAT'S IMPOSSIBLE.
HE WAS ON STAGE WHEN MY CRAP GOT STOLE. I REMEMBER THAT MOST CLEARLY, BECAUSE HE WAS CRACKING PEOPLE UP WITH SOME OF FELIX'S MATERIAL.
NO, HE DEFINITELY— THAT DOESN'T MAKE SENSE. HE PAWNED IT, NOT SOMEONE ELSE. HE HAD THE TICKET. HE BROUGHT THE STUFF IN.

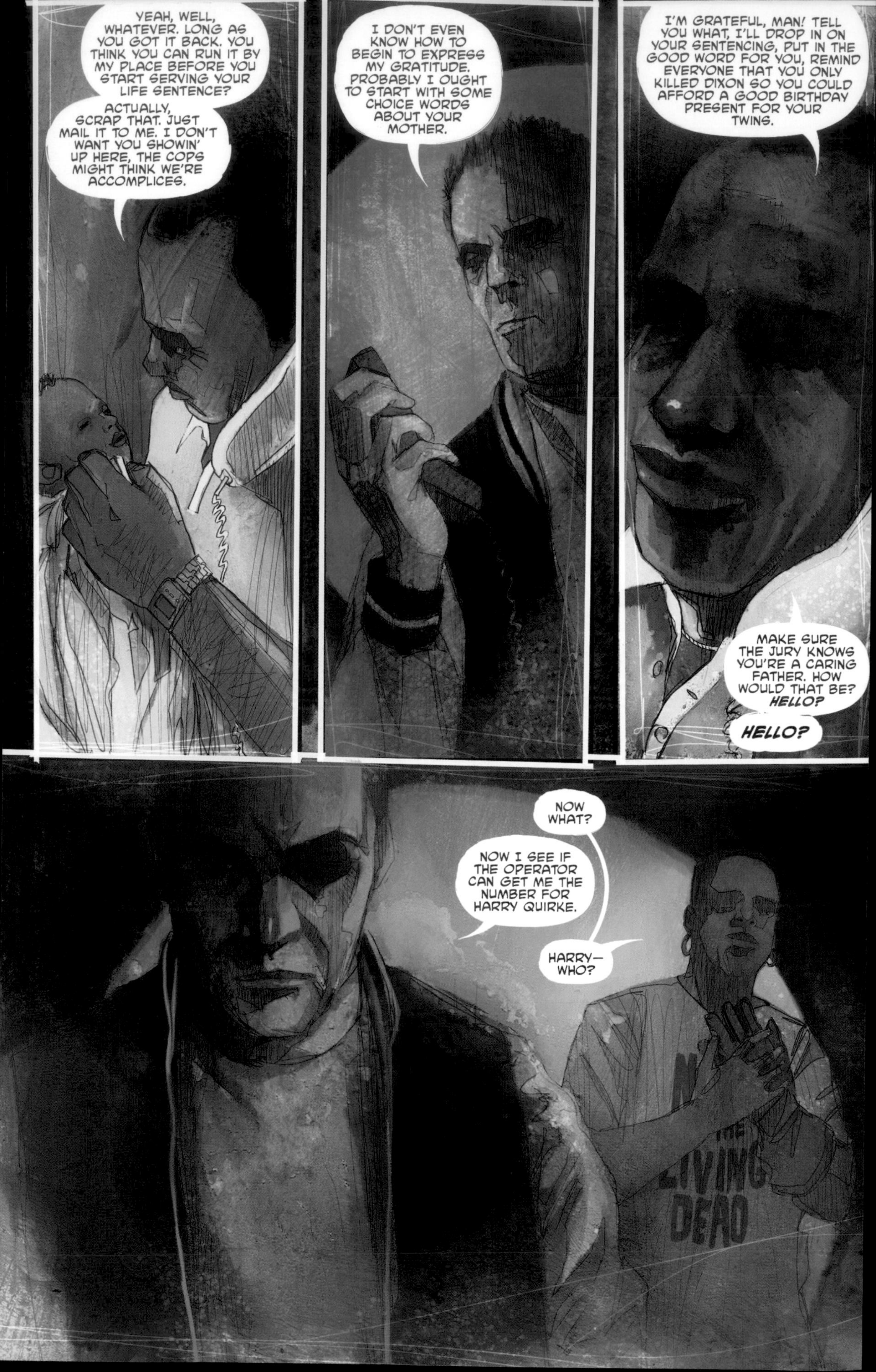
YEAH, WELL, WHATEVER. LONG AS YOU GOT IT BACK. YOU THINK YOU CAN RUN IT BY MY PLACE BEFORE YOU START SERVING YOUR LIFE SENTENCE?
ACTUALLY, SCRAP THAT. JUST MAIL IT TO ME. I DON'T WANT YOU SHOWIN' UP HERE, THE COPS MIGHT THINK WE'RE ACCOMPLICES.
I DON'T EVEN KNOW HOW TO BEGIN TO EXPRESS MY GRATITUDE. PROBABLY I OUGHT TO START WITH SOME CHOICE WORDS ABOUT YOUR MOTHER.
I'M GRATEFUL, MAN! TELL YOU WHAT, I'LL DROP IN ON YOUR SENTENCING, PUT IN THE GOOD WORD FOR YOU, REMIND EVERYONE THAT YOU ONLY KILLED DIXON SO YOU COULD AFFORD A GOOD BIRTHDAY PRESENT FOR YOUR TWINS.
MAKE SURE THE JURY KNOWS YOU'RE A CARING FATHER. HOW WOULD THAT BE? HELLO?
HELLO?
NOW WHAT?
NOW I SEE IF THE OPERATOR CAN GET ME THE NUMBER FOR HARRY QUIRKE.
HARRY— WHO?
THE LIVING DEAD

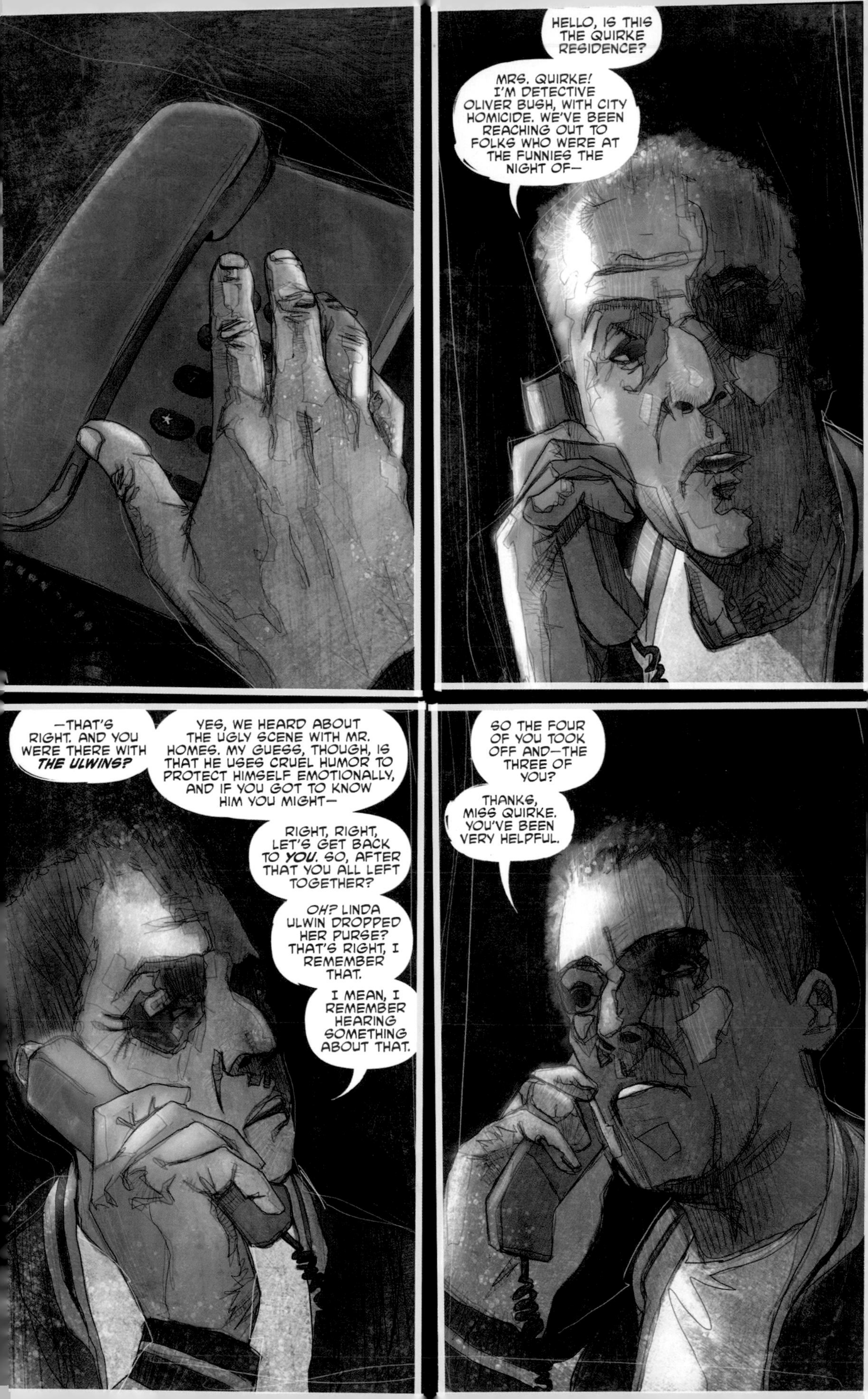
HELLO, IS THIS THE QUIRKE RESIDENCE?
MRS. QUIRKE! I'M DETECTIVE OLIVER BUSH, WITH CITY HOMICIDE. WE'VE BEEN REACHING OUT TO FOLKS WHO WERE AT THE FUNNIES THE NIGHT OF—
—THAT'S RIGHT. AND YOU WERE THERE WITH *THE ULWINS?*
YES, WE HEARD ABOUT THE UGLY SCENE WITH MR. HOMES. MY GUESS, THOUGH, IS THAT HE USES CRUEL HUMOR TO PROTECT HIMSELF EMOTIONALLY, AND IF YOU GOT TO KNOW HIM YOU MIGHT—
RIGHT, RIGHT, LET'S GET BACK TO *YOU*. SO, AFTER THAT YOU ALL LEFT TOGETHER?
OH? LINDA ULWIN DROPPED HER PURSE? THAT'S RIGHT, I REMEMBER THAT.
I MEAN, I REMEMBER HEARING SOMETHING ABOUT THAT.
SO THE FOUR OF YOU TOOK OFF AND—THE THREE OF YOU?
THANKS, MISS QUIRKE. YOU'VE BEEN VERY HELPFUL.

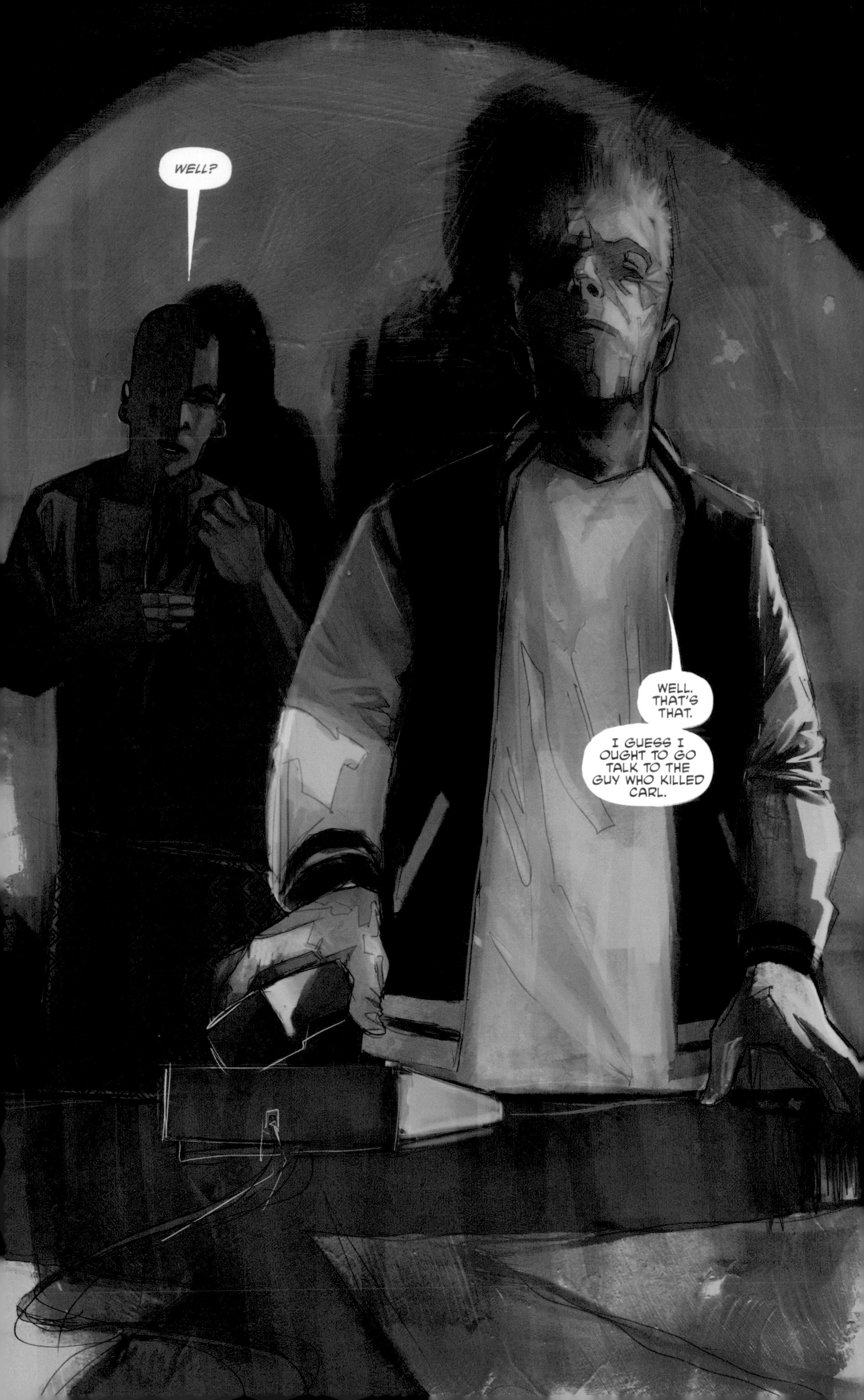
WELL?
WELL. THAT'S THAT.
I GUESS I OUGHT TO GO TALK TO THE GUY WHO KILLED CARL.

art by Gabriel Rodriguez

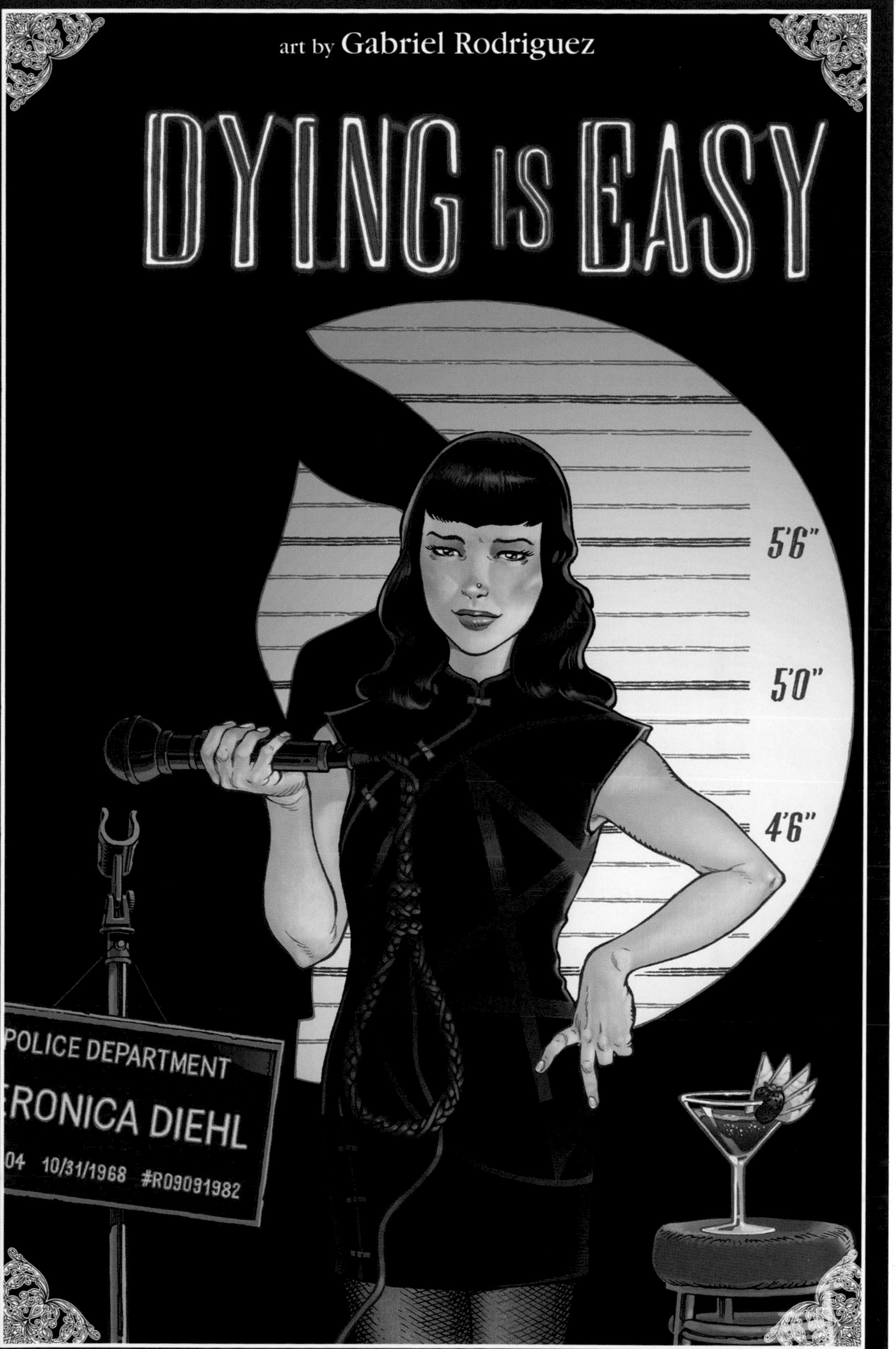

DYING IS EASY
5'6"
5'0"
4'6"
POLICE DEPARTMENT
ERONICA DIEHL
04 10/31/1968 #R09091982

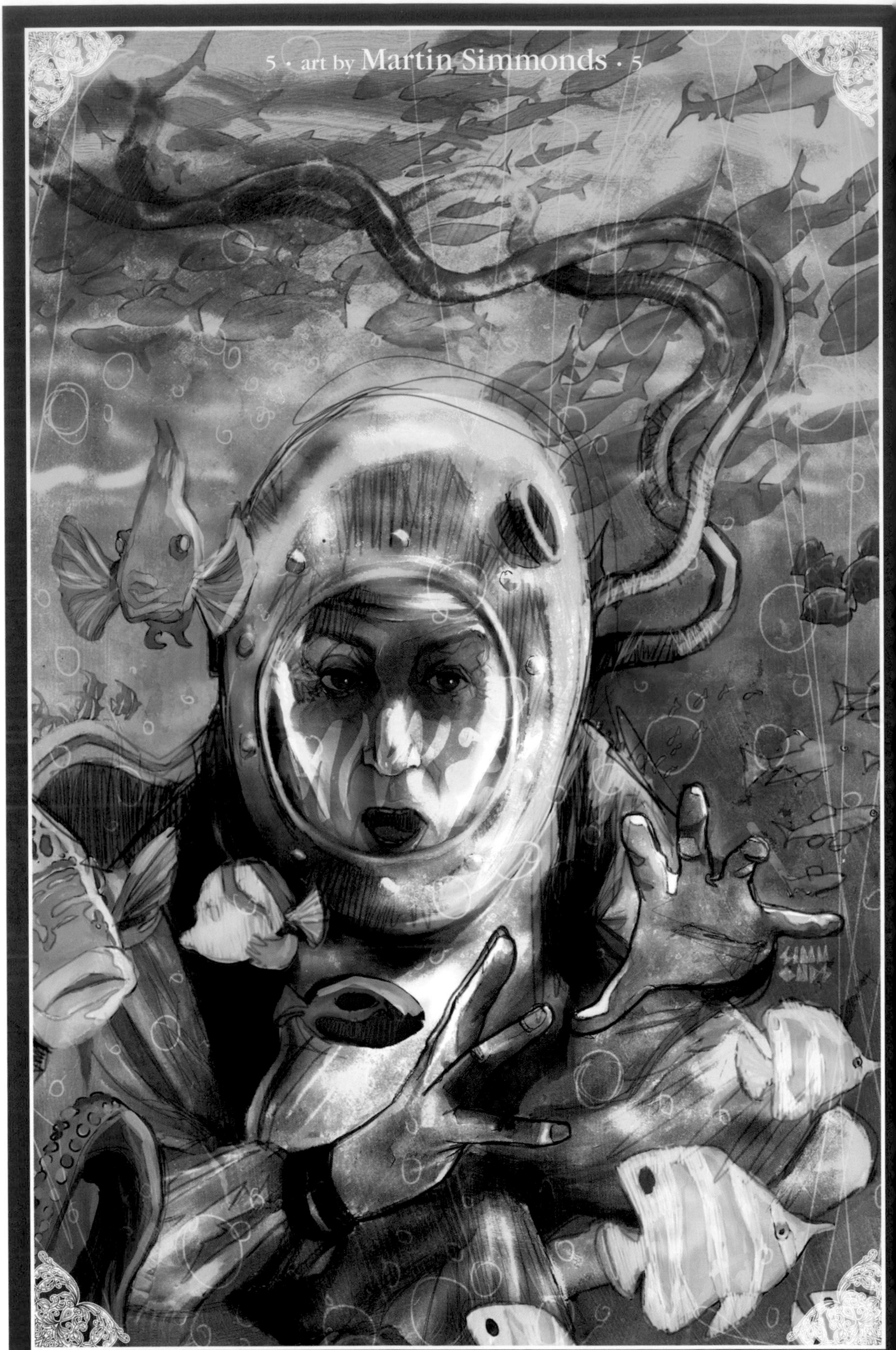
5 · art by Martin Simmonds · 5

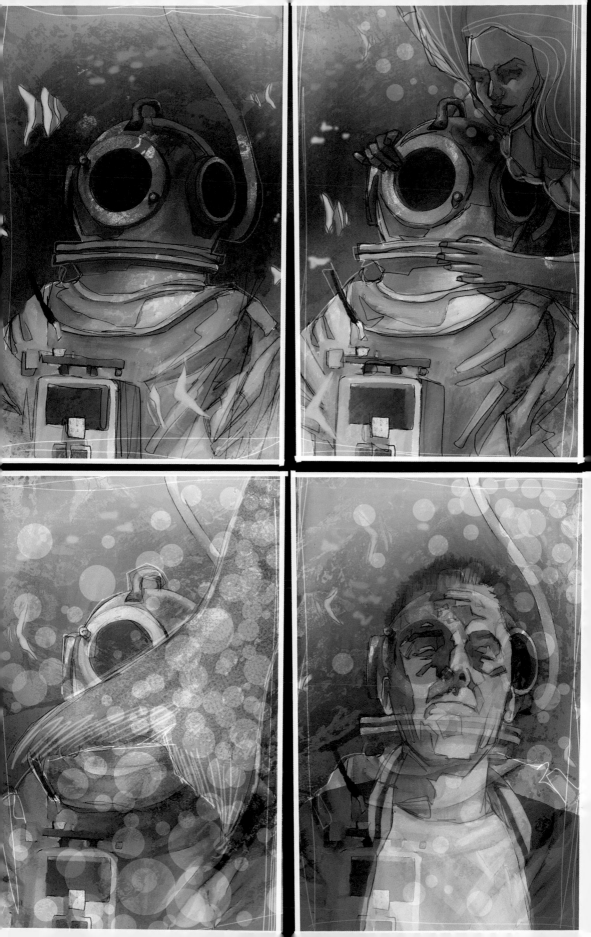

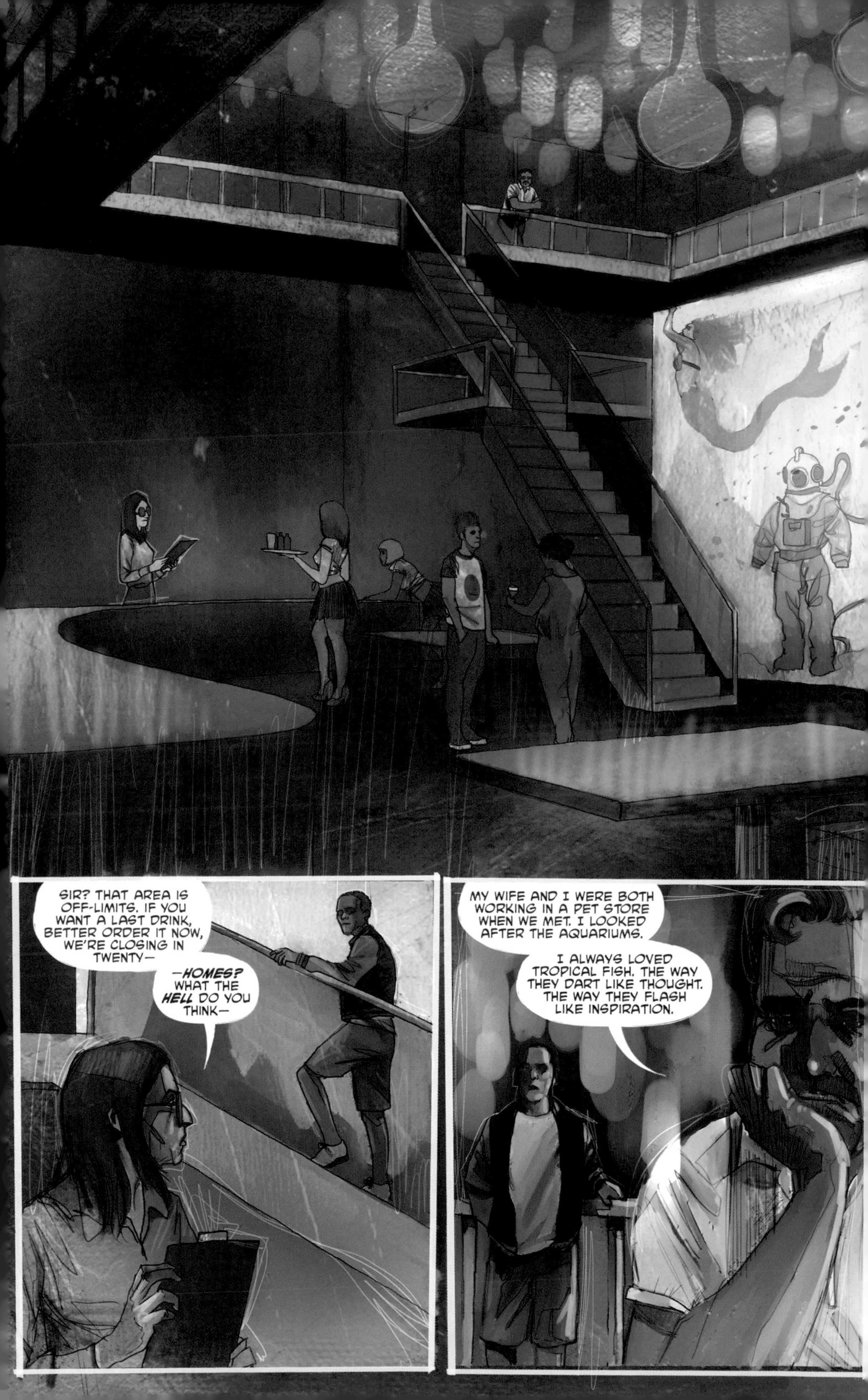
SIR? THAT AREA IS OFF-LIMITS. IF YOU WANT A LAST DRINK, BETTER ORDER IT NOW, WE'RE CLOSING IN TWENTY—
—HOMES? WHAT THE HELL DO YOU THINK—
MY WIFE AND I WERE BOTH WORKING IN A PET STORE WHEN WE MET. I LOOKED AFTER THE AQUARIUMS.
I ALWAYS LOVED TROPICAL FISH. THE WAY THEY DART LIKE THOUGHT. THE WAY THEY FLASH LIKE INSPIRATION.

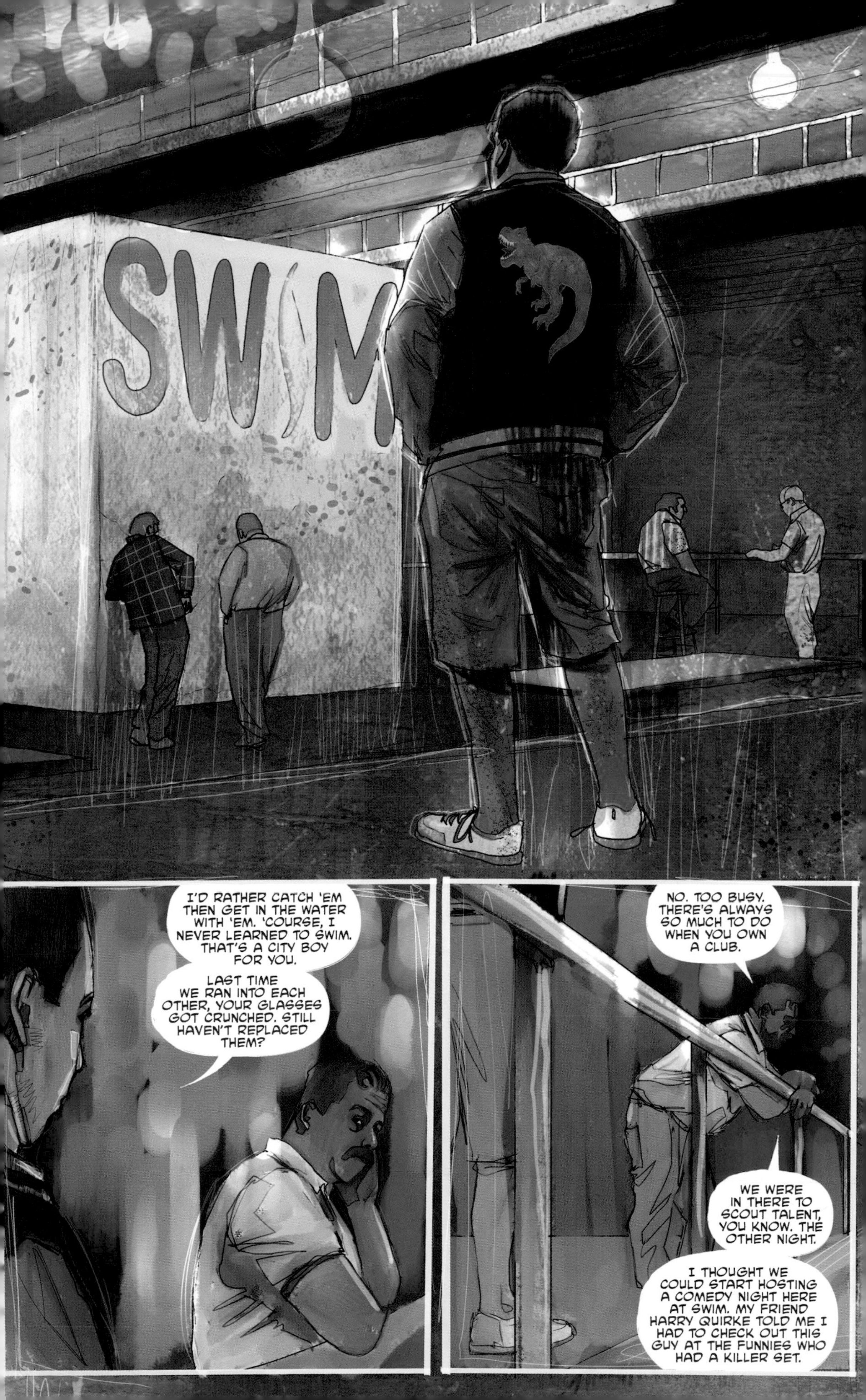
SWIM
I'D RATHER CATCH 'EM THEN GET IN THE WATER WITH 'EM. 'COURSE, I NEVER LEARNED TO SWIM. THAT'S A CITY BOY FOR YOU.
LAST TIME WE RAN INTO EACH OTHER, YOUR GLASSES GOT CRUNCHED. STILL HAVEN'T REPLACED THEM?
NO. TOO BUSY. THERE'S ALWAYS SO MUCH TO DO WHEN YOU OWN A CLUB.
WE WERE IN THERE TO SCOUT TALENT, YOU KNOW. THE OTHER NIGHT.
I THOUGHT WE COULD START HOSTING A COMEDY NIGHT HERE AT SWIM. MY FRIEND HARRY QUIRKE TOLD ME I HAD TO CHECK OUT THIS GUY AT THE FUNNIES WHO HAD A KILLER SET.

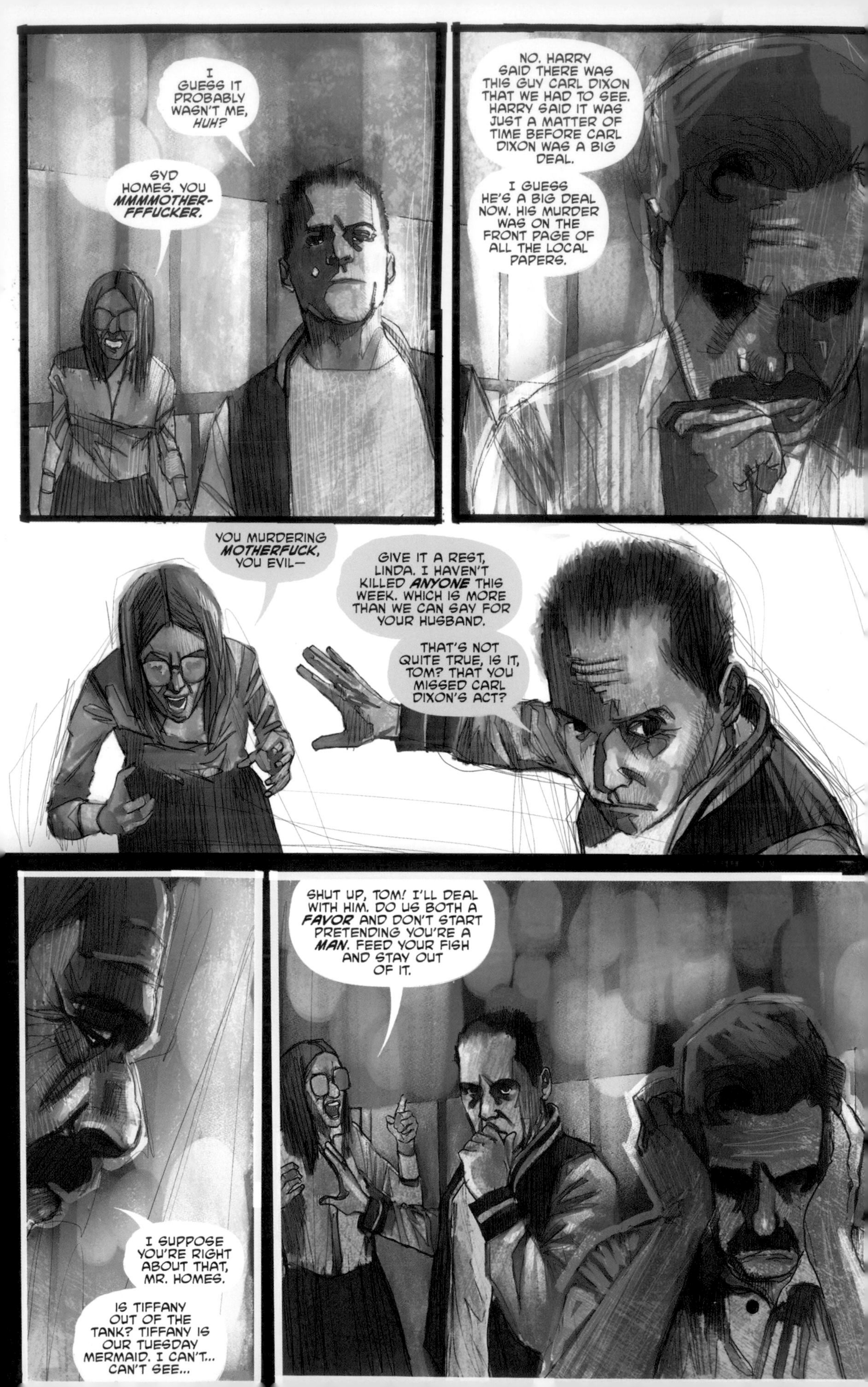
I GUESS IT PROBABLY WASN'T ME, HUH?
SYD HOMES. YOU MMMMOTHER-FFFUCKER.
NO. HARRY SAID THERE WAS THIS GUY CARL DIXON THAT WE HAD TO SEE. HARRY SAID IT WAS JUST A MATTER OF TIME BEFORE CARL DIXON WAS A BIG DEAL.
I GUESS HE'S A BIG DEAL NOW. HIS MURDER WAS ON THE FRONT PAGE OF ALL THE LOCAL PAPERS.
YOU MURDERING MOTHERFUCK, YOU EVIL—
GIVE IT A REST, LINDA. I HAVEN'T KILLED ANYONE THIS WEEK. WHICH IS MORE THAN WE CAN SAY FOR YOUR HUSBAND.
THAT'S NOT QUITE TRUE, IS IT, TOM? THAT YOU MISSED CARL DIXON'S ACT?
I SUPPOSE YOU'RE RIGHT ABOUT THAT, MR. HOMES.
IS TIFFANY OUT OF THE TANK? TIFFANY IS OUR TUESDAY MERMAID. I CAN'T... CAN'T SEE...
SHUT UP, TOM! I'LL DEAL WITH HIM. DO US BOTH A FAVOR AND DON'T START PRETENDING YOU'RE A MAN. FEED YOUR FISH AND STAY OUT OF IT.

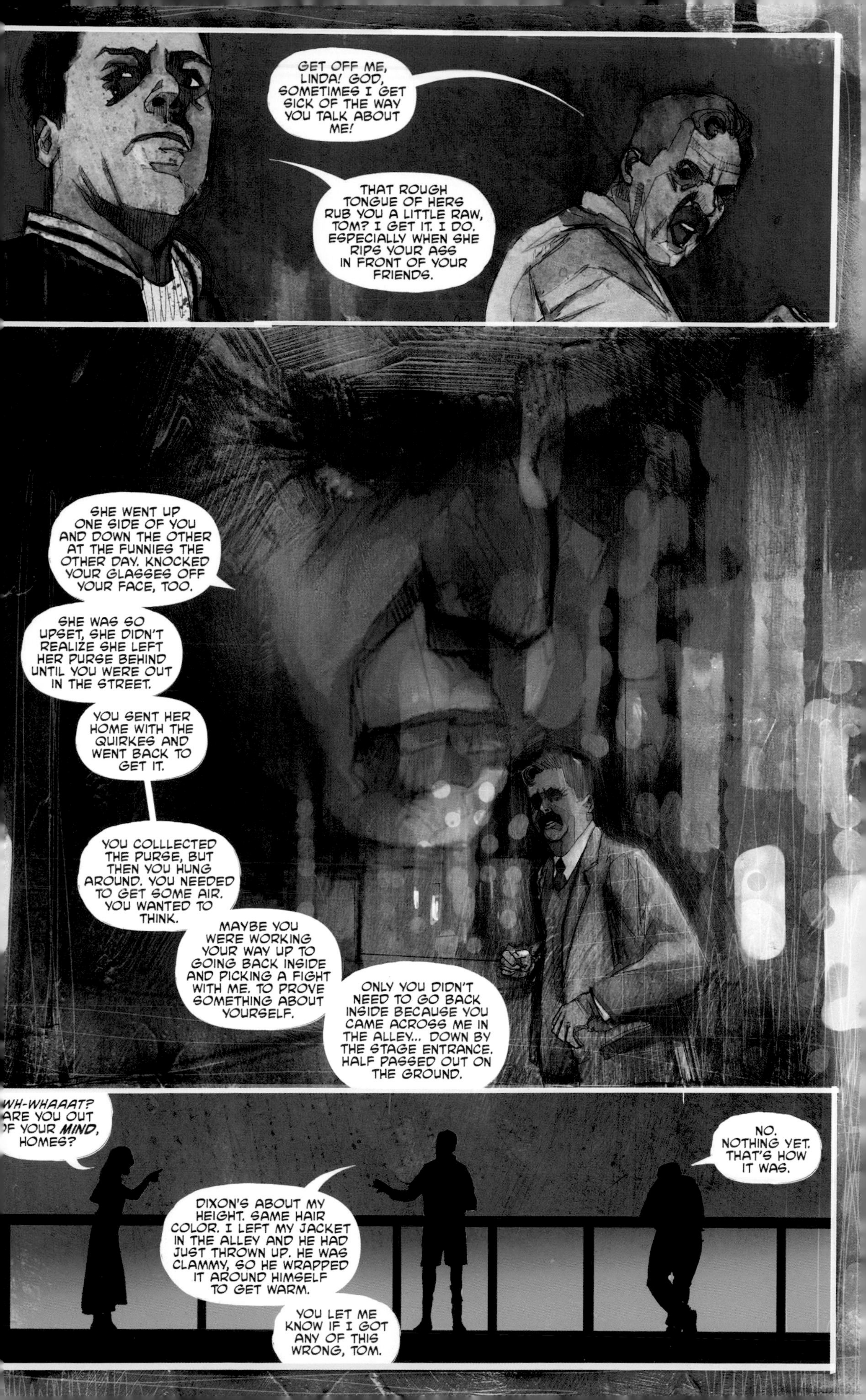
GET OFF ME, LINDA! GOD, SOMETIMES I GET SICK OF THE WAY YOU TALK ABOUT ME!
THAT ROUGH TONGUE OF HERS RUB YOU A LITTLE RAW, TOM? I GET IT. I DO. ESPECIALLY WHEN SHE RIPS YOUR ASS IN FRONT OF YOUR FRIENDS.
SHE WENT UP ONE SIDE OF YOU AND DOWN THE OTHER AT THE FUNNIES THE OTHER DAY. KNOCKED YOUR GLASSES OFF YOUR FACE, TOO.
SHE WAS SO UPSET, SHE DIDN'T REALIZE SHE LEFT HER PURSE BEHIND UNTIL YOU WERE OUT IN THE STREET.
YOU SENT HER HOME WITH THE QUIRKES AND WENT BACK TO GET IT.
YOU COLLLECTED THE PURSE, BUT THEN YOU HUNG AROUND. YOU NEEDED TO GET SOME AIR. YOU WANTED TO THINK.
MAYBE YOU WERE WORKING YOUR WAY UP TO GOING BACK INSIDE AND PICKING A FIGHT WITH ME. TO PROVE SOMETHING ABOUT YOURSELF.
ONLY YOU DIDN'T NEED TO GO BACK INSIDE BECAUSE YOU CAME ACROSS ME IN THE ALLEY... DOWN BY THE STAGE ENTRANCE. HALF PASSED OUT ON THE GROUND.
WH-WHAAAT? ARE YOU OUT OF YOUR *MIND*, HOMES?
DIXON'S ABOUT MY HEIGHT. SAME HAIR COLOR. I LEFT MY JACKET IN THE ALLEY AND HE HAD JUST THROWN UP. HE WAS CLAMMY, SO HE WRAPPED IT AROUND HIMSELF TO GET WARM.
YOU LET ME KNOW IF I GOT ANY OF THIS WRONG, TOM.
NO. NOTHING YET. THAT'S HOW IT WAS.

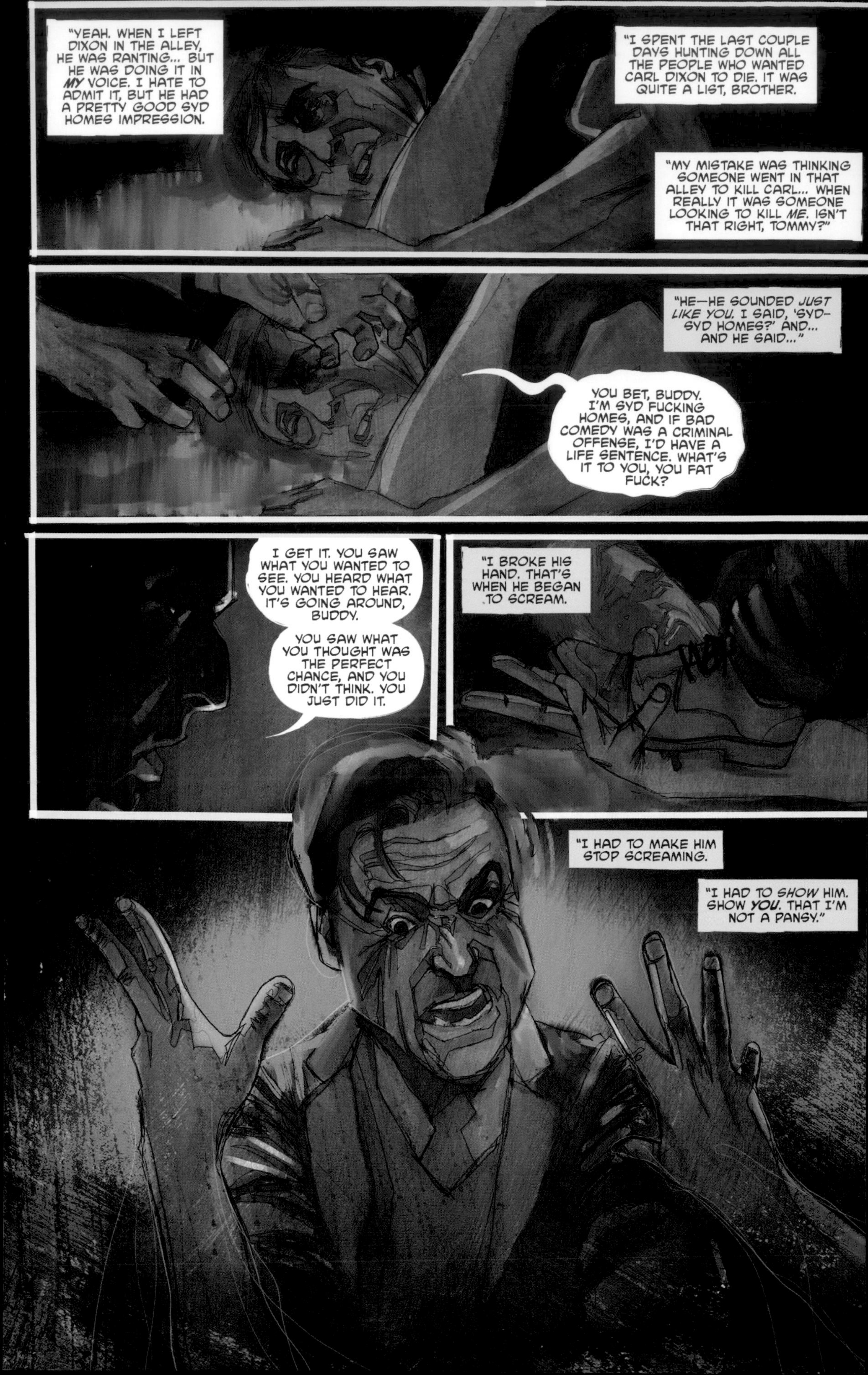
"YEAH. WHEN I LEFT DIXON IN THE ALLEY, HE WAS RANTING... BUT HE WAS DOING IT IN *MY* VOICE. I HATE TO ADMIT IT, BUT HE HAD A PRETTY GOOD SYD HOMES IMPRESSION.
"I SPENT THE LAST COUPLE DAYS HUNTING DOWN ALL THE PEOPLE WHO WANTED CARL DIXON TO DIE. IT WAS QUITE A LIST, BROTHER.
"MY MISTAKE WAS THINKING SOMEONE WENT IN THAT ALLEY TO KILL CARL... WHEN REALLY IT WAS SOMEONE LOOKING TO KILL *ME*. ISN'T THAT RIGHT, TOMMY?"
"HE—HE SOUNDED *JUST LIKE YOU*. I SAID, 'SYD-SYD HOMES?' AND... AND HE SAID..."
YOU BET, BUDDY. I'M SYD FUCKING HOMES, AND IF BAD COMEDY WAS A CRIMINAL OFFENSE, I'D HAVE A LIFE SENTENCE. WHAT'S IT TO YOU, YOU FAT FUCK?
I GET IT. YOU SAW WHAT YOU WANTED TO SEE. YOU HEARD WHAT YOU WANTED TO HEAR. IT'S GOING AROUND, BUDDY.
YOU SAW WHAT YOU THOUGHT WAS THE PERFECT CHANCE, AND YOU DIDN'T THINK. YOU JUST DID IT.
"I BROKE HIS HAND. THAT'S WHEN HE BEGAN TO SCREAM.
"I HAD TO MAKE HIM STOP SCREAMING.
"I HAD TO *SHOW* HIM. SHOW ***YOU***. THAT I'M NOT A PANSY."

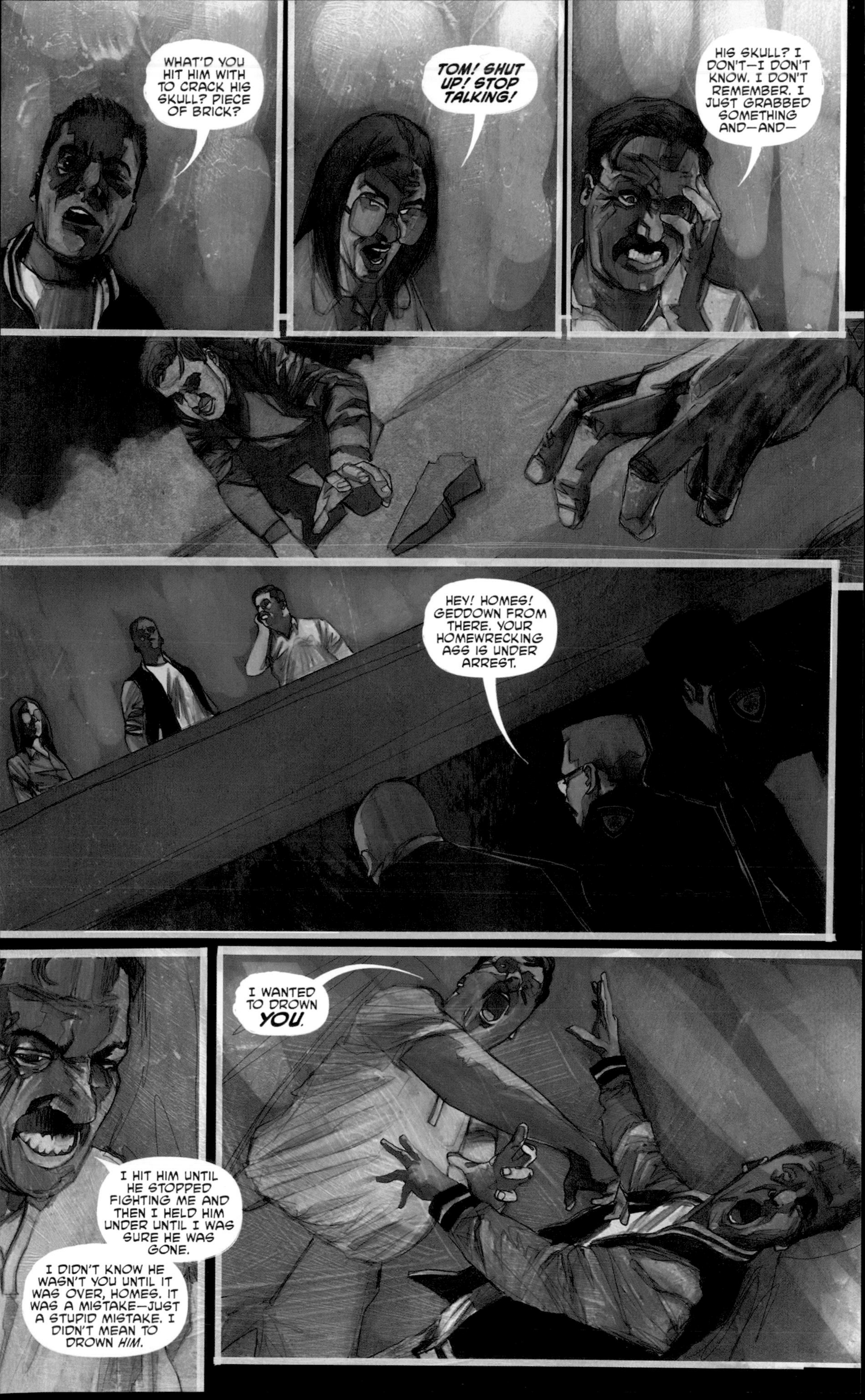
WHAT'D YOU HIT HIM WITH TO CRACK HIS SKULL? PIECE OF BRICK?
TOM! SHUT UP! STOP TALKING!
HIS SKULL? I DON'T—I DON'T KNOW. I DON'T REMEMBER. I JUST GRABBED SOMETHING AND—AND—
HEY! HOMES! GEDDOWN FROM THERE. YOUR HOMEWRECKING ASS IS UNDER ARREST.
I HIT HIM UNTIL HE STOPPED FIGHTING ME AND THEN I HELD HIM UNDER UNTIL I WAS SURE HE WAS GONE.
I DIDN'T KNOW HE WASN'T YOU UNTIL IT WAS OVER, HOMES. IT WAS A MISTAKE—JUST A STUPID MISTAKE. I DIDN'T MEAN TO DROWN *HIM*.
I WANTED TO DROWN ***YOU***.

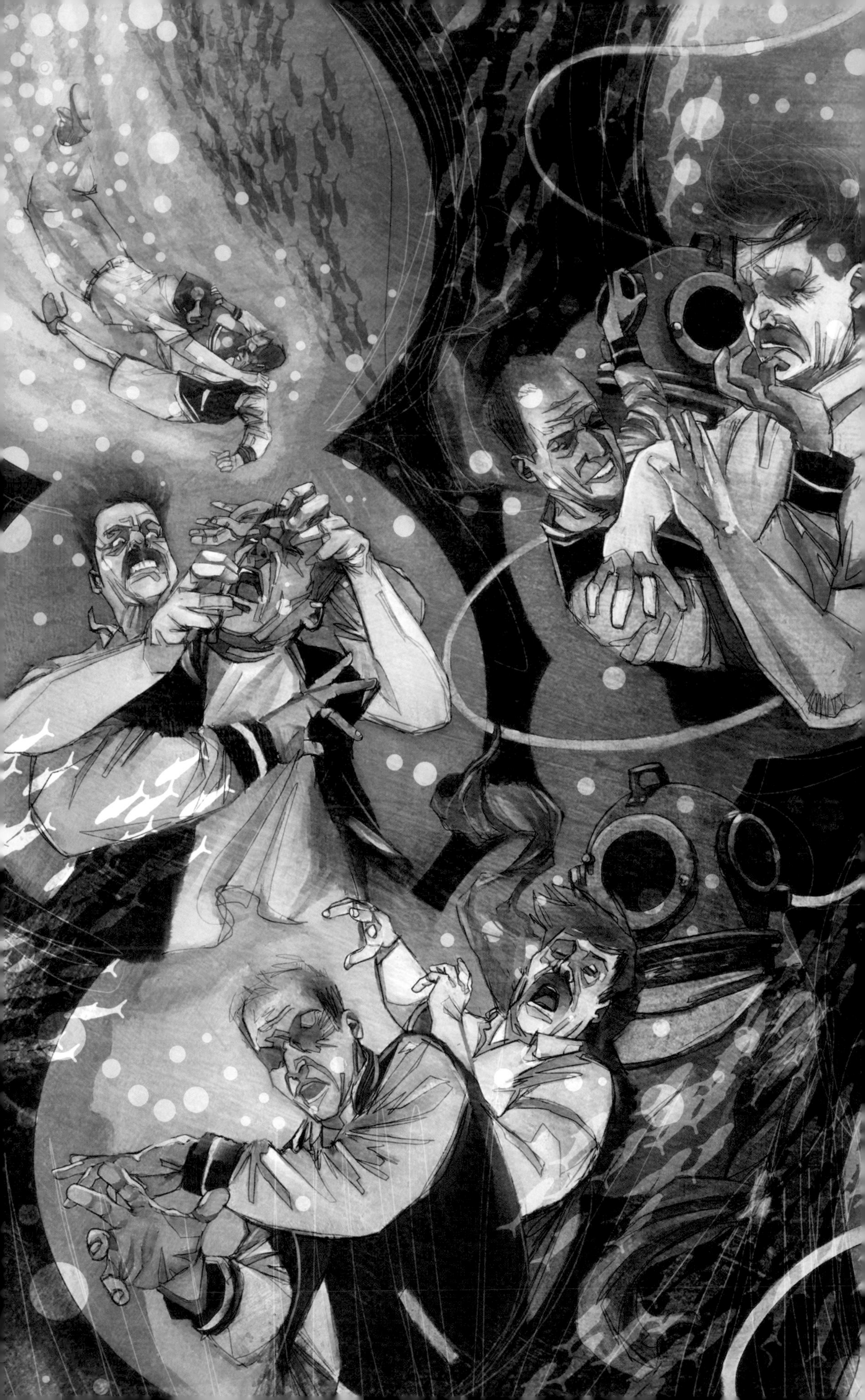

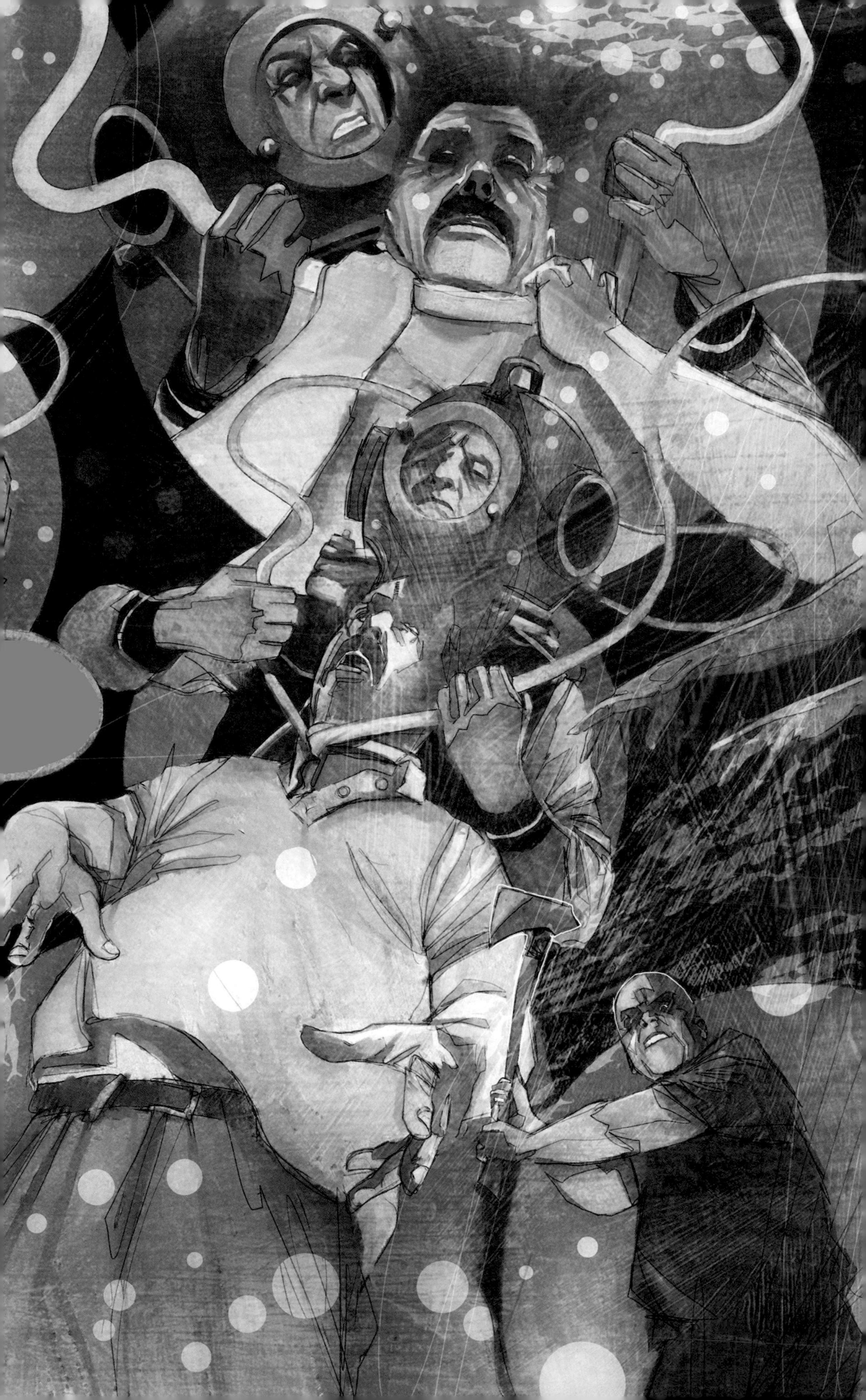

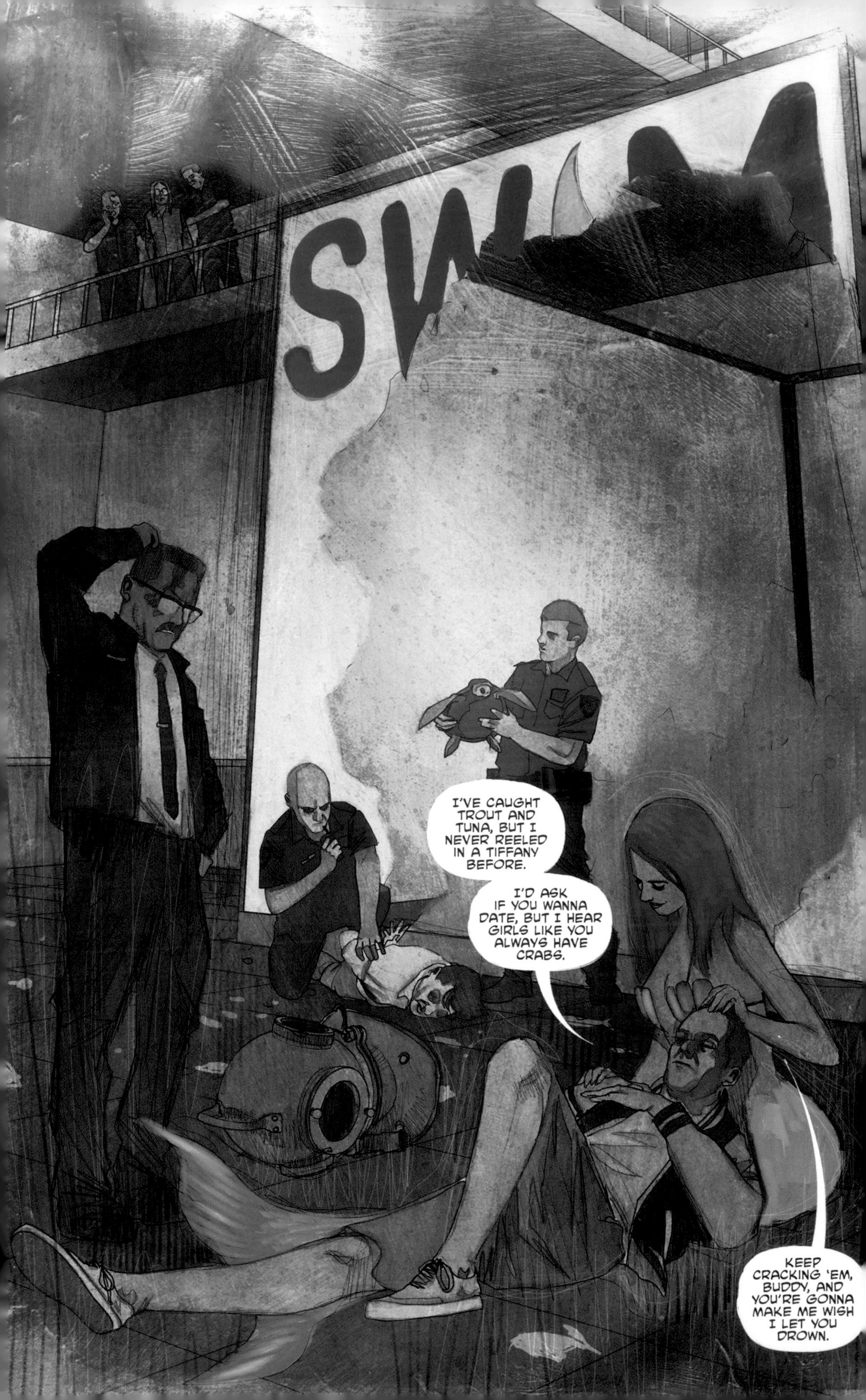
SW
I'VE CAUGHT TROUT AND TUNA, BUT I NEVER REELED IN A TIFFANY BEFORE.
I'D ASK IF YOU WANNA DATE, BUT I HEAR GIRLS LIKE YOU ALWAYS HAVE CRABS.
KEEP CRACKING 'EM, BUDDY, AND YOU'RE GONNA MAKE ME WISH I LET YOU DROWN.

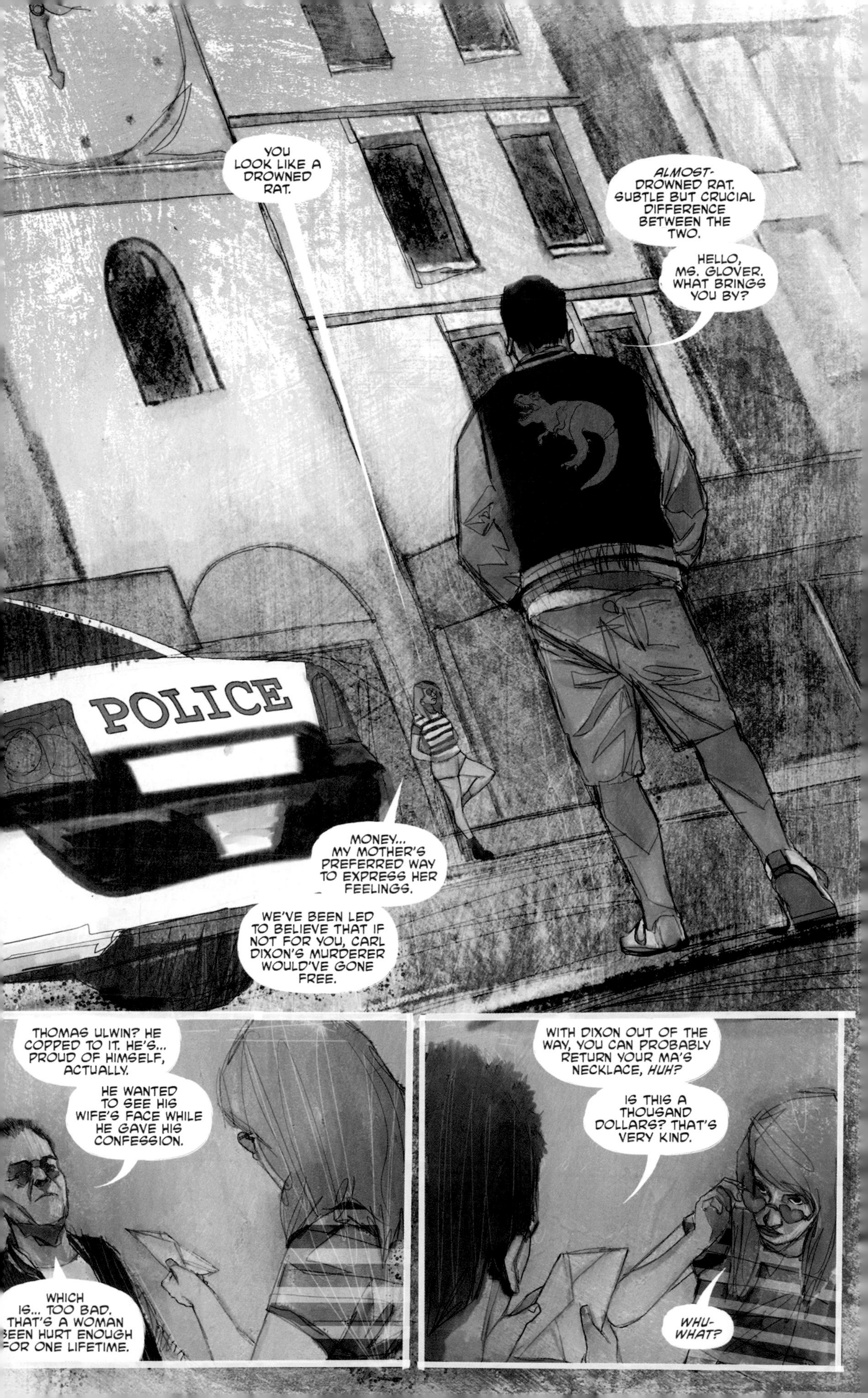
YOU LOOK LIKE A DROWNED RAT.
ALMOST- DROWNED RAT. SUBTLE BUT CRUCIAL DIFFERENCE BETWEEN THE TWO.
HELLO, MS. GLOVER. WHAT BRINGS YOU BY?
POLICE
MONEY... MY MOTHER'S PREFERRED WAY TO EXPRESS HER FEELINGS.
WE'VE BEEN LED TO BELIEVE THAT IF NOT FOR YOU, CARL DIXON'S MURDERER WOULD'VE GONE FREE.
THOMAS ULWIN? HE COPPED TO IT. HE'S... PROUD OF HIMSELF, ACTUALLY.
HE WANTED TO SEE HIS WIFE'S FACE WHILE HE GAVE HIS CONFESSION.
WHICH IS... TOO BAD. THAT'S A WOMAN BEEN HURT ENOUGH FOR ONE LIFETIME.
WITH DIXON OUT OF THE WAY, YOU CAN PROBABLY RETURN YOUR MA'S NECKLACE, *HUH?*
IS THIS A THOUSAND DOLLARS? THAT'S VERY KIND.
WHU-WHAT?

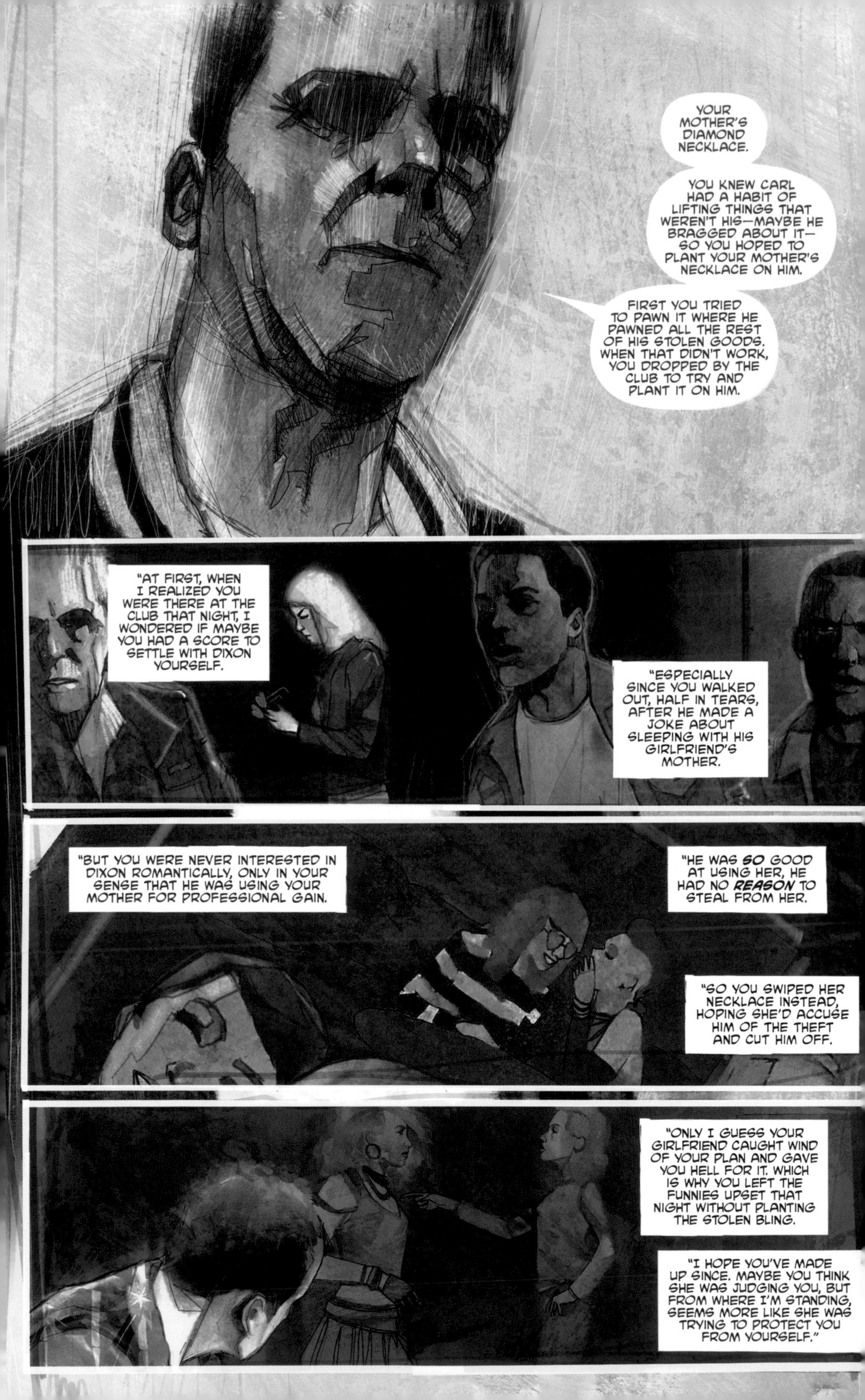
YOUR MOTHER'S DIAMOND NECKLACE.
YOU KNEW CARL HAD A HABIT OF LIFTING THINGS THAT WEREN'T HIS—MAYBE HE BRAGGED ABOUT IT—SO YOU HOPED TO PLANT YOUR MOTHER'S NECKLACE ON HIM.
FIRST YOU TRIED TO PAWN IT WHERE HE PAWNED ALL THE REST OF HIS STOLEN GOODS. WHEN THAT DIDN'T WORK, YOU DROPPED BY THE CLUB TO TRY AND PLANT IT ON HIM.
"AT FIRST, WHEN I REALIZED YOU WERE THERE AT THE CLUB THAT NIGHT, I WONDERED IF MAYBE YOU HAD A SCORE TO SETTLE WITH DIXON YOURSELF.
"ESPECIALLY SINCE YOU WALKED OUT, HALF IN TEARS, AFTER HE MADE A JOKE ABOUT SLEEPING WITH HIS GIRLFRIEND'S MOTHER.
"BUT YOU WERE NEVER INTERESTED IN DIXON ROMANTICALLY, ONLY IN YOUR SENSE THAT HE WAS USING YOUR MOTHER FOR PROFESSIONAL GAIN.
"HE WAS ***SO*** GOOD AT USING HER, HE HAD NO ***REASON*** TO STEAL FROM HER.
"SO YOU SWIPED HER NECKLACE INSTEAD, HOPING SHE'D ACCUSE HIM OF THE THEFT AND CUT HIM OFF.
"ONLY I GUESS YOUR GIRLFRIEND CAUGHT WIND OF YOUR PLAN AND GAVE YOU HELL FOR IT. WHICH IS WHY YOU LEFT THE FUNNIES UPSET THAT NIGHT WITHOUT PLANTING THE STOLEN BLING.
"I HOPE YOU'VE MADE UP SINCE. MAYBE YOU THINK SHE WAS JUDGING YOU, BUT FROM WHERE I'M STANDING, SEEMS MORE LIKE SHE WAS TRYING TO PROTECT YOU FROM YOURSELF."

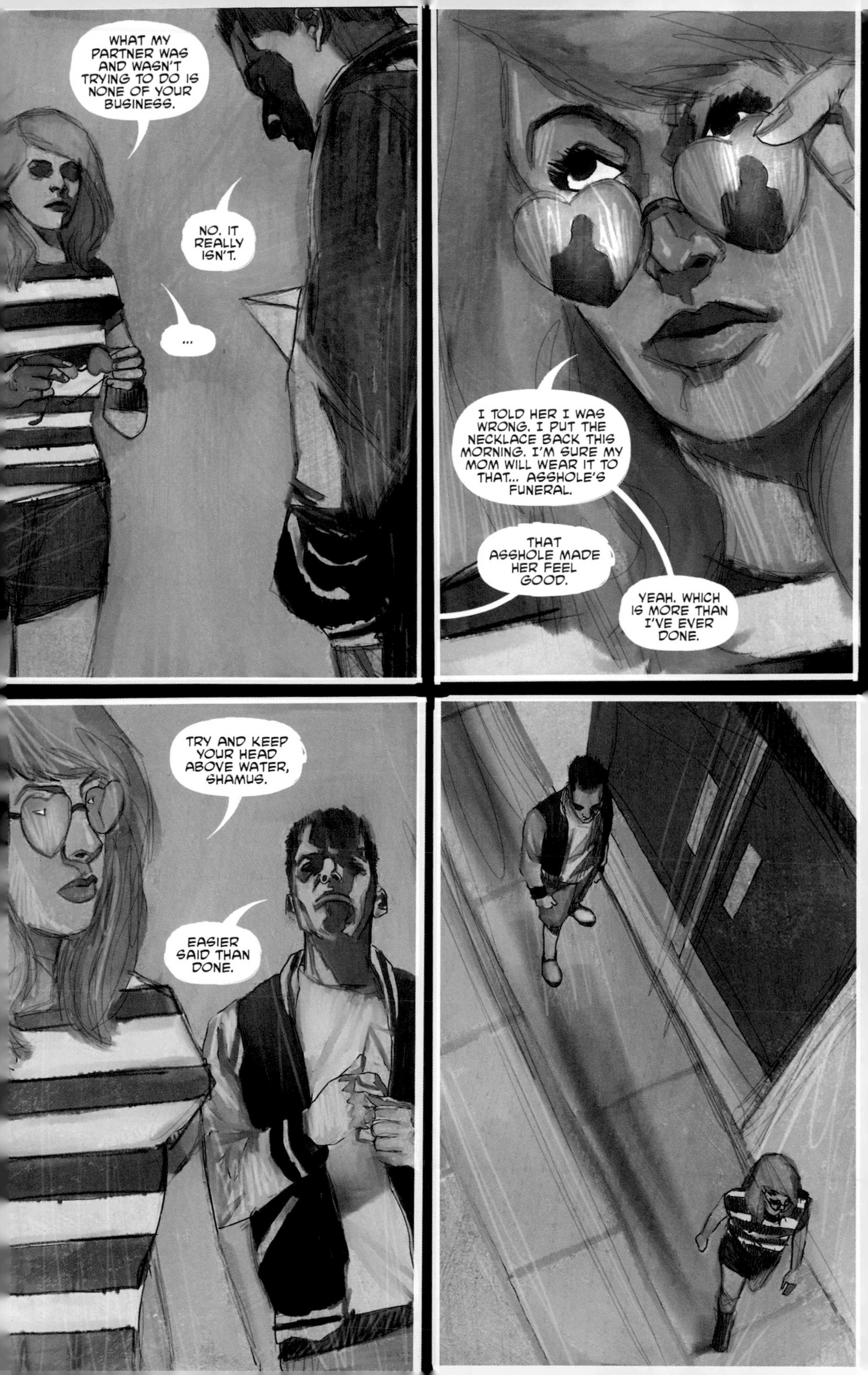
WHAT MY PARTNER WAS AND WASN'T TRYING TO DO IS NONE OF YOUR BUSINESS.
NO. IT REALLY ISN'T.
...
I TOLD HER I WAS WRONG. I PUT THE NECKLACE BACK THIS MORNING. I'M SURE MY MOM WILL WEAR IT TO THAT... ASSHOLE'S FUNERAL.
THAT ASSHOLE MADE HER FEEL GOOD.
YEAH. WHICH IS MORE THAN I'VE EVER DONE.
TRY AND KEEP YOUR HEAD ABOVE WATER, SHAMUS.
EASIER SAID THAN DONE.

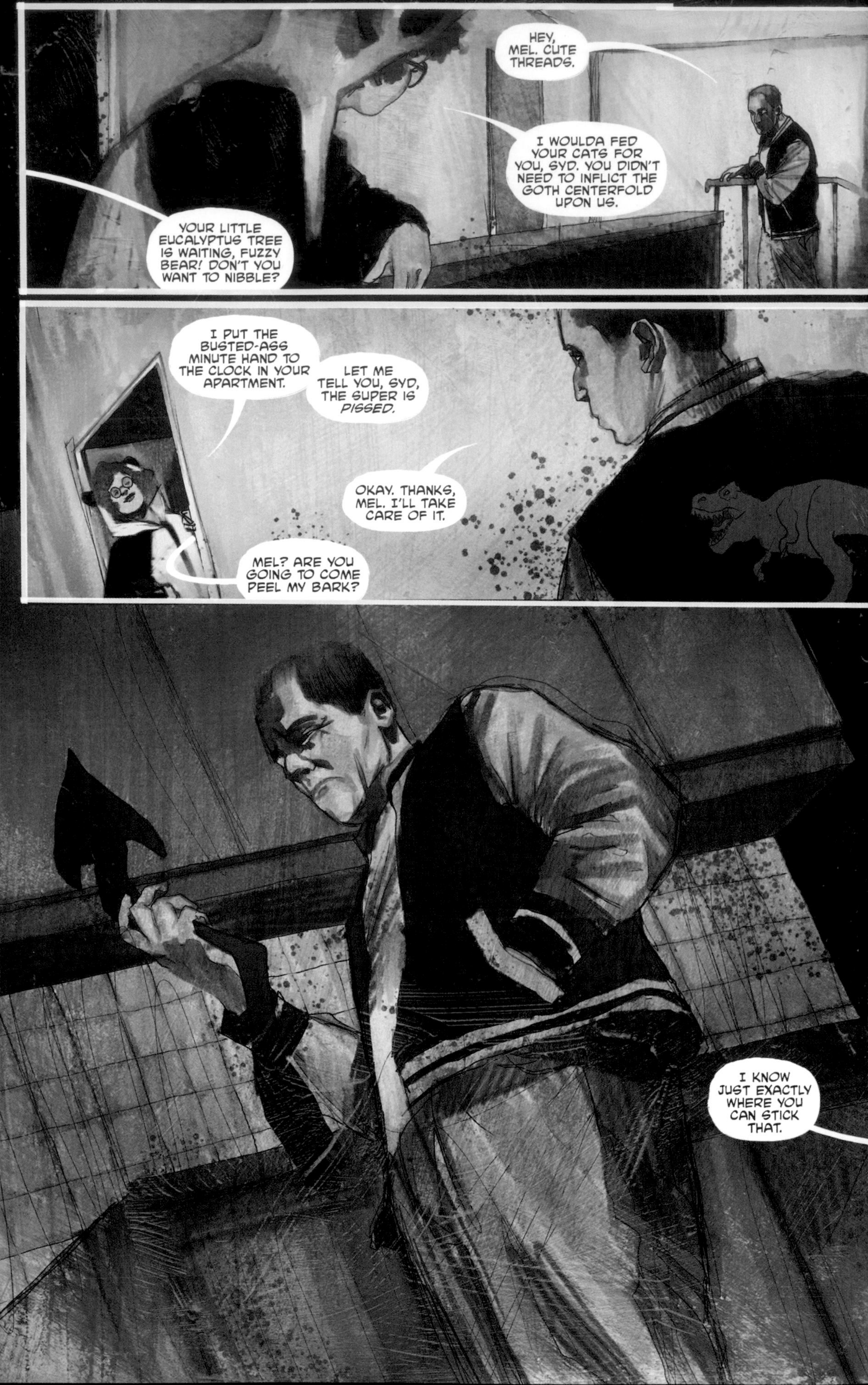
HEY, MEL. CUTE THREADS.
YOUR LITTLE EUCALYPTUS TREE IS WAITING, FUZZY BEAR! DON'T YOU WANT TO NIBBLE?
I WOULDA FED YOUR CATS FOR YOU, SYD. YOU DIDN'T NEED TO INFLICT THE GOTH CENTERFOLD UPON US.
I PUT THE BUSTED-ASS MINUTE HAND TO THE CLOCK IN YOUR APARTMENT.
LET ME TELL YOU, SYD, THE SUPER IS *PISSED*.
OKAY. THANKS, MEL. I'LL TAKE CARE OF IT.
MEL? ARE YOU GOING TO COME PEEL MY BARK?
I KNOW JUST EXACTLY WHERE YOU CAN STICK THAT.

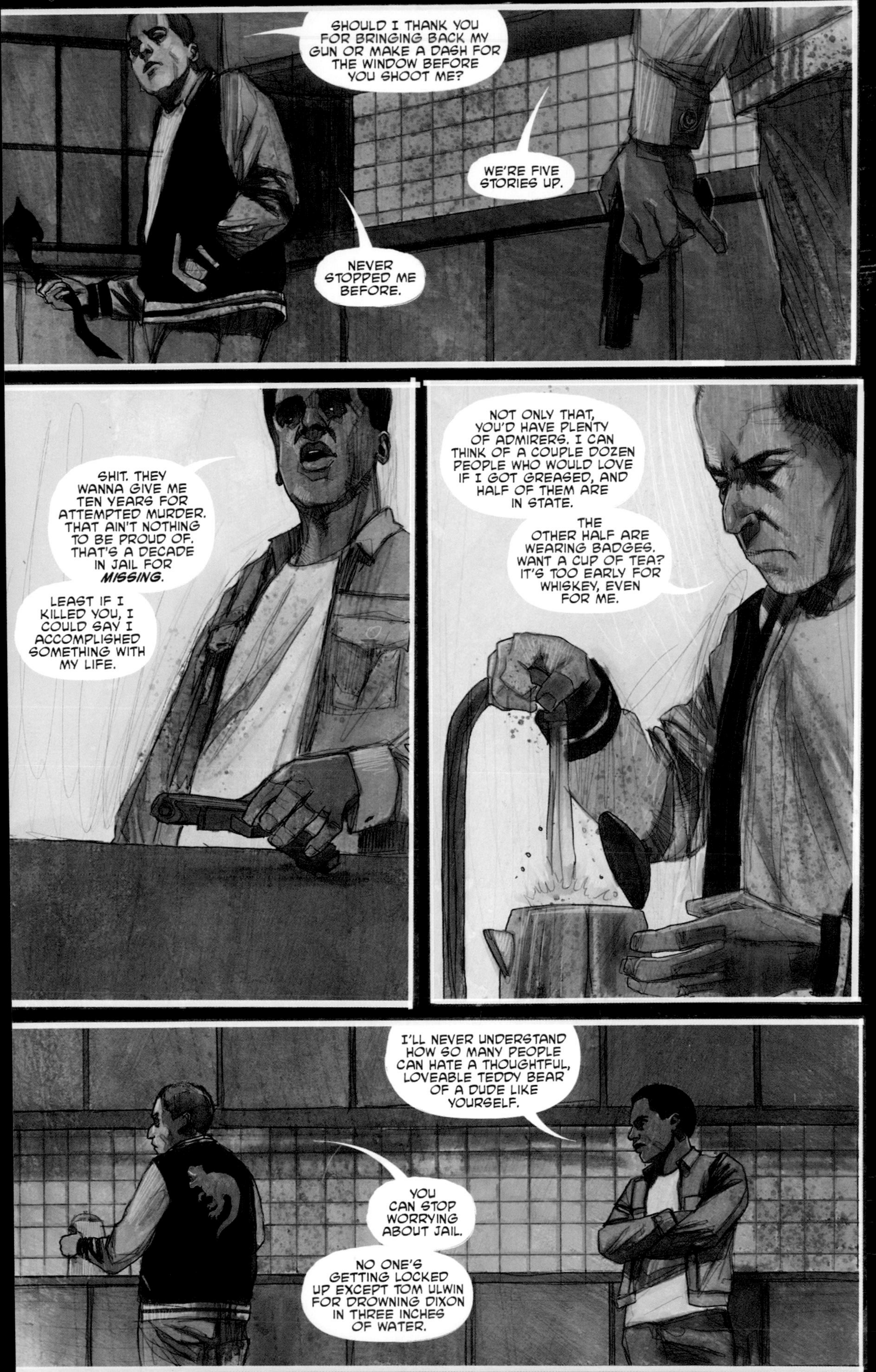
SHOULD I THANK YOU FOR BRINGING BACK MY GUN OR MAKE A DASH FOR THE WINDOW BEFORE YOU SHOOT ME?
WE'RE FIVE STORIES UP.
NEVER STOPPED ME BEFORE.
SHIT. THEY WANNA GIVE ME TEN YEARS FOR ATTEMPTED MURDER. THAT AIN'T NOTHING TO BE PROUD OF. THAT'S A DECADE IN JAIL FOR *MISSING*.
LEAST IF I KILLED YOU, I COULD SAY I ACCOMPLISHED SOMETHING WITH MY LIFE.
NOT ONLY THAT, YOU'D HAVE PLENTY OF ADMIRERS. I CAN THINK OF A COUPLE DOZEN PEOPLE WHO WOULD LOVE IF I GOT GREASED, AND HALF OF THEM ARE IN STATE.
THE OTHER HALF ARE WEARING BADGES. WANT A CUP OF TEA? IT'S TOO EARLY FOR WHISKEY, EVEN FOR ME.
I'LL NEVER UNDERSTAND HOW SO MANY PEOPLE CAN HATE A THOUGHTFUL, LOVEABLE TEDDY BEAR OF A DUDE LIKE YOURSELF.
YOU CAN STOP WORRYING ABOUT JAIL.
NO ONE'S GETTING LOCKED UP EXCEPT TOM ULWIN FOR DROWNING DIXON IN THREE INCHES OF WATER.

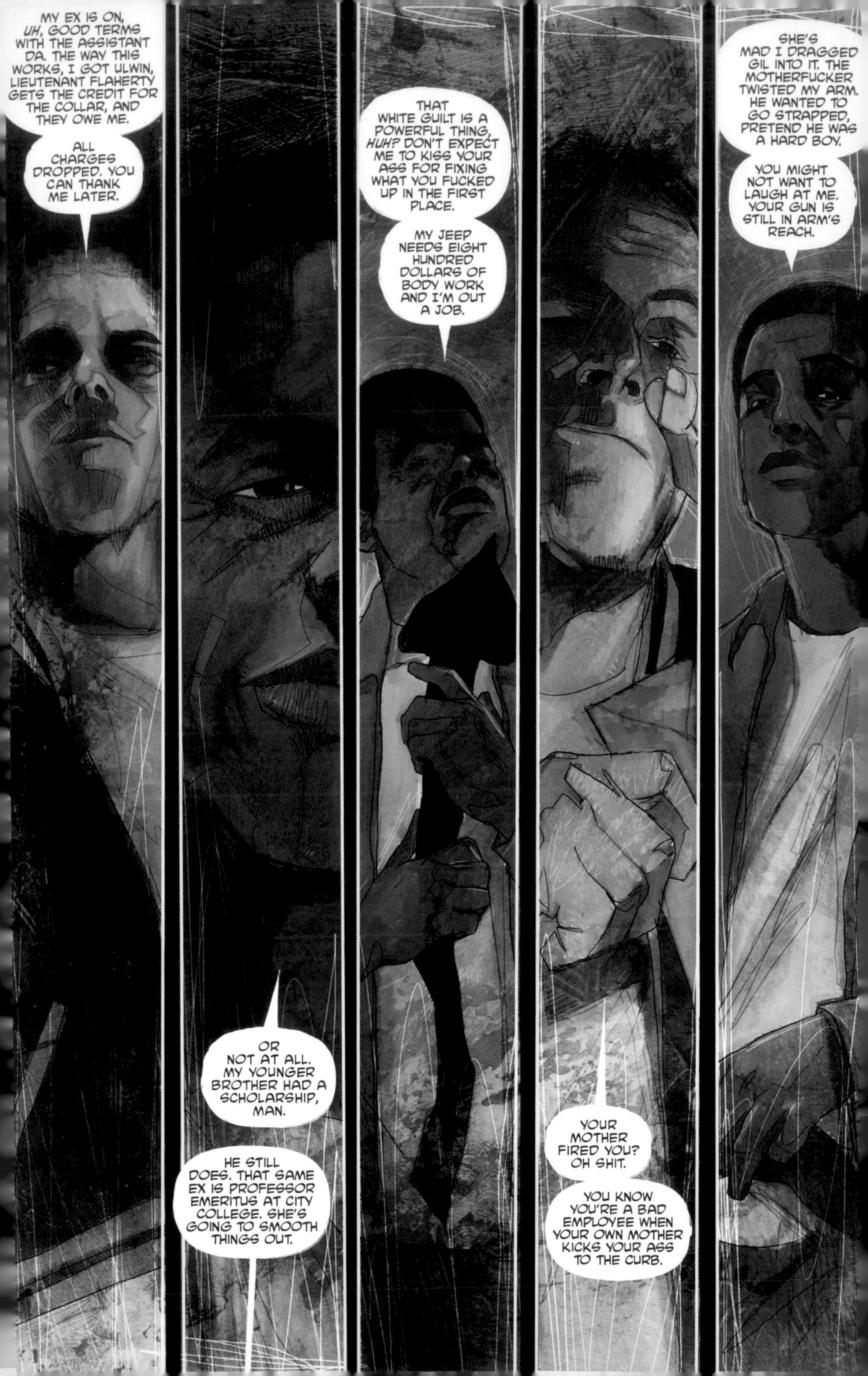
MY EX IS ON, *UH*, GOOD TERMS WITH THE ASSISTANT DA. THE WAY THIS WORKS, I GOT ULWIN, LIEUTENANT FLAHERTY GETS THE CREDIT FOR THE COLLAR, AND THEY OWE ME.
ALL CHARGES DROPPED. YOU CAN THANK ME LATER.
OR NOT AT ALL. MY YOUNGER BROTHER HAD A SCHOLARSHIP, MAN.
HE STILL DOES. THAT SAME EX IS PROFESSOR EMERITUS AT CITY COLLEGE. SHE'S GOING TO SMOOTH THINGS OUT.
THAT WHITE GUILT IS A POWERFUL THING, *HUH?* DON'T EXPECT ME TO KISS YOUR ASS FOR FIXING WHAT YOU FUCKED UP IN THE FIRST PLACE.
MY JEEP NEEDS EIGHT HUNDRED DOLLARS OF BODY WORK AND I'M OUT A JOB.
YOUR MOTHER FIRED YOU? OH SHIT.
YOU KNOW YOU'RE A BAD EMPLOYEE WHEN YOUR OWN MOTHER KICKS YOUR ASS TO THE CURB.
SHE'S MAD I DRAGGED GIL INTO IT. THE MOTHERFUCKER TWISTED MY ARM. HE WANTED TO GO STRAPPED, PRETEND HE WAS A HARD BOY.
YOU MIGHT NOT WANT TO LAUGH AT ME. YOUR GUN IS STILL IN ARM'S REACH.

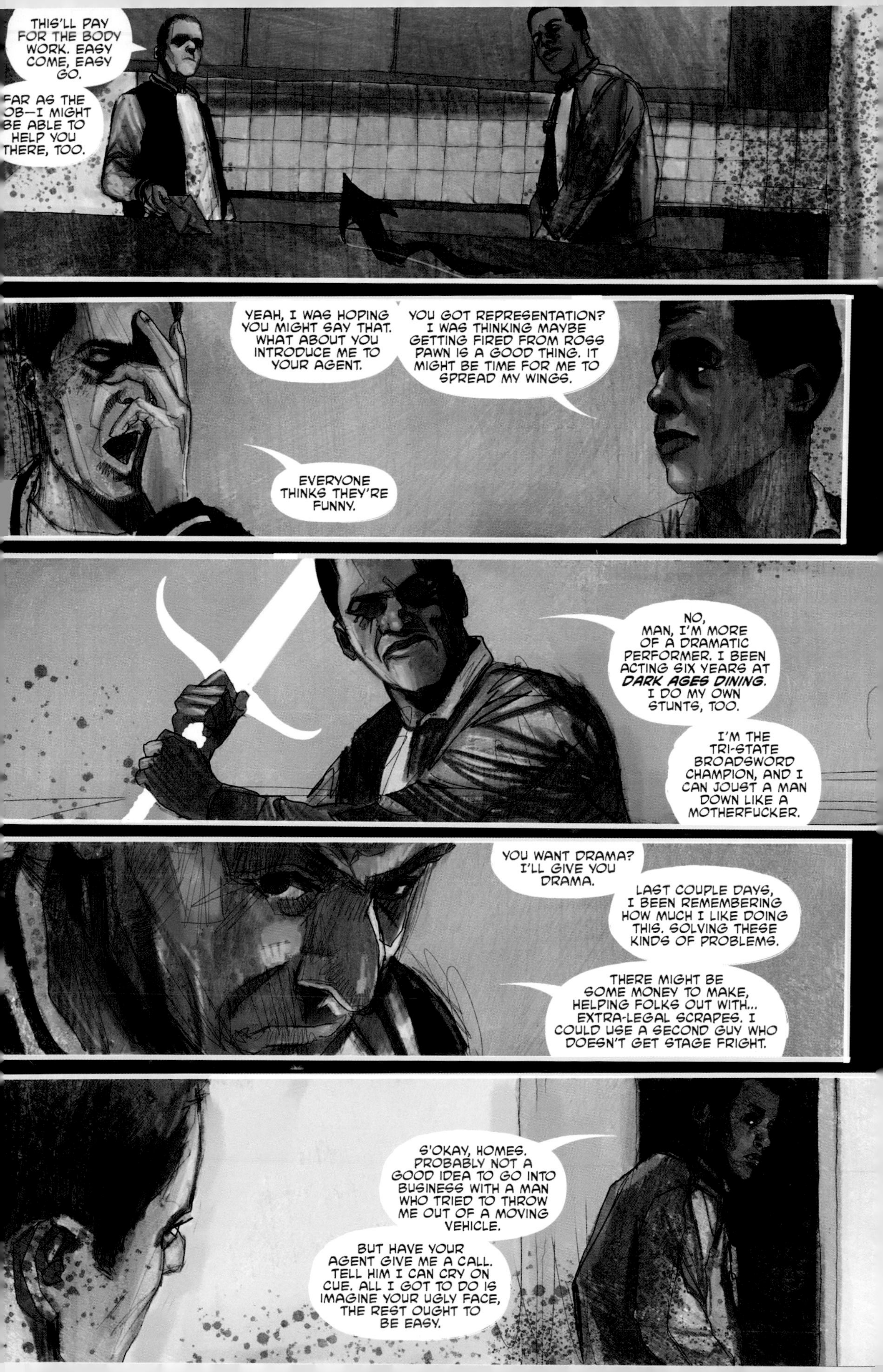
THIS'LL PAY FOR THE BODY WORK. EASY COME, EASY GO.
FAR AS THE JOB—I MIGHT BE ABLE TO HELP YOU THERE, TOO.
YEAH, I WAS HOPING YOU MIGHT SAY THAT. WHAT ABOUT YOU INTRODUCE ME TO YOUR AGENT.
YOU GOT REPRESENTATION? I WAS THINKING MAYBE GETTING FIRED FROM ROSS PAWN IS A GOOD THING. IT MIGHT BE TIME FOR ME TO SPREAD MY WINGS.
EVERYONE THINKS THEY'RE FUNNY.
NO, MAN, I'M MORE OF A DRAMATIC PERFORMER. I BEEN ACTING SIX YEARS AT DARK AGES DINING. I DO MY OWN STUNTS, TOO.
I'M THE TRI-STATE BROADSWORD CHAMPION, AND I CAN JOUST A MAN DOWN LIKE A MOTHERFUCKER.
YOU WANT DRAMA? I'LL GIVE YOU DRAMA.
LAST COUPLE DAYS, I BEEN REMEMBERING HOW MUCH I LIKE DOING THIS. SOLVING THESE KINDS OF PROBLEMS.
THERE MIGHT BE SOME MONEY TO MAKE, HELPING FOLKS OUT WITH... EXTRA-LEGAL SCRAPES. I COULD USE A SECOND GUY WHO DOESN'T GET STAGE FRIGHT.
S'OKAY, HOMES. PROBABLY NOT A GOOD IDEA TO GO INTO BUSINESS WITH A MAN WHO TRIED TO THROW ME OUT OF A MOVING VEHICLE.
BUT HAVE YOUR AGENT GIVE ME A CALL. TELL HIM I CAN CRY ON CUE. ALL I GOT TO DO IS IMAGINE YOUR UGLY FACE, THE REST OUGHT TO BE EASY.

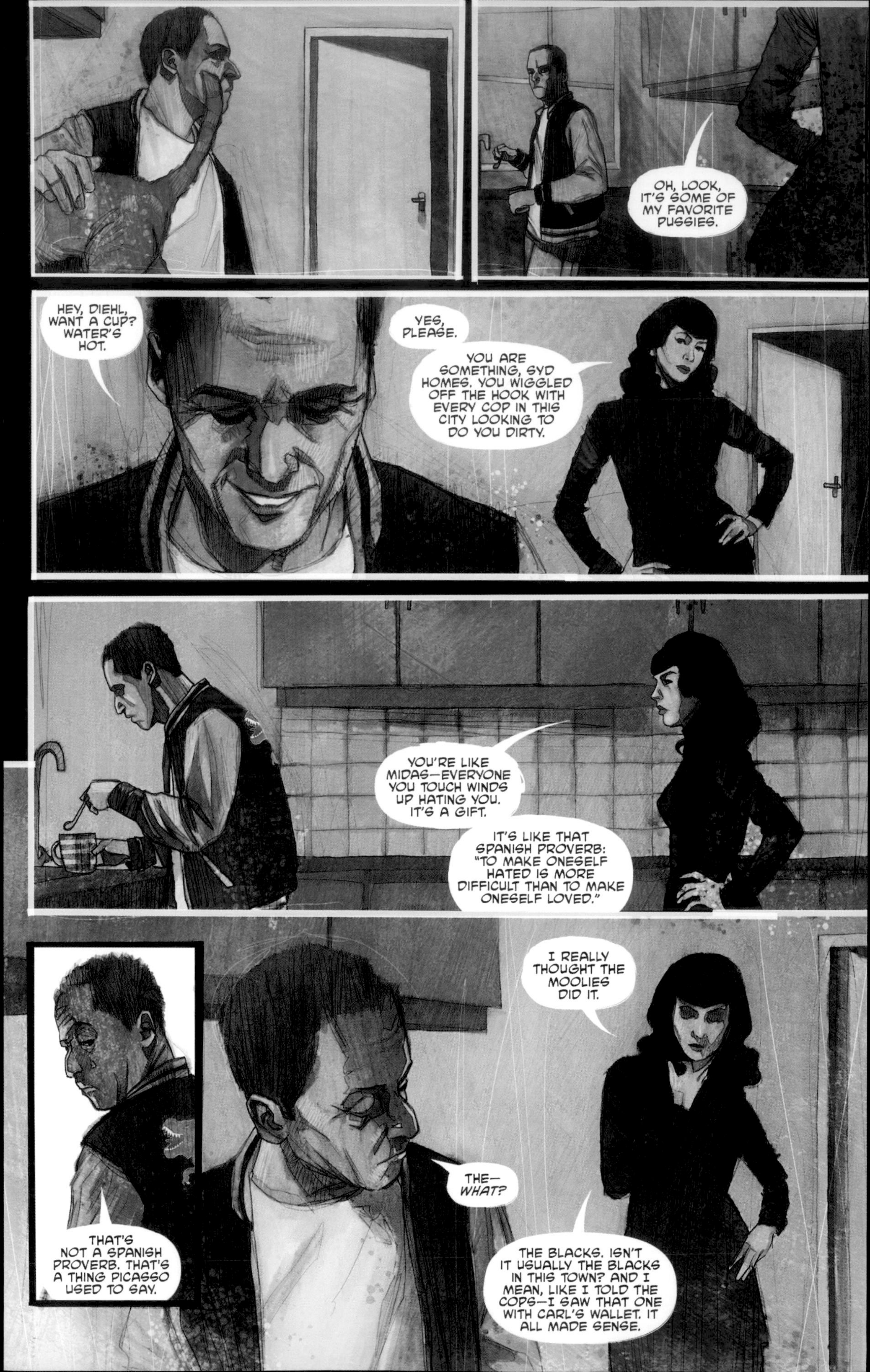
OH, LOOK, IT'S SOME OF MY FAVORITE PUSSIES.
HEY, DIEHL, WANT A CUP? WATER'S HOT.
YES, PLEASE.
YOU ARE SOMETHING, SYD HOMES. YOU WIGGLED OFF THE HOOK WITH EVERY COP IN THIS CITY LOOKING TO DO YOU DIRTY.
YOU'RE LIKE MIDAS—EVERYONE YOU TOUCH WINDS UP HATING YOU. IT'S A GIFT.
IT'S LIKE THAT SPANISH PROVERB: "TO MAKE ONESELF HATED IS MORE DIFFICULT THAN TO MAKE ONESELF LOVED."
THAT'S NOT A SPANISH PROVERB. THAT'S A THING PICASSO USED TO SAY.
I REALLY THOUGHT THE MOOLIES DID IT.
THE— *WHAT?*
THE BLACKS. ISN'T IT USUALLY THE BLACKS IN THIS TOWN? AND I MEAN, LIKE I TOLD THE COPS—I SAW THAT ONE WITH CARL'S WALLET. IT ALL MADE SENSE.

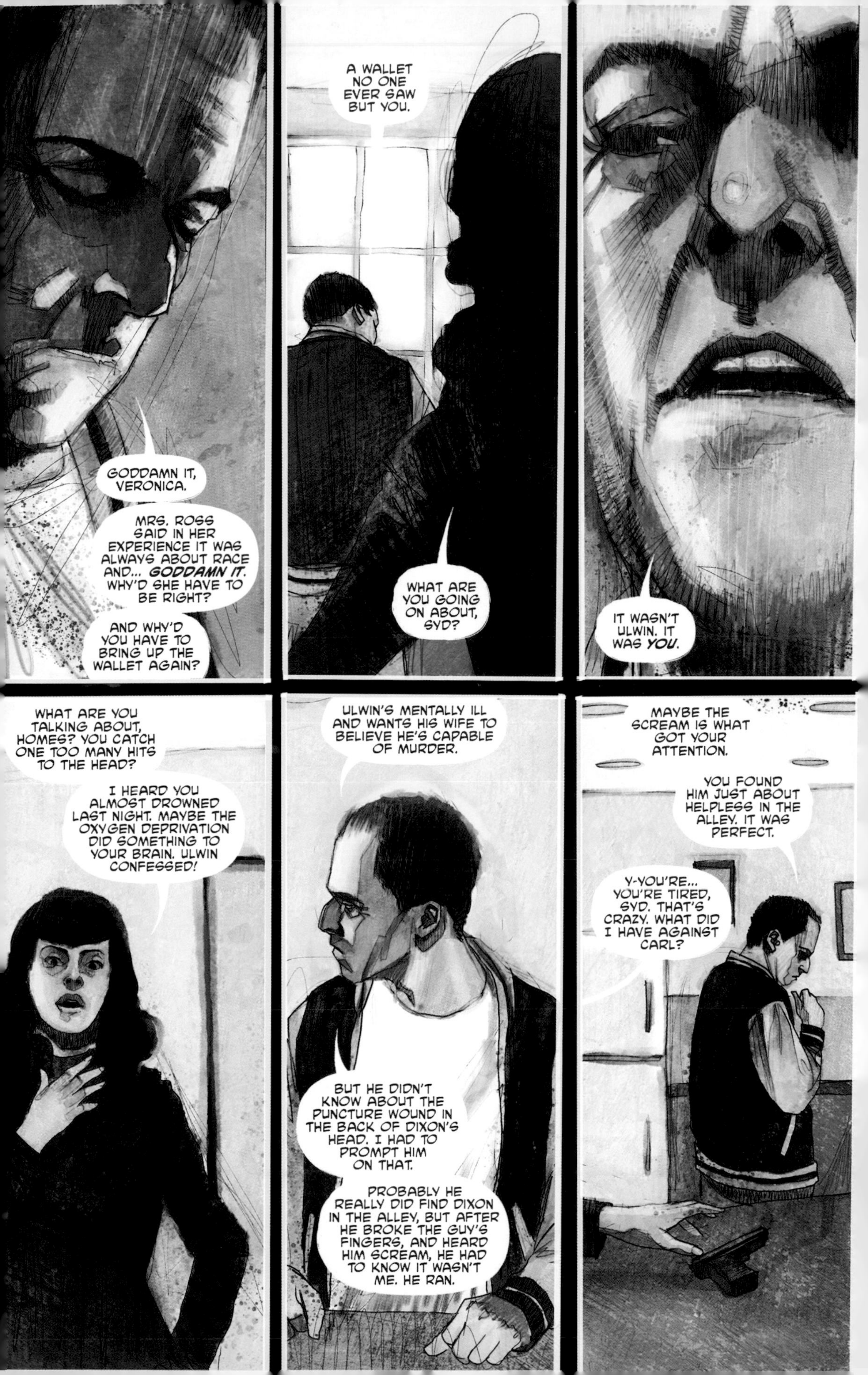
GODDAMN IT, VERONICA.
MRS. ROSS SAID IN HER EXPERIENCE IT WAS ALWAYS ABOUT RACE AND... *GODDAMN IT.* WHY'D SHE HAVE TO BE RIGHT?
AND WHY'D YOU HAVE TO BRING UP THE WALLET AGAIN?
A WALLET NO ONE EVER SAW BUT YOU.
WHAT ARE YOU GOING ON ABOUT, SYD?
IT WASN'T ULWIN. IT WAS *YOU*.
WHAT ARE YOU TALKING ABOUT, HOMES? YOU CATCH ONE TOO MANY HITS TO THE HEAD?
I HEARD YOU ALMOST DROWNED LAST NIGHT. MAYBE THE OXYGEN DEPRIVATION DID SOMETHING TO YOUR BRAIN. ULWIN CONFESSED!
ULWIN'S MENTALLY ILL AND WANTS HIS WIFE TO BELIEVE HE'S CAPABLE OF MURDER.
BUT HE DIDN'T KNOW ABOUT THE PUNCTURE WOUND IN THE BACK OF DIXON'S HEAD. I HAD TO PROMPT HIM ON THAT.
PROBABLY HE REALLY DID FIND DIXON IN THE ALLEY, BUT AFTER HE BROKE THE GUY'S FINGERS, AND HEARD HIM SCREAM, HE HAD TO KNOW IT WASN'T ME. HE RAN.
MAYBE THE SCREAM IS WHAT GOT YOUR ATTENTION.
YOU FOUND HIM JUST ABOUT HELPLESS IN THE ALLEY. IT WAS PERFECT.
Y-YOU'RE... YOU'RE TIRED, SYD. THAT'S CRAZY. WHAT DID I HAVE AGAINST CARL?

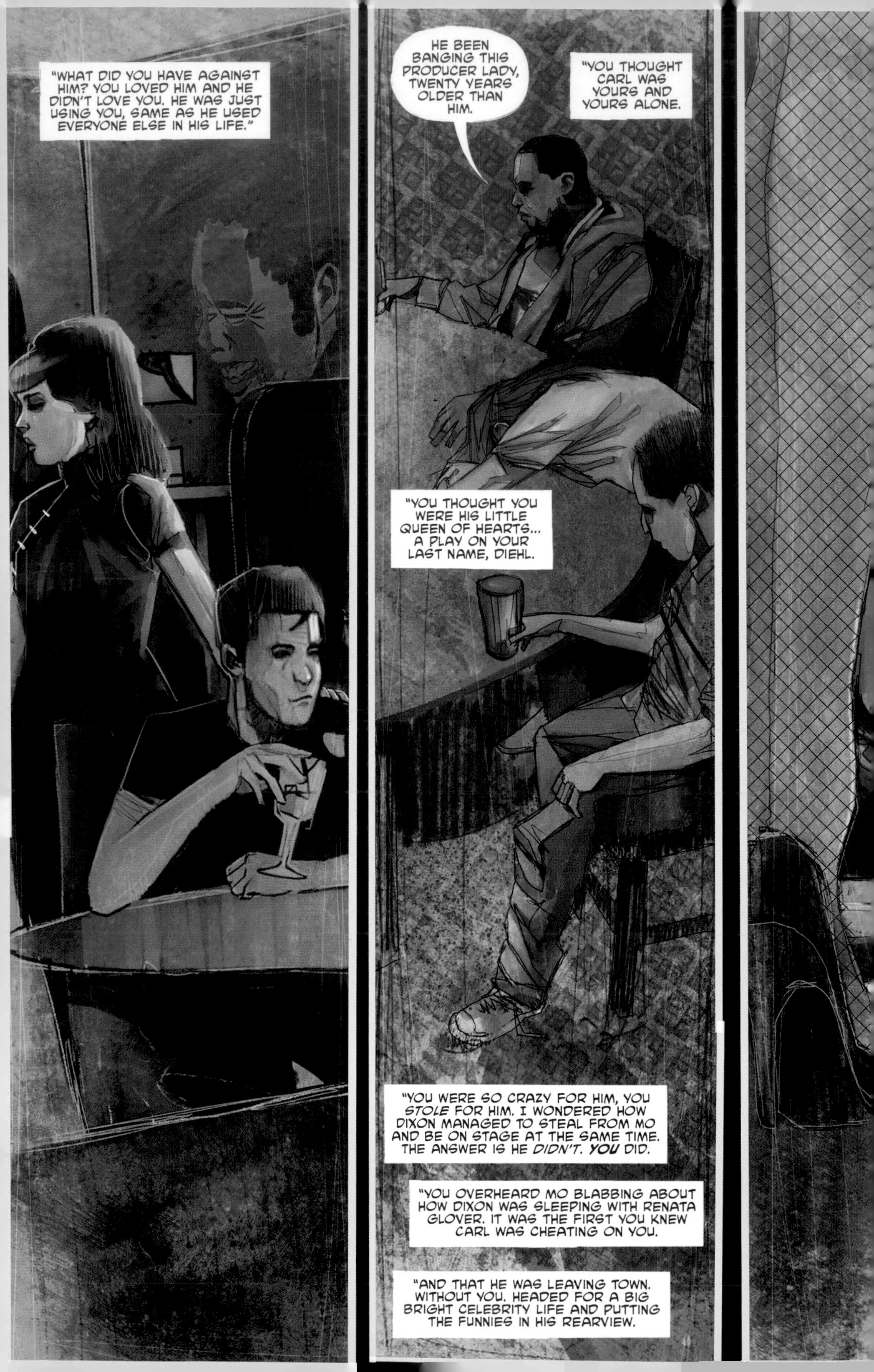
"WHAT DID YOU HAVE AGAINST HIM? YOU LOVED HIM AND HE DIDN'T LOVE YOU. HE WAS JUST USING YOU, SAME AS HE USED EVERYONE ELSE IN HIS LIFE."
HE BEEN BANGING THIS PRODUCER LADY, TWENTY YEARS OLDER THAN HIM.
"YOU THOUGHT CARL WAS YOURS AND YOURS ALONE.
"YOU THOUGHT YOU WERE HIS LITTLE QUEEN OF HEARTS... A PLAY ON YOUR LAST NAME, DIEHL.
"YOU WERE SO CRAZY FOR HIM, YOU *STOLE* FOR HIM. I WONDERED HOW DIXON MANAGED TO STEAL FROM MO AND BE ON STAGE AT THE SAME TIME. THE ANSWER IS HE *DIDN'T*. ***YOU*** DID.
"YOU OVERHEARD MO BLABBING ABOUT HOW DIXON WAS SLEEPING WITH RENATA GLOVER. IT WAS THE FIRST YOU KNEW CARL WAS CHEATING ON YOU.
"AND THAT HE WAS LEAVING TOWN. WITHOUT YOU. HEADED FOR A BIG BRIGHT CELEBRITY LIFE AND PUTTING THE FUNNIES IN HIS REARVIEW.

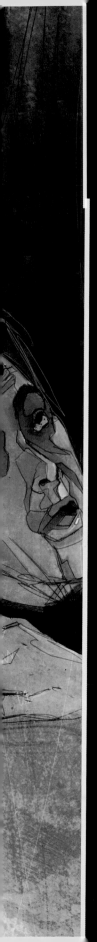

"THAT MUST'VE STUNG. AFTER SPENDING YOUR WHOLE LIFE IN ONE COUNTY AND DREAMING OF GETTING OUT.

"MAYBE YOU DIDN'T EVEN MEAN TO KILL HIM. YOU WERE ANGRY. YOU WANTED TO SCARE HIM. WHO DROWNS IN THREE INCHES OF WATER?

"THEN YOU HAD TO THROW THE BLAME ON SOMEONE ELSE, AND DECIDED A COUPLE BLACK KIDS WOULD DO. BECAUSE THEY WERE THERE.

"'COURSE, I SHOULD'VE KNOWN AFTER THE COPS SHOWED UP LOOKING FOR ME WHEN I HUNTED DOWN RENATA GLOVER.

"YOU WERE THE ONLY ONE WHO KNEW WHERE I WAS GOING AND THE ONLY ONE WHO COULD POINT THEM AT ME. BY THEN, YOU KNEW IT WASN'T GOING TO STICK TO THE ROSS BOYS.

"SO YOU HAD TO HANG IT ON ME AFTER ALL."

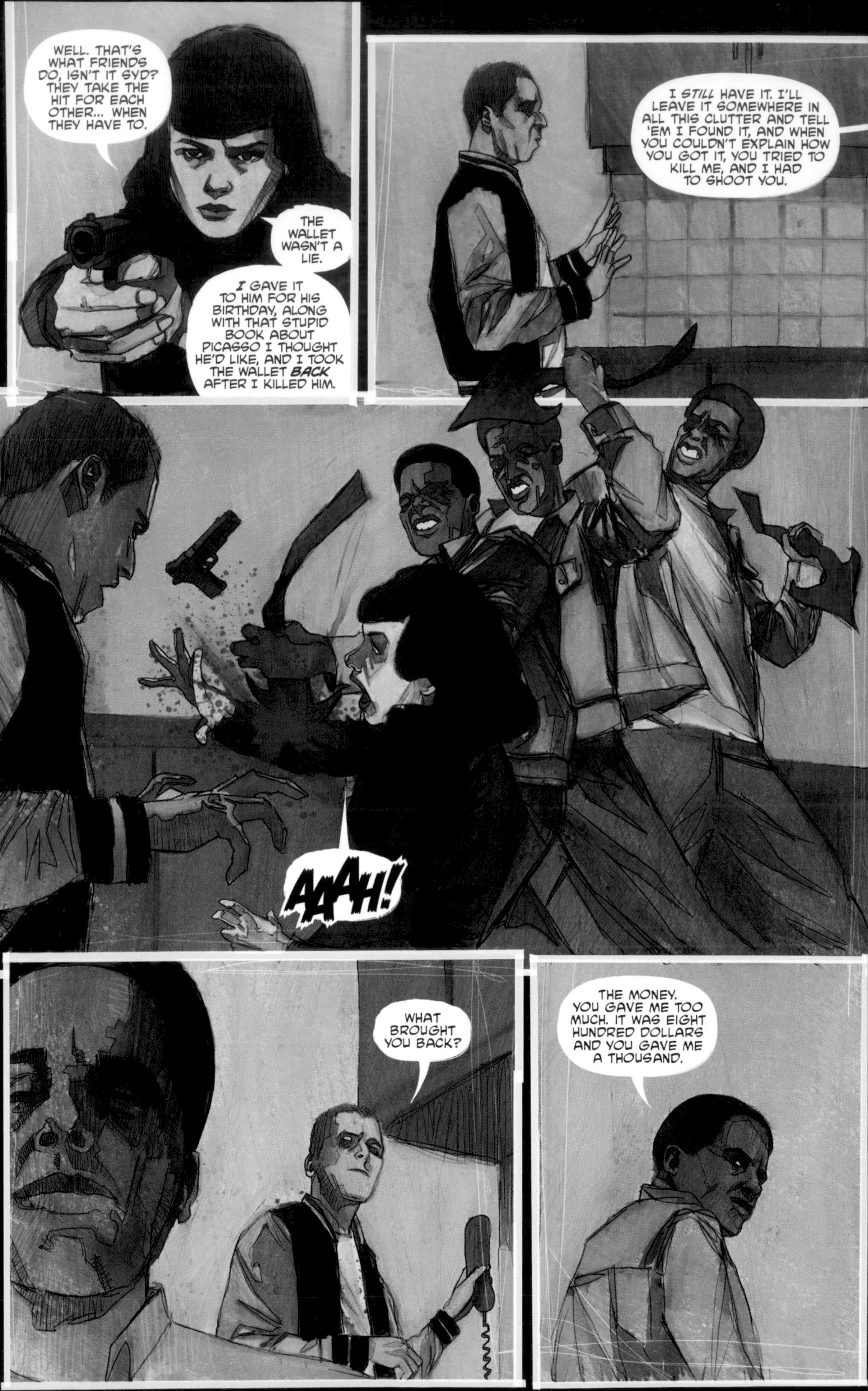
WELL. THAT'S WHAT FRIENDS DO, ISN'T IT SYD? THEY TAKE THE HIT FOR EACH OTHER... WHEN THEY HAVE TO.
THE WALLET WASN'T A LIE.
I GAVE IT TO HIM FOR HIS BIRTHDAY, ALONG WITH THAT STUPID BOOK ABOUT PICASSO I THOUGHT HE'D LIKE, AND I TOOK THE WALLET ***BACK*** AFTER I KILLED HIM.
I *STILL* HAVE IT. I'LL LEAVE IT SOMEWHERE IN ALL THIS CLUTTER AND TELL 'EM I FOUND IT, AND WHEN YOU COULDN'T EXPLAIN HOW YOU GOT IT, YOU TRIED TO KILL ME, AND I HAD TO SHOOT YOU.
AAAH!
WHAT BROUGHT YOU BACK?
THE MONEY. YOU GAVE ME TOO MUCH. IT WAS EIGHT HUNDRED DOLLARS AND YOU GAVE ME A THOUSAND.

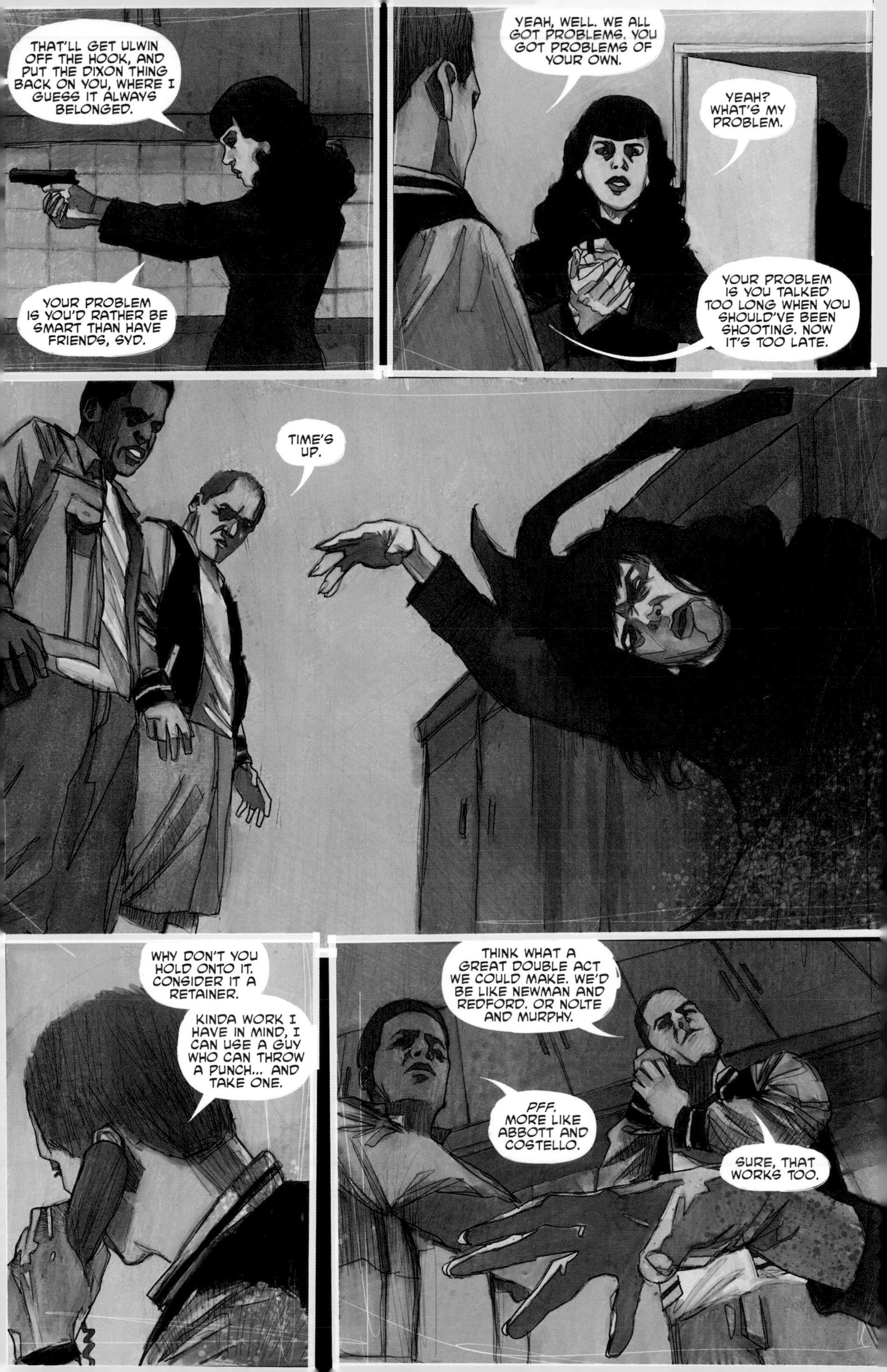
THAT'LL GET ULWIN OFF THE HOOK, AND PUT THE DIXON THING BACK ON YOU, WHERE I GUESS IT ALWAYS BELONGED.
YOUR PROBLEM IS YOU'D RATHER BE SMART THAN HAVE FRIENDS, SYD.
YEAH, WELL. WE ALL GOT PROBLEMS. YOU GOT PROBLEMS OF YOUR OWN.
YEAH? WHAT'S MY PROBLEM.
YOUR PROBLEM IS YOU TALKED TOO LONG WHEN YOU SHOULD'VE BEEN SHOOTING. NOW IT'S TOO LATE.
TIME'S UP.
WHY DON'T YOU HOLD ONTO IT. CONSIDER IT A RETAINER.
KINDA WORK I HAVE IN MIND, I CAN USE A GUY WHO CAN THROW A PUNCH... AND TAKE ONE.
THINK WHAT A GREAT DOUBLE ACT WE COULD MAKE. WE'D BE LIKE NEWMAN AND REDFORD. OR NOLTE AND MURPHY.
PFF. MORE LIKE ABBOTT AND COSTELLO.
SURE, THAT WORKS TOO.

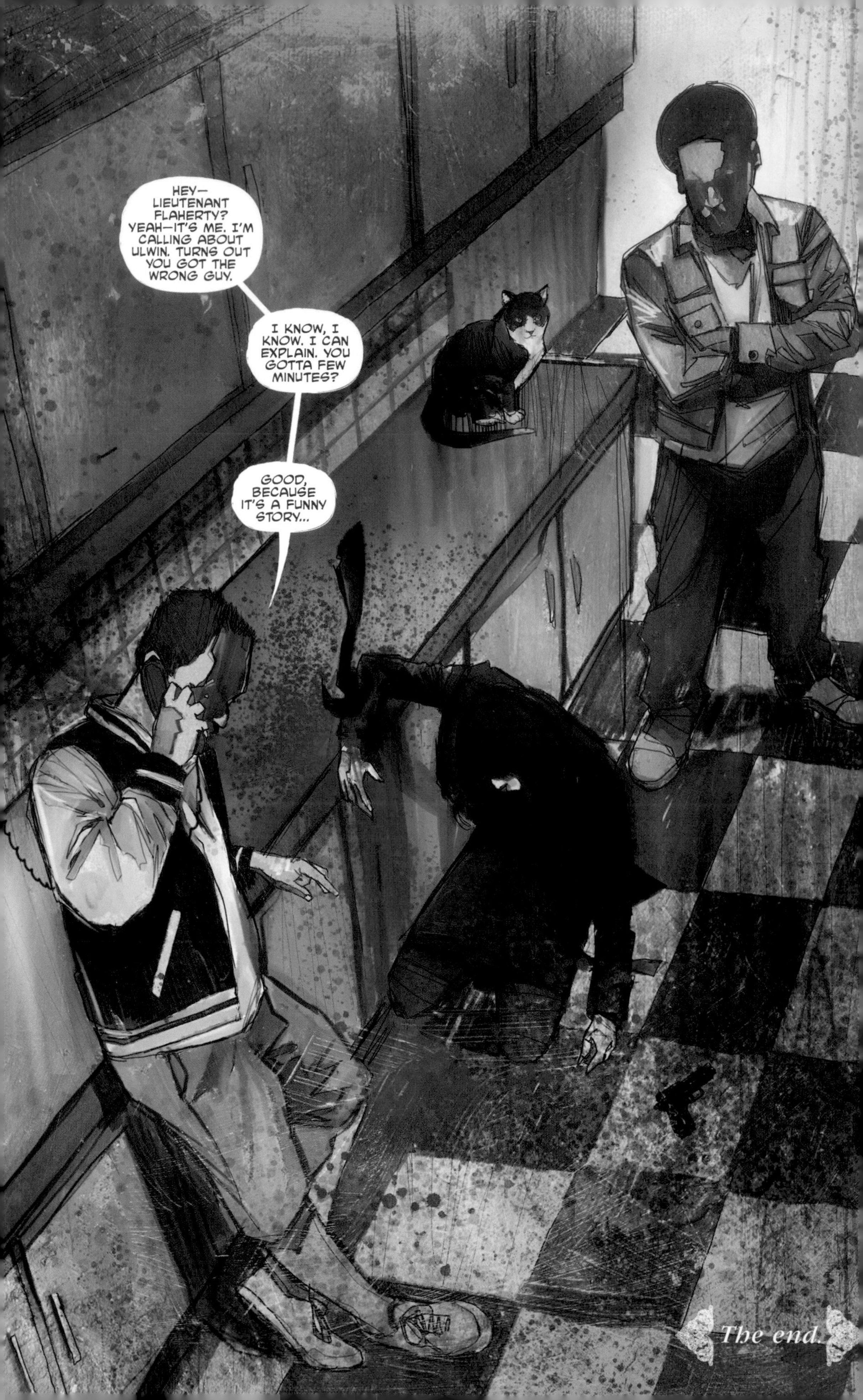
HEY—LIEUTENANT FLAHERTY? YEAH—IT'S ME. I'M CALLING ABOUT ULWIN. TURNS OUT YOU GOT THE WRONG GUY.
I KNOW, I KNOW. I CAN EXPLAIN. YOU GOTTA FEW MINUTES?
GOOD, BECAUSE IT'S A FUNNY STORY...
The end.

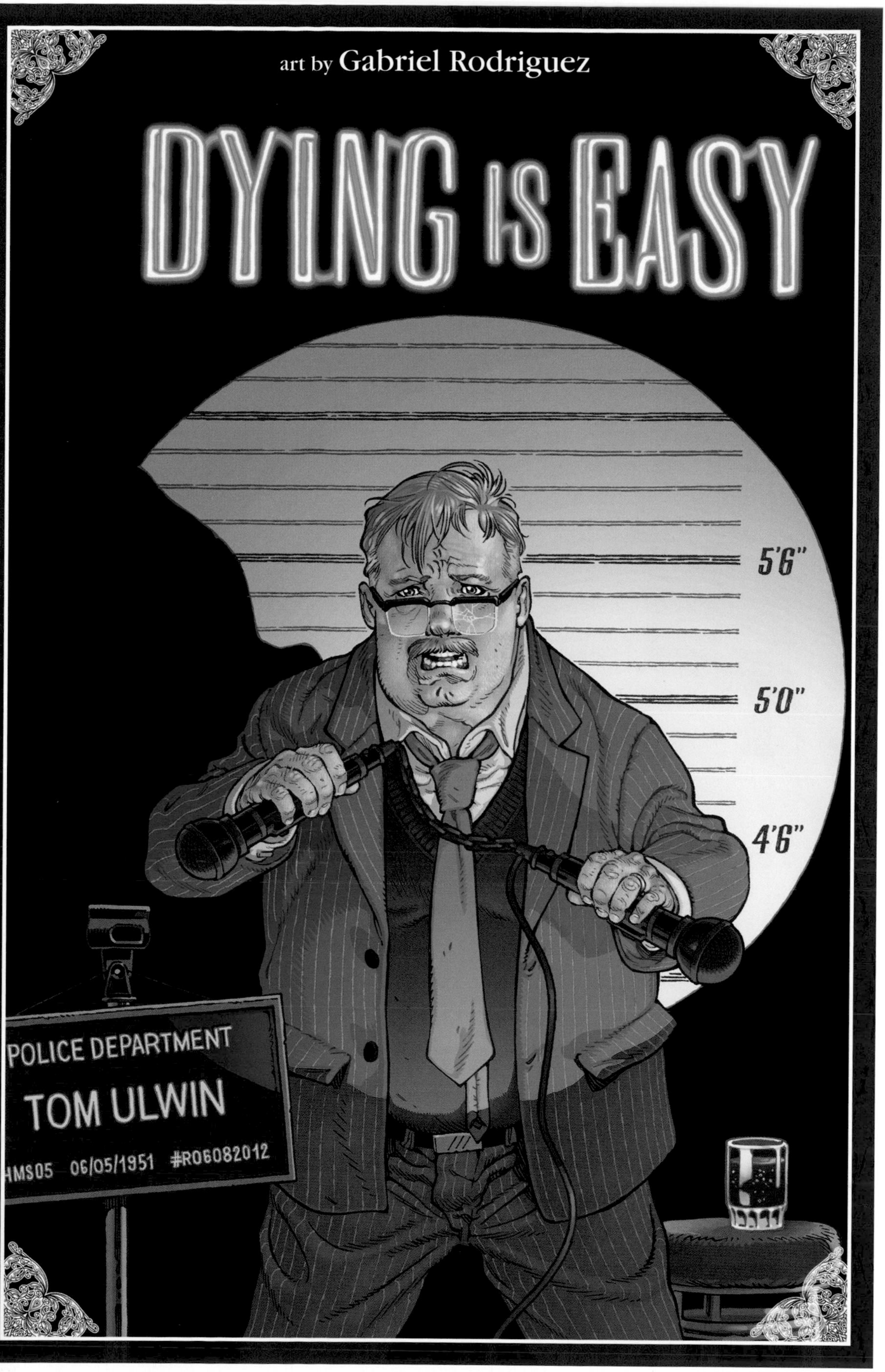
art by Gabriel Rodriguez
DYING IS EASY
5'6"
5'0"
4'6"
POLICE DEPARTMENT
TOM ULWIN
HMS05 06/05/1951 #R06082012

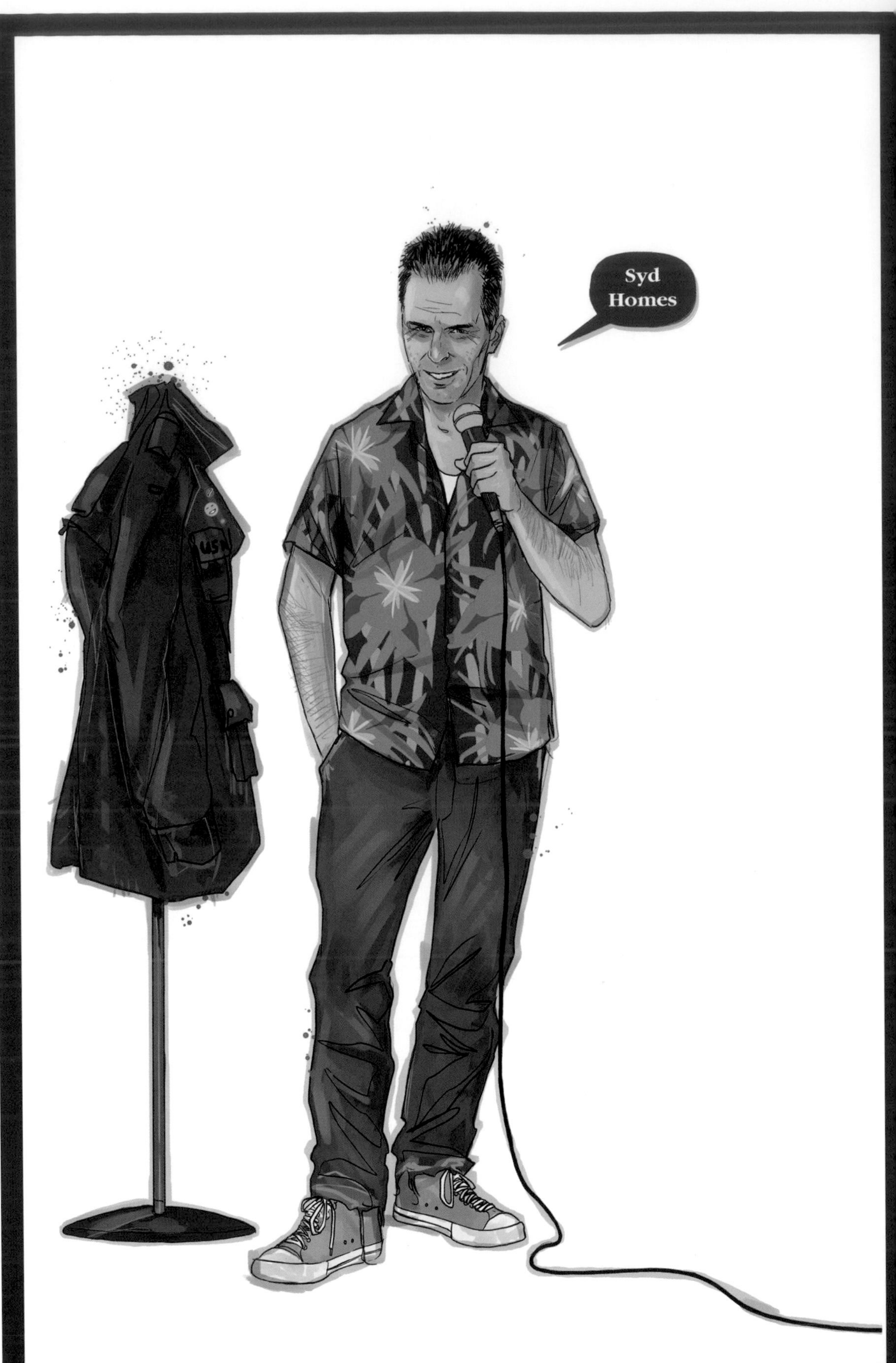
Syd Homes

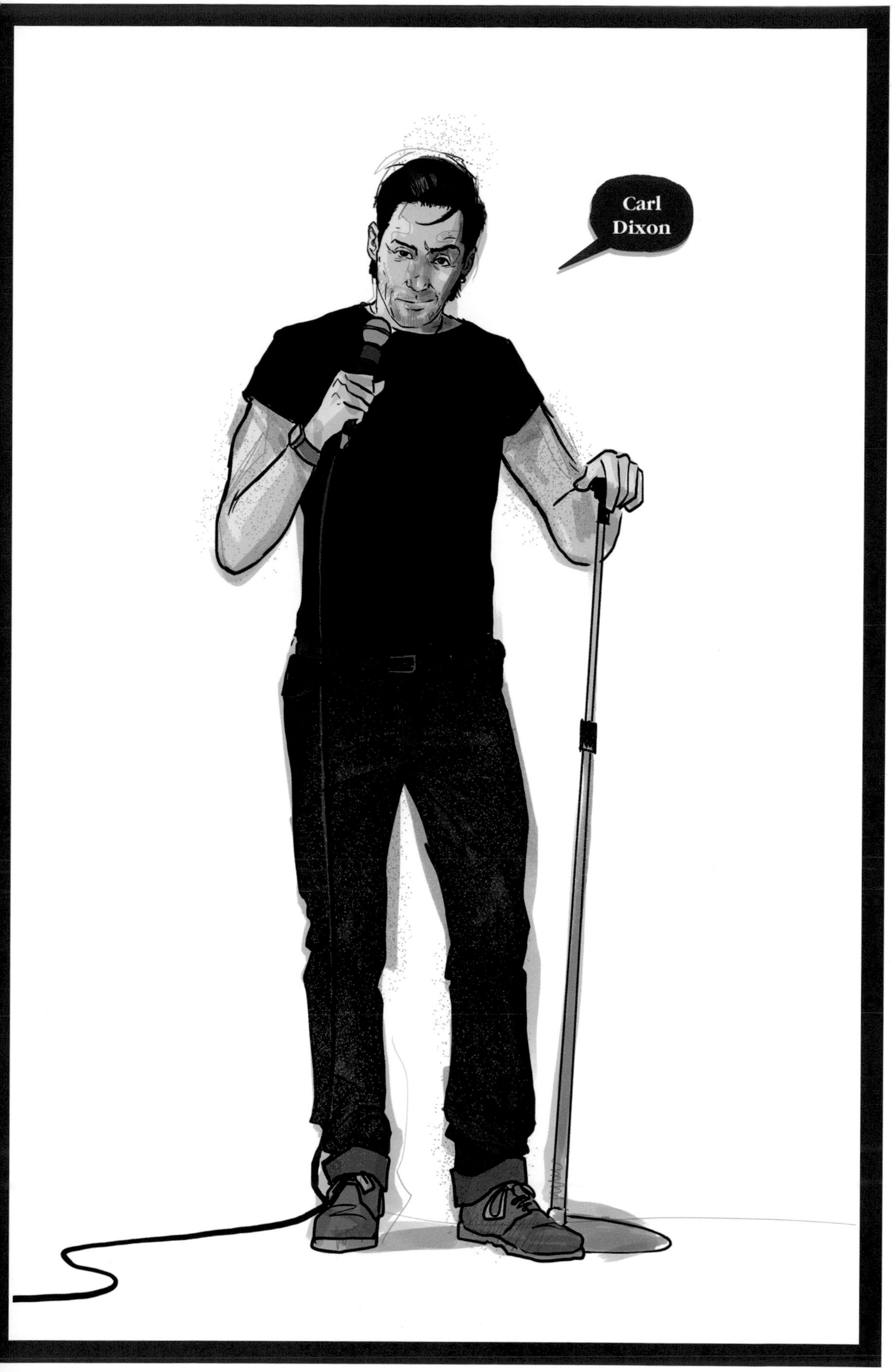
Carl Dixon

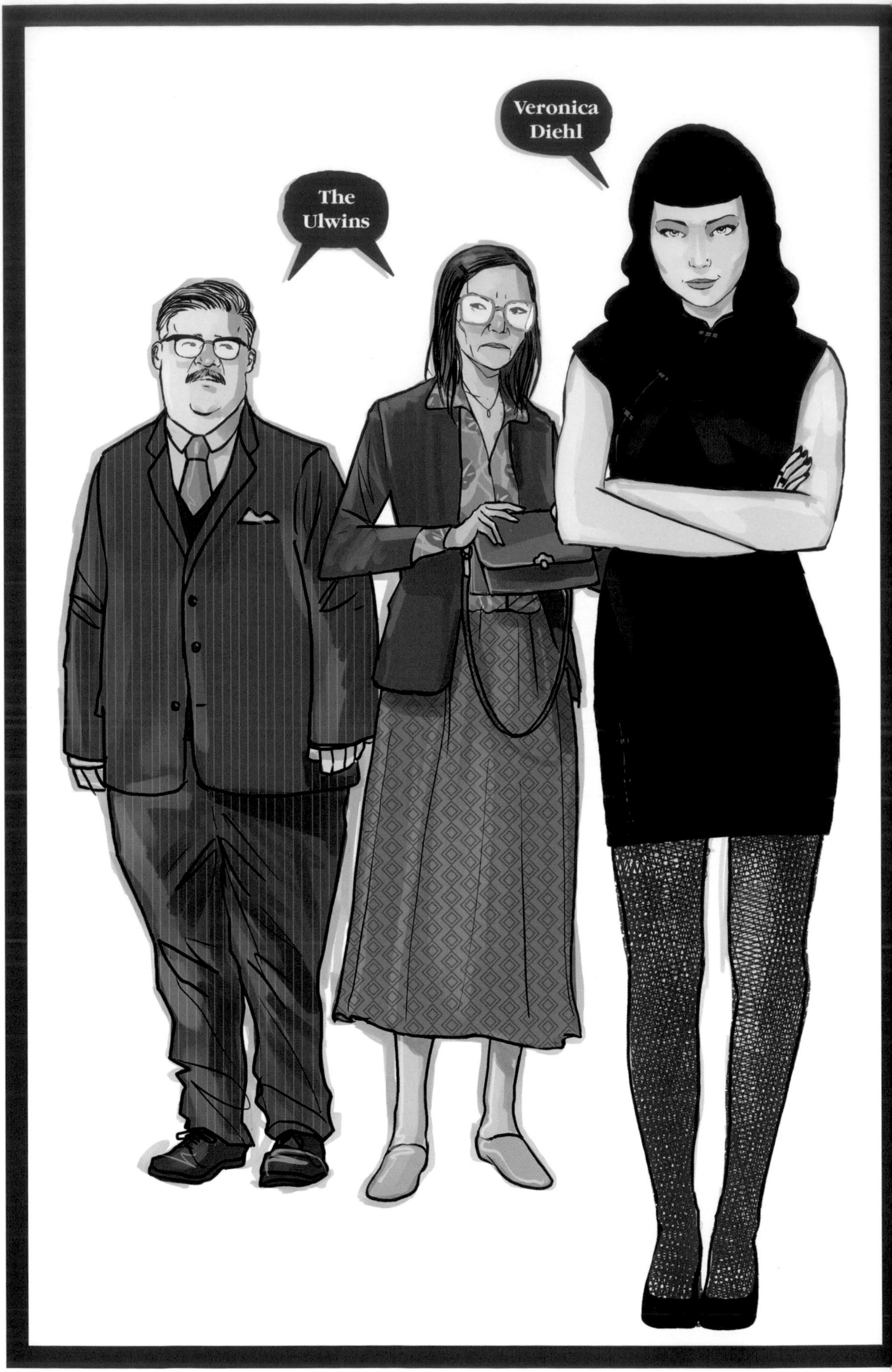
The Ulwins
Veronica Diehl

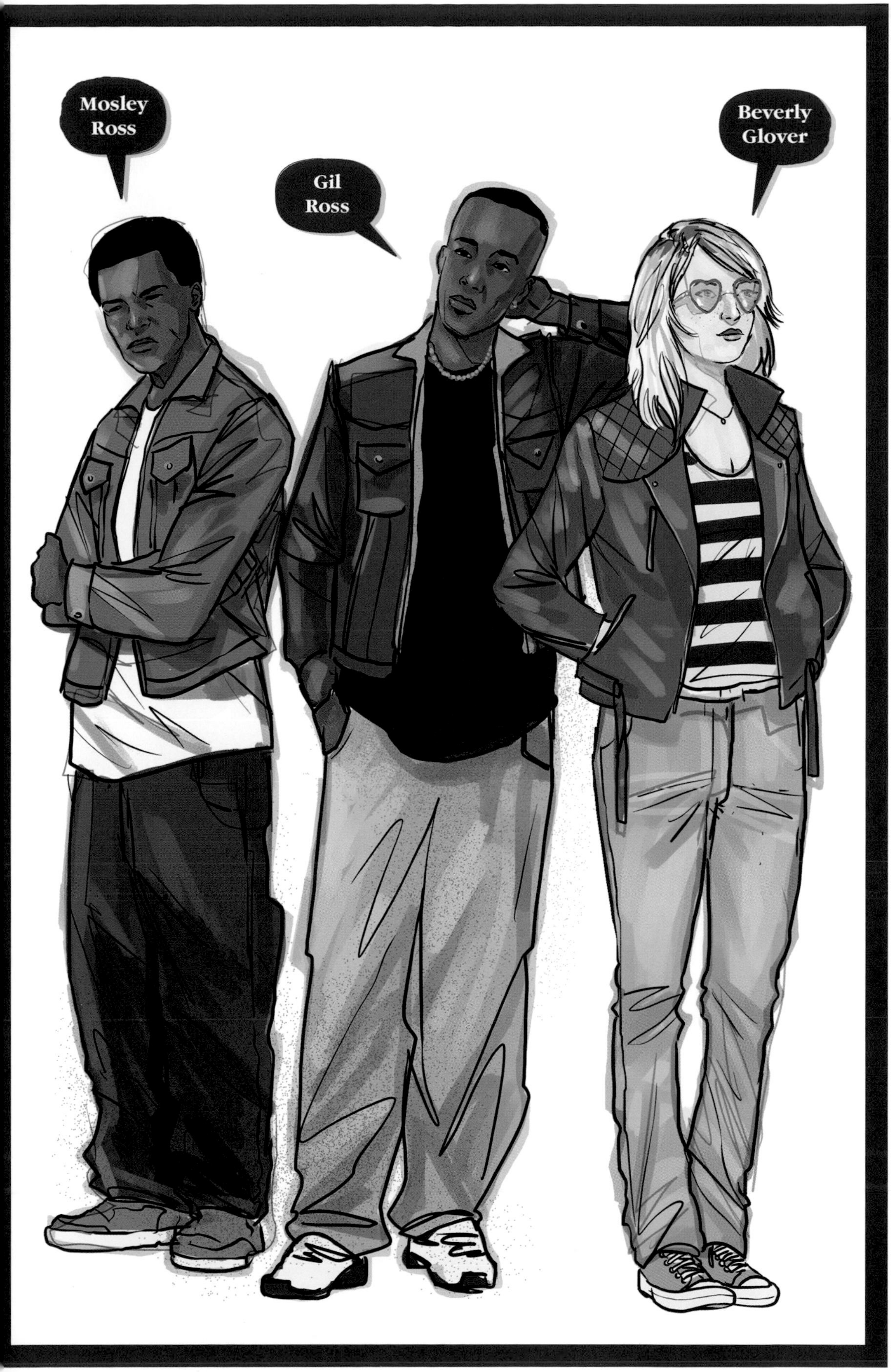
Mosley Ross
Gil Ross
Beverly Glover

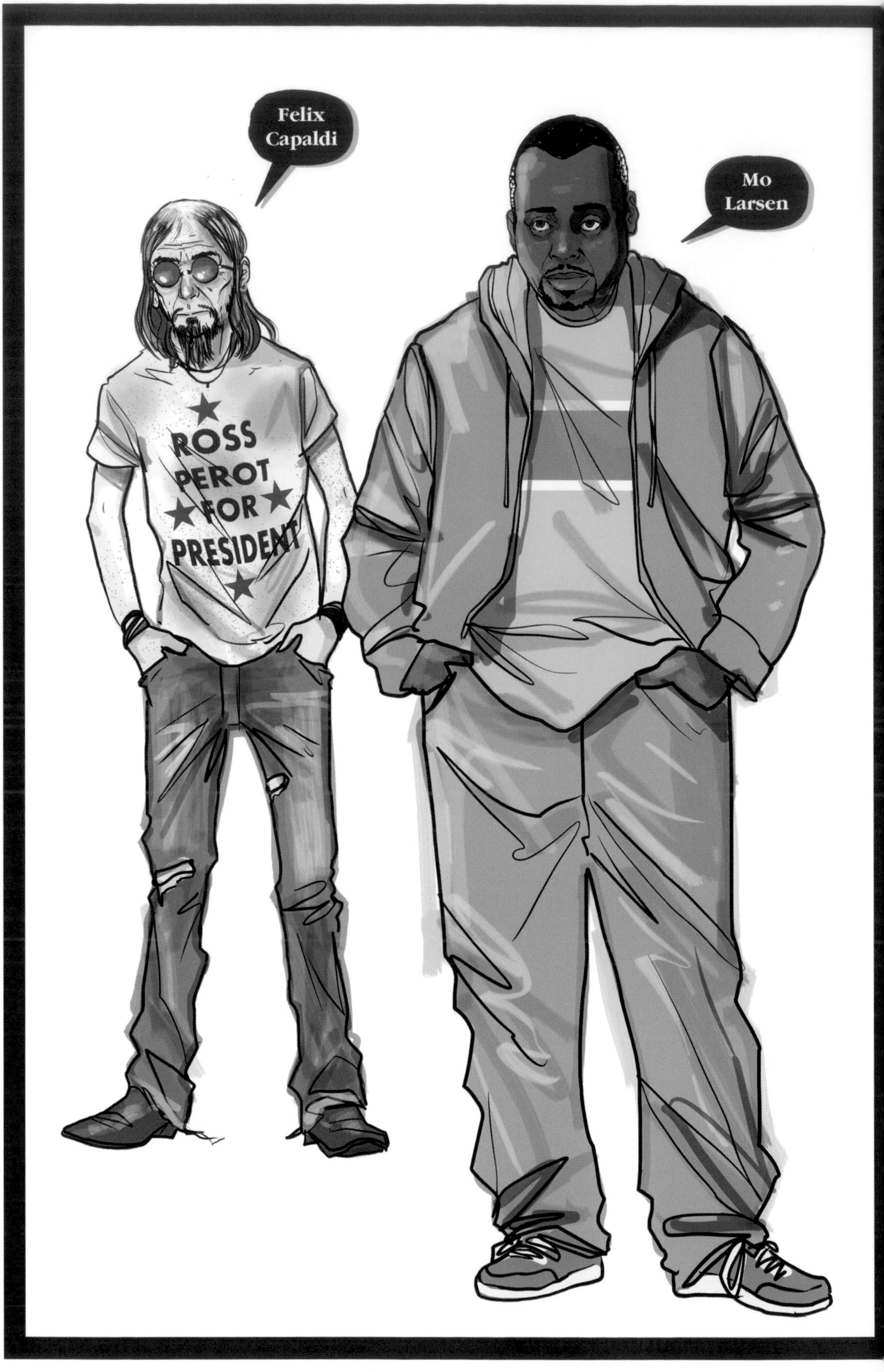
Felix Capaldi
Mo Larsen
ROSS PEROT FOR PRESIDENT

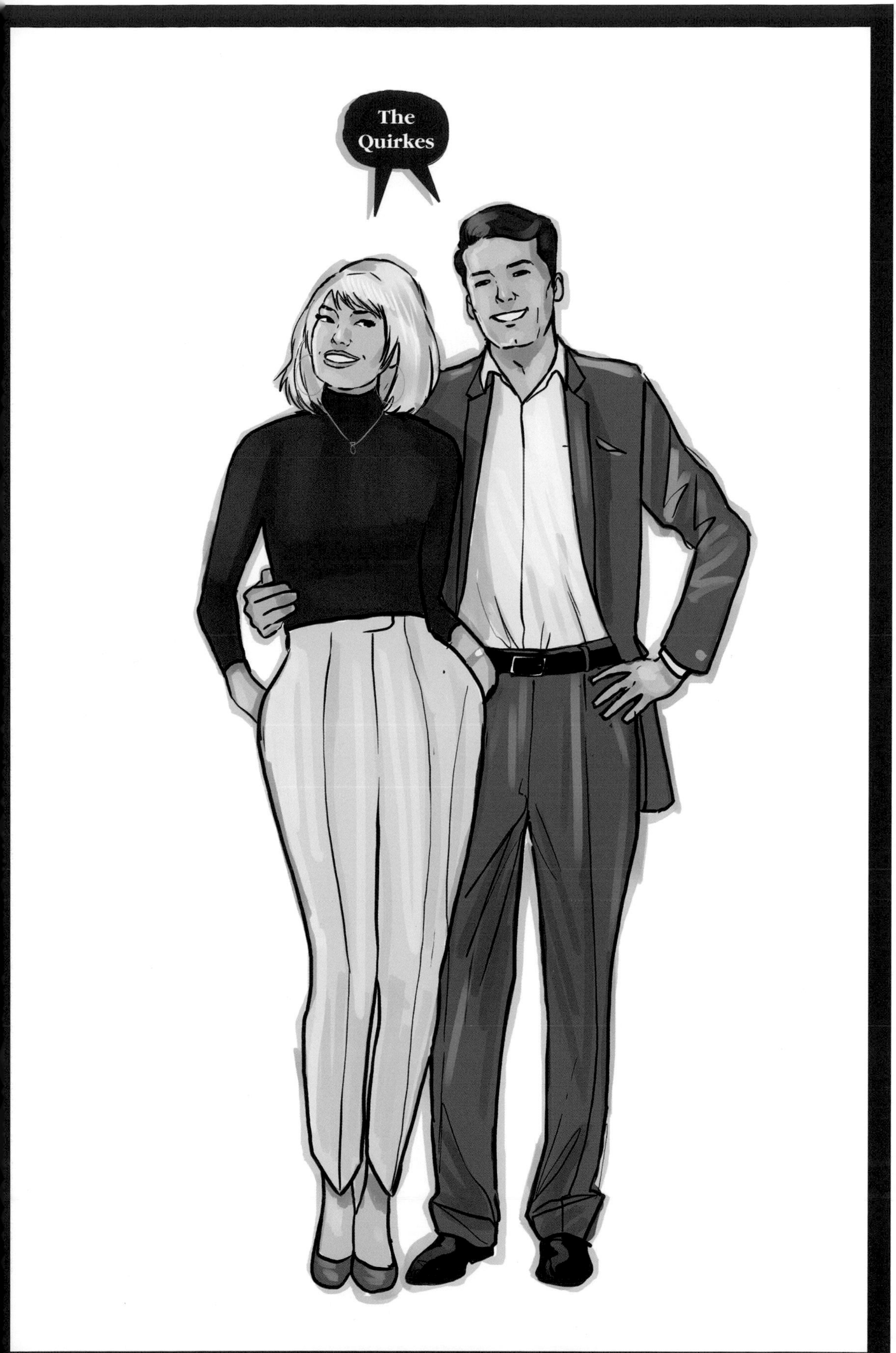
The Quirkes

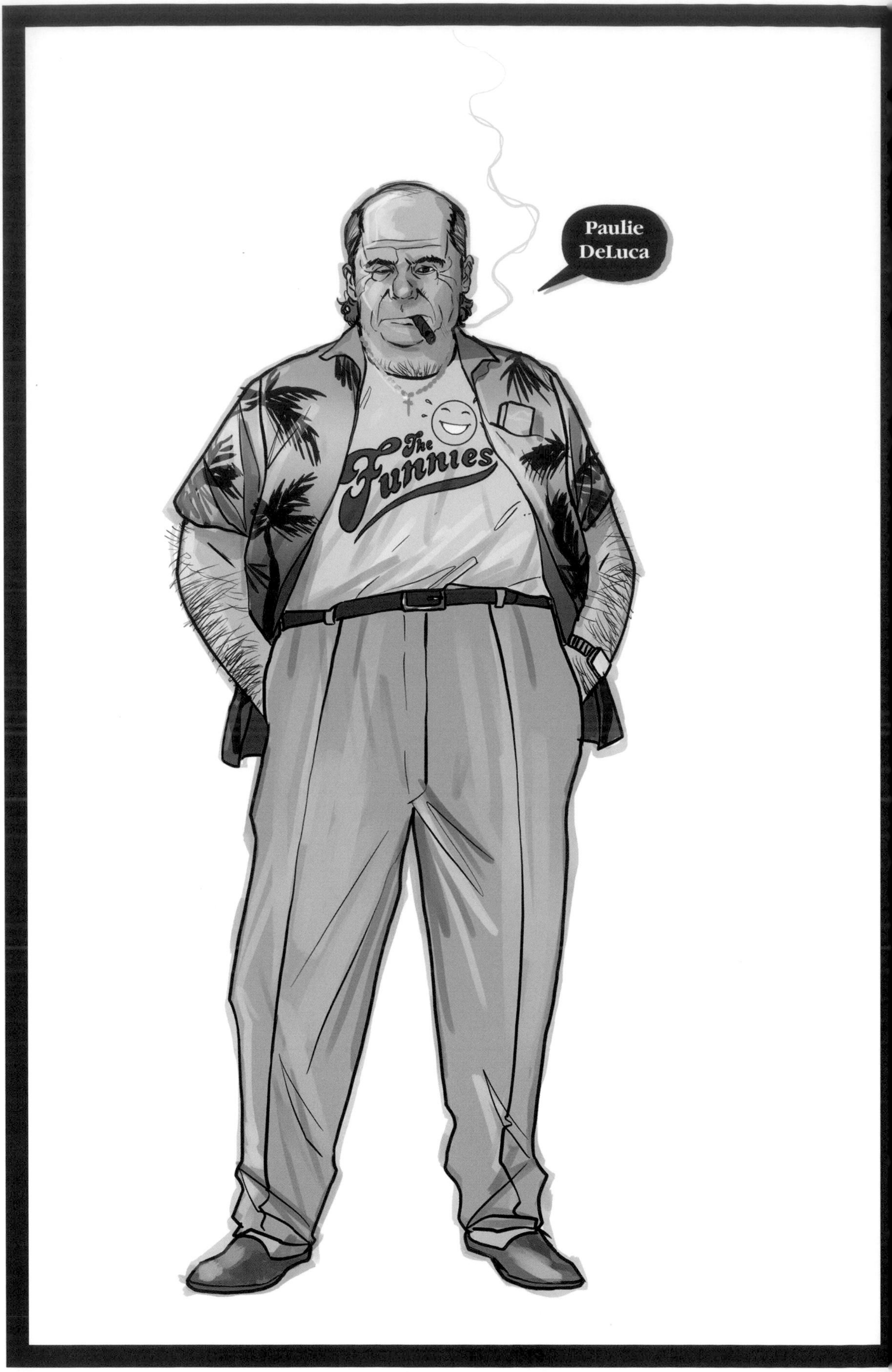
Paulie DeLuca
The Funnies